THE
IRON CODEX

THE DARK ARTS SERIES
BY DAVID MACK

The Midnight Front
The Iron Codex
The Shadow Commission (forthcoming)

THE IRON CODEX

A DARK ARTS NOVEL

DAVID MACK

TOR

A TOM DOHERTY ASSOCIATES BOOK
NEW YORK

This is a work of fiction. All of the characters, organizations, and events portrayed in this novel are either products of the author's imagination or are used fictitiously.

THE IRON CODEX

A Tor Book
Published by Tom Doherty Associates
175 Fifth Avenue
New York, NY 10010

www.tor-forge.com

Tor® is a registered trademark of Macmillan Publishing Group, LLC.

Library of Congress Cataloging-in-Publication Data

Names: Mack, David, 1969- author.
Title: The Iron Codex / David Mack.
Description: First edition. | New York : Tor, 2019. | "A Tom Doherty Associates Book."
Identifiers: LCCN 2018044551| ISBN 9780765383211 (trade paperback) | ISBN 9781466890855 (ebook)
Subjects: | GSAFD: Adventure fiction. | Occult fiction
Classification: LCC PS3613.A272545 I76 2019 | DDC 813/.6—dc23
LC record available at https://lccn.loc.gov/2018044551

Our books may be purchased in bulk for promotional, educational, or business use. Please contact your local bookseller or the Macmillan Corporate and Premium Sales Department at 1-800-221-7945, extension 5442, or by email at MacmillanSpecialMarkets@macmillan.com.

First Edition: January 2019

Printed in the United States of America

0 9 8 7 6 5 4 3 2 1

for the dreams that carry us onward against the current

FAUSTUS: How comes it, then, that thou art out of hell?
MEPHISTOPHILIS: Why, this is hell, nor am I out of it.

—Christopher Marlowe, *Doctor Faustus,* Act I, Scene 3

1954

JANUARY 8

Anja's knee kissed gravel as she leaned her motorcycle into the turn at speed. The demons in her head sniggered at the prospect of her sudden demise, as rocks kicked up by the front tire pelted her riding leathers and bounced off her goggles. The edge of her rear tire scraped the dirt road's precipice. Pebbles rolled down the cliff into the fog-shrouded jungle far below. Around the bend, she straightened her stance and twisted open the throttle.

Ahead, beyond drifting veils of mist, her prey accelerated and widened his lead. Anja's 1953 Vincent Black Shadow had been touted by its maker as the fastest motorcycle in the world, but that didn't matter much on Bolivia's infamous Death Road. The one-lane dirt trail snaked along a mountainside covered in tropical forest. Waterfalls often manifested without warning and filled the road with lakes of mud, and the jungle below was said to have been blanketed with fog since before mankind first arrived in South America.

Condensation clouded the bike's gauges. Anja had to trust her feel for the Black Shadow as she pushed it hard through an S-turn, and she prayed for a straightaway on the other side so that she could close the gap between her and her escaping Nazi target.

Bullets zinged past her right shoulder. Bark exploded from slender tree trunks. Stones leapt from the muddy earth and tumbled into the road behind Anja.

She glanced at her right mirror. A line of four motorcycles—souped-up BMW touring bikes, the same kind as the one she was chasing—were pursuing her.

They knew I would hunt him, Anja realized. *This is a trap.*

The quartet was closing in. They were only seconds behind her now.

Anja berated herself for getting careless. She shifted her weight with the direction of the next curve and got so low that she felt the road grind against the side of her leg. More bullets ripped past above her and vanished into the mist. Swinging into the back of the S-turn, she plucked her last grenade from her bandolier. She squeezed its shoe in her left hand. "DANOCHAR," she said to her invisible demonic porter, "take the grenade's safety pin—and *only the pin*." In a blink, the safety pin vanished.

She let the grenade fall from her hand onto the foggy road.

After she rounded the next turn she heard the explosion—coupled with the screams of riders caught in the blast or thrown with their broken bikes into the haze-masked treetops far below. Men and machines crashed through branches with cracks like gunshots. Then there was only silence on the road behind her.

Ahead of her, the man she had come to kill fought to extend his lead.

The roar of the wind and the growl of the Black Shadow bled together as Anja pushed the British-made motorcycle to its limits. The bike cleaved its way across a deep puddle. Anja used what mass she had to pull her bike around a close pair of perilous turns, and then she bladed through a wall of fog to see a straight patch of road with her prey in the middle of it.

She gunned the throttle and ducked low to reduce her wind resistance. Her long sable hair whipped in the wind like serpents.

Just have to get close enough before he makes the next turn . . .

At last the Black Shadow lived up to its reputation. It felt like a rocket as it brought Anja to within five meters of the fleeing Nazi. She followed him through the next turn—then dodged toward the cliff wall on her right as he flung a hunting knife blindly over his shoulder. The blade soared past her head and then it was gone, out of mind.

Enough. I came for the kill, not the hunt.

Calling once more upon her yoked demonic arsenal, Anja conjured the spectral whip of VALEFOR. A flick of her wrist sent the massive bullwhip streaking ahead of her. Its barbed tip wrapped around the neck of her target, and Anja squeezed the Black Shadow's brake lever.

Her bike skidded to a halt on the dirt road, and her whip went taut. It jerked the Nazi off his ride, which launched itself off the cliff into the gray murk between the trees. As the Nazi landed on his back, his bike vanished. From the impenetrable mists came the snaps of it crashing through heavy branches, a sound that made Anja think of a hammer breaking bones.

She shifted the Black Shadow's engine into neutral, slowed its throttle to a rumbling purr, and then lowered its custom side stand. Her magickal whip remained coiled around her target's neck as she prowled forward to lord her victory over him.

A jerk of the whip focused his attention on her. "You are Herr König, yes?"

He spat at her. "You're the Jungle Witch."

It amused her that the Nazis whom she had spent the better part of a decade hunting throughout South America had somehow mistaken her for a local. The error was forgivable, she supposed; her prolonged exposure to the sun and weather had tanned her once-pale skin, effectively masking her Russian heritage. She drew her hunting knife from its belt sheath and leaned down. "Move and I'll cut your throat."

He remained still, no doubt in part because the demon's whip was still coiled around his throat. The strap of the man's leather satchel crossed his torso on a diagonal. She sliced through it near its top, above his shoulder and close enough to his throat to keep him cowed.

"Don't move," Anja said. With a spiral motion of her hand, she commanded VALEFOR's whip to bind the German fugitive war criminal at his wrists and ankles. Certain he was restrained, she picked up his satchel and pawed through its contents. Most of it was exactly what she had expected to find: extra magazines for the man's Luger, which was still in its holster on his right hip; a few wads of cash in different currencies, all of which she pocketed. She shook the bag upside down. From it fell an ivory pipe, a bag of tobacco, a pencil, an assortment of nearly worthless coins, and a battered old compass. The bag appeared to be emptied, but it still felt heavy to Anja. She muttered, "What are you hiding in here?"

With her hands she searched the interior of the satchel. She found hidden pouches concealed under large flaps. Her prisoner squirmed on the ground as she untied the laces of the flaps. One pouch contained what looked like assorted resources of the Art. From the satchel's other clandestine pouch she pulled a leather-bound journal. "Well," she said, flipping open the book to peruse its handwritten contents, "this is interesting." The few full words and sentences it contained were scribbled in German, but her yoked spirit LIOBOR made it possible for Anja to read any human language with ease. Unfortunately, the spirit was of no help when it came to parsing the acronyms and abbreviations that littered most of the pages.

She showed the open journal to her prisoner. "Explain your acronyms."

"Burn in Hell, witch."

"In time, yes." She flipped another page and admired its high-quality linen paper. "I know your Thule Society dabblers have re-formed under the name

Black Sun, as a nod to Herr Himmler. But what is Odessa? Is that your network here in South America? The one that brought you all to Argentina when the war ended?"

He maintained his silence as a faint growl of motorcycle engines echoed in the distance.

It was evident to Anja that Herr König was not going to provide any useful intelligence. At least, not in the limited time she had remaining before more of his cohorts arrived. Normally she would not have feared a confrontation with his ilk, but she had been holding yoked demons for too long. Her headaches had worsened and become nearly constant in the past week, and she feared increasing her morphine dosage past what she knew to be a safe measure. Soon she would need to release most of her yoked demons, spend a week recovering her strength, and then yoke them or other spirits all over again. It was time for her to fall back and plan her next move.

But first she needed to address the problem of Herr König.

A flourish of her left hand released him from the demonic whip. Free but still on his knees, König smirked at Anja. "We'll find you, Jungle Witch."

"Your minions will try. But before I send you to Hell, I want you to know my name." She made a fist with her right hand, and the unholy talent of XENOCH racked the Nazi with torments worse than the human imagination could conceive. She raised his body off the ground with the telekinesis of BAEL and savored his contorted expression of agony. "My name is Anja Kernova." She flung him high into the air as if he weighed nothing, and as he plummeted toward the jungle she blasted him in midfall with a fireball courtesy of HABORYM. His burning corpse vanished through the fog and jungle canopy and was swallowed by shadows.

Eerie silence settled over the valley. Anja took a moment to enjoy the solitude. Rugged mountains towered around her, but the jungle's misty atmosphere had imbued them all with the quality of fading memories.

Then she heard far-off motorcycles drawing closer.

She tucked the Odessa journal inside her jacket and got on her bike. The Black Shadow rumbled as she shifted it into gear, and she sped south, Hell's dark rider alone on Death's Road.

◆◆◆

Like most gentlemen's clubs in metropolitan London, The Eddington was defined by its subdued ambience. Its interior looked as if it had been hewn from the finest mahogany and black marble, and the only things in the main hall older than the leather on its chairs were its founding members' portraits, which lined the walls and looked down with perpetual disdain on those who had been cursed with the misfortune of being born after the Industrial Revolution.

Tucked in a semiprivate anteroom, Dragan Dalca stood to greet his three smartly attired guests as they were ushered into his company by The Eddington's chief steward, Mr. Harris.

"Gentlemen." Harris gestured toward Dragan. "Your host, Mr. Dalca."

"Thank you, Harris." Dragan gestured toward the open seats around his table. "Please, have a seat." Noting an unspoken prompt by Harris, Dragan said to the three briefcase-toting businessmen, "You must be parched. What can we bring you?"

"Gordon's martini," said the Frenchman. "Dry as the Gobi." Harris nodded.

The American asked, "Do you have bourbon?"

Harris tried not to look put out. "I'm afraid not, sir. Can I offer you scotch whisky?"

"A double of The Macallan Twenty-five," the American said.

Harris approved the order with a nod, then looked at the Russian. "Sir?"

"The same."

Dragan caught Harris's eye. "Double vodka, rocks."

In unison, the businessmen tucked their briefcases under the table.

Harris stepped back, pulled closed the anteroom's thick maroon curtain to give the men some privacy, and departed to fill the drink order, leaving Dragan alone at last with his guests. The trio greeted Dragan with faltering smiles. The Frenchman was the first to speak. "Your message implied this meeting would be private."

"I disagree," Dragan said. "And I am not responsible for your inferences."

The ever-present voice nagged Dragan from behind his thoughts: «*Get on with it.*»

Dragan settled into his high-backed chair and folded his hands together. "The three of you are here because I've promised to raise your stock prices and market shares."

"We know what you promised," the American said, his impatience festering. "Now we want details." The Frenchman and the Russian nodded at their peer's declaration.

«*Skip the small talk,*» needled the voice in Dragan's psyche.

Stay quiet and let me do this. Dragan sat forward and plastered an insincere smile onto his face. "You three represent aircraft manufacturing companies that recently have fallen behind in the race to secure clients on the international market. And I'm sure you all know why."

"Those pricks at de Havilland," groused the American.

The Frenchman nodded. "Indeed. The Comet 1, to be precise."

"It is the only thing my clients talk about," the Russian said. "They overlook its weaknesses and see nothing but its jet engines. 'This is the future,' they tell me."

"And it is," Dragan said. "Unchecked, de Havilland will dominate the market for at least another decade, if not longer. Assuming, of course, that nothing . . . *unfortunate* happens."

This time his unsubtle implication drew raised eyebrows from his guests. The Russian leaned forward. "What sort of misfortune could derail such potential?"

Dragan reached inside his jacket and pulled out a slender gold cigarette case. He opened it, plucked out a Gauloises, and lit it with a match stroked against the table's edge. Waving out the match's flame, he took a deep pull of the rich Turkish tobacco, and then he exhaled through his nostrils. "If you gentlemen are interested in reversing de Havilland's fortunes and improving your own, it might interest you to know that the Comet 1, despite its early success, is plagued by two fatal flaws, both of which de Havilland has worked hard to conceal."

This revelation stoked the American's interest. "What sort of flaws?"

"Let it suffice to say that one is a matter of engineering, the other of materials. Together, they could be exploited to undermine de Havilland's position in the marketplace."

Skepticism infused the Frenchman's mood. "And you know this . . . how?"

"A pair of incidents," Dragan said. "Last March, a Comet 1A crashed during takeoff from Karachi Airport. The flacks at de Havilland blamed it on pilot error—"

The Russian cut in, "The Canadian Pacific Air accident?"

"Yes," Dragan said. "Just under two months later, another Comet 1 crashed, just minutes after takeoff from Calcutta. All six crew and thirty-seven passengers were killed."

"I read that report," the American said. "It blamed the crash on a thundersquall."

Dragan shrugged. "I don't deny the storm was a factor. But it was not the cause. Sooner or later, a Comet 1 will experience an in-flight disaster that it can't blame on pilots or weather." He goaded them with a sly smirk. "Sooner, I hope, for your employers' sakes."

The Frenchman sharpened his focus, clearly intrigued. "So what has this to do—"

The curtain opened, revealing Harris. Balanced on one hand was a tray bearing the men's drinks. As he passed out the libations, he said discreetly to Dragan, "Phone call for you, sir."

"Thank you, Harris." Dragan stood and offered his guests an apologetic smile. "Forgive me, gentlemen. I shall return promptly." The others excused him with polite nods.

Dragan crossed the main hall at a quick but dignified pace. Just before he reached the concierge's desk, he caught his reflection in the glass door of a trophy case and paused to push his black hair back into place and to smooth a few rogue whiskers back into his thin mustache. Then he accepted the phone's receiver handset from the concierge, and he stretched its cord around a corner into the coatroom so that he could take his call with a modicum of privacy.

Knowing that only one person on earth knew to reach him at The Eddington, he snarled, "What is it, Müller?"

"I apologize for the interruption," replied Heinrich Müller, sounding nothing at all like the man who just a decade earlier had been the commandant of Hitler's feared Gestapo, *"but there's news out of Bolivia."*

Hope swelled inside Dragan, the product of unjustified optimism. "She took the bait?"

"Yes. Well, no. Not exactly." Müller's tone was heavy with shame. *"You were right, she was watching the roads to La Paz. But she didn't fall for the decoy."*

"If she didn't go after the decoy, how do you know she—" Realization struck Dragan like a hot shower turning ice-cold without warning. "What happened? What went wrong?"

Müller breathed a leaden sigh. *"König and his guards. She took them all on the Death Road."* After a pause gravid with shame, he added, *"And she captured his journal."*

Profanities logjammed in Dragan's mouth, the flood of invective too great for him to give it voice. He knew not to make a spectacle of himself inside

The Eddington. Instead he clenched a fist and counted to five while drawing deep breaths.

His irritating inner voice was not so considerate.

«*This is a disaster. Contain this, now!*»

Silence! I will handle it.

"Müller," he said at last, "round up everyone we can spare, and bring them to La Paz. Find the woman as soon as possible. Take her alive if you can, but your chief priority—"

"*Is to recover the book,*" Müller said. "*I remember, sir.*"

"See that you do. If you or your men kill Anja Kernova before we find that book, I'll bury your body so deep the Devil himself couldn't find it."

Müller was still mouthing hollow assurances as Dragan handed the receiver back to the concierge, who set it back onto the phone's cradle behind his podium.

Twenty-one steps back to the anteroom, Dragan told himself. *Breathe and put your smile back on before you step through that curtain.*

Low chatter filled the space between his guests as he sidled back into his chair. "Thank you for your patience, gentlemen. I asked you each to bring the first half of my fee, as a retainer. And I brought you here together because I want to make sure that all of you who stand to benefit pay your fair share— I won't tolerate freeloaders. You all pay, or the deal is off."

"And what are we paying for?" asked the Russian.

"To inflict a very public setback on your most dominant competitor. One that will ruin it, and for which it will take all the blame."

The American turned cagy. "And when might such an event take place?"

"Midafternoon, the day after tomorrow. In Rome."

Wary looks of conspiratorial intent were exchanged among the guests at Dragan's table. The Russian nodded. "That would be a most valuable twist of fate."

"And now you know why my fee is so high," Dragan said. "My terms are simple. Half your payment up front, in cash. The remaining half will be due upon delivery of my promise. If I fail to deliver, your deposits will be returned in full, without question." He steepled his fingers and leaned forward. "But in case any of you might be thinking you can renege on the second half of your payment, know this: I have *never* been bilked, nor will I be. Do you all understand me?"

Fearful nods confirmed that his guests knew that his threats were not idle ones.

"Splendid. Thank you for coming. I'll look forward to seeing you all again on the eleventh."

The businessmen downed their drinks with steep tilts of their glasses, and then they rose from the table to beat a quiet retreat through the main hall and then out the front door.

Dragan stole a look through the table and inside the briefcases, using Raum's gift of the Sight. He was gratified to see that each briefcase was packed full of cash—American dollars, French francs, and Russian rubles, respectively.

He sipped his vodka, and then he beckoned the steward.

The dignified, middle-aged Englishman arrived at his table. "Sir?"

"The cases under my table," Dragan said. "Please see them to Mr. Holcombe, and tell him I want the entire sum invested in short sales of de Havilland stock."

"I shall see to it at once, Mr. Dalca."

"Thank you, Harris."

Dragan enjoyed the enveloping silence of the club while Harris and a member of his staff toted the briefcases full of cash to the waiting hands of Dragan's broker.

Twenty-four hours from now, I'm going to be a very wealthy man, he mused. *All I need to do now is get the book from that Russian bitch . . . and then justice will be done.*

JANUARY 9

Living a lie had proved a pleasant state of affairs for Briet Segfrunsdóttir.

It had been over eight years since the OSS had found her in self-imposed exile in northern Finland. When its agents had knocked on her door, she'd thought her day of reckoning was at hand, that they had come to take her to The Hague—or to put a bullet in her head—for her complicity in the Nazis' war crimes. Instead, all her sins had been redacted under the auspices of Operation Paperclip, an American secret initiative to find the scientists and engineers—and also, as it turned out, the sorcerers—of the defeated German Third Reich and recruit them into the service of the world's new master: its lone atomic superpower, the United States of America.

They'd since given her a life far better than what she deserved.

She had a nondescript bordering on meaningless job title, coupled with a generous salary and fringe benefits. A three-story brownstone in the heart of Georgetown. Immunity from international prosecution. Vast reserves of equipment, personnel, and money at her disposal, to facilitate her magickal research. The Americans had even let her keep her Icelandic citizenship despite having naturalized her as one of their own.

All they asked in return was that she be their shield, sword, and all-seeing eye. It was the best deal Briet was going to get on this earth, and she knew it.

So, she wondered as her alarm clock rang at the stroke of seven, *why is my stomach a bottomless pit of dread?* A slap of her hand silenced the alarm. As the only member of her household with a job that insisted on semiregular hours, Briet slept on the left side of the king bed, nearest the end table and clock. Her lovers—Alton Bloch, a former accountant and aspiring Beat poet, and Park Hyun, a Korean woman who had escaped her war-torn country to come to America six months earlier as a refugee—took turns being islanded in the middle of the bed.

Today it was Hyun's turn. She snoozed on, blissfully oblivious as Briet and Alton dragged themselves out from under the covers into the unforgiving chill of a winter morning. A shrill wind rattled the bedroom windows.

Alton scratched his hirsute chest. "I'll put a kettle on."

Briet kissed his stubbled cheek. "You're the best." She slipped away to the bathroom to brush her teeth and shower.

Half an hour later she padded downstairs, dressed for work in a simple dark blue dress, her fiery red hair coiled atop her head under a towel. As she passed through the sitting room on her way to the kitchen, a jazz melody of Lester Young with the Oscar Peterson Trio spilled softly from the stereophonic speakers of the record player cabinet.

In the kitchen Alton had prepared a simple breakfast of poached eggs, rye toast, and tea. His insistence on getting up each morning to cook breakfast for Briet had been one of many tiny kindnesses that had endeared him to her. He wasn't much to look at—he was pushing forty, his brown hair was thinning, and he had exactly the physique one might expect of a longtime office worker—but Briet loved him for the art in his soul.

And for his prodigious cock. She was only human, after all.

They ate without small talk, because he respected her preference for silence, especially in the morning. Afterward, while he washed the dishes, she took a few minutes to retreat upstairs to finish her hair and makeup. Then she visited her study to dote on a companion who had been by her side since before the war: her rat familiar, Trixim.

Born of magick, Trixim had outlived his mundane kin by an order of magnitude. Briet credited his longevity at least in part to the degree to which she spoiled and doted on the crimson-eyed black rodent. He stood on his hind legs and nibbled eagerly as she fed him small morsels of Gruyère, and he licked chicken-liver paté from her fingertip without nipping at her. "Good boy, Trixim," she said, scratching his head before petting him down his back. "Don't be a troublemaker—stay in your cage until I get home tonight." He affirmed her instruction by nuzzling her wrist with the side of his face.

Outside the house, a horn honked.

From the first floor Alton called out, "Your car's here!"

"Coming." She dropped a few last bits of cheese in Trixim's cage, and she locked her study's door as she hurried out.

At the bottom of the stairs she kissed Alton, who held her dove-gray overcoat as she shimmied into it. "Thank you, my love," she said.

He opened the front door, admitting a wash of cold morning air. "Call me when you leave tonight. I'm making a beef Wellington."

"I will. Tootles." She waved farewell as she bounded down the steps and across the walk to a black Lincoln Continental that idled outside her brownstone's front gate. Its chauffeur stood beside its passenger door.

The driver opened the door, and Briet climbed inside the car, which was pleasantly warm. On the bench seat were copies of that morning's editions of *The New York Times* and *The Washington Post*. A creature of habit, Briet reached for *The New York Times* and skimmed the headlines to take the day's temperature.

As was typical for a Saturday paper, there was no banner headline. The most prominent item was tucked into the top left corner: U.S. STAND ON REDS AND JAPAN DRAWS SEOUL BROADSIDE. In the center column, PRESIDENT TO TAKE A STRONGER ROLE IN PUSHING POLICY. The other top stories were similarly drab: proposals for new taxes, a threat of a labor strike in the nation's ports, Thailand pushing for Indochina to join it to form an anti-Communist bloc . . . and then, just above the fold, the buried lede:

NEW BOMB TESTS SLATED IN PACIFIC
Greatest Hydrogen Explosion May Be Produced

The article's opening sentence treated the matter as if it were blasé: "The Atomic Energy Commission announced plans tonight for another series of tests for atomic and probably hydrogen weapons at the government's Pacific Proving Grounds."

Is that why they asked me to come in on a Saturday?

She dismissed the notion as quickly as she'd conjured it. Atomic weapons terrified Briet, and she frequently needed to remind herself that they and the issues they raised were explicitly beyond the scope of her duties. Fission bombs were temptations to brinksmanship in her opinion, not the sort of thing any sane person would want to see used ever again.

Two bombs on Japan was more than enough, she brooded.

At any rate, the United States had tasked Briet with managing a more personal brand of defense. One tailored to her rare and dangerous talents.

She finished her review of both newspapers by the time her driver stopped the car outside the North Rotary Road entrance of the Pentagon. Not a word had passed between them during the trip, making it the same as every other ride they had shared. There was, after all, no point in trying to engage a lamia in conversation. The nameless demons were creatures of low intelligence and pure spite; they were reliable for simple tasks as long as they remained under firm control, but they would never be known for having "people skills."

Briet left the newspapers behind on the seat as she left the car and breezed through the first of several security checkpoints between her and her final destination.

Officially, she was listed as a civilian research assistant to some midlevel naval officer, and that was what she had told both of her lovers. There was nothing to be gained by telling them the truth about who she really was, or the true nature of her work for the Department of Defense.

After a long walk through the Pentagon's seemingly endless corridors, almost all of which looked alike, a lengthy and slow elevator—whose basement access point was guarded by no fewer than three armed marines—delivered her to a sublevel not documented on any official blueprints of the Pentagon. More than six hundred feet belowground another trio of marines with permanent frowns guarded a massive round steel door.

One marine checked her credentials while another stood ready to shoot her dead if they failed to pass muster. When the marine in charge cleared her to proceed, the third man opened the door and ushered her through the massive portalway, into America's best-kept secret.

The Silo.

The main space was humbling in its sheer size. The pentagonal pit measured five hundred feet across, and from its water-filled nadir to its ceiling it stood nearly a thousand feet tall. One-third of the way up from its bottom, a steel-grate widow's walk led to the conjuring stage, a platform shaped like an equilateral pentagon suspended above the pit's center. Mounted on the ceiling were industrial lights that bathed the catwalk and the stage in a white glare. The sides of the platform were ringed by coal-fed braziers atop six-foot-tall stands.

During magickal rituals orange flames would dance from the braziers, and the overhead lights would be turned off, shrouding all beyond the stage's edge in darkness. With the lights on, the high-speed cameras and electromagnetic sensors that festooned the walls were clearly visible. As daunting as the Silo appeared, however, Briet knew that its true marvels were hidden behind its multitude of two-way mirrored observation windows.

Dozens of sublevels surrounding the Silo were packed with thinking machines the scientists called computers. They ran on electricity and stored information on reels of magnetic tape. Inputs from the sensors and cameras were monitored by an army of technicians, physicists, engineers, and—most surprising to Briet—lawyers. While the scientists labored to quantify the exotic particles and energies of magick in order to reduce it to mere science, the lawyers concerned themselves with untangling the convoluted terms and verbiage of demonic pacts. They seemed convinced that they would find ways to exploit loopholes in Hell's contracts and by so doing trick the Devil himself into granting special advantages to the United States.

Standing alone on her conjuring stage, Briet felt a pang of nostalgia.

I miss the days when I could work magick without a fucking audience.

Footsteps on the widow's walk echoed in the cavernous space. Briet turned to see the Silo's director of operations, Frank Cioffi, crossing the bridge. Frank was the epitome of pedestrian, in Briet's opinion. Pale from decades spent indoors, a stranger to the sun. Balding and bespectacled, with a face so plain it could vanish into any crowd. He favored the attire that had become the stereotype of engineers and scientists everywhere: black trousers, a white short-sleeve button-down shirt, a narrow tie, a pocket protector loaded with pens and a folding slide rule, black socks, and dull black Oxfords.

Behind him followed two men and two women, none of whom Briet had ever seen before. *Strangers. That doesn't bode well.*

It took the group a couple of minutes to reach the platform. Briet blamed their sloth on Frank's short legs, ill-fitting pants, and poor health. He wasn't a bad man, as far as Briet had been able to discern, but he was no paragon of integrity or courage, and she had never seen anyone who possessed his knack for making good clothes look bad.

Frank tried to preempt criticism with a jolly "Good morning, Briet!"

"Spare me the bullshit, Frank." She lifted her chin to gesture toward the four strangers at his back. "Who the fuck are they?"

"Your new tanists." He pivoted and tried to segue into introductions. "This is—"

"No," Briet interrupted. "I'm not doing this again."

His smile evaporated, leaving his jowls slack in defeat. "I have my orders."

"I don't care. This is the third time in nine years! Every time I whip a team of adepts into shape, they get transferred and some bureaucrat sends me four novices. I'm sick of it, Frank."

"You know the drill, Bree. It's all about creating redundancies in our defense plan. If Washington ever gets hit by a Russian A-bomb, we'll need magickal defense teams in safe locations, ready to carry on after we're gone."

She stepped around Frank to assess the latest batch of dilettantes. One of the men looked Chinese; the other was pale and blond. Both were lean and sinewy with features chiseled by deprivation. Briet singled out the quasi albino. "You. What demon was bound by Solomon's forty-third seal?"

He looked like a rabbit about to become roadkill. "Um. . . ."

"Shut up." Briet pointed at the Chinese man. "You?"

"Sargatanas?"

"Are you asking me or telling me?"

He steeled his nerve. "Telling you. It's Sargatanas."

"Wrong. It's Sabnock. Don't speak again unless I give you permission."

Briet turned toward the two female aspirants. The taller of the pair was dark-skinned and wore her hair in a dramatic Afro. "I like your hair. So will demons. Wear that to an experiment and I guarantee you a spirit will rip it out of your scalp. Cut that off, today."

As the chastised woman shrank, Briet faced the last new adept. The second woman was short, muscled, and wore her hair in a tight bun. Her fingers were callused, and her eyes were keen. She seemed to burn with the promise of competence. But Briet had to be sure.

"To speak through the flames of Parago, what must one sacrifice?"

"Rock salt and Mercurial incense of powdered black dianthus."

It was the correct answer, provided without hesitation or equivocation. It was already clear to Briet which of her four new adepts would quickly rise to fill the group's senior role.

Still, she took Frank aside. "I don't like this."

"Neither do I. But it's not like the government gives us a choice."

"At least tell me where the latest group was sent."

Frank shook his head. "You know I can't. Even if they told me, which they don't, it'd be top-secret." He lowered his voice and put on an apologetic air. "Do us both a favor: Don't rock the boat. Every time this happens, you pitch a fit. That makes the brass nervous. And trust me—you don't want that. Something scares the brass, their first instinct is always the same: Kill it." He glanced at the new adepts. In a whisper: "Just do what they pay you for."

He patted her shoulder, as if they were conspirators who had come to an arrangement, when the reality was that Briet felt ready to erupt in violence. But she knew there was a legion of soldiers, scientists, and specialists observing her every action. If she rebelled, or cast herself in the role of a dissident here in the Silo, the marines between her and the exit would make certain she never left the Pentagon alive.

She faced her adepts. Behind them, Frank waddled across the steel-grate bridge, headed back into the walls of the Silo. Briet clapped her hands to get her adepts' attention. "With one exception, you are the most poorly prepared group of adepts I have ever been saddled with. So we're going to start today by reviewing the basics of ceremonial magick. Pay attention to what I tell you, because this knowledge is what will keep you alive long enough to try to master the Art.

"All magick, from the simplest trick to the grandest miracle, is predicated on the conjuring and control of demons. No exceptions. Make a mistake in your glyphs, your wards, or the material elements of your ritual, and you will very quickly end up dead."

She circled the adepts, sizing them up and gauging their reactions as she continued. "A person who practices magick is an *adept*. The lowest order of adept is a *novice*. After that comes *acolyte*. Then the highest class, which is called *karcist*. I am a master karcist. Three of you are so pathetic that I think you should be called aspirants rather than novices. If any of you makes it through the first week of training alive, I might be bothered to learn your fucking names.

"Conjuring a Presence, whether Infernal or Celestial in origin, is called an *experiment*. The magician conducting an experiment is called the *operator*. Those assisting the magician are called *tanists*. Making a demon do a task, especially one performed at a distance, is called a *sending*. If a karcist sends a demon to harm or abduct a person, the target is known as the *patient*. If these terms seem quaint and antiseptic to you, blame Aristotle. But don't tell me, I don't care.

"Karcists get power from signing demonic pacts. When you make a deal with a minister or governor of Hell, you earn the right to strike pacts with all of the demons that are subordinate to it. But choose your patron wisely. There are six ministers of Hell, but you can have only one as a patron. Choose a lesser minister and it might be easier to sway, but it won't have as much to offer. Choose one of the greater spirits, and you might find yourself enslaved for eternity."

Briet finished her orbit of the adepts and placed herself in the center of her assigned place on the conjuring stage, the operator's circle. "The most difficult feat in magick is known as *yoking*. This is done by compelling a demon to let you bind its spirit to your flesh so that you can wield its powers as your own. Some of these unions will be limited by the terms of your pact with the spirit; in some cases a demon will stay bound for as long—and only as long— as you remain strong enough in body and mind to hold it in thrall. But be warned:

"Yoking a demon is miserable work. Holding even one in thrall will turn your guts to mud. You'll have nightmares, nosebleeds, and your life will feel like a permanent fucking hangover. A demon trapped inside you will make you scratch holes in your skin and rip out your hair. Bind too many spirits, or hold them too long, and the strain can drive you mad. And it is the nature of demons to abandon you the moment your strength fades or your concentration slips. It's when you need them the most that they will *always* betray you." She clapped her hands and concealed her amusement when all four adepts blinked, as if freed from a spell. "So . . . any questions?" The four amateurs shook their heads. Briet gestured at the men and the tall woman. "You three, go read Waite's *Book of Black Magic*. Don't even think of setting foot in here again until you know it by heart." She asked the short woman, "Have you made your tools yet?"

"No, ma'am. But I've been trained in metalwork and glassblowing. I'm ready to start."

"Report to Sergeant Chapman on sublevel nine. She'll set you up at the electric forge. The sooner we get you equipped, the better." Waving both hands, she shooed her adepts toward the bridge. "That's all for today. Everyone out. Go."

Briet stood alone on the platform and watched her newest students depart. *How long will it take me to train these bumblers? And once I do, how long until they vanish through the same revolving door that robbed me of my last twelve adepts?* Taking care not to let her face betray her anger or her mounting suspicion, she looked up at the myriad windows and cameras.

Redundancies, my ass. What are these people not telling me?

It was a question that no one in the Silo would answer, but Briet was tired of waiting for them to read her into their schemes. One way or another she was going to get the truth—whether her masters liked it or not.

JANUARY 9, PART II

By any legal definition, El Alto was its own city, completely separate from the adjacent Bolivian capital of La Paz. In practice, however, Anja was certain that without the vitality of La Paz to sustain it, the city of El Alto would evaporate like sweat in a desert.

Most of the city's population consisted of indigenous American peoples, but no one seemed to live in the dilapidated sector of the city in which Anja had chosen to establish her safe house. It was a narrow box, three squat stories tall, with an encircling three-meter-high wall, all of it made from the same cheap red brick. The house was protected by an iron gate at its main entrance and corrugated steel barriers in front of its cramped street-level garage. The middle floor was a wide-open space with walls and a floor of bleached concrete. Its blank, empty nature made it an ideal space for use as a conjuring room, as did the house's location at the northwest corner of the El Alto International Airport. Any loud or disturbing noises that might be noticed by Anja's far-flung neighbors or random passersby would be blamed on the airport long before anyone thought to suspect they had heard the roars of demons or the cries of the damned.

She lived in seclusion on the house's top floor, an L-shaped space that framed the north and east sides of its large rooftop terrace. There were almost no furnishings to speak of. Very few rental apartments in the La Paz area were available in a furnished state. Anja had learned to adapt without complaint to situations such as this; she had her bedroll, a roof above her head, and a working electric bulb dangling by a frayed wire from the stuccoed ceiling. Compared to nights she had spent with the Red Army during the Great Patriotic War, this was luxury.

A vodka bottle in her left hand, Anja used her right to peruse the Odessa journal.

The pages of the leather-bound book were packed with initials, addresses, strings of letters and numbers absent of context, and marginalia in a variety of languages—mostly German, but also Latin, Greek, Arabic, Hebrew, Japanese, and a few that Anja didn't recognize. There were also crudely drawn representations of obscure demonic sigils and conjuring circles, followed by footnoted instructions. It was a book of riddles, mysteries, and secrets.

Some of its content, on the other hand, was as clear as could be.

Poring through long passages in German, Anja found herself engrossed in the hidden workings of the "ratlines," an underground network organized by the Roman Catholic Church after the Second World War. Its purpose had been to help Nazis of all stripes—from minor clerks to the most wanted of war criminals—escape Europe and adopt new identities in South America. The participation of a Nazi-sympathizing Catholic bishop named Alois Hudal had been exposed in 1947, but not the true scope of the conspiracy. The Catholic prelate had facilitated the escapes of thousands of Nazis into Argentina, Uruguay, Paraguay, Chile, and Bolivia.

I knew it, Anja fumed while she read. Throughout the Second World War the Catholic Church and Vatican City had steadfastly maintained their neutrality with regard to the conflict. But if the Odessa journal was a truthful account, the Catholic Church had lied to the world. *Neutral, my ass. They sided with the fascists. With the war criminals.*

She indulged a momentary fantasy of revenge against those members of the Catholic Church who had aided the Nazis, but then she remembered the terms of the Covenant. The same truce that prevented White and Black magicians from interfering with one another's delicate experiments also prohibited her from direct assault upon the clergy.

A diabolical notion weaseled into her thoughts.

Israel's Kabbalists are not bound by the Covenant.

Just as quickly as she had considered the idea, she dismissed it. *The Israelis live on the razor's edge as it is. The last thing they will want to do is make an enemy of the Vatican.*

She set down the journal and dug through the rest of the contents of the leather satchel she took from the German motorcyclist. There were small vials of essential oils both common and rare—sandalwood, camphor, Abramelin, Roman chamomile, and jasmine absolute; quills crafted from the feathers of such birds as an eagle, a crow, a snowy owl, and a goose; and three vials of ink labeled, respectively, SQUID, INDIA, and PACT INK.

Tonight's target was definitely a karcist, Anja concluded. *Maybe even the leader of one of the new Black Sun traveling covens I have been hunting. That and the intel on the ratlines would make this book valuable to the Mossad.* She flipped to the end of the book and studied the Black Sun mandala drawn on the inside of its back cover. *But how valuable? Enough to convince them to help me translate the Iron Codex?*

Nine years. That was nearly how long Anja had been struggling to make sense of the ancient grimoire known as the Iron Codex. It had been bequeathed to her by her late master Adair Macrae, the only person she'd ever known who had actually learned how to use the book for angel-based magick. He had used it once to yoke angels to himself and to her, and he had coached her through the details of a specific ritual in order to liberate her fellow karcist—and Adair's prized pupil—Cade Martin from a six-month exile in Hell.

Since then, she'd failed to translate so much as one fucking word of that book.

She knew it was a resource of tremendous power. Adair had told her as much, and she had seen firsthand some of what it could be used to do. But its pages were devoid of easy content such as diagrams. All of its instructions were written in proto-Enochian, the language used by angels in the epoch before the Fall. Consequently, demonic assistance was useless when trying to interpret the tome's lengthy passages. As her brother-in-arms once put it, for demons, trying to read proto-Enochian was tantamount to rubbing lye into one's eyes.

And so the book lay in its hiding place, unopened and untouched, mocking her.

I was so sure I could master it. Instead it makes a fool of me.

For a time the book had been in the care of a group of Kabbalah scholars. As practitioners of White magick, the Pauline Art, they could employ Celestial aid to read the book. But the few masters of the Jewish mystic tradition who had survived the Nazi holocaust were not interested in helping a Goetic magician like Anja unlock the secrets of the codex.

There was another alternative, of course. One that might prove quicker and less costly. She could simply reach out to Cade and ask for his help. But it would demand that Anja swallow her pride by the mouthful, and that was a prospect even more galling than bribing the Mossad.

It wasn't just because of the young American's preternatural ease at reading proto-Enochian. Or because he had continued after the war to increase his power as a karcist at a rate Anja found humbling and daunting. Or because Anja had risked entangling herself with him in a short-lived torrid fling a few years ago, one in which Cade had seemed deeply invested but that had left Anja feeling exposed, vulnerable, and deeply confused. . . .

Do not lie to yourself, she chided her ego. *Your romance-gone-wrong is precisely why you do not wish to talk to him. You would rather risk getting shot by the Mossad to have even one page of the codex translated, than have to look Cade in the eye and tell him the truth.*

It was childish. Cowardly. Beneath her.

But it was easy, and there was no one to force her hand.

Anja emptied the last of the vodka with a long vertical tilt of the bottle. *An entire liter in one sitting. I am getting as bad as Cade.* She let the empty bottle roll away into a corner while she splayed herself backward atop her bedroll and pillow.

Staring straight up at the naked bulb above her, but too tired to stand, she borrowed BAEL's hand to pull the light's chain and plunge her tiny living space into humid darkness. It and shield demon AMYNA were the last ones she had held in thrall after purging all her others. She knew that she would recuperate more quickly if she were fully free of spirits, but paranoia and experience compelled her to keep yoked at least one spirit for defense and one for attack whenever possible.

Come morning she would venture into downtown La Paz. Although the still-nascent state of Israel had no consulate or embassy in Bolivia, there were dead-drop postboxes in an office building in the Sopacochi district where Anja knew she could leave messages that would be received and answered in good time. She would let her Mossad contact know what she had found and try to gauge whether the Israelis were interested in it—and if so, to what degree.

Until then, it would be all she could do to sleep free of nightmares.

Listen up, she warned her troublesome pair of yoked spirits. *One bad dream, one nosebleed, or even one second of migraine, and I will make sure you both suffer an excess of torments the next time I yoke you. If either of you crosses me, you both suffer. Understood?*

Her mental challenge was answered by a sullen silence.

That is what I thought.

Her nightly ultimatum delivered, she shut her eyes and slipped into a deep, black sleep.

JANUARY 10

"Take your places," Dragan said to his four tanists. "It's time."

The banquet room had been prepared with a painstaking eye for detail. A grand circle of protection had been drawn in virgin chalk on the parquet floor. Inside it was etched a pentagram, which contained four stations reserved for Dragan's tanists and his operator's circle at its head. Flames twisted in slow dances atop tapers cast from the beeswax of a new hive; freshly consecrated charcoal smoldered in the brazier beside Dragan's lectern, upon which rested his grimoire, open to the requisite page for the morning's experiment. A mixed perfume of camphor and sandalwood lingered in the cold morning air.

His tanists stepped inside their circles and pulled the hoods of their albs low in front of their faces. Dragan shook his head at them. *As if that can hide their souls from the hosts of Hell. Standards of training have slipped since the Thule Society became the Black Sun.*

He adjusted the belt of his alb and fixed his paper miter into place atop his head, taking care to make sure its inscribed name of EL faced forward. Then he stepped inside the operator's circle and used the tip of his sword to ceremonially close the circle. "From this moment until the end of the experiment, none of you is to move. Do not speak to the demon, even if addressed or questioned. One word, one movement out of true, and you will condemn yourself to death—and possibly the rest of us with you. So hold fast, and remain silent." The tanists acknowledged his instruction with slow, deep nods. "Let us begin."

Knowing what was to come, Dragan was thankful the rest of the manor house was empty. Its master, family, and servants all were away on holiday. Their absence, and the half mile of empty space between the main house and the next occupied dwelling, promised him and his cohort some much-needed privacy.

Dragan set his sword across the tops of his feet, which were shod in white leather slippers. Taking care not to dislodge the sword from its perch, he straightened and focused his mind upon the open page of his grimoire. Then he initiated the ritual.

From beneath his vestments he produced a small crucible and set it down in front of his feet. As soon as the vessel touched the floor, licks of green flame crept upward from its bowl. Dragan took a pinch of incense from a pouch on his belt and cast it into the flames. Then he raised his wand and intoned in a level voice, "Holocaust. Holocaust. Holocaust."

The emerald flames danced higher and brighter.

"We are to call upon GŌGOTHIEL, a great duke of the Descending Hierarchy. Before he fell, he belonged to the Order of Principalities. His virtue is that he follows directions in good faith. Stand fast, now." Dragan thrust his wand into the brazier's rising flames.

A fountain of violet sparks erupted from the crucible, bounded off the high ceiling, and scattered about the room, which resounded with bloodcurdling howls and bansheelike wails. A foul odor washed over Dragan and his tanists, and at once the great circle was surrounded by a swirl of thick fog flickering with spectral light.

Above the Infernal clamor, Dragan shouted:

"I adjure thee, great GŌGOTHIEL, as the agent of the Emperor LUCIFER, and of his beloved son LUCIFUGE ROFOCALE, by the power of the pact I have with thee, and by the names ADONAY, ELOIM, JEHOVAM, TAGLA, MATHON, ALMOUZIN, ARIOS, PITHONA, SYLPHAE, SALAMANDRAE, GNOMUS, TERRAE, COELUS, GODENS, AQUA, and by the whole hierarchy of superior intelligences who shall constrain thee against thy will, *venité, venité, submirillitor* GŌGOTHIEL!"

The noise assaulting the circle grew louder, and the vapors curling from Dragan's brazier began to reek of burning fish gall and festering excrement. Outside the circle the wall of fog climbed higher and spun faster, driven by a wailing wind.

"I adjure thee, GŌGOTHIEL, by the pact, and by the names, appear instanter!"

Dragan stabbed his wand into the glowing coals at his feet.

The room screamed, but the demon remained at large.

"Now I adjure thee, LUCIFUGE ROFOCALE, whom I command, as the agent of the Lord and the Emperor of Lords, send me thy messenger GŌGOTHIEL, forcing him to forsake his hiding place, wheresoever it may be, and warning thee—!" Another thrust of his wand into the flames provoked a clap of thunder, and the ground beneath the house shook with terrible violence.

He was about to continue when Something Else said:

CEASE YOUR PETTY TORTURES. I AM HERE.

The beast manifested inside a glyph of containment several feet northeast of the grand circle. Its cloven feet were bound securely inside the glyph's inner triangle, and it could not venture beyond its bounding circle without the express direction and permission of the operator. Unlike many of the Fallen, GŌGOTHIEL did not resemble some unholy marriage of mismatched fauna. Its form was vaguely human, but gaunt as if it had been starved down to its bones, and its skin was leathery and black. Most disturbing of all was its distorted head, which was stretched into a curving phallic shape devoid of eyes but boasting a mouth filled with sharklike teeth.

It radiated contempt as it regarded Dragan and his tanists.

WHY DOST THOU DISTURB MY REPOSE? WHAT DOST THOU SEEK OF ME?

"A sending suited to your talent and temperament. I charge thee, by those Names I have invoked and on pain of those torments thou hast known, to regard the likeness of the specific vessel whose eidolon I hold in my mind, and that when I release thee, thou shalt straightaway go unto that vessel, not making thyself known to any within her or without her, and accompany her as she embarks upon her next journey. At such time as that vessel finds itself above waters deep enough to ensure its wreckage will be unrecoverable, you are to rend that vessel to pieces and guarantee not only its destruction, but the demise of all the souls on board. Furthermore, you will share your vision of this sending with me as it transpires, so that I might know for certain that it has been performed to my satisfaction."

He felt the spirit's hatred of him. It was as boundless as it was profound.

I CANNOT GIVE THEE WHAT THOU REQUIREST.

"Refusal will not avail thee," Dragan warned. "Either shalt thou go without delay and perform what I command, or I shall in no wise dismiss thee, but rather keep thee here unto my life's end, tormenting thee daily, as thy father permitteth."

The beast bared its fangs in a taunting grin. THY LIFE IS BUT A DAY TO ME,

Eve-spawn. Thy torments but a feeble imitation of those I have suffered ere the cosmic egg was hatched.

Time was running out to complete this commission. Unwilling to be
bullied into negotiation, Dragan jabbed his wand into the coals. Gōgothiel
shook the manor with a plangent howl. Then it regarded Dragan with a pal-
pable aura of hatred and resentment.

I shall do as thou commandest.

"Splendid. Be it executed to my satisfaction, and for thy recompense thou
shalt carry off the immortal parts of all those victims not under Heaven's express protection."

A great prize, the demon said, but not yet enough to satisfy me and
mine. Thou must also give to me of thine own hoard, as it is written
in the pact.

"Thou art slow to recall the pact," Dragan said, "but I will deal fairly with
thee, great duke." From under his robe he retrieved a small, opalescent vial
with a matching stopper. It contained a dram of his own tears, shed after reflection and meditation, and consecrated. He lobbed the vial to the beast,
which plucked it from the air with a snap of its monstrous jaws.

The demon grinned.

When I have thee in Hell, magician, I shall drink thy tears dry.

"Thy threats are empty—I am not marked for thee. Now cease thy prattle
and discharge thy commission! I send thee!"

Observe then, and be satisfied.

A pillar of fire consumed the monster—and then both flames and demon
vanished.

Dragan closed his eyes and concentrated upon Gōgothiel's perceptions.
He was rewarded with a dizzying image of flight at a great altitude. He recognized the shape of Spain and the shores of North Africa. Next came a blur of
passage over the Mediterranean . . . and as the demon passed over Corsica it
descended. Its apparent plunge toward the Tyrrhenian Sea quickly revealed
the target toward which Dragan had set the beast: BOAC Flight 781, a Comet
1 jet airliner cruising north-northeast through clear early-afternoon skies
along the Italian coast.

Gōgothiel wasted no time. It landed atop the aircraft, sussed out the weak
spot noted in Dragan's mental image of the vessel, and proceeded to tear it
asunder.

Shrieks of deforming steel pierced the roaring of wind, which together drowned out the cries of the thirty-five souls the jet had carried to their doom: men, women, and children, not one among them important enough for the hosts of Heaven to give a damn about their fate.

Dragan took a perverse satisfaction in watching GŌGOTHIEL rip the aircraft apart. It would have been enough for the beast to inflict a single rent in the jet's hull; from there physics would have finished the job. But the demon took a special glee in shredding the vessel and tormenting its doomed passengers as they fell—those who were still conscious, anyway.

Bodies and wreckage slammed into the sea and sank into the briny black.

"I am satisfied," Dragan told the demon. "You are dismissed. Go in peace, doing harm to none, and return to thy repose, returning when, and only when, I shall call for thee."

The demon did not deign to acknowledge its dismissal in words. Dragan felt the beast's reply in a wash of cold antipathy that reeked of dog shit.

He opened his eyes and said to his tanists, "It is done." As they pulled back their hoods, he addressed the one that had served as his legal counsel for the past few weeks. "Broeking, contact our friends at the airlines and let them know the second halves of their payments are due." To the one who had served as his accountant: "Auerbach, start monitoring our call options against de Havilland's stock. Once our profits reach ten million American dollars, cash out."

The men stripped off their ceremonial garb and hurried out of the banquet room. The tanists who remained, Schlesinger and Hess, were his chief lieutenants in the ranks of Black Sun. Ulrich Schlesinger was a stocky man with a nervous manner; Juliana Hess, his senior tanist, was a severe blond woman to whom tender emotions seemed an alien concept.

"Did it work?" Schlesinger asked.

"Perfectly," Dragan said.

Hess seemed neither pleased nor displeased. "What next, Herr Dalca?"

"Now," Dragan said, "the war begins anew."

※

I have gazed into the essence of power only to see it transformed into impotence.

The ritual of divination was ended, and twists of bitter smoke curled from snuffed tapers. Father Luis Roderigo Pérez sat alone on a bench at the back of the conjuring room, apart from his brethren of the Monte Paterno monastery.

Father Bernardo D'Odorico, the sixtyish head of the monastery, packed up his tools, setting some aside for later exorcism and fumigation. At the other end of the room two young monks, Father Malko and Father Hakkila, both of whom sported pale skin and blond hair buzzed to crew cuts, pulled off their albs and miters. They put away the white ceremonial garments inside a cedar wardrobe that stood in the room's southwest corner.

The fourth tanist for that morning's ritual, Father Pantelis, busied himself opening the shutters on the conjuring room's north-facing windows, which looked out upon the majesty of the Dolomites' towering peaks of jagged rock. Reflected sunlight filled the conjuring room as the paunchy Greek cleric carried out his task, but even that radiance could not dispel from Luis's memory the terrible spectacle that he and the others had witnessed only minutes earlier.

Their circle, led by Father D'Odorico as the operator, had invoked the Celestial Presence known as SAZQUIEL, the spirit with dominion over the daytime's fifth hour. In a rare display of Divine favor, the spirit had appeared—an occurrence far more rare in the practice of the Pauline Art than it was in the Goetic Art.

Luminous and frightening to behold, SAZQUIEL had bestowed upon the monks a vision: it had compelled them to bear witness to the destruction of a jet-powered passenger aircraft, BOAC Flight 781 from Rome, by a demon known as GŌGOTHIEL.

Luis's blood had run cold as he watched hatred incarnate shred the plane in midair. He had wanted to cry out, to plead with Father D'Odorico to take action, to save the plane, to rescue the passengers, to at least take mercy on the children. But for a tanist to speak out of turn during a magick ritual was a recipe for disaster even when dealing with angels, and so Luis had kept silent, swallowing his grief and his fury as the monster from the Abyss destroyed the jet and gorged itself on all the hapless souls trapped within it.

Luis stared at Father D'Odorico, who went about his business—packing up his grimoire, locking away his tools, noting the day's revelations in his journal—with a dispassion that struck the dismayed forty-six-year-old monk as heartless at best. He watched Father D'Odorico palm sweat from the bald oasis in the center of his tonsure; the rest of his hair had long since silvered, giving his classic monk's haircut the aspect of a crown. That and his aquiline visage, when seen in profile, reminded Luis of the portraits of Caesars and of great Roman generals of antiquity.

Seated in the older man's shadow, Luis felt self-conscious about his own dark brown skin and his closely shorn head of wiry black hair—his inheritance from generations of intermarriage between his Spanish ancestors and those who had been indigenous to his native Brazil.

Not many men of the cloth from Luis's part of the world had ever reached the higher echelons of the Catholic Church, and as far as he knew he was the first adept that Monte Paterno had ever recruited from either Central or South America, and one of very few Jesuits. And because Monte Paterno was the last—and as far as Luis knew, the only—bastion of White magick research clandestinely sanctioned by the Pope, he was wary of saying or doing anything that might jeopardize his place among its fraternity of sensitives, scholars, and karcists.

But he couldn't witness an unopposed slaughter and say nothing.

"We stood and watched," Luis said.

Father D'Odorico turned. He wore a look of surprise, as if he hadn't realized Luis was still in the room. "*Scuse?*"

It took effort for Luis to hide his anger and keep a respectful tone. "We watched a demon destroy that plane. And we did nothing as it murdered innocent people. It killed *children.*"

He registered a fleeting sorrow behind D'Odorico's dark eyes, a ghost of regret. The older man sighed. "You know the rules, Luis. All we can do is bear witness." He picked up his quill and resumed making that morning's entry in his journal of experiments.

The Church's policy was as familiar to Luis as it was vexing. "I know," he said, "'interference is forbidden.' Heaven forefend we defy the Covenant."

"It's as much for our protection as anyone's." From beneath the elder priest's furrowed brow came a look of reproach. "If we were to start tampering with the experiments of Black magicians, they would certainly sabotage ours. Either one would risk loosing malevolent spirits upon the earth without instruction or restriction. The damage could be incalculable."

Luis had heard that argument before, but measured against the nearly three dozen innocent lives he had just seen snuffed out, Father D'Odorico's rationale rang hollow. "I think I might find it easier to see the value of the Covenant," Luis said, "if someone could tell me what, precisely, the dark magicians had to sacrifice to secure the truce."

The Italian shrugged. "Their cost was the same as ours: the noninterference pact."

"We gave up the right to fight Evil. They gave up the right to sabotage Good. Those hardly seem equivalent, especially in light of our reticence to act."

D'Odorico finished his entry in the journal, set down the pen, and closed the book. He turned to face Luis, his demeanor more collegial than confrontational. "You raise good points, Luis. Which is to be expected, given your Jesuit training. But you should know that trying to unravel the wisdom of the Covenant is not unlike grappling with the Problem of Evil itself."

"Perhaps they are both proof that the Devil has the best lawyers."

The older man smiled. "Far be it from me to presume to know whose souls are damned and whose are saved, but I'm relatively certain the Devil has *all* of the lawyers."

"Seriously, Father," Luis said. "Why did the Church ever agree to the terms of the Covenant? It ties our hands. Makes us into mere spectators."

"I know." D'Odorico steered Luis toward the conjuring room's exit, whose door currently stood ajar. "Given the Church's apparent inspirations, it can be hard to understand why it insists on preserving our sanctuary's tactical and political impotence. All I can tell you is what my superiors told me when I was a new adept: Put your trust in God, and in His Holiness the Pope." As they stepped into the Spartan confines of the hall, he added, "And meditate more."

The director made a small gesture over his left shoulder that caused the conjuring room's heavy oaken door to swing closed behind him with a resounding thud. Though there was no sound of bolts being thrown or tumblers turning, Luis knew the door was then locked, its contents secured by potent magicks—which of course meant the forced presence of demons inside a place consecrated as holy ground. As offensive as that notion was to him, he imagined it must be orders of magnitude less pleasant for the spirits held there in thrall.

His master asked, "Anything else on your mind, Luis?"

"No, Father. Thank you." Luis pressed his palms together and honored D'Odorico with a small bow before they parted. He made his way back toward his cloister, his thoughts haunted by images of a jet aircraft torn to scrap and thirty-five human beings shredded with callous ease . . . all while five karcists of the Church watched and did nothing to help.

There must be a better way than this, he told himself. *There has to be.*

JANUARY 21

Rifle fire marked the stroke of midnight in Luang Prabang, the war-stricken capital of Laos. Miles Franklin darted out of a shanty house's pitch-black yard through its open gate. He crossed an unlit, unnamed street to hurdle over a picket fence and through low-hanging branches into another hovel's front yard. The plot was thickly wooded and badly neglected, like so many others on the sliver-thin peninsula that ended where the rivers Nam Khan and Mekong met.

Sweat beaded upon every inch of Miles's body. His clothes stuck to his dark brown skin as if he were human flypaper. He raised his MI6 standard-issue Walther PPK and held the compact pistol at eye level, his grip and gait steady as he moved past the darkened house, whose backyard abutted the rear of the Lotus Villa Hotel on Kounxoua Street.

He reached the fence behind the hotel. Nearby pops of gunfire made him duck. The North Vietnamese troops who had occupied the town weren't his enemies, per se, but at night anyone moving in the dark was suspect—perhaps a looter, or a sniper—and a valid target. He had no plans on catching a bullet tonight. *Not if I can help it.*

In the distance, something exploded. A flash of orange light blazed for half a second in the tiny gaps between the trees, and then everything was dark again.

Miles checked his back and his flanks, and then he vaulted over the fence into the narrow strip of rocky dirt behind the Lotus Villa. All the way to its back door he waited for a sniper shot that never came. The door was unlocked. He drew a grateful breath as he slipped inside.

As soon as he inhaled he regretted it. The air inside the run-down hotel was rife with demon stink. It was a foul odor—a medley of rotten eggs, excrement, meat left in the sun, the ferric tang of blood, and the reek of burnt hair and feathers—and one that he knew all too well after more than eight years of traveling the world with his pal Cade Martin, a real-life sorcerer who trafficked in demonic power and called it "magick."

Miles pushed onward, deeper inside the hotel. The first-floor hallway was quiet and empty. Likewise its kitchen, laundry, and other support areas were deserted. The closer he got to the main staircase at the front of the hotel, the ranker the odors that assaulted his nose. As he checked the front sitting room, he saw one reason for the overpowering stench: all of the hotel's windows were closed. *I know it's a sauna out there, but why shut the bloody windows?*

He looked up the stairs. The second floor was bathed in black and radiated menace. Common sense and every primitive survival instinct in his body told him to turn back, to get as far from this hotel as he could. Instead he forced himself to climb the stairs.

Cade had been missing without explanation for several weeks. It wasn't the first time he had gone AWOL from his role as an unofficial operative of MI6. In fact, Cade had vanished so many times over the past eight years that Miles had started to consider it closer to being Cade's status quo. All the same, he was responsible not only for making sure Cade stayed within the bounds of the law, but for making certain the impulsive young American stayed *alive*.

Teak steps groaned under Miles's feet as he climbed to the second floor. He pulled from his pocket a small torch—or "flashlight," as Cade insisted on calling it—and switched it on. All the bedroom doors stood open save one. Was that an invitation, a distraction, a warning, or a trap?

Treading lightly but with haste, Miles moved past all the open rooms and swept the beam from his torch through them. They were all unoccupied.

Miles's patience was fading. *After all I paid for this tip, if Cade isn't here—*

From under the closed door came a stink of vinegar that made him wrinkle his nose. *What the bloody hell . . . ?* Then he heard a hiss, followed by a growl that made his guts feel as if they'd turned to mud. *That can't be good.*

He kicked open the door.

Then he wished he hadn't.

Cade was sprawled in his boxers on a stained mattress, a tangle of sheets at his ankles. His left hand cupped an empty syringe and hypodermic needle, and the detritus of his latest heroin fix—spoon, Zippo, and rubber tourniquet—lay scattered on the bed beside his bare torso.

But the real horror loomed above him.

Hovering over Cade's bed in the sweltering night was a Southeast Asian woman's detached head and spine. Her mouth was crowded with jagged teeth, and her hate-filled eyes glowed yellow as she spun in midair to face Miles. He struggled to aim his pistol with shaking hands as she floated toward him, her hair caked with blood and writhing like snakes. Swollen organs and viscera dangled beneath the shredded flesh of her throat, all of it dripping blood. The monster reeked of vinegar, and when it hissed at him its breath stank like an open sewer.

It picked up speed and raced toward him.

He fired, put six bullets into its center mass. The slugs passed through the creature and buried themselves in the wall above Cade's bed, but the monster didn't slow down.

His weapon clacked empty as the fiend lunged—

A whip of lightning struck the monster from behind and coiled around its throat. Miles dodged right and saw Cade rise from his bed. With his left hand Cade controlled the crackling whip of electricity, and a wave of his right hand closed and locked the shutters on his window.

The abomination screeched and hollered in some obscure Laotian dialect as Cade reined it in and used his lasso of energy to force it to the floor. It was facing him as he pinned it. Then Cade held out his right hand, and from a corner of the room his black-handled ceremonial dagger—an athamé, he called it—flew to him and planted itself in his grip. He squatted over the creature, which continued to struggle but could not break free of his spectral whip.

He pressed the tip of his knife to the underside of its jaw. "End of the line, Makala."

It spat in Cade's face and then shouted at him in rapid-fire Vietnamese.

Cade thrust his dagger through the monster's jaw and into its brain. It twitched for a moment, and then the eerie yellow light in its eyes dimmed and expired. The young American gave his blade a final twist inside the wound for good measure, and then he pulled it free. "That ought to do it." As he wiped the athamé clean on his bedsheets, he asked Miles, "You okay?"

Miles realized he hadn't blinked in nearly a minute. "What the bloody hell was that?"

"A *penanggalan*," Cade said. "Or as the Laotians call it, a *phi-kasu*."

Unable to take his eyes off the creature's fangs, Miles asked, "Some kind of vampire?"

"Not quite. The undead are just a myth." He tucked his dagger back into its spot inside a leather roll-up he used to transport his various tools of the Art. "That was a karcist named Makala Savang. She's been working for the Vietnamese, stirring up shit all down the Mekong."

"Hang on, mate. You're telling me that thing is *human*?"

"It was. She yoked Pazuzu for one of its lesser-known abilities, one it grants only to women." He rolled up his leather kit and tied it closed. "She's been cutting a swath through the French troops down in Dien Bien Phu. I told them I'd take care of it." He grabbed up some clothes and started to get dressed. "And I just did."

"And painted a bull's-eye on your back in the process."

Cade shrugged as he put on his shirt. "Couldn't be helped." He sat on the bed to pull on his pants. "I needed her to come after me so I could ambush her."

"Some ambush. You were on the dark side of the moon when I came through the door."

An irreverent grin. "A cunning ruse. I had her right where I wanted her."

"Five seconds more, she'd have had you for supper." Miles loaded a fresh magazine into his Walther. "Speaking of which, I was only a few minutes ahead of some folks from the KGB and the MSS, both of whom have standing orders to neutralize you on sight."

Cade looked up as he tied his boots. He seemed untroubled by Miles's report. "So much for extending my vacation. And I had a front-row seat to the war and everything."

"Save your jokes for the plane. We need to leave." Miles made sure that his baritone conveyed the true urgency of their situation as he added, "*Now.*"

"Whatever you say, *sahib.*" Cade retrieved his Beretta from under his pillow, tucked it behind his waistband at the small of his back, and draped his wrinkled linen shirt over it. Then he grabbed a quarter-full bottle of gin off the dresser as he moved to follow Miles out the door.

Through the muddled odors of sweat and cooked opium, Miles caught a whiff of juniper on Cade's breath. "Christ, mate, are you pissed right now?"

"No more than usual. Why?"

Miles beckoned Cade to follow him out of the room. "You're a piece of work, old boy. I can count on one hand the number of times I've seen you sober since the war."

"I probably faked at least one of those," Cade said as they hurried downstairs.

As they reached the ground floor, a burly bruiser with a classic Russian crew cut lurched through the villa's open front door, a silenced Makarov pistol in his hand. He raised it in Miles's direction and almost had time to aim before Miles shot him through his left eye.

The dead Russian fell as Miles noted a moving shadow blocking the moonlight spilling through the slats of a nearby window's shutters. He put three bullets through the shutters and watched the shadow collapse. He went out the front door and held it open for Cade. "Let's go."

"One second," Cade said. He extended his right arm and made a slicing motion in the air with two fingers. A third Russian staggered out of a dark corridor with his throat slashed open. Blood sheeted down his chest and soaked his shirt while his mouth twitched in a futile attempt to speak. Three steps out of the hallway he dropped his Makarov and fell dead onto his face. Gesturing toward the street, Cade added, *"Now* we can go."

Fucking hell. No matter how many times Miles saw Cade wreak havoc with magick, it never ceased to unnerve him. He turned his back on the carnage in the villa and crossed the short walk to the gate that separated the villa's property from the street. He raised his miniature torch and snapped it on and off a few times in a simple signal. From a few dozen meters up the road, the proper response signal came from a car's headlights. He motioned for Cade to join him.

Half a minute later they clambered into the back of a black Peugeot 203 sedan, one with rearward-opening "suicide doors" in the front. The driver, Akamu, was a local MI6 asset Miles had met only that morning, but he had found the skinny young man to be extremely helpful, even in the face of deadly violence. "The airport, Akamu," Miles said as he pulled the door shut behind him. "Don't stop for anyone or anything." He passed the man a fistful of crisp new twenty-kip banknotes. "Understand?"

"Not stop," Akamu said, slamming his foot down on the accelerator.

Outside the car the shadowed streets of Luang Prabang blurred past. Cade and Miles ducked low in the backseat, as wary of being spotted as they were of ending up on the wrong end of a stray bullet. "I suppose you have a ride lined up at the airport," Cade said.

"Naturally. You don't think I'd saunter into a shithole like this and not have a plan for getting out, do you?" He fished a crumpled pack of Player's Weights cigarettes from his pants pocket, dug out one that was still intact, and lit it with his next-to-last match. Then he passed the smokes to Cade, who exhumed a crooked but unbroken cigarette and lit it with a snap of his fingers. The two old friends savored their nicotine in silence as the car hurtled through the night.

Between drags, Miles asked, "Care to tell me where you've been the last eight weeks?"

"Tracking the *penanggalan*."

"For part of it, maybe. But my sources insist you arrived in Laos only six days ago."

Cade shot a cagy side-eye look at Miles. Then he finished his cigarette with a final pull and flicked its smoldering stub out the open window on his right. "Wake me at the plane." He shut his eyes and offered up a fairly good impression of a corpse.

Wide awake, Miles kept his concerns to himself, just as he had for years.

Cade's had a streak of melancholy ever since the war ended, he reflected, *but I can see it's getting worse, no matter how much he denies it.*

He watched his old Oxford chum sleep—or maybe just pretend to sleep, not that it mattered—and worried that the troubled young American was not going to be able to pull himself out of this nosedive toward self-destruction.

Miles lit a broken half of another cigarette and swallowed his frustration at being unable to help Cade in any way that mattered.

I keep hoping he'll exorcise whatever personal demons are haunting him. But from what he tells me, demons are what keep him in business. . . . And I'm pretty sure they're also what's killing him, day by bloody day, from the inside out.

Libraries had always unnerved Anja, and La Paz's Biblioteca Municipal was no different. The narrow white building sat at the convergence of Calle Cañada Strongest and Calle Mexico, a pair of boulevards that terminated—or originated, depending upon one's point of view—at the Plaza del Estudiante. Its exterior fused Art Deco curves and angles with stately Doric pillars, but its interior was as dark, musty, and cramped as every other library she had ever seen.

And the silence. The oppressive, smothering silence.

Anja could enjoy peace and quiet, especially when she was free of demons. Having it imposed upon her rankled her. Being shushed stoked a spark of rebellion deep inside her heart.

For the sake of survival, she embraced the discretion that came with using the library as a meeting point. Her contact from the Mossad had selected this location several months earlier, and so far it had served them well. She would request meetings by placing coded ads in the classified section of *O Estado de S. Paulo,* Brazil's newspaper of record, which was generally available in major cities throughout South America. Usually within a few days, her contact would respond with a similarly coded ad that she then deciphered to determine the day, time, and specific location for their meeting inside the library.

Today she had been instructed to meet him on the third floor, in the stacks of the Philosophy section. She had been sent to subsection 110, Metaphysics, and told to seek him in 111, Ontology. When she found the shelf, it was configured just as she had expected: subsection 110 occupied one side of a towering shelf and 111 stood on the other. In the interest of discretion and plausible deniability, a wall of books would stand between Anja and her contact.

As usual he was late. She passed the time paging through a book of Buddhist philosophy that touched upon but ultimately dismissed most metaphysical queries as "spiritually unhelpful." She could only nod in sympathy. *There is much truth in the old ways.*

A book was cautiously removed from a spot on the far side of the bookshelf, creating a narrow gap from one aisle to the next. All that Anja could see of Yaakov Stern through the sliver of space was his eyes and formidable brows, but those and the wiry fortyish Israeli's voice were all she needed to be sure it was him. "Find something of interest?" he whispered.

She leaned close to the gap and matched his hushed tone. "A journal. Taken from an ex-Nazi. It proves Odessa is real."

"Of that we did not need to be convinced." Yaakov pretended to leaf through whatever book he had opened. "Why should this concern us?"

She looked around, paranoid that they might acquire an eavesdropper. Satisfied they were still alone, she continued. "It has names. Addresses. And more I cannot decode. It is a map to hundreds of Nazi war criminals hiding in South America."

Yaakov lifted one eyebrow in consideration. "You're sure it is genuine?"

"Positive."

He fixed her with an intense one-eye stare. "Did you bring it?"

Anja was reluctant to share her leverage, but how else was she to entice the Israelis? She took the leather-bound journal from inside her satchel and pushed it through the gap in the wall of books. Yaakov plucked it free from the other side and assessed its contents in short order. "It is . . . interesting." He closed the journal and sent it back to Anja, who anxiously snatched it back off the shelf. Yaakov asked, "What do you want for it?"

She saw no point in playing coy. "Your promise that the Kabbalah scholars in Jerusalem will help me translate the Iron Codex."

Yaakov shook his head. "I can't give you that. The journal is a good find, but its clues are vague. It would take time, maybe years, to unpack its true value."

"More excuses," Anja muttered in anger as she put away the journal. "Same old lies."

"I won't make promises I can't keep," Yaakov said. "If you had a solid lead on someone like Mengele, or Alois Brunner, maybe I could make a case for bringing you to the rabbis. But as it stands, my supervisor doesn't think I should *ever* trust a Russian as an asset."

She glared through the empty space on the shelf and suddenly noted how much it resembled the murder holes of a medieval fortress. "You are not much use to me alive, are you?"

He sighed. "If you want to give me the journal, I can arrange for a drop of some money and weapons, like we did for you last year in Asunción."

"Stop wasting my time. I took the journal off an Odessa cell leader. I *know* it has value."

There was guilt and resignation in Yaakov's expression. "You may be right. But the truth is, the Mossad isn't ready to act on that kind of intelligence. It might be years before we'll have the strength and experience to move against escaped Nazis. All we can do for now is watch, listen, and keep good records."

"If that is all you can do, your efforts amount to nothing."

She returned her book of Buddhist thought to the gap on the shelf and strode away, eager to put this waste of time and effort behind her. As she emerged from between the stacks, Yaakov gently took her arm to stop her. "Anja, please—"

She confronted him with a promise of violence in her eyes. "What?"

"Our sources in Moscow say the KGB knows you're here. They've been tracking you since you left Cochabamba." He telegraphed his concern with a frown that looked rehearsed. "It might be a good time for you to leave La Paz."

She pulled her arm from his grasp. "I will leave La Paz when I know its Nazis are dead."

6

JANUARY 22

Briet was safe inside her operator's circle, and her patron spirit ASTAROTH was secured inside a triangular ward several yards away. Around them yawned the vast cavity of the Silo, all of it except the conjuring stage lost in darkness. Though the cavernous pit's myriad sensors, cameras, and witnesses all were well out of sight, Briet never let herself forget, not for a moment, that they were there, ever vigilant. *No doubt waiting for the one time I make a mistake.*

The only illumination on the pentagonal platform came from the coal-burning torchères that ringed its periphery, and from the great swirling cloud of violet flames exhaled by the demon between answers. A sullen inflection tainted the beast's elegant baritone, which it delivered in a normal human register, unlike so many of its Infernal kin. "Are thy questions nearly exhausted? I grow weary of this inquisition."

"I shall ask as many questions of thee as I need and desire."

She refused to be bullied or wheedled by the demon. It had wasted enough of her time this day by appearing in three consecutive false forms—by turns grotesque, indistinct, and patronizing—before presenting itself in its true shape: that of a nude, beautiful angel with flowing golden hair, feathered wings smeared with blood and ash, and a huge, semi-tumescent coal-black penis. In its right hand it held a writhing viper; a ten-pointed crown glittered with painful brightness upon its brow. It sat astride a beast that sported a hyena's head, a lion's paws, a feathered torso, leathery wings, and a serpent's tail.

Fire spilled from its mouth as it sighed. "Ask thy questions, Eve-spawn."

"Share with me any portents to which you have been privy, especially those that concern activity Below as directed from here on earth. Confess to me dark tidings, the schemes of my enemies and allies alike, and any tales of war or rumors of war."

It was a routine inquiry during rituals of divination, a catch-all solicitation for bad news and warnings of danger. Briet much preferred the more esoteric queries she sometimes got to ask when the scientists would prepare questions for her in advance—requests for insight into realms metaphysical or subatomic. But this was not that kind of session. This day's scheduled experiment was all about America's foreign policy and national defense.

So it struck Briet as odd when ASTAROTH hesitated to answer.

The great duke of Hell had a well-earned reputation as a spirit that would give true answers of all things past, present, and to come, and regarding all matters of science. But a routine supplication for a general warning seemed to have left the tarnished angel tongue-tied.

Briet pointed her wand toward the brazier of burning coals at her feet. "Speak! Or I shall torment thee without respite until you comply! By the names ADONAY, ELOHIM, JEHOVAM—!"

STAY THY ROD, the beast commanded, its voice swollen into a roll of thunder. I SHALL ANSWER THY QUESTION. The viper in its hand writhed as if desperate to escape back to Hell. OMENS OF A GREAT CALAMITY HAVE ALL HELL CLAMORING TO RISE.

A chill snaked down Briet's spine. "What kind of calamity? Natural? Or man-made?"

THE LATTER. A HOLOCAUST ABORNING.

"From whence comes this danger?"

FROM WITHIN THY MASTERS' BORDERS. A CASTLE OF FIRE—

Red warning lights mounted on the Silo's walls snapped on, and a man's voice boomed from unseen loudspeakers, "BRIET! ABORT!"

ASTAROTH belched a cone of green flames that Briet deflected with her raised wand. Twisting to and fro within the confines of its triangular ward, the beast demanded, WHO DARES TO ADDRESS ME WITHOUT INVITATION? SHOW THYSELF AND FACE MY WRATH!

Briet stabbed her wand into the coals at her feet. "Hold, demon!" The beast howled, its wails of pain mixed with roars of fury. "The Law applies only to my tanists, and as you can see"—she motioned at the otherwise empty conjuring stage behind her—"I have none. Hold fast to thy appointed place!"

Again the voice bellowed from the hidden speakers: "BRIET! TERMINATE THIS EXPERIMENT NOW!"

The command was still echoing as the demon threatened to break free of its magickal restraints, its eyes ablaze and fixed upon Briet. YOU WILL PAY FOR THIS BREACH!

I have to end this while I still can.

She raised her wand, met the demon's burning stare, and spoke quickly. "Our business is done for today, great ASTAROTH! I dismiss and discharge thee by the terms of our pact. Depart in peace and return when, and only when, I call for thee. Begone, spirit, in the name of ADONAY, ELOHIM, ARIEL, and JEHOVAM!"

Her patron roared as the floor inside the triangle beneath it vanished, plunging the creature into a starless void. As soon as the tips of its soiled wings passed from sight, the floor reappeared, accompanied by a clap of thunder that dimmed the flames in the torchères. A leaden silence settled over the great emptiness of the Silo, and in her moment of solitude Briet felt a great tide of anger rise from deep within the darkest parts of herself.

The overhead lights snapped on, harsh, cold, and white. Briet squinted. Shielding her eyes, she walked off the stage and crossed the bridge with murder on her mind.

Minutes later she stormed through the technology-packed confines of the Silo's control suite, which she considered to be little more than an overhyped observation deck. Half a dozen sergeants and junior officers tried to block her path, but she brushed them aside with sheer force of personality and a glare that could carve diamonds. One wall was full of windows that looked down into the Silo from several levels above the conjuring stage. The opposite wall was lined with towering gray steel cabinets that housed computers whose endless labors took the form of tape reels that jerked and spun, back and forth, ad infinitum.

She was shaking with fury by the time she reached the elevated console reserved for the director of operations. Still dressed in her ceremonial alb and miter, and clutching her wand, Briet looked like a character out of a fairy tale confronting the essence of modern banality.

"You fucking prick," she said.

She wondered whether Frank might clear the room in a bid to demonstrate his authority. Instead, he acted as if her presence in the control suite was nothing of consequence, despite the fact that she had made a point of never coming here unless she had to. Poking at buttons on his console, he asked with affected boredom, "Something I can do for you, Bree?"

"You can tell me why you nearly just got us all killed."

"The experiment had to be terminated."

"You broke protocol." Briet planted her hands atop Frank's console and leaned over it to get in his face so he couldn't keep ignoring her. "You know the rules. When there's a Presence on the conjuring stage, no one speaks inside the Silo but the operator. You could've gotten me killed in there—and set loose a minister of Hell in the process." He refused to make eye contact with her, so she grabbed him by his necktie and yanked him forward so they were nose-to-nose. "I want an answer, asshole. And the explanation you're about to give had better be phenomenally fucking good, or I will gut you like a fish I don't even want to eat."

He extricated his tie from her grasp with methodical precision, his expression a cipher. Seemingly unfazed, he sat back, meeting her stare the entire time. "Long story short? The whole program's going dark."

"Why?"

"McCarthy," Frank said, invoking the specter of Senator Joseph McCarthy, the most-feared man in American politics. "His witch hunt is threatening to become dangerously literal."

"He doesn't know about the Silo, does he?"

"Not yet," Frank said. "But it's only a matter of time. He's papering the DOD with subpoenas. Digging into anything he can find: testimony, budgets, operational records—"

"If he digs into the ODP—"

"That's why we've gone dark. We're pretty sure we've covered our tracks, but if his dragnet pulls in enough paper, someone's going to notice the budgets don't add up. And if he connects that to the Occult Defense Program, he'll want records of all our personnel. Especially those who might be concealing . . . *alternative* lifestyles."

His warning was as effective as it was blunt. McCarthy's subcommittee and its paranoid hunt for communists, homosexuals, and other "subversives" had been the talk of Washington for months, but until that moment Briet had never really thought he could pose any danger to her, thanks to the secretive and dangerous nature of her work. But now, the mere thought of McCarthy digging into the private details of her life as a drug-using, polyamorous, bisexual practitioner of Black magick left her feeling decidedly . . . *vulnerable.*

"Just do us both a favor," Frank said. "Lay low and stay quiet."

"For how long?"

"I don't know. A while." He adopted a more reassuring manner. "This'll blow over. Sooner or later, McCarthy'll move on, and when he does, we'll get back to work. But until then, the best thing you can do is take a long vacation, *capisce*?"

Briet nodded. She hated the idea of being bullied out of her domain; after all these years, she had come to think of the Silo as her stronghold, as the center of her world. To be expelled from it, forced into the shadows by the obsessions of the petty and small-minded, reminded her of the years she had spent among the Nazis and their perverse campaign of global conquest and genocide. That was not a journey she wanted to repeat.

"Say the word and I can put an end to McCarthy right now."

"If that's a joke, it ain't funny. And if it isn't, I'll just pretend you never said it." He beckoned a pair of armed marines and directed them toward Briet with a nod. "Please take Miss Segfrunsdóttir back to her office. After she changes back to street clothes, show her out." To Briet he added, "Don't come back until I call for you. And don't skip town—I might need you back in the Silo on short notice."

"Wouldn't dream of it."

Briet stewed as the marines ushered her out of the control room.

Not many aspects of working for the U.S. Department of Defense bothered Briet. She had never had trouble carrying out violent, amoral orders. She'd hardly ever balked at killing, as long as she'd known who her targets were and why they had been marked for death. Espionage, blackmail, extortion—none of those tasks had ever elicited from her any serious reservations.

But the one thing she could not—*would* not—abide from anyone was lying.

Her ride home was tainted with anxiety. She had known that McCarthy had been digging into the army's affairs, but what could have led him to expand his inquiry into the Pentagon's classified operations? Was he so overzealous that he no longer cared who he antagonized? Or had someone in the ODP broken their vow of secrecy? Was it possible that McCarthy already had some idea what he was looking for? And what would he do if he found it?

Reviewing all of her questions in her imagination, Briet found no answers, only more reasons for worry. By the time the taxi reached the front of her brownstone, she had arrived at a seemingly inescapable conclusion: *Someone is lying to me.*

———

"Come in," said Father D'Odorico, beckoning Luis with one hand. "Shut the door."

Luis heeded the director's summons and stepped inside the office, a space marked by its austerity. In keeping with the nature of their order, Father

D'Odorico had kept his sanctum plain. It contained simple wooden furniture, an unassuming desk, and no curtains on the sole window, which was located behind his chair and looked out upon the snowcapped Dolomites. Pine bookshelves stood along the two walls to either side of the door; they were packed with a variety of old reference works, none of them the least bit exotic.

The director sat behind his desk, his hands folded in front of him. Standing in front of the desk, to Luis's left, was a tall, rail-thin man he didn't recognize. His features had a Mediterranean cast, and he looked to be in his midsixties. However, the detail of his appearance that dominated Luis's attention was his attire: the vestment of a Catholic cardinal. A long black cassock with crimson piping and an elbow-length shoulder cape, and a broad scarlet sash of silk around his waist. Wisps of his thinning white hair poked out from beneath his tight-fitting scarlet *zucchetto,* or skullcap.

Father D'Odorico gestured toward the visiting dignitary. "Father Pérez, this is Cardinal Umberto Lombardi, from the Pauline Synod."

Lombardi offered his hand. Luis shook it, momentarily in awe. *I should have realized it was him.* He couldn't believe he had failed to recognize the cardinal. Lombardi was a principal of the body within the Church that supervised all activity by its handful of remaining Pauline karcists and higher-level exorcists. As the cardinal released his hand, Luis bowed his head in humility. "God be with you, Your Eminence."

The cardinal's voice was deep and commanding: "And also with you, Father." Lombardi motioned toward a pair of chairs in front of the director's desk. "Let's sit, please."

The cardinal took the chair on the left, and Luis sat beside him, facing the director, who picked up a manila folder that sat atop another, similar file on his desk. "The cardinal came here to task our order with a holy mission," Father D'Odorico said. "I've assured him that you are the best qualified to see it accomplished." He set the folder in front of Luis. "He brought us two dossiers that you need to see, starting with this one." A small nod. "Open it."

Luis opened the folder, whose cover was marked in Latin, *de secreto.* The first page he saw was headlined *Libro Ferrum.* Out of habit, he translated it. "The Book of Iron?"

"*Si,*" the cardinal said. "Or as it is sometimes called in English, 'the Iron Codex.' It is, among other things, a guidebook to the practices of Pauline magick. It was created in secret several hundred years ago, a product of

Divine inspiration, by the combined research and efforts of Albertus Magnus and Roger Bacon."

Paging through the file, Luis saw nothing that resembled the contents of such a grimoire. Instead, he found only page after page of notes indicating cities and dates spanning centuries. "What am I looking at here, Your Eminence?"

"To the best of the Synod's knowledge," Lombardi said, "that is a record of every known sighting of the codex itself, or of an event that we believe was made possible by its use." He glanced at the file as Luis continued to leaf through it. "As you can see, we've been searching for the codex for quite some time. Over four hundred years, in fact."

Curious, Luis skipped to the end of the file. "Wewelsburg, Germany, 1942," he read from the logs. "Buenos Aires, Argentina, 1949." He closed the file. It was difficult for him to mask his skepticism concerning the logs' value. "That's a fairly large gap between the final two entries."

"It's far from the largest span of unaccounted time," Lombardi said. "What's vital to know at this juncture is that we have a new lead on where to find the codex. Or at least, to find the last person known to be in possession of the tome." The cardinal gestured with a curling of his hand for D'Odorico to pass him the second manila folder. The director put the file in Lombardi's hands, and he presented it to Luis. "We think this woman has the book."

Luis opened the second folder.

Its top sheet was a government form written in Russian. In its upper right corner was a black-and-white photograph of a young woman, perhaps in her late teens or early twenties, with raven-black hair and a piercing gaze. A Y-shaped scar marred her left cheek, its branches linking the corners of her mouth and eye to the curve of her jaw beneath her ear. He squinted at the page's Cyrillic characters and struggled to remember what little he had learned of Slavic languages as he read the woman's name from the top of the file: "Anja Kernova."

"A Russian peasant girl," Lombardi said. "Fought with the Red Army's Central Front at Stalingrad, Kharkov, and Kursk before she deserted in 1944. She's also a trained karcist who served in Europe with an Allied special warfare group known as the Midnight Front."

Subsequent pages of the dossier listed various known associates of Miss Kernova, though most of their photographs were grainy and indistinct at best.

Most were marked KIA—killed in action—during the Second World War. The only one that was still considered alive and active was an American man named Cade Martin. Skimming the plethora of information, Luis asked, "How did a Russian peasant girl end up in possession of the Iron Codex?"

"Inheritance, we think." Lombardi plucked one of the pages out of the dossier and held it up. "This man, Adair Macrae, was her teacher. We're relatively certain he had possession of the codex until after the war ended. Though we can't prove he's dead, there are witnesses who say he died in British Honduras in September of 1945. And that he willed the codex to this girl."

Luis put the second file back on the director's desk. "How does this concern me?"

"We have credible intelligence that places Miss Kernova in La Paz, Bolivia," Lombardi said. "Since you hail from South America—"

"I'm from Brazil," Luis corrected. "That's a far cry from Bolivia."

The director leaned forward. "I've already informed the cardinal that you're fluent in both Spanish and Portuguese, as well as a smattering of indigenous tongues spoken in several countries of South America. And that you know the local terrain, as well as its politics, better than anyone else who belongs to our *unique* community within the Church. That, plus the training you received during your missionary years, makes you an ideal candidate."

Luis started to feel as if he were being railroaded. "Be that as it may, Father—"

Lombardi interrupted, "The Church wants you to go to La Paz, find Miss Kernova, and recover the Iron Codex by any means necessary." He shrugged. "If you don't succeed, so be it. But we insist that you make the attempt in best faith." He shot a troubling look at Father D'Odorico, then returned his focus to Luis. "In return for your cooperation, Father Pérez, the Synod will continue to look favorably upon your order's future requests for special dispensation and autonomous discretion in its magickal research." Lombardi intensified his intimidating stare. "But time is of the essence, Father. So I suggest you embark upon this holy mission with all due haste. Do I make myself clear?"

Luis knew there was no way to refuse a direct order from Cardinal Lombardi, especially not one delivered with the authority of the Synod itself. At the same time, Luis was all too aware that he was being tasked with a mission far beyond his aptitude. Despite his talent with magick within the conjuring circle, he had not yet dared to attempt yoking even a minor spirit, since such practices were banned by the Church. Without the powers that came from yoked spirits, Luis knew he could never be remotely qualified to confront an experienced battle mage like Anja Kernova and hope to survive long enough to regret it.

He was still grappling with his doubts when Lombardi asked, with an edge of anger, "Father Pérez? Do you understand the mission with which you've been charged?"

A nervous nod. "Yes, Your Eminence."

"Good. I'll leave the rest of your preparations to Father D'Odorico." Lombardi stood, so Luis and the director did the same. The cardinal patted Luis's shoulder on his way out of the office. "God be with you, Father. Try not to come home dead."

Humbled and terrified in equal measure, Luis struggled to muster a faltering smile and a weakly uttered valediction of "Amen."

JANUARY 23

Knowing it was a nightmare didn't make it feel any less real.

All around Anja, Dresden burned. Tens of thousands of souls lay inciner-ated, charred into slag, torn apart by explosions and shrapnel. Overhead, waves of Allied aircraft continued to carpet the once-glorious medieval city with incendiary bombs, leveling entire city blocks that had already been re-duced to blackened skeletons. Each blast shook the ground beneath Anja's feet as she clung to her wounded master, Adair, who lay dying in her arms.

In front of Anja, a massive vortex of flames swirled at the center of what had been the manicured grounds of the Zwinger palace. It churned like a wound in the earth, a conduit for the ascent of Hell's vengeful legions, even as Cade Martin plunged into it, a willing sacrifice in order to undo Anja's wrathful mistake. She had cast their nemesis, Kein Engel, into the pit, think-ing it a fitting punishment for all his evils, which had included opening the vortex. Only after the deed was done had Adair been able to tell Anja that by casting Kein into the abyss she had completed the dark magician's ritual for him—and that the only means of reversing it was to make a sacrifice equal in measure. Kein had been a man soul-bonded to a demon; Cade had been soul-bonded before birth to an angel. And so it was that for the thousandth time Anja watched in mute horror as Cade died to undo her blunder.

The moment he vanished into the burning depths of the hellmouth, the vortex shrank and vanished, leaving only solid smoking ground in its wake.

She struggled to lift Adair, whose strength was fading. "Can you walk?"

Blood sprayed from Adair's mouth in hard, lungsore coughs. "Forget me, lass."

"Never." She pulled his right arm across her shoulders so she could com-pensate for the damage to the crude prosthetic that had taken the place of his lower right leg. When she tried to stand, Adair's dead weight felt immovable. "Get up!"

Adair shook his head. He lifted his left hand from his gut to reveal a deep, ugly wound. His eyes were closed, his face a twisted mask of grief and rage. "I cannae go on."

A procession of explosions marched across the burning city, advancing directly toward Anja and Adair. Panic filled her thoughts and fueled her limbs. Desperate to survive, to escape, to cheat death even if for just one more minute, she hefted her master's weight and dragged him through a labyrinth of fire in search of a route to the river. *I can keep us safe if we reach the water,* she told herself as the detonations closed in.

But the master wasn't moving his feet, wasn't fighting to survive. All he was doing was weighing her down, dragging her with him to a fiery doom.

The rational thing to do was to drop him and run.

But she'd already abandoned him once; it was a sin she would never commit again.

One step after another, she trudged toward the River Elbe, the burden of her half-dead master no more than the penance she knew she had brought upon herself.

Explosions toppled the scorched façades of buildings all around her, and a wall of flames stood between her and the Elbe. The whine and thunder of falling bombs was about to overtake them . . . and then time slowed around her, like a moment becoming trapped in amber.

Jolted out of the dream, Anja became aware of the fact that she was sleeping, caught in a nightmare. Then an ethereal, golden radiance enveloped her from behind—something that had never before been a part of this dreamscape. She turned to face its source.

A human figure stepped forward, as if emerging from within the light itself. As he moved closer, Anja saw that it was a man—or, more precisely, his astrally projected shade. He appeared to be in his seventies and had the oak-toned complexion and facial features of an Arab, which were distinct in spite of his white beard and the tufts of white hair that poked out from under the edges of his kufi. He wore pale desert robes and leather sandals, and his very presence exuded peace and calm. He met Anja's bewildered stare with a kind smile. "Hello, Anja."

He knows my name? How?

As if compelled, Anja took a step toward the man. "Who are you?"

"I am Khalîl el-Sahir."

"Khalîl?" She recognized his name from the countless late-night stories Adair had told her of his old master—the one who had disappeared so long ago. "Adair told me you had died."

Regret faded his smile and colored his words. "I had to let him think so for my ruse to fool Kein. I wish there had been a better way to keep safe the secrets entrusted to me."

She continued to drift closer to him, drawn as if by gravity. "How did you find me?"

He looked around at the hellscape that surrounded them, and then down at her memory of Adair. "Your love for him. I felt its pull, like a magnet. I loved him like a son, just as he loved you like a daughter." They were near enough now that he reached out and gently stroked her cheek. "You meant everything to him."

Tears stung her eyes. They were only phantasms of tears, but they burned all the same. "And he was the world to me."

Concern darkened Khalîl's expression. "Unfortunate, then, that he never found the courage to tell you the truth."

"About what?"

"Of who and what you are." Perhaps noting her confusion, he added, "A *nikraim*. Not one of Adair's forced savants, but a true *nikraim*, one of Heaven's chosen."

She recoiled. "What? No. You have me confused with Cade."

The old master shook his head. "There is no mistake, Anja Kernova. It was no accident that you and your brother stumbled into Adair's duel with Kein that night in the forest. They'd come in search of you—Kein to take your life, and Adair to save it."

Anja shook her head and backed away. "No. That would mean—" She looked around at the frozen memory of death of destruction. "That night in Dresden . . . I could have been the one to close the portal. But Adair said I was not—"

"He lied." Khalîl stepped forward and took Anja's hand to halt her retreat. "He loved you too much to sacrifice you, just as I'd feared. And the fact that I had to seek you out means that even on his deathbed he denied you the truth." With genuine remorse he continued, "I'm sorry."

She yanked her hand free of his. "I do not believe you."

"The truth does not change based upon one's belief." He held up his hands, palms out, as if pleading for her patience. "When you came to live with Adair, you were all but illiterate. And yet you learned magick, an accomplishment that even scholars treat as a labor." There was a troubling ring of truth in his calm, almost lilting voice. "Did you think you accomplished that feat by nothing more than the sweat of your brow?"

His revelation left Anja in a state of shock. Part of her wanted to trust him, but letting go of everything she thought she knew about herself was not so easy. "If I am special like Cade, why did it take me so much longer to learn magick? And why is he so much stronger than me?"

"Because he had every advantage you were denied. He is a man in a world tailored to men. He came from wealth and social privilege. While you grew up in poverty, he attended an elite English boarding school and university." Khalîl cocked one eyebrow. "If you'd been born with half his opportunities, you would now be at least his equal, and likely his better." Once more he gently took her hand. "That is why I've come to you now. To invite you to find me in India, so that I can help you realize your potential and become the karcist you were born to be."

It was a tempting offer, but it sounded too good to be true—and Anja had learned to be suspicious of gifts too freely offered. She withdrew her hand, this time with respect. "I mean no offense, Master Khalîl, but I think I can best achieve my potential by killing fugitive Nazi karcists until they go extinct."

"You really think that's a fitting use for an artifact like the Iron Codex?"

She froze at his mention of the grimoire she had inherited from Adair. After all of the stonewalling she had endured from the Kabbalah masters in Israel, could Khalîl be the one to help her unlock the tome's mysteries? The urge to ask him what he knew of the book was powerful, but she knew that venturing down that road would come with a condition: he would withhold any information he might possess about the codex until she joined him in India. Which would mean putting her mission of vengeance against the Black Sun on hold indefinitely.

"Thank you for your invitation," she said, "but I have made my choice."

"For now." He regarded her with an unflappable calm that suggested he knew more than he was prepared to say. "Ere the next full moon, you will seek me out."

His certainty both amused and annoyed her. "Oh, will I?"

"Yes, you will. When the time for your journey comes, remember this as your guide: 'Follow the needle true, and thread your way to the Key, on the bank of the river, where five lands meet as three.'" He took in their surroundings once more, this time with a disapproving frown. "Until then, the least I can do is release you from this prison you've built for yourself." With a wave of his hand, the fires and carnage of Dresden vanished. Night's curtain was drawn aside to reveal the pure blue sky of a perfect spring day. Where moments earlier there had been nothing but smoking debris and ravaged bodies, there now stretched a serene vista of grassy plains around a lake of mirror-perfect blue waters. In the distance rose the glaciated mountain peaks of northern Sweden. When Anja looked over her shoulder she saw the cabin in which she had taken refuge during her sojourn from the Great Patriotic War. Smoke curled from the stovepipe of the quaint house—the last place Anja had ever felt truly at peace.

She turned back toward the old master. "How did you know about—"

The astral shade of Khalîl faded from sight. His disembodied voice echoed after his departure from Anja's newly idyllic dream.

"*Your journey is just beginning, Anja Kernova, and greater than you can imagine. Until we meet again . . . may God be with you in all the empty places you walk.*"

～

The key to any good ambush, in Dragan Dalca's experience, was patience. An advantageous location was also vital, as was knowing the schedule of one's target, but the virtue that enabled one to spring a trap with élan was the ability to sit still and wait in silence, free from anxiety.

This afternoon's target had made Dragan's task easy. The karcist had poured himself a triple rye on the rocks from the well-stocked liquor cart in his prey's home office. Then, drink in hand, he'd settled into a high-backed leather chair in a corner that would be blocked from view when the door opened, and he'd planted his feet on the chair's matching ottoman.

After that, there had been little for him to do but sip his libation, admire the man's vast collection of leather-bound books and memorabilia from around the world, and enjoy watching fat snowflakes trace winding paths from sky to ground outside the office's many tall windows. The grounds of the posh estate were slowly erased from nature's canvas by the heavy snowfall. Only tree trunks and the vaguest suggestion of the landscape remained to be seen by the time the office's door finally opened.

Just as Dragan had expected, the senator entered the room alone except for his martini.

The thin elected official startled and spilled his drink as Dragan spoke: "Balzac tells us that 'behind every great fortune lies a great crime.' I'm paraphrasing, of course, but I think we both know that in your case the axiom holds true. Don't we, Senator?"

The senator was a pale man, so it gave Dragan a rush of schadenfreude to see the man's aquiline face blanch a ghostly white. A bit of his color returned as he marshaled enough outrage to overcome his fear. In a tremulous, nasal voice, he demanded, "Who the hell are you? What are you doing here? Do you know who I—"

Dragan slammed shut the office door with a wave of his hand—from across the room. He snapped his fingers, and the martini glass in the senator's hand shattered, dousing the sleeve of his beige cardigan with chilled gin and the faintest hint of dry vermouth.

"You're a smart man, Senator. Don't waste my time with futile posturing."

The senator set the orphaned stem of his glass on his desk. He took a kerchief from his pocket and dried his hand. "It'll take more than parlor tricks to scare me, sir."

"I didn't come here to frighten you. I came to secure your assistance."

His confidence returning, the senator tucked away the kerchief. "Why would I help someone who's broken into my home?" He took a step toward Dragan. "Tell me why I don't summon the police and have you carted out of here in a paddy wagon."

"You know why. The answer's on your desk."

The senator glanced toward his desk, where a large envelope awaited him.

"Go ahead," Dragan said. "Open it. I'll wait."

It took willpower for Dragan to suppress his urge to smirk as he watched the senator open the envelope and sift through its copious evidence of the man's illegal business dealings with the Nazis before and during the Americans' involvement in the Second World War. Nearly half a ream of paper, every page brimming with evidence of willful collusion and war profiteering by the senator and his family. High crimes bordering on treason.

By the time the senator had finished reading and put all of the evidence back into the envelope, Dragan had nearly finished his rye. The senator looked deflated. He took off his wire-frame eyeglasses, rubbed his eyes, and sighed. "What do you want? Money?"

"Nothing so vulgar." Dragan took another sip of his drink and savored its notes of spice, orange, and pepper. "I need a base of operations. One remote yet defensible, preferably with critical infrastructure and military fortifications already in place."

The wiry older man put his glasses back on. He fixed Dragan with a knowing look. "Let me guess. You already have a place in mind?"

"I do." Dragan stood, walked to the senator's desk, and from inside his suit coat took a small folded piece of paper. He handed it to the senator. "I want full control of this site no later than eight days from now."

The senator unfolded the note and read it. "That's outrageous."

"You're a well-connected man, Senator. People on the Hill owe you favors. Use them."

Shaking his head, the senator said, "It's not that simple. A U.S. military facility can't be handed over to private control that quickly. These things take months to arrange, or years."

"I disagree. Life has taught me that overcoming obstacles is all about two things: money and motivation. Money is not the issue. I have more than enough to grease the gears of this deal. So the question becomes one of motivation. Specifically, is yours strong enough to make this happen on my schedule? If it is, I will add a significant sum to your tainted fortune. If not, I'll be forced to see which provides you the greater impetus." He glanced at the envelope on the desk between them. "The threat of blackmail?" He punctuated his threat by clutching the senator's throat with the fist of ORNIAS. "Or the promise that I'll have a demon slay your family, burn down your home, and rip out your spine and show it to you before you die?"

Dragan released the man, who collapsed, gasping, into his chair. He fought to recover his breath, then nodded in acquiescence. "I know who can get this done. I'll take care of it."

"Good." Dragan downed the last of his rye, which had become diluted by melted ice, and set the empty tumbler on the desk. "Cheer up, Senator. If you perform even half as well for me as you did for the Nazis, I see no reason you can't come out of this alive—and maybe even intact."

The senator didn't hide his resentment. "You're too kind."

"Eight days, Senator. Come February first, I'll either be walking the halls of my new fortress, or I will be *here*. And if it's the latter"—making his exit, Dragan tossed his parting shot over his shoulder—"our next conversation will be *far* less cordial than this one."

More than a day had passed since Luis had been dismissed from the director's office. An evening of prayerful reflection had yielded nothing but a night of troubled sleep, and that morning's meditation had brought Luis no closer to accepting his new mission for the Church. The sensitive nature of the assignment had precluded any chance of his discussing it with the other members of the order, though he had no idea in whom he might have confided even had it been allowed.

Plagued by his unquiet mind, he had ventured out after the evening meal in search of the director. Just as he had expected, Father D'Odorico was once more in the monastery's conjuring room. The director had set out his magickal tools atop a clean sheet of linen, arranged in the order of their creation: boline; white-handled knife; black-handled knife, or athamé; sickle; lance; staff; pen; wand; the four swords of the Art; and the needle.

The air in the candlelit room was rich with the perfume of incense, suggesting to Luis that the director had already finished exorcising, fumigating, and blessing his implements. Father D'Odorico stood over them, his posture bowed slightly, hands pressed together and eyes shut. After a few moments he muttered a soft "Amen" and opened his eyes to see Luis. "Father Pérez," he said with a genial smile. "Shouldn't you be resting before your fast?"

"If you'll forgive me, Director, that's the reason I've sought you out."

A sage nod. "I see." Father D'Odorico shook a gold aspergillum over his tools, sprinkling them with holy water. "Having doubts, are you?"

"I think I have good reason. With all respect to the Holy Father and the Synod, I'm not sure I'm the right person to send after the Iron Codex."

The director replied while he wrapped his tools in sheets of clean linen and bound them with ties of scarlet silk before tucking them into his leather roll-up. "I thought that I offered a compelling argument for your suitability. Was anything I said of your abilities erroneous?"

"Not as such," Luis said. "But I'm not qualified to confront an experienced karcist like Anja Kernova. She yokes demons and uses their powers in combat. I've yet to serve as an operator, and Ecclesiastical Law forbids me to yoke fallen spirits."

Still putting away his tools, D'Odorico said, "How does that disqualify you from acting as the emissary of the Church?" He shot a conspiratorial look at Luis. "No one says you need to take the book by force. Have you considered that the Synod's rationale for sending you might rest in your rhetorical skills? Or your gifts of suasion?"

"Frankly? I haven't." He searched for any sign that the director might be testing his gullibility. "Do you and the cardinal really think that I can talk an unrepentant Goetic magician into handing over one of the world's most powerful tomes of the Art without a fight?"

Father D'Odorico put his linen-wrapped needle into its place in his leather tool roll-up, which he closed and bound with a leather string. "To tell the truth, Luis? . . . No. We don't." He picked up his leather roll. Luis followed the director, who carried his tools to his cedar wardrobe at the back of the conjuring room. "But you should have a little faith. If not in the Church, the cardinal, or me, then in yourself." He put away his tools, closed the wardrobe, and locked it to keep safe his consecrated tools until he next came for them. Facing Luis, he continued, "There's a reason we told you to begin fasting. Five days from now, we're going to arm you for your journey. By the time you leave Monte Paterno, you'll be ready to face anything—even a battle-trained renegade karcist."

"So you *do* mean for me to take the book by force."

The director put on an air of long-suffering. "We mean for you to recover the rightful property of the Church in a manner consistent with its philosophy."

"Which philosophy would that be, exactly? The pacifism of the New Testament? Or the sadism of the Inquisition?"

The director's strained patience surrendered to vexation. "And just like that, I'm forced to recall why it is that we train so few Jesuits in the Art."

⁂

Like most of the audience scattered among the table seats in the Bohemian Cavern, Briet and her lovers had paid their cover charge expecting to see a forgettable lineup of local jazz acts. Even though it was a Saturday night, it was the end of January in Washington, D.C., a period of miserable wet and cold that scared most of the best performers south to Miami or west to Los Angeles for the season.

Consequently, it had come as a surprise to Briet when, shortly after pairing a glass of Chianti with a hand-rolled cigarette of marijuana—or "tea," as it was called by the Beatniks who had come to populate the capital's late-night jazz scene—the stage's spotlight had snapped on to showcase none other than the famous but troubled young trumpet player Miles Davis.

Backed by a swinging trio of bass, drums, and piano, Davis was performing songs he had recorded in recent years. He'd opened his set with "'Round Midnight," followed by "Morpheus." Now he was deep into a new rendition of "Whispering" that so mesmerized Briet that she forgot about the joint in her hand until it dwindled to a stub that burnt her knuckles. She dropped the smoldering remnant and kissed away the pain from her burned fingers.

Alton sat between Briet and Hyun, who likewise seemed entranced by Davis's virtuoso musicianship. Alton leaned close enough to Briet to confide without irking the other patrons, "Miles is on fire tonight! He hasn't sounded this good since before he went to Detroit."

He was right. There was a renewed vitality in Miles's performance, a keen edge in his style that had felt dulled in recent years. It was a phenomenon Briet knew all too well in the context of magick. She leaned toward Alton and replied, "He's finally off the heroin."

"You think so?"

She nodded. "Positive."

Around the room, the audience was enraptured. Though they were few in number, they knew they were being treated to a rare treasure: an unannounced, almost private show by one of the most acclaimed names in jazz. Even the waitresses and bartender had come to a halt, nearly hypnotized by the masterful performance unfolding on the other side of a narcotic haze.

A pair of eyes in the darkness caught Briet's attention.

She squinted to see who was staring at her. He appeared to be a handsome older man of Middle Eastern ancestry, perhaps in his sixties or seventies but still lean and trim. He stood near the door to the backstage areas, his gray wool overcoat open to reveal his dark three-piece suit. Atop his head rested a wide-brimmed black hat with a matching band. His left hand rested on the dragon's-head finial of a black cane, though he didn't seem to need it to support himself.

With his free hand he beckoned Briet.

Confusion rooted her in place. She had no idea who the stranger was. Did he want to talk with her? Was this an invitation to a back-room tryst? Or just a blatantly telegraphed ambush?

Overcome by curiosity, she glanced toward Alton and Hyun to see if they had noticed the stranger. To her relief, both of her lovers were caught up in Miles's spirited playing and seemed oblivious of anything else that might transpire in the room.

Briet got up and walked away without saying a word. No one seemed the wiser. As she made her way toward the backstage access door, the dignified-looking old stranger opened the door and slipped through it. Briet reached the door a few seconds later to find it still ajar. One more look back confirmed that no one was paying any attention to her, so she opened the door just enough to slip past it, and she closed it gently behind her.

On the other side stretched a dim corridor lined with closed doors. A bare lightbulb dangling from a frayed wire dimmed with a soft crackle and buzz as Briet passed under it. Through the graffitoed walls of chipped paint and cracked plaster she heard the music from the club's main room, though it was muted. The concrete floor was carpeted with discarded cigarette butts and used prophylactics. And every door that Briet tried to open as she worked her way down the hall was locked.

Old instincts returned to her. Something about this situation felt off. She reached into her coat pocket, pulled out a switchblade, and opened it with a push on the release. Its long, razor-sharp blade snapped into place. It wasn't as comforting to hold as a pistol, but Briet had come to accept that practices she had taken for granted during wartime had no place in times of peace.

As if there's ever truly a time of peace, she brooded.

At the end of the corridor, a short flight of steps led to the locked backstage door, which was marked AUTHORIZED PERSONS ONLY. To its left, a door labeled STORAGE stood ajar. A light burned on the other side of the open door. She nudged it open with her foot.

It was exactly as advertised: a room packed with stage equipment, lights, cables, and assorted junk. Briet saw no other way in or out of the room, but she was the only one in it. Lying in the middle of the room's only patch of open floor, however, was a folded sheet of paper with her first name scrawled upon it. She kneeled beside it and lifted its edge with her knife. There were no glyphs or other magickal symbols on it, just a handwritten message, so she picked it up.

Its missive was short and to the point.

> *Briet,*
>   *Your masters are lying to you. Get out of the capital while*
> *you still can.*

It wasn't signed. There was no calling card, no claim of authorship.

She folded the note, closed her knife, and stuffed them both into her coat pocket. Walking back the way she had come, she knew that her boss would call her crazy if told that she believed the words of a stranger who refused even to deliver his warning in person. But as peculiar as this encounter had been, it had served only to affirm what Briet already knew: She was being lied to by those whom she'd trusted. And she didn't like it.

Not one fucking bit.

8

JANUARY 27

In retrospect, Anja realized, her first hint that something was wrong should have been how easy it was to spot and surveil her target. He was a young man with blond hair and chiseled features, a veritable stereotype of the Nazis' vaunted Master Race. He spoke Spanish with a German accent, a trait that might not attract notice in other parts of South America but which had made him stand out from the mostly local patrons of La Paz's Mercado de las Brujas, or Witches' Market.

The market, which carried a variety of bizarre and hard-to-find ingredients for local folk-magic recipes, had on occasion been useful to Anja. There was a small degree of overlap in the needs of ceremonial magick practitioners, such as herself, and those of the native traditions. Unlike the German, however, Anja had made an effort to blend in with the locals. Despite her Russian ancestry, she had spent enough time in the South American sun to acquire a deep tan. Coupled with her black hair and lean physique, her sun-browning served as social camouflage.

A car driven by another German, one with light brown hair and a round face, had picked up the blond man around the corner, on Calle Linares. Using traffic for cover, Anja had followed them on her motorcycle. At the time it had seemed a reasonable tactic. *If I am lucky,* she had thought, *they might lead me to their Black Sun lair in La Paz. Then I can plan its destruction.*

Dusk had swiftly turned to darkness while she tailed the Germans. First south to the Avenida Mariscal Santa Cruz, and then generally east along the Avenida Saavedra. At the Plaza Uyuni they veered northeast along the Avenida Héroes del Pacífico, and then due north on the Calle Paraguay, into a more desolate section of the city.

That was where the traffic had thinned, forcing Anja to drop back to avoid being spotted. Several times after making the turn onto Calle Walter Portocarrero, the car had vanished around one distant curve in the road, only to reappear moments later, continuing its climb up the lonely dirt road that hugged a steep rock formation rising from the city's basin. Then it made a sharp turn onto Villa Imperial, an even narrower dirt path up the hillside, one that led into a dead-end warren of half-finished—or, in most cases, abandoned—construction.

Anja had paused before making the turn. She hadn't ventured into this part of La Paz more than once or twice during her short time in the city, but she had a feeling that the Germans were driving into a dead end. Anxiety and demonic mischief had churned the acid in her gut.

A good place to hide a coven's lair, she had reasoned. *Or a good place to lay a trap.*

Her sense of caution had collided with her mounting frustration. She had tracked the Black Sun to several locations in Paraguay and Bolivia in recent months, only to finalize her attack plans just after the coven had moved on, forcing her to start her hunt over from scratch.

If I could catch them off guard even once, she had thought, *I could end them for good.*

Gambling that this might be her moment of advantage, she'd switched off the headlamp of her Black Shadow and eased open the throttle for a slow roll up the dead-end dirt road, with moonlight as her only guide. All had seemed quiet as she had rounded the final curve in the road and passed a staircase-access gap in the low curb on her left. Ahead of her, a few dilapidated shacks stood dark and silent.

Muzzle flashes lit up the hillside—bullets were flying.

Anja surrounded herself with AZOTH's shield as she clutched the brake, gunned the throttle, and forced the motorcycle through a 180-degree pivot on its front tire. Then she let go of the brake, and her rear tire spit gravel as she raced back the way she had come—

Only to see headlights snap on in the darkness ahead. A truck wide enough to fill the road was hurtling straight at her with no room to slip past on either side.

That was when she knew she'd driven into a trap.

Like a damned amateur, she castigated herself.

From the terminus of the dead end she heard motorcycle engines, and the truck picked up speed as it closed in on her. There was only one way to go.

She gunned her engine and drove over the low curb—and then she hung on for dear life as the Black Shadow plunged down a steep, scrub-covered hill-side, harried by gunfire every inch of the way. She invoked the Sight of Vos SATRIA to pierce the dark just in time to swerve past a utility pole at the bottom of the slope.

Above her, men scrambled out onto corrugated-steel rooftops—but instead of guns these men were armed with magick. Forks of lightning and orbs of fire rained down on her and exploded against her shield. The force of the blasts knocked her off balance and into a skidding turn as she hopped another curb to get back on a dirt road.

Behind her, seven motorcycles charged down the same hillside she had just descended, but now its dense scrub was aflame. Above them, the truck on the upper road had stopped—and a man standing on its flatbed swiveled a mounted machine gun toward Anja.

She ducked forward, head down, and opened up the throttle.

An angry stutter echoed off the cliffs. Large-caliber rounds ripped into the road just shy of Anja's accelerating motorcycle. She leaned low into a hard left turn as bullets and spectral flashes flew over her head and blasted away the front of a scrapwood house.

Wind whipped at her face as she raced up a street flanked on the left by a wall of stone and on the right by a high chain-link fence. Her pursuers' engines roared behind her.

Taking the curves wide to maintain her speed, Anja stole a look at her side mirrors. All seven of the Nazis' bikes had made it down the hill and were on her tail. Rounding an S curve, she caught the flash of headlights above her. The truck was coming back down the high road.

Trying to cut me off. A garbage-strewn gulley beckoned on her right. *Time to take the low road.* She swerved off the dirt path and into the ravine.

The Black Shadow fishtailed and hopped down the rocky trail. It took all of Anja's strength and experience to keep the bike upright. More bullets and magickal projectiles peppered her faltering shield and the ground on either side of her.

At the bottom of the slope she hit another dirt road that within a few meters became a cobblestone path. Her bike shuddered as she sped over the bricks. A few seconds of reckless acceleration later she was back on a paved road that hugged the face of another tall cliff. She pushed the bike through another wide left turn, onto a long and winding downhill stretch of road.

As she sped through a four-way intersection, she saw the lights of the city's center in the middle distance, and for a moment she dared to think she had slipped the Germans' noose—

A car narrowly missed broadsiding her, but not for its driver's lack of trying. The passenger in front was half out of his door's window and firing a pistol over his roof at Anja, and another Nazi in the back of the car was hurling fireballs carelessly into the street as the driver skidded and swerved into a bootlegger's reverse maneuver.

A blast of flames made Anja's magickal shield crackle and stutter. One more direct hit and it would collapse for sure.

The Black Shadow growled like a demon, protesting as Anja pushed it to its limits. The buildings on either side of Avenida Burgaleta were nothing but blurs as she fought to put as much distance as she could between herself and her pursuers.

The farther she drove, the denser traffic became. A close call with a delivery truck sheared off her bike's right-side mirror in a flurry of shattered glass and bent steel. Then she was swerving around cars, dodging between near collisions, and playing chicken with oncoming trucks just to maintain her lead over the Germans—who, she was dismayed to see, were not only keeping up but adding reinforcements.

They must be calling them in by radio, she realized. *Fuck.*

She hooked a wild right turn around snarled traffic onto Calle Walter Portocarrero and then opened her throttle to the max. Instead of slowing down as she neared a hard switchback turn, she continued straight and rode a natural ramp of packed dirt into a daredevil jump over a rocky slope and a brick house built up against it, and off of the house's flat steel roof.

Her bike slammed down onto Calle Costanera hard enough to make her grind her teeth. She veered left and pushed the Vincent for all it was worth.

Scenery melted past—narrow roads, abandoned storefronts, a rotary, playgrounds boxed inside chain-link fences—each detail bleeding into the next at breakneck speed until Anja found herself somewhere in the Los Guindales barrio, on a road with no name, speeding south still hounded by the mad buzzing of her pursuers. Ahead of her, the road forked. She veered right, then opted to skip the multiple switchback turns ahead and steered off the pavement, down a slope of loose rock and heavy brush. *Nothing like a shortcut that doubles as camouflage.*

She pointed her bike uphill toward Calle Villalobos and continued her retreat.

In her left mirror, she saw the seven Nazi bikers taking her shortcut down the hill. Behind them, two cars and the flatbed truck with the machine gun navigated the switchback turns, swerving madly through oncoming traffic to make up for lost time.

She was about to cross Avenida Argentina when a bullet tore open her bike's rear tire. She rode the Vincent into a hard slide, and then she rolled away, trusting her riding leathers to keep her safe. The road burned and ripped at her, and by the time she came to a stop, the Germans were barreling up the street, hell-bent to run her down.

I am not that easy to kill.

She marshaled the powers of HABORYM and LERAIKAH. A flourishing forward wave with both hands unleashed a flight of demonic arrows, all of them ablaze with hellfire.

The Black Sun bikers raised their shields—the lucky ones, at least.

Three of the seven hit the ground skewered and aflame. Fiery missiles bashed through the windshields of the two cars following the bikers, and a second volley sent the remaining German dabblers running for cover.

Time to close the road.

Anja summoned the burning whip of VALEFOR and with a snap of her wrist coiled it around the base of a nearby utility pole. One tug on the whip broke the pole like a toothpick. It toppled across the street, bringing with it a sparking tangle of severed electrical wires. They danced and crackled on the pavement like serpents spitting lightning.

A bullet from out of the dark slammed against her shield, which stopped the round but fizzled away, its protection expended. AZOTH's shield could be useful in battle because it required no concentration to maintain, but its durability and longevity left much to be desired.

Anja sprinted past Avenida Argentina and turned north on Calle República de Cuba. On the run, she reached inside her jacket and fumbled to retrieve an old keepsake, an enchanted hand mirror given to her long ago by her late master. Holding it in her right hand, she struggled to both speak and breathe while running. "*Fenestra,* Cade!"

Her reflection vanished from the mirror and was replaced by churning vapors in a rainbow of colors. Then the image of Cade appeared within its frame. "*Long time no—*"

"Shut up," Anja snapped. "I need your help. *Now.*"

He seemed oblivious of her urgency. "*Can it wait? I'm smoking a cigarette.*"

Her voice shook as she ran and dodged bullets from behind. "What?"

"I mean, don't get me wrong. I love it when you boss me around, but—"

She had no time for his bullshit. "Cade! I am in trouble!"

He sighed. *"What kind? Bullets or brimstone?"*

"Both!" A bullet caromed off a brick wall as she ducked left around the corner onto Calle Diaz Romero.

"All right, gimme a minute. Keep the mirror open."

She darted off the sidewalk into the street so she could use traffic for cover. Shots rang out on the narrow street. Around her, car windows became storms of shattered glass mingled with sprays of blood and brains.

She made a diagonal sprint through four lanes of moving cars onto Calle Genaro Gamarra. At its far end rose the outer wall of the Estadio Olímpico Hernando Siles.

The growl of a motorcycle's engine resounded down the street. Anja drew her trusted Browning nine-millimeter pistol, spun, and fired three shots. The first went wide. The second pierced the windscreen of the German's motorcycle and slammed into his chest. Her third shot went through his throat and launched him backward onto the street.

She didn't linger to admire her marksmanship. Pistol in hand, she darted between cars as she ran for her life toward the stadium.

The street resounded with the metallic crunches of vehicles colliding behind her, accompanied by the musical breaking of glass and the shrieks of the wounded.

A dozen meters before she reached the stadium she realized it was closed. A barrier of green iron blocked Gate 11, the nearest entrance. She reached the end of Calle Genaro Gamarra and stumbled into the middle of Calle Hugo Estrada, which ringed the stadium.

The German truck with its flatbed-mounted machine gun bore down on her from the left, and a car full of armed Black Sun dabblers sped in from her right.

Three motorcycles charged up the sidewalks of Genaro Gamarra behind her. She was surrounded.

Her Browning had a thirteen-round magazine.

She had ten shots left. She made them count.

She put two into the closest motorcyclist. Two into the rider behind him.

The truck skidded to a halt and stopped lengthwise across the road. Its gunner swiveled his .50-caliber machine gun toward Anja—

She put a round in the gunner's left knee, another into his face. He tumbled off the back of the truck. One of his comrades in the truck's cab scrambled out to take his place. Anja put a bullet in his back.

Gunfire lit up the street, forcing Anja to take cover between two parked sedans. Glass shards stung her face as the cars' windows disintegrated.

She rolled under the more durable-looking of the two vehicles. Peering out from beneath its chassis, she saw the Germans' boots as they advanced on her position.

She took a deep breath, steadied her aim, and fired three careful shots.

Each found a different man's ankle and turned it to splintered bone and mangled flesh. The three men collapsed in the road as Anja's weapon *clack*ed empty with its slide extended.

Bullets raked the cars above her. Their ravaged frames rang like bells beaten into submission. Then the terrifying buzz of the machine gun drowned out every other sound on the street as it began slicing through the car behind Anja.

If only my shield had not failed me—

Thick gray smoke jetted from her mirror as she winced in anticipation of meeting the machine gun's assault.

Then the smoke solidified into Cade, who stood tall behind Anja, his automatic rifle chattering like a jackhammer, its storm of lead shredding the third motorcyclist.

Anja twisted around in time to see Cade switch his rifle for a grenade launcher in a blink with help from his demonic porter. He launched a grenade at the truck. As soon as the explosive was away, that weapon vanished and his Browning automatic rifle returned to his hands.

The light machine gun's report was deafening at close range, and it made quick work of the Germans' car, whose engine block burst into flames. Then the grenade detonated on the other side of the intersection and ignited the truck's gas tank. The fireball flipped the truck and reduced it and its machine gun to a heap of burning debris, and its lone troop to a charred corpse.

Out of the burning car came a trio of Black Sun dabblers, all radiating arrogance as they escaped the flames unscathed, each launching a magickal attack at Cade. Spectral blades flying as if shot from a cannon. A burning skull meant to erupt on contact. A bolt of lightning—

Cade swatted away the swords.

Snuffed the burning skull in his fist.

Then he caught the lightning—and hurled it back threefold.

The bolts slammed into the Nazis' shields and knocked them on their asses. None of them had the good sense to stay down. In a mad scramble they fumbled for wands and fresh attacks.

Cade spread his hands. Their car exploded into a cloud of shrapnel that engulfed them—but went no farther. He set it spinning like a tornado. The Nazis screamed for a few seconds as they were shredded in Cade's blender of fire and steel. When the whirlwind ceased and fell in a heap onto the street, its flames had been drowned in blood.

Police sirens wailed from far off, but they were growing closer.

Cade sprinted from the entranceway to Anja's cover and kneeled beside it. "You okay?"

"We need to go." She climbed out from under the car.

"Roger that." He lifted the Browning rifle, which vanished into the invisible care of his unseen demonic porter. Moving without apparent concern, he waded through the wreckage and carnage that choked the street until he reached the nearest German motorcycle. "This should do." He raised it with a wave of his hand and then held it steady. "Want me to drive?"

"You don't know La Paz." Anja mounted the bike. "Get behind me."

"Just like old times," Cade quipped.

She started the stalled motorcycle and shifted it into gear. "Hang on."

He held her waist as she weaved a path out of the battle zone. Seconds later they were several blocks away, cruising at a respectable speed that wouldn't attract attention, and after a few minutes without bullets or magick harassing her, Anja accepted that they had gotten away. But she kept on driving, not satisfied with having survived the ambush.

It was time to get out of La Paz.

She drove in silence, and for once Cade was smart enough to keep quiet.

They rode together, not talking, for over an hour. By the time Anja had tired of listening to the wind, they were far west of the city, on a deserted stretch of Highway 2. She pulled off onto the shoulder and parked the bike with its engine idling.

Cade got off the motorcycle and stretched. "Not the wildest ride you've ever given me, but it was good for a few laughs."

"I am not laughing."

Her dark turn took Cade off guard. "Hey, seriously: You all right? You seem . . . I don't know. Conflicted?"

Damn him. How does he read me so easily?

She shook her head in denial. "I am fine. Just got in over my head."

"If you say so." He sighed. "Hell of a mess back there. Gotta be careful throwing magick around in front of the rabble. That shit'll bite us in the ass someday."

"I did not see *you* holding back."

"I was fired upon, so I returned the fire." He softened his approach. "Look, if things here are getting too hot for you, you could always throw in with me and Miles. French Indochina's a pretty wild place. You might like it."

"Thank you, but no."

He didn't take her rejection in stride. "I get it. You'll call when you need something, but if you have to choose between spending time with me and hunting Nazi dabblers—"

"This is not about *you*. I know that must come as a shock." She was reluctant to share too much with Cade, for fear that he might use it in some ill-considered bid to revive their failed romance. "There is something I need to do. For myself. Alone."

"I should've guessed. *Alone* is your thing. Always has been."

He stepped away and brushed dust and blood off of his weathered bomber jacket. "If your mirror's still open, I ought to skedaddle. Miles worries when I go AWOL."

An awkward moment hung between Anja and Cade. She wanted to tell him about Khalîl, about how she felt she had reached the limits of what she could be as a karcist, and about what the old master had said about her being a *ni-kraim,* like Cade except natural in her origin. Instead, she averted her eyes from his and frowned. "This is it, then."

"Yeah." He took a breath and focused his thoughts. "See you when I see you."

She caught his arm. "Wait."

Anja mentally instructed her demonic burden-bearer DANOCHAR to give her the Odessa journal, which appeared in her hand. She offered it to Cade. "Take this."

"What is it?"

"A book of leads to all the Nazis in South America, including their new Black Sun coven and more. I do not have the time or the resources to make proper use of this—but I think maybe you do." She pushed it into his hands. "Take it."

He accepted it with reluctance. "You'd give this up? What about your Nazi hunt?"

"I have to put it down for a while," she said. "I trust you to do the right thing."

Cade nodded, seemingly aware of the seriousness of her request. "I will."

He nodded once, and then he transformed into a spire of smoke that snaked its way through her hand mirror, back to wherever he had been before she'd summoned him. As soon as he was all the way through, she heard him say from the other side, "*Velarium*," and the mirror returned to its normal reflective state.

Anja got back on her motorcycle, put it in gear, and continued west. Then there was nothing behind her but darkness, and nothing ahead of her but the night, which welcomed her with open arms.

As it always had.

As it always would.

9

JANUARY 28

The experiment was scheduled for dawn. It was an auspicious time for an operation of White magick, one that would be an extraordinary undertaking even by the lofty standards of the Pauline Art. Luis kept to himself on the periphery of Monte Paterno's conjuring room while Father D'Odorico and his senior tanists, all in ceremonial garb, finished their preparations.

Most of the spacious room's floor was now occupied by an enormous pentacle unlike any Luis had ever seen, either in person or in the grimoires he'd studied. In its center the astrological symbol for Saturn had been drawn twice, side by side. Outside the circle were drawn, in counterclockwise order, the symbols of the other six classical celestial entities, starting with the fastest, the Moon, and ending with the slowest, Jupiter. A majority of the symbols scribed around the pentacle's perimeter were proto-Enochian. Though Luis had made progress in his study of the original angelic language since joining the order, these glyphs were foreign to him.

Or maybe I'm just not concentrating, he speculated. He had fasted for five days to prepare for this morning's experiment, and the ordeal had left him light-headed. All of his thoughts and perceptions had an ethereal, dreamlike quality. When he moved, he felt as if he were floating, his body an insubstantial idea rather than a corporeal prison for his soul.

Fathers Malko and Hakkila circled the pentacle, each positioned opposite the other, as they lit the various tapers, all of which had been cast with the first wax from a new hive. Father Pantelis shuffled around the room's outer perimeter, opening its windows. As the portly priest locked open the shutters, Luis saw the predawn sky brightening. A pale glow was chasing the twilight into retreat.

Standing in for Luis as the fourth tanist that morning was Father Sayles, a fortyish Briton whose hair had turned prematurely gray a decade earlier.

Because he spent most of his time as a researcher rather than as a tanist, he stood with Father D'Odorico at the lectern, reviewing the plans for that morning's operation. His contribution would be limited to one pour of Abramelin oil, but only if something went wrong, and then the timing would need to be precise.

Luis knew the consequences of making an error in the circle when a demon was involved. He was less clear on what might happen if a transgression occurred while a Celestial Presence was in the restraining pentacle. Would an angel be as quick to slay them for a minor mistake of protocol? For all of their sakes, Luis hoped this would not be the occasion to learn the answer.

Daybreak strained at the horizon as Father D'Odorico declared, "It's time, everyone. Places." He assumed his station inside the operator's circle, and the four tanists moved to their respective posts around the great pentacle. Luis stepped carefully over the chalk lines that defined his circle of protection, one separate from the karcists' pentacle and the spirit's restraint. When they all were in position, Father D'Odorico closed the circle by pulling a small reserve of chalk into place with the tip of his sword. Then he unfurled a scroll atop his lectern.

"Today we plan to beseech and invite into our presence none other than SAMAEL, one of the seven archangels. He rules over the first hour of the day and presides over the Fifth Heaven. He was the guardian spirit of Esau, and the Celestial patron of the Roman Empire. He serves the Almighty as an accuser, a destroyer, and a harbinger of death. The Kabbalah tells us he remains a servant of the Divine in spite of the fact that he condones the sins of Man, but some believe that SAMAEL acts as a bridge between Heaven and Hell, between good and evil. He can serve as a conduit of great power, but make no mistake: this spirit is *not* one of mercy. Let us begin."

The four tanists covered their eyes with blindfolds of white silk.

Father D'Odorico passed his wand over the brazier at his feet, igniting its newly consecrated charcoal. Orange flames peeked out from inside the broad vessel; they danced higher as Father D'Odorico teased them with three dribbles of holy oil. He drew a breath.

The director's voice took on operatic dimensions as he began the conjuration.

"O thou mighty and potent angel SAMAEL, who rulest the first hour of the day, I, the servant of the Lord thy God, do conjure and instruct thee in the name of the immortal host of hosts, JEHOVAH TETRAGRAMMATON, and by the seal to which you are sworn.

"By the seven angels that stand before the Throne of YAHWEH, and by the seven planets and their seals and characters, I beseech thee to be graciously pleased with our entreaty, and by Divine permission to come from whereso-ever you may be, show thyself visibly and plainly before this circle, and speak with a voice intelligible and to my understanding.

"O thou great and powerful angel SAMAEL, I petition thee to come forth, to inform and direct us in all things good and lawful to the Creator, by the power of the divine names ADONAY, ELOHIM, ZEBAOTH, AMIORAM, HAGIOS AGLAON TETRAGRAMMATON, and by the name PRIMEUMATON, which com-mandeth the whole host of Heaven."

As the director spoke his conjuration's final word—"Amen"—the morning's first golden ray of sunlight breached the horizon and spilled into the room through its open windows. A cold breeze wafted in with it and trembled the flames on the tapers. Then came a rumbling like thunder, and at once the con-juring room seemed to have no ceiling—just an endless expanse of cosmic darkness salted with cold stars. A single pinprick of light amid the multitude flared and filled the room with white radiance. Luis had to close his eyes and turn his head away from the light; he found its glare too painful to behold.

The world seemed to quake as the angel spoke with the voice of a storm.

AVE. THE BLESSINGS OF JEHOVAH BE UPON YOU. WHY HAVE YOU SUM-MONED ME?

"O great and terrible angel SAMAEL," the director said. "Please accept our humble gratitude for thy presence. We seek thy aid to gird one of our faithful with powers Divine for a mission most holy—a quest that will take him into conflict with agents of The Adversary."

Beyond the angel's tempest of a voice sang a choir of cacophony.

I SEE THE OBJECT OF YOUR DESIRE. THE IRON CODEX.

"Yes. Please, take mercy upon us and our mission, O great angel SAMAEL. Grant thy servant Luis Roderigo Pérez the aid of three of thy dukes, so that he might smite the enemies of the Lord our God and succeed in this venture most sacred."

WHICH OF MY DUKES DOST THOU HOPE TO PRESS INTO THY SERVICE?

"By the grace of JEHOVAH TETRAGRAMMATON, and by thy Divine and infinite patience," Father D'Odorico said in an unwavering voice, "we would beseech thee to intercede on our behalf to secure the willing services of DAROCHIEL, BENOHAM, and MALGARAS."

WISELY CHOSEN, the angel said. IS THE VESSEL PREPARED?

"He is," the director said. "Will your dukes consent to be yoked to his will?"

THEY BEND TO THE WILL OF THE DIVINE, WHICH HAS GRANTED THY BOON. When the spirit next spoke, its words seemed to pierce Luis's flesh and reverberate in his bones. FEAR NOT THE FIRE OF THE DIVINE, LUIS RODERIGO PÉREZ. SO LONG AS THY CAUSE BE RIGHTEOUS, OUR POWER SHALL SERVE THEE IN TRUE FAITH.

Luis cried out as the spirits fused themselves to his mortal frame. It was like inhaling a hurricane, swallowing lightning, or injecting lava. Then his fear passed through him, and he realized that there was no pain, only a heady rush of power followed by a shocking clarity in his purpose and perception.

Then he looked down and saw he was floating three feet above the floor, his entire body wreathed in a blue halo of supernatural energy, with his arms spread wide in a pose that he realized belatedly bordered on the blasphemous.

He drew a deep, calming breath and centered himself in the quiet core of his faith. Within a few seconds, his feet settled back onto the floor inside his protective circle. To speak during the ritual was forbidden, but he couldn't let the moment pass without giving silent thanks.

Glory be to God. Hosanna in the highest. Amen.

From the other side of the great pentacle, the angel said, IT IS DONE. HE IS READY.

Father D'Odorico bowed to the spirit. "We thank thee, O great angel SAMAEL, messenger of JEHOVAH TETRAGRAMMATON, for delivering unto us this blessing most holy. May its use be lawful and good in thy sight, and pleasing to thee and to YAHWEH, the Lord Almighty. Thy boon having been fulfilled, I dismiss thee, great SAMAEL, with the deepest gratitude, and I charge thee to depart directly, doing harm to none, and to return when, and only when, I shall call for thee. In the name of ADONAY, ELOHIM, ARIEL, and JEHOVAM, depart!"

The angel vanished in a pillar of white flames that ascended into the void overhead—and then, with a clap of thunder, the ceiling reappeared, and there was no sound in the conjuring room except the whispering of a winter breeze through the windows.

"We're secure," Father D'Odorico said. "Tanists, you may remove your blindfolds and leave the circle." He stepped out of the operator's circle and walked over to stand with Luis. "How do you feel?"

"Electrified," Luis said, trying not to let on that his mood verged on giddy. "Like I could move a mountain, or wrestle the Devil himself."

"Don't go overboard," the director said. "You've just been imbued with a tremendous amount of power, which will be yours until you release it, or until your strength falters. But you must use it wisely—which means sparingly, and with discretion."

Luis nodded. "I understand. So, if it's not impertinent to ask: What powers have I just been given? And how do I use them?"

"To be clear, I haven't so much given *you* powers as I've made it possible for you to borrow those of three angels for a short time. The spirits DAROCHIEL, BENOHAM, and MALGARAS have been yoked to your mind and body as willing servants. DAROCHIEL will do its best to guide you with its gift of intuition. BENOHAM will let you conjure, shape, and wield angelic fire for a variety of purposes. And MALGARAS will give you the ability to teleport yourself instantaneously to anywhere on earth." He lowered his voice. "The spirits are strong, but they're also fickle. If you become too weak, either physically or mentally, to serve as their vessel, they might abandon you for your own protection. And MALGARAS's power is exhausting to use, so don't waste it."

"I won't," Luis said.

He was still savoring the narcotic rush of holding angels in thrall as the tanists left the conjuring room—and then Cardinal Lombardi entered. The Synod emissary looked pleased. "I am told the experiment was a success."

Father D'Odorico beamed. "It went exactly as hoped."

"Splendid." Lombardi faced Luis. "We'll give you a day to acclimate to your new status quo before we send you forth."

"If you think that's best," Luis said. "Though to be frank, Your Eminence, I feel . . . *amazing*. I'd be willing to leave today if—"

"Not yet," Lombardi said. "I know all too well the excitement of one's first yoking experience. Give yourself a day to recover your equilibrium and presence of mind."

Luis acquiesced with a bow of his head. "Of course, Eminence." He looked up, apprehensive. "Is this what yoking always feels like?"

"Far from it," Lombardi said. "Yoking an angel is usually agony. Mortal flesh can crack and burn from such a plenitude of power it was never meant to hold. It's only because of Father D'Odorico's decades of experience with SAMAEL that you were granted this much power without being cooked to a cinder on the spot. As for yoking demons . . . well, let's just say it's no accident that the Goetic Art drives most Black magicians to the bottle, the needle, or both."

The director gave Luis a reassuring pat on his shoulder. "You must be starved after five days of fasting. Go get something to eat."

"Will you join me?"

"The cardinal and I have other business to discuss. We'll be along directly."

"Of course."

Luis left his superiors to confer as he made a fast walk to the sanctuary's dining room in search of sustenance. It was just after eight o'clock, too late for breakfast—but as he watched tendrils of angelic power crackle between his fingers and climb the hairs on his forearm, he had a sneaking suspicion that he wouldn't have much trouble persuading someone to fry him an egg.

Or maybe even two.

Bangkok was known for many things but a dry heat had never been one of them. Sweat rolled down Cade's back as he and Miles followed a long line of passengers across the tarmac to their waiting flight. Traversing the black pavement felt to Cade like walking on a hot griddle; its searing presence radiated through the soles of his shoes even as the late-morning sun beat down upon his head, for which he had only the scant protection of a straw Panama hat. He winced behind his sunglasses as the strap of his leather tool roll chafed against his shoulder and chest through the gauzy fabric of his linen shirt, but his attention was on the Odessa journal, in whose contents he had been submerged since the previous night.

"Anja wasn't kidding," he said to Miles, who lumbered beside him, with a suitcase in either hand threatening to dislocate his broad shoulders. Cade held out the book to show a page to his friend. "It's a map to some of the most-wanted Nazi fugitives in the world."

Miles replied through teeth gritted with effort, "You don't say."

"I'm serious. If I'm reading this right, she had a lead on Heinrich Müller."

That made the lanky Brit perk up. "The former Gestapo chief?"

"The very one."

"Impressive," Miles said, "but I doubt that'll interest the boys back at HQ."

Cade lowered his sunglasses enough for Miles to note his look of reproach. "*Pardonez-moi.* I thought we *wanted* to bring war criminals to justice."

"Not our department."

Cade sniffed and wrinkled his nose at a musky scent. "Smell that?"

"All I smell is jet fuel, mate."

Another deep breath. "I think there's a rabid mongoose tracking us."

"That's just the mescaline talking." Miles heaved a sigh born of long-suffering patience. "I told you not to spike your coffee."

"Lucky for you that I did. I think the bastard has friends. And they're closing in."

"Bloody hell, old boy. There isn't a mongoose within a thousand miles of here." He frowned. "We need to get you on that plane before you cause an international incident."

"I still say you should have let me jaunt us to South America."

"We've been over this. We need the paper trail—"

"—to nix suspicion. I get that. But what sadist booked this trip? We're on, what? Five different flights over the next three days?"

"Six," Miles corrected him. "This bird takes us to Tokyo. From there we continue on to Honolulu, Mexico City, Caracas, Brasília, and finally Buenos Aires."

"Fuck me. I'm tired just *listening* to that itinerary."

"Carry these bloody cases for even a minute. *Then* you can whinge to me about tired."

"Touché."

Miles handed his suitcases to an airline employee who was loading a luggage bin to be moved inside the aircraft's cargo hold. The aircraft's engines sputtered and then roared to life. The pull of the propellers nearly tugged the hat off of Cade's head. He tucked the journal to his side with one hand and clutched his Panama hat with the other. He and Miles climbed the mobile staircase and ducked through the hatchway to enter the Vickers Viscount 700.

Inside, Miles showed their tickets to a stewardess, who pointed them toward their seats. Miles settled in beside a window. Cade stowed his tool roll atop the cheap pillows in the open overhead bin, and then he flumped into his aisle seat. Even before Miles had a chance to loosen his necktie, Cade thrust the open journal in front of him again. "How about this?" He pointed at a series of peculiar illustrations that combined occult glyphs, pentacles, and astrological charts with formulae that Cade vaguely recognized as calculus. Or maybe physics.

An arched eyebrow signaled Miles's disinterest. "What about it?"

"I don't know what this means, but it looks pretty advanced, whatever it is. Even if we had no other reason for wanting to hunt down the names in this book, I'd think we'd want to know what the fuck this is, and why they're working on it."

"Has it occurred to you that it might just be gibberish?"

"Nobody puts this much effort into a doodle."

"Then how do you explain all that chicken-scratch marginalia?"

"That's Anja's handwriting. She made notes all through this thing, linking parts of it together." He took off his sunglasses and tucked them into his shirt pocket. "But she couldn't make heads or tails of these diagrams, and neither can I."

Miles took another weary look at the pages. "Fine. I'll have our man in Caracas photograph these pages and send the film back to London for analysis. Satisfied?"

"I'd say 'mollified.'" Cade lit a Lucky Strike and blew a smoke ring that spread out against the back of the seat in front of him. "I'm about four double bourbons away from 'satisfied.'" He threw an anxious look aft over his shoulder. "How long is this flight?"

Reclining his seat, Miles said, "Relax, mate. They have enough booze on board to keep you lubricated all the way to Japan."

"What makes you so sure?"

"I had Her Majesty's Government send a memo to the airline."

"Did you, now?"

"No one wants a repeat of the Helsinki Incident." Miles closed his eyes as the aircraft taxied onto the runway for takeoff. "Me least of all, I assure you."

⁓

From a legal standpoint, the house had no owner of record except a shell company. Briet had paid a princely sum to a skilled team of lawyers to make certain no one would ever be able to link the house to her, or vice versa. Located at the end of a long dirt path off a remote road in St. George, West Virginia, roughly a five-hour drive from Washington, D.C., the converted farmhouse had appealed to her because of its isolation and its voluminous interior, which she had all but gutted. She had replaced its wooden floors with poured concrete, bricked up its windows, and soundproofed its walls and roof.

It was the backup plan she had hoped she would never need.

Tonight she had driven there with her backup set of karcist's tools, which she had made years ago in anticipation of the day the government turned against her. Then she had spent several painstaking hours preparing this room for a Goetic experiment.

Now she and the room were ready.

The early stages of the ritual she performed by rote: the donning of her vestments, the lighting of the brazier, the invocation of her patron spirit ASTAROTH. Next followed the din and tumult that accompanied the compulsion of the spirit to appear, complete with fearsome peals of thunder and expulsions of foul vapor that now annoyed more than they frightened her.

When, after two refusals, ASTAROTH manifested at last, it insulted Briet by wearing a false form, that of a young girl draped in a blood-soaked nightshirt and clutching fistfuls of writhing worms. Disgusted, Briet dispensed with the usual exhortations and stabbed her wand into the burning coals at her feet. The demon wailed in impotent rage, but Briet felt no pity for the beast. It was a creature of spite, hatred, and petty villainy imbued with extraordinary power.

Why would I ever waste an ounce of mercy on a beast such as this?

In time she grew bored of its baleful howls and withdrew her wand from the flames. "Art thou ready to present thyself in thy true form and take thy appointed place inside the triangle?"

Resentful fury oozed from the spirit as it shifted into the visage she knew all too well. The naked fallen angel with filthy wings tossed its mane of golden hair. Then, with one hand it adjusted the sparkling crown on its head, and with the other draped its squirming viper across its shoulders. In a rare display of petulance overcoming bravado, its normally turgid black member dangled flaccid. Equally odd, the chimera that so often served as its mount was absent.

The demon trudged to its place inside the bounding ward. WHAT A PEDESTRIAN SETTING.

"Great ASTAROTH, I adjure thee to hold thy tongue until I direct thee to speak." She waved her wand toward the brazier. "Disobey and thy pains I shall increase a thousandfold."

It surrendered to her will with a grudging bow. HOW MAY I SERVE THEE?

"Our last conference was rudely interrupted. I would know what intelligence thou meant to share at that time. You spoke of a castle of fire."

AYE. BUT THIS IS A CASTLE OF THE AIR.

"Speak not in riddles, or I shall punish thee."

HELL HAS NO WORDS FOR WHAT YOUR KIND HAS WROUGHT IN NEW MEXICO.

"Where in New Mexico? Be specific."

TRAVEL TO THE CITY CALLED SANTA FE. SEEK THERE TWO MEN, WOLFGANG KRUEGER AND DRAGAN DALCA, AND THE ENDEAVOR THAT BONDS THEM.

Briet froze. The second name she recognized: Dragan had been one of her first adepts in the Silo. Well educated and fearsomely talented, the Yugoslavian man had always struck Briet as an enigma. She had never been able to ascertain the truth of his loyalties or his agenda.

"What can you tell of the man named Wolfgang Krueger?"

ONLY THAT HE IS THE ARCHITECT OF THE BLACK DAWN THAT SWIFTLY DRAWS NEAR.

"Why can you tell me nothing more? Are you ignorant of his truths, or are you constrained from speaking what you know?"

The minister of Hell bared a razor-blade smile that told Briet it was the latter.

"How long do we have until this 'black dawn'?"

NOT LONG NOW, EVE-SPAWN. ANOTHER CYCLE OF THE MOON AND NO MORE.

"And what of Dragan Dalca? Is he acting in his capacity as an agent of the American Occult Defense Program?"

ASTAROTH laughed. It was a cruel, mocking sound.

HE SERVES NONE BUT HIMSELF. SO HAS IT BEEN SINCE HE LEFT THY TUTELAGE.

Confusion clouded Briet's thoughts. If the demon was speaking truthfully, then it was possible that everything her superiors at the Silo had told her about the adepts who were transferred out had been a lie. She needed to know.

"Answer me with truth most direct, or I shall torment thee to the ends of thy strength: How many other covens like mine currently serve the United States of America?"

THINE IS AS IT EVER WAS: THE FIRST AND THE ONLY.

Frank and the Pentagon brass have a lot of explaining to do, Briet fumed. *Just as soon as I put a lid on whatever the fuck is going wrong in New Mexico.*

"Thy counsel has been most illuminating, O great ASTAROTH. Only one more service do I require of thee this night."

SPEAK YOUR WILL, THAT I MIGHT SATISFY THEE AND BE RELEASED.

"Rouse thy legions, great ASTAROTH. I suspect a labor of violence lies ahead of me, and I shall require some of thy Infernal hosts to be bound to my service ere the sun rises."

As THOU COMMAND, SO SHALL IT BE DONE.

It had been a long day and a long night, and now it was going to become longer still. But as Briet braced herself for her first serious attempt at yoking demons in nearly a decade, she no longer harbored any doubt that whatever her superiors had hidden from her, it was very likely going to kill them all unless it was reined in—and that she was very likely the only person in the world who comprehended the true scope of the threat, or who had the skills to confront it.

She opened her grimoire to begin selecting which spirits to yoke.

If memory serves, this is going to hurt. A lot. I hope I brought enough morphine. She steeled her resolve by focusing on something positive. *I can hardly wait to see the look on Frank's face when I bill him for this.*

JANUARY 29

The train to Rome kept a steady rhythm as it rushed southward, the clacks and thumps of its wheels on the tracks a steel lullaby. Luis found it soothing. He had barely slept since the previous day's yoking ritual; he had felt too energized to relax, and there had been no time for him to practice using his new temporary abilities. The past day had been a whirlwind of preparation, from packing his tools of the Art to filling a small ruck with toiletries and a thin brick of cash composed of notes from several nations' currencies.

He did not expect to have much need of the cash. The Vatican had made his travel arrangements and paid all of it in advance. All he'd been expected to do was show up on time for his departures and connections. So far that had worked out. That morning, an hour before dawn, he had descended the winding road from Monte Paterno to find a chauffeured car waiting for him at the edge of Misurina. The drive to Venice had taken just over four hours on snow-packed roads. In contrast, by train the journey from Venice to Rome would likely take only half as long. Once he reached Rome, he was to check in at Vatican City, where he would stay the night before boarding an early morning flight to Brazil the next day.

Outside his window, the Tuscan countryside was a colorful blur.

A conductor passed Luis's seat and tried to conceal his grimace of disapproval. It had become something of a ritual at this point; the man had struggled to suppress the same reaction each of the half dozen or so times he had passed by in either direction. It had taken Luis a few repetitions to realize what was putting the man off: Luis's bare feet.

Like all the members of his sanctuary, Luis honored a vow of poverty that required him to remain discalced whenever possible. Other orders granted their members dispensation to don sandals when traveling outside of their hermitages, but the brothers of Monte Paterno did their best to adhere to the old ways, no matter how inconvenient they might be in the modern world.

I'm sure this will draw a few comments on the plane tomorrow, he thought.

The crinkle of a newspaper's pages being turned was followed by the crack of the paper being snapped taut. Turning toward the sound, Luis saw a pale man in a dark suit sitting across the aisle from him, in a rear-facing seat that enabled the men to look each other in the eye. Upon closer inspection, Luis saw that the man appeared to be in his thirties, sported a thin mustache, was of a lean build, and wore his black hair cropped close to his scalp.

Luis tried to mask his confusion with a polite smile. He was certain the stranger had not been there just a moment earlier. He was about to avert his gaze back out the window when the dapper man lowered his newspaper and said in a Slavic accent, "You should turn back, Father."

"*Scuse?*" He had heard the man clearly but refused to accept the threat at face value.

The stranger folded his newspaper with crisp precision. "The real world is no place for those who know only theory. Out here, practical application is the key to success."

Refusing to be bullied, Luis adopted a brave face. "I think you've mistaken me for—"

"There is no mistake, Father Pérez. I know where the Synod means to send you, and I also know why." He flashed a predator's smile. "You're out of your depth, Father."

"That is for the Lord alone to judge. And I won't be threatened by the likes of you."

"I made no threats, Father. Just recommendations. I bring warnings, nothing more."

Luis clenched his hands into fists. "Only because the Covenant constrains you."

The man bit back on a derisive laugh. "Hardly. The Covenant is a miserable farce. One that ties your hands far more than it does mine."

So my guess was right—he is a Black magician. Luis forced himself into a semblance of calm. "Who are you, and what do you want?"

"You can call me Dragan. And what I want is the same thing you do: the Iron Codex." He discarded his immaculately folded newspaper on the empty seat in front of him. "Don't pretend you've not heard of it. We both know you've been tasked with its recovery."

"Then you also know that to impede my quest is to incur the wrath of the Holy See."

"As if that were any cause for concern. Your Church is impotent, just like your sanctuary at Monte Paterno." Dragan stood. "And while my compatriots are truly thankful for all the help the Church gave to see them safely out of Europe after the war, do not mistake our gratitude for obligation." He leaned down, intruding into Luis's personal space. "Sentimentality will not stay my hand should a filthy Jesuit like you come between me and the codex."

Luis refused to back down. Instead he leaned into the challenge. "The codex is not yours to claim. It belongs to the Roman Catholic Church, to which I will see it safely returned."

His rebuff broke Dragan's cool façade and exposed the simmering fury underneath. "The codex is mine, Father. Don't make me warn you again."

"Now *that* sounded like a threat."

Dragan grinned. "No, Father." His hand shot forward, plunged through the rough fabric of Luis's cassock, pierced his breastbone—and then jerked back, holding Luis's beating, bloody heart. "*This* is."

Luis awoke with a yelp and a mad flurry of kicking legs and flailing arms.

In the seats across from him, a woman and her two young children recoiled from him in shock. There was no sign of the Slavic stranger in a suit, and when Luis touched his chest, he found both his cassock and his sternum intact. Before he could apologize for frightening the woman and her toddlers, they had retreated rearward into the next train car.

Luis breathed a heavy sigh and turned to watch the countryside fly past outside his window while he silently recited the *Ave Maria*. He repeated the prayer in his thoughts until his stampeding heart slowed to a mere mad gallop.

Apparently, he realized with mild dismay, *my secret mission for the Church is not so secret after all.*

Good thing it's winter, Briet decided. The cold weather had made it almost imperative that she wear her overcoat, whose deep pockets were ideal for concealing her rat familiar, Trixim. She had stopped at her brownstone just long enough to pack a bag, scoop up the magickal rodent, and say a hasty farewell to Alton and Hyun. She had hated to lie to her lovers, but no good would come of telling them her true destination or purpose, so she had concocted a lie that blamed her travel and incommunicado status on her work.

Better this way, she told herself. *Safer for everyone.*

Sitting in the departures area of National Airport, Briet had seen some of the capital's better known political operators and social mavens drift past, no doubt bound for ski resorts in the mountainous states or beach resorts along the coasts. It had been a busy morning at the airport. Thanks to her early arrival Briet had witnessed several flurries of activity. She was thankful none of them had involved her. Yoking eleven spirits in one night had left her head aching and her stomach soured. All she wanted now was to leave town without fuss or bother.

She broke off a chunk of a muffin's crown and snuck the morsel into her pocket for Trixim, who gratefully gobbled up the treat, then nuzzled her hand.

In all of Briet's studies of magick, she had never read of familiars showing such affection for their summoners. She couldn't deny that she had developed a tender affinity for the creature, who throughout the war had watched over her every night while she had slept. More than a dozen times Trixim had saved her life by rousing her when it detected a threat or an intruder.

She wondered sometimes whether her bond with Trixim was unique. Like all familiars, it had a life span that was greatly extended to match that of its master, and its presence helped diminish some of Briet's discomfort when she held yoked spirits. But how many familiars slept on their masters' pillows at night? Trixim was more than a magickal servant. It was her friend.

She palmed another generous piece of the muffin and delivered it sub rosa to Trixim.

As the rat nibbled the muffin debris from her hand, she smiled.

Then she heard Frank Cioffi's voice behind her right shoulder, quiet and close.

"Don't turn around," he said. Next came the rustling of a newspaper's pages being turned. "Just look ahead, or off to one side. If you have something to read, pick it up."

Briet retrieved a large magazine from her shoulder bag, the only item she seemed to be bringing onto the aircraft. The check-in lady had found Briet's lack of luggage curious. How was Briet to explain, without sounding crazy, that she had a demon to fulfill her needs of portage?

She opened the magazine, lifted it in front of her face, and replied to Frank in a low voice, "What are you doing here?"

"The more pertinent question is, Why are *you* here? I told you not leave town."

"You also told me to take a vacation."

"I thought you knew that was a euphemism for 'lay low and stay quiet.' Guess I was wrong." More dry scratching of shifting pages. "Why can't you just stay off the radar until this McCarthy mess blows over?"

"Because I made contact with ASTAROTH," Briet said. "Something ugly is being born in a joint effort of earth and Below. And I need to know what it is."

Frank sighed. "You never could take good advice, could you? Sit this one out, Bree. It's been a long time since you got your hands dirty on this kind of thing."

He wasn't wrong. It had been years since Briet had yoked spirits for anything more than instructional purposes, and this morning she was feeling the deleterious effects of her decision to take so many spirits in thrall the night before: the pounding in her head, the sick swirl of nausea in her gut, the cold sweat on her back like a layer of frost—they all were underscored by sinister whispers lurking beneath her conscious thoughts and a growing urge to twirl strands of her red hair around her index finger and violently yank them out.

But she had no intention of admitting that to Frank.

"Maybe it's time I got back to basics," she said, masking her discomforts.

Her supervisor did not sound convinced. "What you ought to do is go home. If you get on that flight, I guarantee you'll be met at the other end by agents from divisions so secret they don't even have acronyms. And once they lay hands on you—let's just say there won't be much I can do to help you after that."

"I never asked for your help. Or your advice."

"Well you should fucking take it anyway. Because I'm trying to save your life."

His insistence on her surrender fueled her anger like gasoline on a fire. "Why shouldn't I be able to travel like anyone else?"

He lowered his voice. "You mean aside from the fact that you're a Nazi war criminal who lives and works in this country only by the grace of the Department of Defense? And *that* only contingent upon your obedient service? How stupid do you think we are? We respect you, and we value your skills. Because of that, we're willing to overlook some of your . . . let's call them *idiosyncrasies*. But those are exactly the sort of colorful details that will put you in Senator McCarthy's crosshairs. We can't afford to let that happen."

"Then don't."

Frank folded his newspaper over upon itself, clearly in a bid to stall for time until he was ready to respond. "You have no idea how much shit you're stirring up here. Step even one foot out of bounds, Bree, and I promise you, there are hard cases at the FBI, CIA, and NSA who are just itching to tell your 'housemates' Alton and Hyun the whole truth about who you really are. How do you think your Jewish lover Alton would react if he found out you used to fight for the Nazis? You think Hyun will forgive you when she learns you put people into death camps?"

A long pause betrayed that Frank had struck a nerve.

"Your point is well taken," Briet said at last.

"I'm glad we understand each other."

"Now tell me: How did you find me?"

"The fake ID you booked your flight with. We flagged it a year ago."

That made sense. She castigated herself for being careless. "Which ones do you know?"

"We have alerts in place for your Lankford, Guilfoyle, and Tierney identities. If you have a newer one, you might consider using it on a less closely monitored mode of transportation."

"Understood." She was about to leave, but her curiosity nagged at her. "Frank, why are you helping me?"

There was an undercurrent of grudging respect in his reply. "Because even though you're a massive pain in my ass . . . I'm pretty sure you're the only person in the Pentagon, and maybe the entire government, who's never lied to me. That's got to count for something."

She closed her magazine and abandoned it on the empty seat next to hers as she stood. She turned and saw Frank look obliquely in her direction, just enough that they could acknowledge each other. She thanked him with a subtle nod. He returned the gesture in kind.

There was nothing else to say. Briet made sure Trixim was secure inside her overcoat's deep pocket and she walked away from the waiting area without looking back.

She had a train to catch.

It was late morning when Anja entered the city of Arica, Chile, on foot, following a lonely road out of the foothills. The sun beat down upon her, its warmth a welcome relief from the cold breezes that had haunted her every step since the night before, when she had abandoned her stolen motorcycle in a deep ditch beside a high mountain road.

Anja had come to Arica by a circuitous route, one filled with detours and reversals, to thwart anyone who might have sought to follow her out of La Paz. There were coastal towns in Peru she might have reached more directly, but she had needed to be sure she was really alone.

Her feet ached and her stomach rumbled, but she ignored their pleas for attention. She needed to move quickly and minimize her interactions. There were certain to be Odessa spies on the lookout for her in Arica, and she couldn't afford the delay or the risk that might come from an altercation with any of them. There was somewhere more important she needed to be.

On the outskirts of town she traded her riding leathers for the clothing of local peasants that she took off of a backyard laundry line. She didn't think of it as stealing, because she left behind a few notes of local currency—enough to replace what she had taken and feed a family of four for a week.

I am desperate, not cruel.

Moving through the city proper, Anja resembled most of the other women crowding its street markets and food stands. An artfully draped head scarf, worn by the locals to keep the sun's glare at bay, also served to hide her facial scar, her most easily identified characteristic. Even so, she did not trust her disguise to see her safely out of peril. With every step she remained alert for any sign that she had been spotted, or that she was being followed. She had become careless in La Paz, overconfident. Those were not errors she would let herself make again.

By midday she reached the western edge of the coastal city. Following a boulevard whose grassy median was populated by squat palm trees, she made her way to the beach without incident. There weren't many people out that afternoon, despite the mild weather—a trademark that had earned Arica the nickname "city of the eternal spring." A highway ran parallel to the shoreline but its traffic was sparse. Anja darted across the road with confidence and climbed over its railing, down to the sandy beach.

She surveyed her surroundings. No one took any interest in her. She walked toward the ocean, focusing her thoughts with each step as she called upon the talents of a demon known as EGROS. It was a minor spirit by the standards of Hell, one with limited dominion over water. Anja had learned to shape its yoked abilities in tandem with those of PELGARAS, a weak spirit whose special talent was teleportation, but with the caveat that it could perform only when its power was linked to those of another demon, for reasons long lost to antiquity.

After years of careful research and experimentation, Anja had merged the two spirits' gifts to create a mode of travel she referred to as a "water jaunt."

It was a simple trick, really. She could utilize any body of water deep enough to submerge herself in as a portal to any other similar body of water, anywhere in the world. From a lake to a lake, or a river to a river. As long as she had some idea of where she was going, it was a great time-saver. Best of all, in spite of the medium of her conveyance, she always emerged completely dry on the other side of the jaunt.

Waves lapped at her ankles as she waded into the crashing surf. The water of the Pacific was every bit as cold as she had remembered, and as hypnotically blue. Forcing herself to ignore the numbing chill, she continued walking forward, deeper into the ocean with each step. She shivered uncontrollably as she sank in up to her chest, and her teeth chattered as the frigid salt water enveloped her neck. Then, with just two more steps, she submerged into the mysterious roar of the sea and marshaled the power of the water jaunt.

In her mind's eye she pictured her destination. She had seen it only ever in photographs, but she was confident enough of its location that even though she had never been there before, the water jaunt would deliver her on-target to its shores. She felt the weightlessness of transition. The quality of the light around her shifted, from refracted daylight to shimmering moonglow.

Anja surfaced and paddled for a few seconds until her feet found purchase on the seabed. Above her the night sky sparkled with starlight, and ahead of her the city of Bombay twinkled with the same radiance. Though its skyline had no shapes she considered familiar, the fact that the ocean reeked of a backed-up toilet made her certain she was in the right place. As much as the Indian Ocean stank, it was at least warm—though she realized that might not be a good thing.

Thank EGROS *none of this will stick to me,* she thought as she held her breath and waded ashore. Just over a minute later she strode onto the beach, dry and unobserved.

Somewhere nearby a church bell rang eleven times.

I made it, she congratulated herself. *If only I had the faintest idea where to go next.*

JANUARY 30

"I'm just saying, I think you'd like this book if you gave it half a chance." Cade tried to hand Miles a copy of *Casino Royale* by Ian Fleming as they queued up to disembark from their last connecting flight. The spy novel had been left behind by another passenger when they had landed in Caracas, and Cade hadn't hesitated to appropriate it in order to pass the time on the next two legs of their journey.

Miles evinced no interest in the pulp thriller. "I'll pass, mate."

"Suit yourself. I'm not saying it's Hemingway or Joyce, but it gets more right than you might expect." He handed the book to a stewardess at the exit and adjusted his Panama hat to block the sun that was trying to cook his face. "When did Buenos Aires get so fucking hot?"

"It's hardly a new phenomenon," Miles said, sounding grouchier than usual. Cade noticed that the journey had seemed to take a slightly heavier toll on his friend than such trips had in the past—and he was reminded of the fact that, while he himself enjoyed dramatically slowed aging thanks to his compact with Lucifuge Rofocale, his best friend did not. As a result, time was already taking its toll on Miles, despite his being only in his midthirties.

Another ten years and I'll look more like his trainee than his partner.

They descended the steps to the tarmac. The air was thick with the fumes of aviation fuel and machine oil. Drifting curtains of black smoke were tainted with the unique odor of diesel petrol. It was a short walk to the terminal, followed by an excruciatingly long wait at a carousel for Miles's luggage. Cade sighed. "Whatever happened to traveling light?"

"I forfeited that luxury the moment I became responsible for your sorry arse."

Cade's irritation mounted as he watched scores of other passengers from their flight depart with their luggage while Miles's bags had yet to appear.

"Seriously. We could have driven into town and bought you a whole new wardrobe by now."

Under his breath, Miles said, "And where do we go to replace our gear from Q Branch?"

"You say that like gun dealers and hobby stores are hard to find."

"I'm not going to dignify that with—" He craned his neck, and his eyes widened. "There it is. About bloody time." Relaxing a bit, he asked, "Why don't you go scare us up a ride?"

"Taxi or a loaner?"

"Loaner. We'll need to stay mobile while we're in town."

"Copy that. Meet you out front."

As Cade turned to go steal a car from the airport's long-term parking lot, Miles caught his arm. "We need to avoid attention. You understand what that means?"

"Don't worry, I'll find us something suitably low-key."

"You? Keep a low profile? That'll be a first."

Cade pulled free of Miles's grasp and left the terminal. As he feared, there weren't many cars in the long-term parking lot that suited their needs. Most were in poor condition. Only a few looked road-worthy, and of those, there was only one that he was willing to spend any time in.

He bypassed the locks on its door and ignition with the talents of ARIOSTO, and he bluffed his way past the lot attendant with a fistful of cash and the suggestive gifts of ESIAS. A few minutes later he pulled the car around the traffic loop to the main entrance of the airport to find Miles at a news kiosk, buying up copies of the local Portuguese-language newspapers.

Miles took one look at the car and scowled.

"A Cadillac Fleetwood 60S? That's your idea of low-profile?"

"It was this or a red Corvette convertible," Cade said. "I didn't think you'd want to pose as international playboys, so I went with the Caddy."

Miles frowned and shook his head, but all the same he got into the car. "Try to keep us under the speed limit. Last thing we need is a brush with the Old Bill."

"Not a problem." Cade shifted the car into gear, checked his mirrors, and pulled away from the curb into traffic. His maneuvers were smoother than glass, his graceful weaves through the dense city traffic sweeter than honey.

All of which made Miles's reaction strike him as odd. The veteran MI6 agent was white-knuckling his door's armrest and the dashboard.

Cade asked, "You okay over there?"

"Christ, mate! Don't you ever fucking slow down?"

Threading the needle of traffic with the Cadillac, Cade was bewildered by Miles's apparent fear. "I'm fine. What're you on about?"

Miles pointed at the instruments in front of Cade. "I told you to watch your speed!"

In a glance, Cade registered that they were hurtling down a busy street at nearly ninety miles per hour. He smiled at his partner. "It's under control."

His friend's face became a mask of horror. "Fucking hell! Are you drunk?"

"Of course not," Cade assured him. "I drive much better when I'm on speed."

"God help us," Miles muttered, his voice nearly lost in the roaring of the engine.

Cade pulled out a pack of Lucky Strikes and offered a smoke to Miles. "Light up. Takes the edge off." Miles was too petrified to respond. "Look on the bright side," Cade said as he put away the pack. "We're making great time to the hotel."

Miles's horror turned to dismay. "Dozens of ops in the most dangerous places on earth, but this is how I meet my end: collateral damage in a junkie's race with Death."

"Quit whining. I've raced Death a dozen times, haven't lost yet. Want to know why?" Cade flashed a manic grin that made Miles slump in his seat. *"Death drives like a pussy."*

⚒

Luis was certain he must have misheard the airline's ticket agent. "I'm sorry, did you say my flight was *canceled*?"

The young lady behind the counter was gratingly chipper as she confirmed the bad news. "Yes, Father. I'm afraid all of our flights to South America have been indefinitely postponed due to a sudden storm cell over the Atlantic."

"But yesterday's forecast—"

"These things happen sometimes," interrupted the charming young woman. "Honestly? I never believe anyone who says they can predict the weather."

"A wise policy, to be sure." Flustered and hoping not to miss his connecting flight, Luis looked down the length of Ciampino Airport's line of check-in counters. "Do you know if any other airline might be making that flight? I really need to get to Buenos Aires."

The ticket agent put on a look of remorse without sacrificing her sunny affect. "I'm so sorry. This was a safety decision made by the government. It's not just our flights to South America that were grounded, it was everyone's." A devil-may-care shrug. "Maybe it's a sign from God, Father. Maybe you're just not meant to go to South America today."

She had spoken the platitude half in jest, but something about her words struck Luis as true. His angelically enhanced intuition latched on to her statement, giving it persuasive weight.

"Perhaps you're right," Luis said. "Mortals make plans, but the Lord decides." He picked up his passport and ticket, then nodded in gratitude. "Thank you for your help."

He walked away from the check-in counter, his ticket in his hand, at a loss for what to do next. *I can accept that one door has been closed,* he reflected. *But if this truly is a sign from Above, then there should be an indication of what door has opened to beckon me onward.*

Moving down the concourse, he cleared his mind of conscious thought. It took effort to purge oneself of expectation, of intention, and to simply exist in the moment. Meditation had a stronger foundation in Eastern philosophy than it did in the study of magick, but the skill had proved useful to Luis ever since he had begun studying it during a missionary tour in Japan.

He compelled himself not to read words or even to see the letters on all the signage around him. In his mind's eye they became shapes divorced from meaning. Around him the world became a wash of color and sound, voices speaking but producing only noise. As a woman passed him, a whiff of her subtle perfume made Luis think of jasmine.

His bare feet padded along the cold tiled floor. He splashed through shallow puddles of cold water, the products of melting snow tracked in by other passengers. Cigarette smoke and pipe tobacco mingled in the air with men's cologne and the astringent bite of ammonia from a custodian's mop bucket. Outside the terminal, horns honked and men exchanged vulgarities. Shrieks of delight prefaced the sudden appearance of excited children, who ran past Luis on either side, giggling as their shoes slapped the floor, filling the long hall with echoes.

In a self-imposed daze he drifted the length of the concourse and back again.

He was halted by a commotion in front of him. Snapped back into the moment, he saw a pair of men from the airport's cleaning staff trying to shoo a bird that had found its way inside the terminal. Their pursuit of the bird as it flapped to and fro was almost comical. More than a few onlookers enjoyed laughs at the janitors' expense. Luis was one of them.

Then he saw that the bird was a dove. A symbol of the Holy Spirit.

It dodged and swooped, evading capture or injury, and it glided past Luis in a graceful arc. He turned to keep his eye on it as it passed. The dove settled atop a pipe that ran along the ceiling and from which dangled a series of banners promoting discounted flights to selected destinations. Luis stepped back to get a clear look at the banner beneath the dove.

It was an advertisement for reduced fares to New Delhi, India.

Outside, a sudden shift in the clouds above the city admitted a sliver of sunlight into the terminal . . . and one such shaft of solar brilliance landed on the banner gently waving.

A feeling of calm and certainty welled up from the part of Luis's soul that was quiet and trusted in God. He knew as he gazed upward that he could not have asked for a clearer message.

He walked back to the check-in counter and placed his ticket in front of the chipper young woman. "When is the next flight to New Delhi, India?"

"Hold on, let me check." She reviewed a printed schedule behind the counter. "Flight Three-eighty departs in about ninety minutes."

"I would like to exchange my current ticket for one to New Delhi, please."

"Of course, sir." She smiled, as if she had no other purpose in this world but to show off her perfectly straight, white teeth. She shuffled papers as she worked, and then she looked up some information that was stored in a three-ring binder. Then she smiled again. "Good news, Father! Because of the discount on our fares to New Delhi, you're entitled to a partial refund on your Buenos Aires ticket. Would you like the difference refunded to the account that purchased the ticket, or would you like to have the balance in cash?"

Luis struggled for a moment with the ethics of the question. After all, the Vatican had paid for the ticket, and the Holy See was entitled to receive any refund that was due. *On the other hand,* he rationalized, *it's not as if they really need the money.*

He mirrored the ticketing agent's smile.

"Cash, please."

<hr />

The streets of Bombay were an assault on Anja's senses. Aromas of turmeric, cumin, coriander, and cardamom from the carts of roaming food vendors mixed with the stink of uncollected garbage and open sewers. People of many ethnicities packed its streets, in which pedestrians, bicyclists, and motor vehicles competed for space. The air was thick with car exhaust and the smell of animal manure, the streets a minefield of garbage and dung from livestock.

On either side of her, modern buildings stood shoulder-to-shoulder with structures from the nineteenth century, suggesting to her that Bombay was a city that had little use for sentimentality. Vintage structures were just as likely to be torn down as they were to be thought of as landmarks.

But the people—there were so many of them! And they practically fell over one another in their mad rushes about the Indian metropolis. Anja had long since accustomed herself to the lower population densities of cities in Argentina, Paraguay, Chile, and Peru. It felt cloying to be hemmed in so tightly by strange bodies, and also alarming. This, she knew from experience, was fertile ground for pickpockets and cutpurses.

She did her best to fit in. Even on the far side of the world from South America she had to assume there were people looking for her. If not the Nazis it would be the Soviets, or the Chinese, or the Americans. She had made her share of enemies. It had become an occupational hazard for karcists who had spent decades meddling in modern wars and politics—entanglements their kind once had been wise enough to avoid. To make matters worse, Anja knew that her facial scar made her more recognizable than most people.

It was fortunate, then, that India was home to a substantial Muslim population. With a deep tan and black hair, all it took for Anja to disappear into the throngs of Bombay was a half *niqaab* of midnight-blue silk. Her taste in attire had long tended to favor modesty, making the disguise an easy one to appropriate. But even concealed, she still felt exposed, and every few blocks she forced her way across the street, or doubled back for half a block, just to make certain she wasn't being followed.

The demons in her head mocked her paranoia. She called it *caution*.

Over the course of her first day in Bombay, she had explored a fair portion of the city in search of a clue as to where she should go next. Master Khalîl's riddle had not left her much in the way of suggestions. Consequently, left to wander without guidance, she found herself in a seedy quarter of the city, one in which unaccompanied women were rare and vulnerable, one whose general atmosphere betrayed its place in the city's criminal ecosystem.

Anja turned around and quickened her pace. This was a street to be avoided.

It felt cowardly, but Anja had given up trying to be the savior of the oppressed. There were too many of them, and their plights too dire, for any one person to help them all, even if that person was trained in magick. She had learned to content herself with being an avenger, with finishing the mission she and Adair had started so long ago.

Killing Nazis—*that's* what she was good at.

And, she had come to realize since meeting Khalîl, that was the problem: It was *all* that she was good at. She had spent so long devoted to her singular mission of destroying the heirs of the Thule Society that she no longer knew who she was beyond that task.

I have lost myself, she'd realized. *I look in the mirror and do not know who looks back.*

Khalîl had been right. She was incomplete. Half a person. Half a magician. If she ever wanted to be whole, she would need to have a reason for living that was nobler than murder; she needed to become something more than an instrument of death. And if what he had said about her being a *nikraim* like Cade was true, there were so many more questions she needed to ask in order to know where her true destiny might lie.

It was almost dusk by the time she found her way to the city's central train station. The crowd that choked the streets around it only grew thicker as she pushed closer to the terminal.

How do these people breathe? she wondered.

Inside the train terminal, the scene was one of narrowly controlled chaos. Packs of people stampeded down the concourse in various directions, shoving past one another to reach their trains before they departed the station. It was a madhouse. Anja couldn't begin to comprehend how people navigated such mayhem even once, never mind daily.

There were a dozen trains or more every hour to choose from. None were listed on the departures board with any kind of helpful information.

Such as "this train goes to Khalîl," she mused sourly.

There was a route to anywhere one wanted to go in India. Surveying the breadth of the Indian rail system on a wall map, Anja felt a grudging respect for the British Empire's devotion to building reliable railroads. But where to go? Calcutta? Chennai?

She forced herself to recall the first part of Khalîl's riddle.

"Follow the needle true . . ."

Staring at the map, Anja wondered if India was home to a geographic feature known as the Needle. Then her eyes stopped on the illustration of the cardinal directions in the lower right-hand corner of the map—and she deduced that Khalîl had meant the needle of a compass.

North, she realized. *He wants me to go to northern India.*

She checked the departures board for the next train that could take her north. To her relief, it was leaving in twenty minutes. Just long enough for her to buy a ticket and climb aboard. She walked to the ticket window.

Behind the window, a middle-aged man with rich brown skin smiled at her. "Yes?"

Anja smiled back at him. "One ticket to New Delhi, please."

JANUARY 31

Feeling like a sewer rat creeping through a palace, Miles crouched low on one of the balcony levels above the main nave of the Buenos Aires Metropolitan Cathedral. The building was modern by the standards of the Catholic Church—its interior dated only to the eighteenth century, and its imposing exterior had been entirely rebuilt in the nineteenth century—but it had the trappings of a place steeped in antiquity. Its gilded dome was adorned with frescoes depicting scenes from scripture, and the nave was flanked on each side by three towering marble arches.

The cathedral was mostly empty in the midafternoon between services. A few worshippers sat apart from one another in the pews, praying or perhaps merely enjoying the silence. Footsteps echoed in the great space's cold emptiness, which was perfumed with sweet incense, the fragrance of melting beeswax, and the scent of wood polish.

A shuffling behind Miles turned his head. Cade made his way to Miles's side and squatted beside him. "All set. Mics hidden in the corners, and I bugged the confessionals."

"The confessionals? Doesn't that strike you as blasphemous?"

The look on Cade's face expressed sardonic reproach. "I use demons as tools. I think it's a bit late for me to start worrying about *blasphemy.*"

"Suit yourself, mate." In truth he knew, as Cade did, that the confessionals had needed to be wired for audio surveillance. If, as their deciphering of the Odessa journal had suggested, ex–Gestapo commander Heinrich Müller met his contact here, one of the most obvious places for such an exchange would be in the privacy of the confessional booths.

Miles glanced at his watch. "He's late. Or else we decoded the journal wrong."

"I'll be impressed if he shows up at all," Cade said.

"You mean on account of his having been declared dead?"

"Exactly. Who knew he and I would have something in common?"

A loud *clack* resounded inside the cathedral as someone opened the front doors to the nave. Miles and Cade ducked low and then peeked over the edge of the balcony railing to see who was walking up the center aisle.

"That's Müller," Cade whispered. "Watch for his contact."

None of the other visitors to the church stirred or even appeared to notice Müller's arrival. Then Miles looked toward the altar and saw a priest moving in quick strides toward the Nazi. "Point the mic at the priest," he said to Cade while fumbling for his tiny spy camera.

Cade put on a small pair of headphones and aimed their miniaturized parabolic microphone at the cleric, who met Müller in the middle of the cathedral, completely out in the open. The men shook hands and exchanged what looked like small talk.

Miles snapped photos of the meeting. Then he nudged Cade. "What are they saying?"

"Müller asked if the priest found the Bible he left behind at morning services." Down below, the priest handed a careworn Bible to Müller. "Now he's thanking him." The priest and the Nazi parted, each walking back the way he had come. "And that's it."

"Must be a note pass in the Bible," Miles realized. "We should get ready to follow him."

"Not so fast," Cade said. "He's making a detour."

Straining to maintain a line of sight to Müller, Miles risked poking his head a bit higher above the railing. On the main floor of the cathedral, Müller carried his Bible over to the tiered stand of memorial votive candles and kneeled in front of it. He opened the Bible and took from it a folded paper, which he opened. It took him only a few seconds to read it. Then, instead of putting it back in the Bible or into his pocket, he touched its corner to a candle's flame and set it ablaze. Tongues of fire consumed the paper in a matter of seconds. Müller dropped the last smoldering fragment to the stone floor. As the flames transformed the paper into black ash, Müller made the sign of the cross, stood, and walked toward the exit.

"Damn," Miles muttered. "I was hoping we could do this without having to take him."

Cade took apart the parabolic microphone. "What do you mean?"

"We need to know what that note said. Assuming the priest is a cutout, he probably never saw it. Which means we'll need to force that information out of Müller."

A sly smile brightened Cade's features. "Maybe not." He put the disassembled parabolic microphone into its case and handed it to Miles. "Pack up the other mics and meet me by the candles." Without waiting for inquiry or permission, he got up and left Miles behind.

A few minutes later, Miles toted the recovered spy gear in a thin briefcase downstairs to find Cade squatting in front of the memorial candles. The young American scraped the last of the black ashes from the floor into a small envelope. He looked up at Miles. "All set upstairs?"

"Shipshape. What's all this, then?"

A devilish smirk. "You'll see." Cade walked toward the exit, and Miles followed him. In the foyer they paused at the stoup. Cade pulled a flask from inside his bomber jacket, and emptied its contents onto the floor. Whiskey fumes filled the air as the puddle spread.

Miles shook his head in disapproval. "You are so going to Hell, mate."

"I wouldn't bet on that," Cade said as he filled his flask with holy water from the stoup. Closing the hinged cap of his flask, he beckoned Miles with a sideways nod to follow him outside. "Let's see what Müller thought was important enough to burn."

The two men walked out of the cathedral, crossed the street, and strolled into the Plaza de Mayo. They made their way to a bench in a tree-shaded nook off the plaza's main pathway. Cade sat first, and then Miles, who watched Cade empty the ashes from the envelope onto the pavement and then sprinkle them with holy water from his flask. As the ashes turned to charcoal-colored sludge, Cade waved his hand over the mess.

Miles felt an electric tingle like the prickling of a thousand tiny needles down the back of his neck. Then, in the blink of an eye, the mud of ashes on the ground reshaped itself into a few small scraps of scorched paper on which a few handwritten words were legible.

"Voilà," Cade said, "courtesy of XAPHAN."

The scraps were tiny, their contents few. Miles threw a dubious look at his friend. "Not much to go on, is it?"

"More than we had before. And more reliable than trusting the word of a Nazi."

The larger of the two fragments read:

Herr Dalca that our American asset has

The smaller piece contained only three words:

the atomic device

Miles and Cade both stared with wide eyes at the smaller note.
"We need to know who that asset is," Miles said.
Cade nodded. "Right fucking now."

⁓

All the lights were off inside the train carriage. It rocked slowly, a massive crib rolling on steel wheels toward the Indian capital. Hypnotized by the steady percussion of track ties passing underneath, Anja sat low in her seat, up against the wall with her rolled-up jacket for a pillow.

The trip from Bombay had been a test of her patience. It seemed there was no end to the things that could delay a train in India. Rockslides. Cows on the tracks. Faulty track switches. Rainstorms that were as biblical in their fury as they were short-lived.

She checked her watch; at its current speed, the train would arrive in New Delhi almost half a day late. Its tardiness frustrated her on principle, though in practice she was grateful for the extra hours of sleep it had afforded her. Still drowsy, she savored the quiet in the train car—

Why is it so quiet? Her eyes fluttered open. It struck her as odd that no one else in her car was talking. She had struggled to tune out their chatter during the first half of the trip. Where was all that idle conversation now that the trip was almost done?

Concentrating, she listened to the sounds inside the train carriage.

There were footfalls, slow and heavy. Two sets of them, at least. There were other people in the car, and they were moving toward her. She squinted and searched for the reflections of other passengers in the windows. To her alarm, she saw that they all were gone.

Who is here? Local thugs? Black Sun?

Under the rattle and rumble of the train's wheels on the track, the *snick* of a switchblade. Then the *ker-clack* of a semiautomatic pistol's slide being primed to put a round in the chamber.

Anja mustered her yoked spirits and tensed to meet her attackers.

They struck quickly, with precision and strength.

Big hands seized Anja's arms in a fierce grip. She flailed as she was pulled from her seat. Two men loomed over her, both fair-skinned and light-haired. Big Hands did his best to subdue her as a thin man lunged at her with a hypodermic needle. Behind Thin Man was another pale man with darker hair and a beard—he was the bearer of the pistol. Big Hands was backed up by a white crew-cut youth wielding a switchblade knife.

The hypodermic needle sank into Anja's thigh but found no purchase thanks to her control of ELIGOS, who made her insubstantial to metal. She twisted clear of the needle before Thin Man could press its plunger, and then she kicked him in his groin. Then she bit into Big Hands's right thumb, deep enough to hit bone.

Thin Man groaned and fell aside. Big Hands howled like a shot bear.

The gunman aimed for Anja's gut and fired.

Big Hands yowled as the bullet passed harmlessly through Anja and ripped into his leg. From the spray of his blood and the way that he hit the floor, she knew the bullet had shattered his femur.

Free, Anja pinned the gunman's wrist against the back of a seat; then she swatted the Makarov out of his hand with a palm strike. Her elbow in his face knocked him backward.

She spun to face the knife-fighter only to find that he had cast aside the blade. His dominant hand emerged from his coat pocket adorned with a set of wooden knuckles.

They've done their homework, Anja realized. *This is no random attack.*

Knuckle Boy swung at Anja, who dodged his first punch and deflected his second. She kicked at his knee, but he sidestepped clear of the blow.

On the edges of her vision she noted movement—more men were entering the train car. She was about to be badly outnumbered.

No more pulled punches.

She slammed the fist of BUER into Knuckle Boy's gut. The demonic blow doubled him over, and she put her knee into his chin. It connected with a satisfying crunch of shattering teeth and the crack of a broken jaw. Then she spun and skewered two men approaching from the front of the train with a triple fork of lightning that dropped their smoking bodies to the floor.

Something solid clocked the back of her skull.

The hard wooden floor bit into Anja's knees as she fell onto them. She looked back at a burly thug winding up to pummel her again with a wool sock full of rocks. She used the hands of BUER to throw the bruiser through the nearest window, into the rushing blur of the night.

Her head ached, and as her strength and consciousness ebbed her hold on her yoked spirits faltered. She reached behind her back for her Browning, only to find its holster empty. Someone had stolen it while she'd slept. *May thieves burn in Hell,* she raged.

Two more men advanced from the rear of the train, and two more came through the door from the front. There was more of the train behind her than ahead, so she charged at the men in the rear, hoping to force her way past them and retreat into another carriage. The closer of the two ducked her punch, and then he snared her arm with a length of rope. When she tried to pull herself free, he bent with her and coiled the rope around her biceps, trapping her arm completely.

He snapped his head forward and slammed his forehead into her nose. The break was a blast of white pain and red heat. Anja struggled to breathe as blood gushed from her nostrils. Marshaling the last of her magickal strength, she used the gift of HABORYM to ignite the rope, which vanished into ashes. Then she used her freed hand to jab Rope Man in his throat. His windpipe went flat with one hit, and he collapsed, unable to breathe.

A booted foot kicked Anja behind her right knee, which buckled. She fell backward and landed hard on the floor. She was about to unleash a fireball when another kick connected with her temple, and her world turned to blurs and echoes.

Through her confusion she felt rope being tied around her wrists and ankles, and a gag was shoved into her mouth. Her vision went soft and dimmed as the men pulled a rough canvas bag over her head and tied it shut around her throat.

Fuck, she fumed. *What now?*

The next voice she heard spoke in Russian.

"Ivan, get her tools and gear," said a man whose voice sounded like a tiger gargling gravel. "Dmitry, call ahead. Tell the *rezidentura* we need to get rid of these bodies. Viktor, grab her. We'll get off as soon as the conductor announces the next 'delay.'"

A rag was pressed over Anja's face from outside the bag. She caught the medicinal scent of ether and knew exactly what had happened: Anja Kernova, the most-wanted fugitive of the Supreme Soviet, had just been captured by the KGB.

13

FEBRUARY 1

The apartment tower stood back from the road. It was protected by a black iron fence and a gate manned by an armed guard. Eyeing the building of red brick and white concrete from across the street in his car's rearview mirror, Cade wondered whether its residents believed they were safe.

They had every reason to think so; they lived in a protected enclave in the heart of Belgrano, one of Buenos Aires's most upscale neighborhoods. They had the best police, concealed fortifications, and private security that money could buy. However, it seemed no one in the building was aware of the real and present danger posed by magick, because Cade was unable to detect a single glyph or ward anywhere on the premises' ground floor.

Next to him in the parked Cadillac, Miles checked his watch. "Getting late."

"The journal says they hold a regular meeting every Monday night at nine." Cade shifted his gaze toward Miles. "Assuming the clowns back at GCHQ deciphered it correctly."

Miles looked ready to defend his peers' honor, but then he ducked low in his seat. "Fuck. Here he comes."

Cade observed Heinrich Müller via the rearview mirror. The former Gestapo chief left the building's lobby and exchanged pleasantries with the security guard as he exited to the street. His image in the mirror shrank as he hurried from one pool of lamplight to the next.

"Relax, Miles. He's walking the other way."

Miles sat up and looked over his shoulder. "About bloody time."

"How long do we wait?"

"Let him get around the corner," Miles said. "Then we move."

In between glances at the mirror, Miles loaded his Walther and Cade checked his Beretta to make certain it was full. As both pistols' magazines clicked back into place, Cade said, "We're clear. Let's go."

They got out of the car. Each man tucked his weapon under his belt at the small of his back and concealed it with the drape of a lightweight sport jacket. The street was dead quiet as they quick-stepped toward the security guard's gate. Inside the cramped booth, behind a pane of bulletproof glass, a portly Argentinian of middling years and silvering hair looked up at the two men. Not recognizing them, he put on a look of menace. "*¿Qué deseas?*"

Cade looked into the guard's eyes and focused the power of ESIAS. "*Dormir.*" The guard's eyes fluttered closed, and he slumped against the booth's rear window. Then Cade waved his hand at the locked gate, which swung open. He ushered his friend past him toward the apartment tower. "After you."

Miles took the lead. Cade followed him inside the tower's brightly lit foyer, and then into the elevator, where Miles pressed the button for the twelfth floor. As the lift car ascended, Cade noted that it looked new and modern, like the rest of the building. "Swank place," he said.

"The Nazis might be monsters, but they don't lack style."

Floor numbers above the doors lit in sequence until they reached the twelfth floor. A soft semi-musical *bing* accompanied the opening of the doors onto a long hallway. The carpet was the hue of champagne; the walls were papered with a sophisticated design and sported framed art. All of it was lit by the subdued glow of evenly spaced wall sconces that bounced their light off the stuccoed ceiling. Broad doors of dark wood with brass fixtures lined the hall, those on opposite sides staggered so that no door opened to face another, but a potted plant instead.

The two men left the elevator and walked down the hallway side by side.

Cade sighed. "Why do bad guys always get the nicest places to live?"

"The same reason fools always seem to wind up as supervisors. To test our faith."

The pair stopped in front of apartment 1217. Miles reached for his lock-picking tools, but Cade stopped him with a raised hand. "Hang on." He waved his hand in front of the door as he marshaled the Sight of SATHARIEL. A warding glyph that was visible only to those armed with magick appeared on the front of the door. "Thought so. The building isn't warded, but the apartment is. Better let me open it." He held out his open hands and willed his demon of burden to deliver his wand and a hunk of hematite.

Miles flinched as the tools appeared in Cade's hands as if from thin air. "Bloody hell. I will never get used to that."

"It's not that big a deal," Cade said. He neutralized the glyph with a few strokes of the lodestone and a tap of his wand. "You're smart enough to learn magick if you want."

"No thank you. I've enough demons of my own. Don't need to go adding more."

Cade unlocked the door with another bit of magickal effort and swung it open. The apartment beyond was dark and quiet. He probed the room with the Sight, which rendered the scene in spectral twilight, like a photo negative backlit by green fire. "Looks okay."

"Close the door behind us," Miles said, stepping past Cade. "I'll check the bedroom. You root around out here." He pulled a compact flashlight from his pocket and clicked it on as he hurried away to the apartment's master suite, leaving Cade alone in the main room.

There wasn't much to see or search. Müller's dwelling had little furniture and almost no decoration. The man seemed to love open space and clear sight lines more than anything else. His kitchen was spotless, its cupboards half bare. There was nothing in the refrigerator except a few bottles of wine lying on their sides between two closely placed shelves.

Not much for cooking, I guess.

Atop an end table beside the front door were a small pad and a pencil. Cade moved closer to check the pad. Its top sheet was blank. He ran his fingers over it and felt the subtle impressions left behind from previous notes. Remembering a trick he had seen in a movie, he picked up the pencil and held it at an oblique angle as he shaded the paper with the edge of the pencil's graphite tip. As his cloud of shade spread, old writings appeared in relief like ghosts. Most of them overlapped too many other sets of characters to be intelligible, but one line came through clearly along the bottom edge of the pad:

unseren Mann in L.A.

Was it connected to the deciphered notes in the journal? He needed to know.

MERSOS was a demon whose talents related to concealment. As Cade had learned since the war, mostly through trial and error, many spirits were equally adept at the reverse of their stated specialty, and MERSOS was no exception. Though it could be called upon to hide secrets and the true natures of things, it could also be compelled to remove such obfuscations.

He tore off the top sheet, held it up, and focused his will upon it.

Show me, he commanded Mersos. *Show me the most recent writing hidden on this page.*

Legible words shimmered into focus, as if surfacing from a sea of scribbles. Cade let his eyes travel across the document, and he discerned four clear lines of text:

> *Atomtest startbereit*
> *Dämon ist vor Ort*
> *Alle Covens nehmen Schutz 28.2*
> *Dragan braucht unseren Mann in L.A.*

He called out to Miles, "I've got something."

Miles returned to him directly. "Spill, mate."

Cade traced the words Mersos had revealed. "I separated the latest note from the rest of the scribbles. Roughly translated, it says, 'atomic test ready to proceed; demon is in place; all covens take shelter twenty-eight point two,' and, last but not least, 'Dragan needs our man in L.A.'" He handed the note to Miles. "What do you think?"

"Anything that combines 'atomic' with 'demon' sounds like trouble to me." Miles squinted at the note. "Who's Dragan?"

"No idea," Cade said. "Send it to MI6. They can check it against known Nazi sympathizers. Maybe get us a new lead by the time we get to America."

A sly arching of Miles's brow telegraphed his suspicion. "And what makes you think we're going to America?"

Cade plucked the note from Miles's hand and pointed at the last line. "Who else has atom bombs and a city named 'L.A.'?" He folded the note and tucked it inside his pocket.

Miles frowned. "Need I remind you that we're still persona non grata in the U.S.?"

"What, you mean the Roswell mess? That was almost seven years ago. I'm sure they've forgotten all about that by now." Cade cracked open the door to check the hallway. It was clear. He opened the door and left the apartment, with Miles following close at his back. "Let's pack our bags, Miles. We're going to Hollywood."

The worst part of Father Luis Pérez's trip to New Delhi hadn't been the interminable layovers between his flights—first in Tel Aviv, and then again in Tehran—but the walk from Safdarjung Airport to the Sacred Heart Cathedral after his arrival.

His flight had landed ahead of a storm front, which broke the moment he set foot outside of the terminal. Within moments every taxi, pedicab, and rickshaw had vanished from sight. Pedestrians had scrambled for cover, and the deserted streets had transformed into swift rivers of mud. After an hour the rain had only worsened, and Luis, fatigued from his long journey and desperate to reach a safe haven, had chosen to brave the deluge.

Half a kilometer from the airport he had succeeded in waving down a taxi. Thanking God for a moment of providence, he had trudged over to the beat-up vehicle. Then the driver saw Luis's bare feet, and before Luis could explain that he wasn't without currency, the car had sped away, leaving Luis once again abandoned before the full fury of the storm.

Lashed by the tempest he made his way north from the airport, following a now-sodden guide map he had purchased during his layover in Tehran. *If I read this correctly,* he assured himself, *I need only follow the Rafi Marg until it meets Ashoka Road, which will lead me to the cathedral.* It was a simple enough plan, but rain, wind, and darkness made the road signs nearly impossible for him to see. *Lord God,* he prayed without resentment or rancor, *please have mercy upon your humble servant and see me safely to shelter.*

A flash of lightning banished the night for half a second—just long enough for Luis to discern the street sign ahead that read ASHOKA ROAD. Encouraged, he pressed onward.

Almost there.

As the map had promised, Ashoka Road soon led him to a roundabout. On the far side of the circle stood the outer gates of the Sacred Heart Cathedral's walled compound. In keeping with the Church's tradition of serving as a sanctuary, the gates were open. Luis stepped through them and instantly felt relief, in spite of still being at the mercy of the elements. He was back on consecrated ground; he could feel the comfort it promised.

He approached a sign mounted at the edge of the cathedral's manicured lawn. An arrow pointed left was labeled MARIA BHAWAN, and an arrow pointing right directed visitors to the Archbishop's House. He headed right, toward the residence.

Nearly all of the lights inside the large brick house were off as Luis knocked on its front door. He waited several seconds. No one answered. He knocked again, harder this time, and for a few seconds more. Through a curtained window next to the door he saw an electric light switch on inside the house. A shadow passed over the curtain.

A man dressed in loose nightclothes opened the door. He looked young and had the close haircut and bare face of a novitiate. He regarded Luis with confusion. "Yes?"

"Forgive the late hour," Luis said in his best English, and hoping his Spanish accent didn't impede their conversation. "I am Father Luis Roderigo Pérez, and I have come to ask for sanctuary during my stay in New Delhi."

A gust of wind spat rain in the young man's face. He winced and asked, "You're who?"

"Father Luis Roderigo Pérez."

"Are we expecting you?"

"No," Luis admitted. "I had to change my travel plans at the last moment." He cast an imploring look past the younger man, toward the warm dry house behind him. "Please. I have come a long way, and I am very tired. May I come in?"

The youth eyed Luis's robes. "Are you a Catholic priest?"

"I am a Jesuit monk, dispatched on a holy mission for the Vatican. I was sent by Cardinal Umberto Lombardi. Please, in the name of Our Lord Jesus Christ, I am asking for your help."

Caution turned to suspicion. "Wait here," said the young man, who closed the door.

Wind and rain slashed at Luis, who now was too soaked to care.

The door opened again. This time Luis found himself facing a tall man in his midsixties. Tufts of gray hair lingered above his ears, but the rest of his head was bald. Loose-fitting pajamas could not conceal his lean and sinewy physique, and he was clearly of Indian ancestry. He studied Luis with a piercing gaze. "You're from the Vatican?"

"No," Luis said, doing his best to sound modest. "I am on a mission for the Vatican." He offered the man his hand in greeting. "I am Father Luis Roderigo Pérez."

Shaking Luis's hand, the older man replied, "Joseph Alexander Fernandes, archbishop of Delhi and Simla. If you're not from the Vatican, what is your parish?"

"I'm a Jesuit monk, Your Excellency, with the Order of Monte Paterno."

The archbishop's eyes widened at the mention of the sanctuary. It was obvious to Luis that the man knew exactly what transpired within Monte Paterno, and, therefore, what Luis was. The archbishop ushered Luis inside the residence and shut the door. He turned to his novitiate. "Please prepare a guest room for Father Pérez. See that he has whatever he needs."

"Yes, Your Excellency."

The younger man started to leave, but the archbishop caught his arm to waylay him. Then he asked Luis, "Are you hungry, Father?"

"I am, Your Excellency."

To his subordinate, the archbishop added, "Once you've shown Father Pérez to his room, go to the kitchen and prepare a plate for him."

The youth nodded in understanding. "At once, Your Excellency."

He let go of the young man, who left to prepare the room. The archbishop looked unsettled as he faced Luis. "Do you know how long you plan to stay, Father?"

"Not yet, Your Excellency."

"Very well. You're welcome as long as your mission requires. But I would ask that you refrain from practicing your Art within the consecrated grounds of the cathedral."

"Of course, Your Excellency. I would not have thought otherwise."

A nod of relief, and then the archbishop lowered his voice. "Also, and please understand that I mean no offense, but I must ask that you sequester yourself and avoid any unnecessary contact with the cathedral's clergy and lay staff, for the duration of your visit."

It was not an unexpected request, given the Church's official doctrine banning the practice of ceremonial magick. Even the existence of Monte Paterno was a fact the Church and its upper echelons found embarrassing.

Luis bowed his head in a gesture of submission. "As you wish, Your Excellency."

They bid each other good night. Minutes later, the young priest returned and beckoned Luis to follow him. As they walked down a narrow hallway to the far end of the archbishop's residence, Luis said, "I never did catch your name."

"Father Anil Dupresh." He stopped at a door and opened it, then motioned for Luis to step past him and go inside. "Make yourself comfortable. I'll be right back with some food."

"Or you could keep me company while I settle in."

An awkward grimace played across Anil's face. "Please don't think me rude,

Father. The archbishop asked me to avoid engaging you in conversation." With downcast eyes he added, "I'll be back directly with your dinner." And with that, he padded off down the hall.

The room was spare and mostly blank, as Luis had expected. It had one window, which faced east. Its narrow bed was against the west wall, and a small desk and chair stood against the south wall beneath a crucifix and a wall clock, opposite the door. On the desk was a small basin of clean water, and beside it were a clean washcloth and small towel.

Nothing more do I require except Your guidance, Lord.

The dinner was cold curried lamb and rice; it more than satisfied Luis's hunger. His only regret was that Anil had not lingered long enough for him to say more than a simple "thank you."

Alone behind a closed door, Luis undressed and draped his robe from a hook on the back of the door so it could dry. Then he dug into his traveling bag and retrieved his Llull Engine. The contraption was a simple one to make. It consisted of three circles of stiff, thin card stock. The largest was the bottom circle; the second-largest was in the middle, and the smallest lay on top. Each was inscribed with symbols that represented, respectively, fundamental questions, philosophical or ontological concepts, and divine qualities. They were joined at their center point with a metal pin, around which they could spin freely.

He held up the Llull Engine, faced north, and waved it once. He repeated this gesture to the east, south, and west, and then he set the wheels spinning in different directions while he held the device by its center pin. The hand-written characters on the wheels were a blur, and he let go of any expectations or hopes he might harbor.

The chief value of a Llull Engine to a karcist was that its operation did not require the invocation of any kind of Presence, either Celestial or Infernal. Its random nature made it an ideal tool for intuition-based reflection and divination through insight.

He needed to know what to do now that he was in New Delhi, and there was no one else he could ask, and no other method he could use, while taking shelter within the cathedral.

The wheels slowed, and at last they stopped. Luis looked to see which elements had aligned above the pin's needle. He was pleasantly surprised to find it had produced an almost poetic result out of its chaos: PATIENCE / CHANGING / REALITY.

It was not the call to action he might have hoped for, but it was an instruction with which his years of service to the Church had made him most familiar: sit, wait, and observe.

If that is Your will, Lord, so be it.

Luis put away the Llull Engine. Washed and dried his hands and feet. Kneeled and prayed for guidance and forgiveness. Climbed into bed. Turned out the light.

Tomorrow would be a new day.

Until then, all he could do was keep the faith—and a low profile.

Consciousness hit with a frigid jolt. Anja gasped at the shock of ice-cold water dripping into her face and running down her back, and she suppressed a shiver as she took in her predicament.

Her wrists and ankles were bound with rope to a metal chair whose legs were bolted into a concrete floor. There was no natural light, just the feeble glow of a low-wattage bare tungsten bulb hanging from a frayed wire above her head. Its sway was so subtle as to be almost imperceptible, like the pendulum of a clock running down the last seconds at the end of time.

Surrounding the chair was a magic circle of protection, one whose configuration she knew well. It was used in exorcisms. Its specific combination of glyphs and symbols indicated that it had been prepared to separate a karcist from yoked spirits. She searched her thoughts for the whispers of demons but found only her own haunting inner silence.

In the room's corner stood her leather roll-up of tools. Its tie was undone, suggesting her implements had been inspected. Her rucksack lay limp and empty on the floor, its contents spread across a folding table against the wall to her right. In the middle of the mess lay her grimoire, its silken cord of binding undisturbed. Beside it was her cameo necklace.

Footsteps snapped on the hard floor behind her.

Someone leaned down close behind her. She felt warm breath on her left ear.

A woman asked in Russian, "Do you know why you're here, Miss Kernova?"

"You have mistaken me for someone else," Anja lied.

"No, we haven't." The female KGB agent circled Anja, who caught only glimpses of the woman's blond hair and angular features. "You're Anja Kernova. Born in Toporok, Novgorodskaya Oblast, on the eighth of November,

1921. Member of the Allies' top-secret magickal warfare unit the Midnight Front, active from 1939 until 1942. Deserter from the Central Front of the Red Army, October 1943." The pale woman stopped in front of Anja and leaned down close to confront her. Her skin looked as if it had been pulled taut against her skull. "In February 1944 you confronted the Red Star—the Red Army's magickal warfare group—outside Toporok. And according to the testimony of a handful of survivors, you single-handedly wiped out the entire unit of more than a hundred karcists-in-training."

Anja remained silent. Everything the woman had said was true, but Anja had nothing to gain by confession. Instead she met the woman's glower of contempt with blank indifference.

From behind Anja came the sounds of more shuffling feet. She and the woman were not the only ones in the room. Anja wondered if she was under round-the-clock guard. If the KGB knew as much about her as it thought it did, they would never leave her unattended, not for a minute. It was just as likely, however, that the KGB woman had a torture expert standing ready.

The stretched-face blonde circled Anja again, as if sizing her up.

"It might interest you to know, Miss Kernova, that you're drawing breath right now only because I countermanded my team's standing orders to terminate you on sight." Another sultry whisper into Anja's ear. "Would you like to know why?"

"Am I supposed to care?"

Her defiance was received by the blonde with a taut, mirthless smile. "I would."

"Then that is one of many things we do not have in common."

The blond woman looked past Anja and nodded.

Cold metal touched the back of Anja's neck. Then a surge of electricity shot through her body, helped along by her damp clothes and the layer of moisture trapped beneath them. Every thought in Anja's head turned white with pain. She jerked and thrashed against her restraints, and her jaw clenched with such violence she feared her teeth might crack.

The spasms ended, leaving behind a hideous burning sensation at the back of her neck. The air was thick with the sharp odor of burnt hair and scorched flesh.

Another cold smile from the blonde filled Anja with hatred. The woman stroked Anja's chin with the red, pointed nail of her index finger. "Our relationship need not be adversarial, Miss Kernova. The reason I insisted you be taken alive was to give you a chance to redeem yourself. To return to Moscow not as a prisoner, but as a Hero of the Soviet."

"Not fucking likely," Anja said between ragged breaths.

"This is no ruse," the woman said. "Your name could be lauded alongside those of Zhukov and Brezhnev, or in the same breath as Fedorov and Zaytsev." She leaned in close enough that Anja could see her eyes. "The Soviet Union is losing the race for occult power. Every day the neofascist Americans grow stronger, and our people fall farther behind."

"What a shame."

"You could change that, Miss Kernova. Come home to Russia, and use your talents to train a new generation of Red Star karcists, and not only will your past be forgiven, you will live a life the likes of which few people on earth will ever enjoy."

Anja shrugged. "You do not need me for that. All you need is in my grimoire."

The woman *tsk*ed. "I am not so easily goaded as Comrade Major Tarpov." A predatory grin of crooked teeth. "Yes, I read about your trick. He cut the cord on your book, and the poor man hallucinated multilegged horrors biting and stinging his flesh. A clever ruse. But not one to which I intend to fall victim."

Heavy steps behind Anja were accompanied by wooden creaks—the sound of poorly carpentered steps protesting a grown man's weight. The slow footfalls and acoustics told her someone was climbing. Noting the room's cracked concrete walls, and sniffing the musty quality of the damp air, Anja concluded she was in a basement. The presence of electric light meant she likely wasn't far from an urban center; in rural India, electrical service was one of the few things rarer than concrete basements and foundations.

In front of her face, the blond skull became impatient. "Well? Are you with us?"

"I made my deal with the Devil years ago. I have no need for another."

"There are only two ways you leave this room," said the KGB woman. "As a hero of the Soviet, or as its victim. The choice is yours." She beckoned one of her colleagues. A short, slim man crossed the room to stand beside her. He had the vaguely Asian features of someone from the eastern territories of Russia. He unfurled a nylon roll lined with surgical blades, dental hooks, and exotic implements whose purposes Anja refused to imagine. "This is Sydir. He will be with you until I return." A malevolent gleam lit up the KGB woman's eye. "Perhaps a few hours in his company will make you more receptive to mine."

"Or maybe it will be the push I need to kill you all."

Behind the woman's smile flickered a moment of admiration. "Reports of your arrogance and courage were not unfounded. . . . Good." She added as she climbed the stairs out of the basement, "Your defiance will make it all the more satisfying when we finally break you."

FEBRUARY 2

Miles followed Cade out of the menswear shop into the glare of California sunlight. Using a wad of cash Cade had scammed from local banks since their arrival that morning in Los Angeles, they had updated their wardrobes to what Cade had insisted was the local norm: Italian suits, bespoke leather shoes, Borsalino hats—a fedora for Miles and jaunty Panama straw trilby for Cade—and, of course, black sunglasses.

Looking up and down Melrose Avenue, Miles saw not one other person sporting an outfit even remotely similar to his and Cade's. "Mate, I'm starting to think you're taking the piss."

Cade drew a deep breath and smiled. "Smell that air, Miles. That's the smell of success."

"All I smell is smog."

His partner scowled. "I don't think you 'get' the vibe of L.A., Miles."

"I'm beginning to doubt your commitment to our craft." He flicked the brim of Cade's hat. "Not exactly keeping a low profile, are we?"

"Low profile?" Cade furrowed his brow. "Who tries to be low-profile in L.A.?"

Under his breath, Miles asked rhetorically, "Spies?"

Cade shook his head and started walking, compelling Miles to follow him. "Trust me. Trying *not* to get noticed is the fastest way to stick out like a sore thumb in Hollywood."

"How the bloody hell would you know? Spend a lot of time rubbing elbows with the glitterati, do you?"

"Where do you think I am when I go AWOL? I'm here, pitching my memoirs."

"Memoirs? You? The man who can't spare ten minutes to write an after-action report?"

"I follow my muse." A pair of young women passing by in the opposite direction smiled at the duo. Cade tipped his hat and smiled back. "Keep your eyes open. We still need a car."

"We had a car at the airport. You said we didn't need it."

"No, I said we *had no use for it.* And we don't—that rolling shitbox would get pulled over every five minutes in Bel Air or Brentwood. We need something that'll let us cruise the city without making people wonder if we belong here."

"There was nothing wrong with the De Soto."

"Are you kidding? It might as well have a neon sign on its roof that flashes 'undercover cops' or 'international spies.' Damn thing's so boring it *begs* to be noticed."

"It's not alone in that respect," Miles said, expecting his criticism to pass unremarked. He was not disappointed. All of Cade's attention was on the cars that lined the street around them. "We could still walk away from this. Let the Yanks handle it."

Just as it had the last several times Miles had brought it up, that suggestion drew a frown from Cade. "This is our lead, Miles. Our op."

"Mate, how many times do I have to tell you? *There is no op.*" He moved closer to Cade and dropped his voice. "The CIA made it very clear last time that we aren't welcome here."

"Pfft." Cade seemed impervious to reason. "Gimme a break, we're allies."

"Yes, and if we want our countries to *stay* allies, we'd best not get caught here." How could he make his impetuous old friend understand? "Seriously, Cade. Let's walk away from this. It's not far to the British consulate. M can hand this off to the FBI and the NSA by lunchtime, and we can be out of the country before anyone knows we're here."

Cade looked at him as if he's sprouted horns. "What fucking fun would *that* be?"

They were walking again, and not toward the consulate. Miles felt like a leaf riding a river, pulled along by Cade's irresistible current. "Give me one good reason we should risk going to jail for the rest of our lives, rather than hand this over to the Americans?"

"Because I know the woman in charge of their Occult Defense Program." There was no more jocularity in Cade's manner, just lethal focus. "She's an ex-Nazi, Miles. I wouldn't trust her any farther than I could throw her. But Truman handed her the keys to the kingdom. And as far as I can tell, Eisenhower hasn't seen fit to replace her, either."

"You're talking about Briet?"

"No, I'm talking about Marilyn Monroe. Of course I'm talking about Briet."

"If she was a security risk, don't you think they'd have ousted her by now?"

Cade stopped and faced Miles. "Even if she was, how the fuck would they know?"

"I suspect they have her under closer supervision than you think." He pinched the fabric of Cade's jacket. "A fate I suspect we'll share once the home office gets our expense reports."

"Why would they care? It's not like I spent *their* money."

"I'll look forward to explaining our acts of grand larceny to M, then, shall I?"

"I always do." And with that the brash young karcist was back in motion. "Look, if this was any other kind of intelligence op, I'd have stuck to protocol. I don't relish the notion of winding up in an American military prison any more than you do. But that journal—it's got more than leads to Nazis. The glyphs and diagrams I saw in there—that's some next-level shit, Miles. I won't pretend I understand all the parts that mashed up magick with physics, but every time I look at them I get a chill down my spine. There's something seriously fucking bad coming down the pike, and I'm afraid Briet might be a part of it."

"Except," Miles said, "we have no proof of that."

"No, but until I'm convinced that she's on our side, I don't want her within a hundred fucking miles of that journal." He paused, looked away—and his eyes lit up. "There we go." Cade jaywalked through traffic on Melrose.

Against his better judgment and his instinct for self-preservation, Miles followed him. Together they arrived beside a cherry-red convertible sports car with an open top that all but screamed *look at me, mortals, and despair.* It was the automotive equivalent of a pinup model.

Miles pinched the bridge of his nose. "Cade. No."

"Are you kidding? It's perfect." He ran his hand lovingly up its windshield frame. "A Moretti 750 Spider Bialbero." He smiled. "You can't tell me this doesn't fit L.A."

Folding his arms to signal disapproval, Miles said, "Steal this car, and we'll be the stars of an all-points bulletin within the hour."

Cade's smile became one of mischief. He cast a quick look around to confirm no one was watching them, and then he snapped his fingers. In the blink of an eye the candied-apple-red car turned black, and all the characters of its license plate changed. Cade vaulted into the driver's seat and grasped its starter. Though he had no key, he used one of his magickal tricks to turn it. The car's engine rumbled to life before settling into a dead-sexy purr.

Miles sighed. He hopped over the door into the passenger seat and surrendered with a grin to the inevitable. "Burn some rubber, mate."

Cade shifted the car into gear, and the duo flew like daredevils into traffic.

Tony Bennett's "Rags to Riches" blared from the car's radio, the sun beat down, and the wind forced Cade and Miles to hold on to their overpriced hats as the convertible roared through downtown L.A. The boys back at HQ would not approve, but today Miles didn't care.

Some battles were not meant to be won.

At high noon everything in the New Mexico desert looked the same shade of bleached white. The sun, close and merciless, stole the world's colors with its brilliance.

Ensconced in the backseat of a taxi, Briet had to squint at the landscape, even through the filter of her black sunglasses. After decades of a mostly nocturnal lifestyle, she found the solar glare brutal almost to the point of being unbearable. Her only comfort was that the monotony of the flat vista, which was bordered by distant mountain ranges that seemed impervious to parallax, left her confident she had not missed much worth seeing.

Her driver had kept to himself during the hour-plus drive from Albuquerque to Santa Fe. Briet had not been concerned about offending him when she had asked for a conversation-free ride, but she still had felt relief at how amenable he had proved to the request. Thin and dark brown with short black hair and a caterpillar of a black mustache obscuring his top lip, young Julio Ortiz had kept his eyes on the road and his hands on the wheel, with only a static-filled radio broadcast of show tunes for company.

Briet watched faint blurs of scrub brush pass by outside. She tucked her handbag close to her side and undid one of its clasps so she could check on Trixim. The rat lay sprawled inside the bag, clearly no more enamored of the

New Mexico heat than Briet was. She stroked the fur between his red eyes until he relaxed. *Just a few minutes longer,* she promised him, knowing he could hear her thoughts. *Almost there.*

She petted his flank and recalled the time, years earlier, when a purse-snatcher had grabbed her bag on a street in downtown Washington. The thief had made what he'd thought was a clean getaway, but when he dug into the handbag in search of his unjust reward, he'd found instead the painful bite of Trixim's front teeth. Guided by her familiar's calls, Briet had found Trixim and the bag just half an hour later—along with the tips of two of the thief's fingers.

Good times, she mused with a smile.

Ahead of the taxi Briet saw an overpass, a sign of civilization. To the west, houses.

"Is that Santa Fe?"

"No, *señora,*" Julio said. "La Cienega. A few miles more."

Briet sat back and let herself be hypnotized by the roaring of wind against the car.

Ten minutes later they slowed and pulled off the highway. She looked around at the sprawl of low ranch houses. A hundred hues of off-white with roofs in more gradations of pink adobe than she would ever have thought possible. As the cab neared the center of town, she kept expecting taller buildings to rise up and embrace the streets, but no matter where she looked she found nothing higher than three stories. Private houses broke up blocks of commercial real estate, and nearly every street was lined with trees in full leaf. Drinking it all in, the only word that Briet could apply to it all was *quaint.*

The cognitive dissonance between her mission and its locale was staggering.

This is where the black dawn of Armageddon is being summoned?

Ahead, hanging from the corner of a building, was a white flag bearing an image of an open hand above which hovered a dove. Beneath the image was printed HOTEL ST. FRANCIS.

"Pull over here," Briet said.

Julio stopped his cab in front of the entrance to the hotel, an unassuming three-story pink building with blue awnings and a deserted covered patio. He and Briet got out. She waited on the sidewalk while he retrieved her bag from the car's trunk. As he set it down beside her, she made a show of peeling off five twenty-dollar bills and holding them up for inspection. "Now, my dear Julio: If anyone should ask about the fare you drove today . . . ?"

"I took two foulmouthed Cubanos out to the Navajo reservation to score peyote."

Briet pressed the bribe into Julio's palm. "Yes. Yes you did."

He smiled, stuffed the cash in his shirt pocket, got in his car, and drove away.

Briet picked up her bag and carried it inside the hotel. The lobby was just as empty as the patio outside, but better air-conditioned. She walked to the front desk and rang the bell.

A bespectacled, fair-haired white man in his thirties poked his head through the doorway of the office behind the desk. He flashed an awkward but engaging grin. "Hello," he said with a mild drawl. He came out to meet Briet and towered over her. Looking up, she realized the genial man was at least six and a half feet tall, perhaps taller. He planted his palms on the counter and leaned forward. "I'm Glenn. How can I be of service?"

"I'd like a room, please."

"Very good." He pulled out a guest book and opened it. "Do you have a reservation?"

"I don't." She looked around the empty lobby. "I hope that won't be a problem."

Another ingratiating smile. "Not at all. You can have your pick of rooms, actually."

"I'd prefer one with a king bed and a northerly view, if possible."

"That's a can-do. Do you know how long you'll be staying with us?"

"I don't. My plans are in flux at the moment."

"No problemo." He made some notes in the guest book, and then he rotated it to face her. "Just sign in right there, and I'll get your key." He retrieved a room key from a pegboard behind the desk while Briet inscribed her traveling alias into the log. He looked at the book as he handed her the key. "Room nineteen, Miss . . . Owens." He raised his eyebrows and pointed at her suitcase. "Should I get the porter?"

"No, thank you. I travel light." She picked up her bag.

Glenn said, "Let me know if you need restaurant reservations."

"I was planning to grab a bite in the hotel restaurant."

"We're happy to open it for you, but you might find it a lonely dining experience."

Briet imagined the mad scramble that America's national-security community was no doubt mired in at that very moment, all in search of her and her agenda. She smirked.

"I suspect I'll have an excess of company soon enough."

In the years that had passed since Luis had answered his calling, he had concluded that prayer, if practiced correctly and with sincerity, was a balm for the soul. Meditation could be a palliative for even the most troubled minds. And there was no better tonic for the stresses of the flesh than the graceful forms of aikido.

It had been many years since Luis had first studied the modern martial art. He had first encountered it in 1933, at the start of his five-year missionary tour to Ayabe, in Japan's Kyoto prefecture. The martial art's grace had been the first aspect to attract his notice. When he had observed some of its students during training, he had come to admire the fluidity of the fighting style, as well as its intrinsically gentle nature.

Persuading his parish host to let him learn the art had been difficult; convincing the master of the dojo to train him had been even harder. But after a time Luis had been welcomed into the school, where he proved to be a quick study.

In his heart he had intuitively embraced the core philosophy of aikido, which sought to resolve violent conflict with as much concern for the well-being of the attacker as that of the defender. Its teachings emphasized defense, meeting assaults and flowing with them until their destructive forces could be redirected. Unlike martial arts that highlighted means of inflicting injury or death, aikido appealed to Luis because it favored holds, joint locks, and nonlethal throws. It was less a fighting style and more a *not*-fighting style—a means of turning the other cheek without passively waiting for another blow to land.

Alone in his room inside the New Delhi archbishop's residence, he concentrated on breathing slowly and steadily while he practiced the forms he had studied for five years in Japan. Most of them involved stretching and preserving his balance while focusing his *ki,* or life energy. It was difficult to execute his *kata* without a partner; the art had been designed to be practiced by students working in pairs. He did his best to visualize his old sparring partner Kiroshi. The man sadly was many years gone, consumed by fire in the atrocity that had leveled Nagasaki.

Luis had just begun rehearsing his *tori* forms when he was startled by an urgent knocking at his door. He straightened, exhaled, and opened the door to see Father Anil Dupresh, the young priest who had shown him to this room the night before, trembling with anxiety. "Yes?"

"The archbishop wants to see you," Anil said. "Right now. I'm to bring you to him."

"I understand." Luis folded his hands so that they vanished into the overlapping sleeves of his cassock. "Lead the way, Father."

Anil led him through the narrow hallways of the residence to a master suite at its far end. The young Indian man pushed open a door that led to an elegantly appointed private office. "Wait here." He walked away without waiting for Luis to acknowledge or thank him.

Alone and curious, Luis ventured inside the office. The books on the high shelves that filled the walls to his left and right were all leather-bound hardcover tomes. Some looked to be works in English, others in Latin, a few in the local languages of India. Two guest chairs sat far apart, near either end of the wide mahogany desk. As Luis crossed the room toward the desk, the floor of polished stone tiles felt cold beneath his bare feet.

A door behind the desk opened, and Archbishop Fernandes entered. He wore street clothes rather than any of his clerical uniforms or vestments; he looked both weary and vexed. "I've just had a most interesting conversation with Cardinal Lombardi," he said.

"I see," Luis said, though he had no idea what to infer from the archbishop's statement. He moved to pull back one of the guest chairs.

Fernandes stopped Luis with a castigating waggle of his index finger. "Don't sit, Father." He pointed at Luis. "You won't be here that long."

"Beg your pardon?" Luis was troubled and surprised by the archbishop's angry tone.

"You aren't supposed to be in India, Father. Your superiors tell me you were bound for Bolivia when they sent you from Rome."

How could Luis explain Divine inspiration without sounding mad? "I was forced to change my plans based on new information. I didn't have time to confer with the Synod."

"Well, you'll have ample time to concoct an explanation on your flight home tomorrow."

"My flight home? I don't understand, Your Excellency."

"It's quite simple, Father. Cardinal Lombardi has directed me to have you driven back to Safdarjung Airport first thing tomorrow morning. I'm to instruct Father Dupresh to see that you are boarded onto a flight that will take you back to Rome by way of Tehran and Istanbul. Emissaries of the Church will be waiting to meet you at both connection points to ensure that you complete this journey as ordered. And when at last you return to the Holy See, I'm to understand that Cardinal Lombardi himself will have some rather pointed questions for you."

How could this be happening? Was the Synod really so doctrinaire that it couldn't understand the need to adapt to changing circumstances? Luis's instincts told him to forge ahead, but after a quarter of a century of service to the Church he knew better than to waste breath on a debate with his superiors. He bowed his head to the archbishop. "Very well, Excellency."

"Father Dupresh will take you back to your room. He will collect you tomorrow morning at sunrise. We will feed you breakfast, and then he will take you to the airport. Understood?"

"Understood, Excellency. Please accept my apologies for any inconvenience my presence might have caused, as well as my thanks for your generous hospitality."

"You're welcome. Now get out of my office."

"At once, Excellency. God be with you."

The archbishop declined to grace Luis with the traditional response. Instead the older man pretended to be distracted by the papers on his desk while his underling, Father Dupresh, entered, caught Luis's eye, and escorted him out of the study.

The two men walked in silence back to the guest room. Anil ushered Luis inside and then closed the door without so much as a simple "good night."

There was little for Luis to pack. Just his Llull Engine and his prayer book. He hadn't bothered to unpack his tools, since practice of even the relatively benign Pauline Art had been forbidden on the cathedral's consecrated ground. He prepped his things for a swift exit come morning, snuffed his room's only light, and then he settled onto his narrow bed.

Some quest, he needled himself. *I've had cheeses that lasted longer than my mission from God.* He watched light and shadows dance on the ceiling above him. *Was all this just a detour? A waste of time? Or was there a reason you guided me here, Lord?*

In the dark, Luis found no answers. Only the tapping of raindrops against his window.

Frustrated, Luis dared to flirt with blasphemy.

"Lord, I know you like to work in mysterious ways. But in the future, you might want to consider a more direct approach." He made the sign of the cross as he added, "Amen."

FEBRUARY 3

Anja awoke to pain in every part of her body. She fought to open her eyes. Her left eyelid was so swollen that it had become a painful bridge linking her cheekbone and brow.

More pain defined the rest of her slight frame. Welts blazed hot along her arms and legs. Bruises throbbed with dull aches on her ribs, and the broken digits on her hands and feet stung as if they had been skewered with needles. Dried blood caked her split lips. Her mouth was haunted by a foul taste. When she tried to run her tongue over her teeth, it was dry and leathery, but strong enough to reveal which of her incisors and bicuspids had been loosened by her captors' regular beatings.

Her skull felt trapped in a battle between crushing sensations and an excruciating inner pressure that threatened to split her head apart. It was worse than any demonic migraine she had ever suffered, and it left her vision doubled and dim. *Must be a concussion,* she realized.

There was no telling how long this bout of clarity would last. Anja knew she needed to make the most of it. She tested the bonds holding her wrists and ankles. They were as secure as ever, and by now they had cut into her flesh, leaving it chafed, raw, and bloody. Struggling against the ropes only tore off her fragile scabs and set her wounds to bleeding anew. In the absence of yoked demons she felt lost, but she refused to accept this as the end.

I will not die here, she promised herself. *Not like this.*

Tugging and squirming, she soaked her bonds in blood as she fought in vain for escape. *Stretch, damn you! Break! Unravel!* She hoped that her blood might make the ropes more pliable. Instead it seemed only to fuse them tighter together. *Fucking hell.*

Despair lurked on the edge of her perception. It was a black presence, felt rather than seen, but no less real. It whispered tales of defeat in her ear. It wanted her to give up.

No, she pledged. *I will not die a prisoner. There is always a way out.* Another testing of her bonds left Anja gritting her teeth as tears rolled from her closed eyes.

Then came a soft chittering sound from the corner of the basement.

She opened her eyes and blinked away her tears. In the darkness, two beady eyes caught the light from the bulb above her head. When she peered deeper into the shadows, she realized she was looking into the narrow pointed face of a gray weasel—no, a mongoose—that had made its way inside through an open drainage pipe. She had heard of the escapades of Indian mongooses, but until that moment she had never seen one in person.

The slender, long-bodied creature squirmed out of the pipe and regarded her with intense curiosity. Looking back into its eyes, Anja felt a sudden and profound sense of connection with the skittish creature, as if they shared a silent language. The longer she regarded the mongoose, the more certain she became that it had come in response to her desperation; on a deep level, she knew that it was there to help her. But why?

She reflected upon her years of studying magick. Before and during the Great Patriotic War, she had demonstrated a keen knack for sorcery that involved communicating with or controlling animals, or for transforming herself into various animal shapes. Of all the various talents conferred by magick, that and the healing arts had always come the most naturally to her.

Now, as she ruminated on Khalîl's revelation that she was one of "Heaven's true chosen," a *nikraim,* she wondered if her bond-spirit was one with an affinity for animals.

One way to find out, she decided.

"Hello, handsome," she whispered to the mongoose. "Can you chew through these ropes for me?" She concentrated on an image of the mongoose biting through the coils of hemp. "I bet they taste delicious. And I would be so grateful, little friend."

As anxiously as a feral cat, the mongoose skulked out of the pipe. It skittered forward, and then it paused to look to either side before continuing toward Anja.

"You are brave, little one," Anja said, her voice a gentle hush. "I am proud of you." The mongoose reached the chair and nibbled at the ropes binding her ankles. "Good job," she said, keeping her tone sweet and full of approval. "Who is the best mongoose ever?"

The quick-footed creature freed her right foot, and then her left.

She nodded over her shoulder. "Now the rope on my wrists."

The mongoose darted under her chair. Within seconds Anja felt the tug of its gnawing fangs against the rope holding her hands to the chair. In less than a minute the rope went slack and she pulled her hands free. Anja stood and cast aside the fragments of rope. She looked down and saw the mongoose staring up at her, its manner eager and expectant. She squatted down in front of it. The ferret-like beast stood up on its hind legs and touched its tiny wet nose to Anja's. She stroked her hand down its back. "Thank you, my friend." She kissed the top of its head. It squeaked once, and then it turned tail and vanished in a blur, back down the drainpipe.

Animals are my friends, Anja noted with satisfaction. *Good to know.*

She retrieved her grimoire and necklace from the table. After she put them in her rucksack, she picked up her leather roll of karcist's tools and slung its strap diagonally across her torso. Then she put on her jacket, followed by her ruck, and pondered her next move.

A proper farewell seems in order, she decided.

She had no magick at her command, but she didn't need it. As she climbed out of the basement, dagger in hand, she remembered all of the throats she had cut for the Red Army during the war, in the rubble of Stalingrad, the ruins of Kursk, and the ashes of Kharkov.

The door at the top of the stairs was not locked.

Why would it be? After all, I am well-tied and without magick.

Anja moved like a panther through the darkened halls of the safe house. The whole place shook as thunder rolled outside. At the end of the corridor she ambushed a KGB guard as he turned a corner into her blade. His throat opened like a flower and painted the floor red.

Moving down another short hall, she melded with the darkness and stabbed a second agent in his back, piercing his heart. Then Anja continued upstairs to the house's second floor.

At the top of the stairs, an agent snored softly while he slept in a chair. Anja cut his throat through the larynx. She caught the shocked man's body as he slumped and went limp, and then she lowered him to the floor. She took his Makarov pistol and both his spare magazines.

Anja peeked through cracked-open doors as she passed a few rooms whose occupants were of no interest to her. Then she found the one who was. She nudged open the door and made her way to the bedside of her interrogator and self-appointed judge, jury, and executioner.

The blond Russian woman was asleep, the depth of her slumber betrayed by the darting motions of her eyes beneath their lids and the soft rasps of her breathing.

Anja put her blade to the woman's throat and pressed hard enough to draw a thin line of blood from the skin above the jugular. "Wake up, Comrade Bitch."

The woman groaned. She shifted in her sleep and pushed her own throat against Anja's blade. Then she woke with a start, and her eyes snapped open, wide with terror at the sight of Anja at her bedside. "You—!"

"Quiet," Anja whispered. "Unless you want me to cut your throat."

The woman lowered her voice. "What do you want?"

"To deliver a message. To you, and to your masters in Moscow." Anja leaned closer and adjusted the cutting edge of the blade as a warning to the other woman. "I am going to take my leave now. But if I ever see you, or so much as a *shadow* of the KGB *ever* again . . . I will slaughter the new Red Star down to its last soul—right after I kill you and every member of your family. Do I make myself perfectly clear"—she picked up the woman's diplomatic credentials from the end table beside the bed—"Comrade Sergeyvna?"

Terror lurked behind the woman's mask of calm. "Perfectly clear, Comrade Kernova."

"Good. When you wake tomorrow, this will all have been just a bad dream. But if you or any of your men try to come after me, I promise you—I will become your final nightmare." Anja jabbed the pommel of her athamé against Sergeyvna's temple and knocked her out.

No one tried to stop Anja as she slipped out of the safe house.

No one tried to follow her down the street into a breaking storm.

Dawn was still more than an hour away as Anja vanished into the back alleys of New Delhi, cloaked in rain, thunder, and darkness. Once more, the night welcomed her.

As it always had.

As it always would.

⁓

Wind pulled open the wooden shutters above Luis's bed. They slammed against the outer wall, their sharp reports waking him from a troubled sleep.

He threw off his sheets and sat up. A cold spray of rain stung his face as he looked out the window—and then, with a cool breeze, the precipitation abated.

The air outside the archbishop's house had the fresh scent of a world cleansed by rain. Overhead, clouds parted just long enough to let the moon wash New Delhi in silver light. Wet streets and rooftops shimmered with reflections, making the deserted cityscape come alive despite the unseemly hour.

Bleary but curious, Luis checked the clock on the wall. It was 4:31 in the morning. Just a few hours away from his forced departure from the Sacred Heart Cathedral.

The logic of his superiors, as always, confounded him. *Why gift me with a spirit of Divine intuition, only to punish me for deviating from the Church's orders?* He despaired of ever truly grasping the politics that seemed to drive so many of the Church's decisions.

He turned toward the window to pull the shutters closed so that he could return to sleep for a short time longer. A mad flutter of white arrested him where he stood.

A dove alighted upon his windowsill.

The bird stared at him, its inhuman eyes unblinking.

To another man the moment might have felt random. A more callous man might have shooed the dove away in the name of sleep. But Luis felt possessed of a deep certainty as he gazed upon the dove, the symbol of the Holy Spirit: this was a message, an omen that he would ignore only at his own great peril. The longer he stared at the bird, the more it seemed to take on a magickal radiance, a luminance not of reflection but of some inner quality.

This was a sign from Heaven. Luis was sure of it.

The bird looked at Luis's karcist's tools. And then it fluttered away.

He sprang to the window. The dove swooped away from the archbishop's residence and came to rest on a low branch of a tree near the edge of the cathedral's property. Then it pivoted on the branch and looked up and back, directly at Luis.

It wants me to follow it, he deduced.

Luis froze. *If I follow the dove, what will happen when Father Dupresh comes to collect me in the morning? What if I'm not back? If I miss the flight to Rome, what will Cardinal Lombardi say? I could be expelled from Monte Paterno. Or worse, defrocked.*

There had been no ambiguity in Luis's orders from the cardinal. Of that he had no doubt. But when he looked back at the dove, the bird continued to face squarely toward him. *I was charged with a holy mission,* he ruminated. *And I'm sure this is a sign from God. That should take precedence over anything— even the orders of the Church. Shouldn't it?* He felt torn between his vows to the institution and his faith in the Almighty. *Ultimately, we all serve the Lord God before all else. If I accept the dove as a sign from the Lord, then it would be blasphemy to ignore His direction just to obey the edicts of men.*

It made sense to Luis. He doubted the cardinals at the Vatican would share his view.

He made his decision and resigned himself to accept the consequences.

He grabbed his rucksack and his roll of karcist's tools. It was time to make a swift but silent exit from the grounds of the Sacred Heart Cathedral. Treading softly on bare feet, he slipped out of his room and stole down the long hallway to the nearest stairs. There was no sound of other activity inside the archbishop's house. Luis nimbly skipped the creaking next-to-last step on the main staircase and hurried to the front door. He undid its locks with all the caution he could muster, and then he eased open the door and snuck outside.

Standing on the front stoop, he closed the door behind him with a gentle *thump.*

Luis looked for the dove. It sat perched on the front gate to the cathedral's grounds. He walked toward it. As he drew near it took flight and circled above him, its circumference widening as it led him away from the cathedral and down deserted predawn streets.

He chased after it like a drunkard pursuing a bank note blown by the wind. The bird led him east past Connaught Place and then north, down long boulevards whose names Luis had no time to note, until at last he found himself standing on the bank of the Jumna River. Its muddy water coursed past him black and serene, a ceaseless flow devoid of memory or intent. The dove swooped in tight circles above a narrow iron bridge that crossed the river.

Summoned onward, Luis walked toward the bridge. As he neared it, he caught sight of someone else approaching it from his right. Suddenly fearful, he ducked to cover in some shrubs that grew thick and tall by the riverside. He watched from his hiding place as the stranger neared the bridge above him. At first he didn't recognize the woman, whose face was bruised and swollen down its left side. Then she turned right and started across the bridge. When he saw the other side of her face, he knew immediately who she was.

It was Anja, the keeper of the Iron Codex, the woman he had been ordered to find. She crossed the bridge with her head held high, as if she had nothing to fear or conceal.

His inspired decision to come to New Delhi had been vindicated. But what now? Luis watched her, paralyzed by indecision. *I could go back to the cathedral before sunrise. But if I do, they'll send me back to Rome, and I might never find Anja again.* That was too dispiriting an outcome for him to accept. But the alternative was not much better. *If I defy the cardinal to follow her, and I fail to recover the codex, I'll be cast out of the Church.* He stared after Anja, who neared the far end of the bridge. *If I don't follow her right now, I'll lose her.*

He had only a moment in which to choose.

He emerged from hiding and turned his steps onto the bridge.

You've led me to this path, Lord, Luis prayed. *Please guide and protect me. Amen.*

FEBRUARY 4

Dirty plates, greasy utensils, and empty glasses littered the hotel suite like casualties of war. California sunlight slanted through venetian blinds and cut through the haze of smoke that lingered between Cade and Miles. The two men sprawled at opposite ends of the luxury suite's sitting room. Cade was draped over an armchair like a discarded sock, blowing smoke rings at the ceiling, while Miles stretched barefoot across the leather sofa.

"I still think this plan is shit," Cade said, his opinion unsolicited.

Miles plucked a mostly empty bottle of Gordon's gin from the floor. "We have no time, no scratch, and we aren't even supposed to be here." He downed the last swig of gin. "If we had a budget and months to work, we could play this safe. But you say we're on a deadline."

"I'm not saying time isn't a factor; it is." Cade blew a small ring of smoke that nested inside a larger one. "But I also thought we were supposed to be *secret* agents. Emphasis on the *secret*. As in, we don't go putting targets on our own backs." He glanced at the empty bottle on the table by his chair. "By the way, we're out of bourbon."

"Of course we are."

"Should we get another bottle?" Miles rolled his head lazily toward Cade, but said nothing. Cade searched his friend's blank stare for any hint of an answer. "You think we should get one more." Miles let his eyes drift halfway to closed, his stare as empty as the fifth of Jim Beam in Cade's hand. Cade seemed to take the silence as assent. "Okay, we'll get one more." He picked up the room phone and dialed 0 for the hotel operator.

Miles understood Cade's concern. In truth, he shared it. But if the crisis hinted at by the Odessa journal was as imminent as it seemed, they didn't have time to follow the normal protocols. They could not afford the luxury of lengthy surveillance programs, wiretaps, and calculated infiltration ops.

If they were to have any hope of flushing out Odessa's agent in Los Angeles before it was too late, they would have to spook him into revealing himself, by making it known throughout L.A.'s underworld of racist subcultures that they were looking for him.

It was an old concept: *The easiest way to find someone is to let them find you.* The flaw in the strategy was that, more often than not, one also ended up being found by any number of hurt-minded thugs and murderous goons, most of whom could offer nothing of value aside from a brief pugilistic work-out and a bit of target practice.

Cade finished his murmured conversation with the hotel's room-service office and hung up the phone. "Refreshment reinforcements are inbound, so check your fire to the west."

"I miss the days when you talked like a regular person."

"Sorry, mate. Blame the army." Cade stuck a fresh cigarette into his mouth and lit it with a snap of his finger. He reclined into a shadow, and the cherry at the end of his Lucky brightened as he inhaled. "Have our boys in London figured out who the fuck 'Dragan' is?"

"Latest word is that their inquiries are hitting roadblocks."

"In other words, they have no idea."

"So it seems."

Three quick knocks on the suite's door. Cade and Miles sat up, inebriation dispelled by adrenaline, their senses sharp and their voices low.

Cade began, "Is it my imagination—?"

Miles finished, "—or is that the fastest room service in history?"

The duo moved quickly, stepping softly in bare and stocking feet. Miles drew his Walther. Cade conjured a ball of fire in his palm. Miles ducked behind an armchair as Cade took cover in the doorway to the suite's master bedroom. Then they traded anxious stares.

"Aren't you gonna answer it?" Cade asked.

"Me? *You're* the one with immunity to bullets."

"I took point last time. You—"

The suite's front door exploded inward with a bang. Splinters shot from its fractured edge and broken jamb, and the door rebounded off the wall as voices full of fear and anger bellowed, "FBI! Drop your weapons and get on the floor!"

As soon as Miles saw the squad of men charge into the suite, he knew they were the real deal. Their suits were too boring, their shoes too scuffed, and their haircuts too unflattering for them to be anything but American federal agents. Most telling of all were their .38-caliber snub-nosed revolvers. Classic U.S. government-issue service weapons. Real bad guys would have come with submachine guns and sawed-off ten-gauge shotguns.

Raising his empty hand, Miles called out, "Hold your fire! British Secret Service! We surrender!" He made a show of slowly setting his pistol on the floor and pushing it away from the armchair, into the middle of the room. Then he shot a glare at Cade, who was still hidden in the doorway, out of the agents' line of sight.

There were rules, after all. Not killing law-enforcement officers was one of them.

With a scowl, Cade extinguished the fireball in his hand. Then he raised his hands and called to the agents, "Hold your fire. British Secret Service. I'm unarmed and coming out." He pivoted slowly around the corner to face the five men who had spread across the suite's main room. Miles could only imagine how hard it was for Cade not to resort to his Ranger training and fight back as the FBI agents took them into custody and pulled their hands behind their backs.

Cold rings of steel closed around Miles's wrists as he asked, "How did you find us?"

The agent in charge wrinkled his aquiline features in mock disbelief. "How could we *not*? You two kicked every hornets' nest from Northridge to Corona."

A younger agent with the blunt features of a punching bag tightened the cuffs on Cade's wrists. "You assholes are lucky we found you first."

Miles knew the drill. They would have to endure some embarrassment in the short term, and very likely a reprimand from their superiors, but arrest in a friendly country was accepted as one of the occupational hazards of their profession. He sighed. "I presume we'll get to call our consulate after we've been processed?"

Only then did he register the agents' conspiratorial glances.

The man in charge smirked. "You're not *that* lucky."

A dull *thud* preceded Cade's unconscious collapse to the floor, and a blow to the back of Miles's head condemned his curse of *fucking hell* to go unspoken as he sank into a black silence that swallowed him whole.

⌇

Tequila was a new experience for Briet. Over the years her tastes had graduated from white and red wines to clear liquors such as vodka and gin. More recently, she had begun to appreciate bourbons and scotch whiskies. But the selections for those libations, so popular on the East Coast and in the capital, were scant in Santa Fe. The bar in the St. Francis Hotel had an abundance of tequilas and mezcals, and its most popular cocktail, the bartender had said, was called a margarita. Never one to shy from novelty, Briet had consented to try one. It had proved to be quite effective at muting the demonic voices that once again plagued Briet's waking hours.

She was on her third margarita of the evening when she heard car doors slam. She looked at the mirror behind the bar and watched a pair of clean-cut men in drab suits—one brown, one gray, both accessorized with matching hats—through a window behind her. They stopped on the sidewalk and adjusted their suit jackets, betraying the bulges of shoulder-holstered pistols. The man in brown flipped open a small notebook, and the pair conferred over it. Gray looked up to check the hotel's sign, and then they headed for its front entrance, moving in tandem with the body language peculiar to paired agents.

The windows of their car had been left rolled down. *I guess they aren't worried about anyone stealing it,* Briet surmised.

Out of the corner of her eye, she clocked them as they strolled through the hotel's lobby and headed toward the bar. They walked straight toward her. Brown stepped to the bar on her left, and Gray mirrored his partner's stance on Briet's right. Each man put his hat on the bar top.

Subtlety did not seem to rank high on their list of concerns.

Briet lit a cigarette, the first from her second pack of the day. "Took you long enough." She exhaled grayish plumes through her nose. "Were you lost?"

Brown flipped open a leather fold to reveal a badge and an ID card. "Miss Segfrunsdóttir, I'm Special Agent Sullivan from the Federal Bureau of Investigation." He lifted his chin toward Gray. "And this is my associate, Mr. Lippoldt."

She looked at Lippoldt. "No badge to show off?" The man maintained a stoic façade. Briet knew his type. "I get it. You were never here, and if anyone asks who you work for, you tell them 'No Such Agency.'" His blank expression darkened just enough to tell Briet she had pegged him correctly as an operative of the newly formed National Security Agency, the U.S. intelligence community's worst-kept secret. She sipped her drink and stole another puff of her cigarette. "What can I do for you boys?"

"For starters," Sullivan said, "you can tell us what you're doing in Santa Fe."

She played it cool. "I'm on vacation."

Sullivan pulled out a pipe with an ivory stem. "Long way from D.C."

"I thought that was the point of a vacation—to get away."

Lippoldt narrowed his eyes. "But why did you choose Santa Fe, specifically?"

Teasing them with a coy smile, Briet said, "I came for the waters." Neither man seemed to know what to make of her response. "This is the part where you point out that Santa Fe is in a desert, and then I tell you, 'I was misinformed.'" The agents exchanged looks of befuddlement. Exasperated, Briet asked, "Neither of you ever saw *Casablanca*?" She shook her head in disappointment. "You need to get out more."

In her mind's eye, she tracked her familiar Trixim as the rat scurried out of her room's open window, down a drainpipe, and across the sidewalk to the agents' car.

Special Agent Sullivan did his best to put on a menacing air while he lit his pipe. "You should know that we're keeping tabs on you, Miss Segfrunsdóttir. We know every place you've been in Santa Fe, and every person to whom you've said so much as two words."

"I've had lovers who paid less attention to me. Are you married, Agent Sullivan?"

Her question made the FBI man cough into his pipe, launching burning tobacco and ash onto the bartop and his own hat. The NSA man took over the conversation without missing a beat. "I hope you've enjoyed your stay in Santa Fe, because as of tomorrow, it's over."

"I beg to differ," Briet said. "I'm booked through next Tuesday."

She sensed Trixim as the rat leaped onto the fender of the agents' car, scampered across its trunk, climbed onto its roof, and then tumbled through the open passenger-side window. Once inside the car, Trixim retreated into the backseat and concealed itself under the driver's seat.

Lippoldt plucked Briet's cigarette from its perch in the crenellations of an ashtray and plunged it into her half-finished drink. "This is not a game. We're not making suggestions. We're telling you, in clear, simple English: Go back to Washington. Tomorrow."

"And if I refuse?"

"Then our next visit won't be so cordial," Lippoldt said.

"A shame, since this one has been *such* a delight."

The two men picked up their hats and turned to leave.

Briet called out, "Excuse me." They turned back. "One of you owes me a new drink."

Neither dignified her demand with a response. They turned and resumed walking. She watched them exit to the lobby, and then she picked up their reflections in the bar mirror as they got back into their car. Merging her senses with Trixim's, she eavesdropped magickally on the agents' conversation inside the vehicle:

"*What a bitch,*" Sullivan said.

"*Cheer up, Ted,*" Lippoldt said. "*If she's still there tomorrow, we get to pop her.*"

"*That's on you, Erik. You spill blood, you get to mop it up.*"

"*Don't be such a nancy. Let's get moving. We have to be back on the hill by five.*"

"*Fine. Do me a favor and try to find something on the radio besides that Mexican shit. If I have to listen to one more song in Spanish, I'm gonna shoot the next mariachi I see.*"

The engine turned over with a rumble, and the car pulled away from the curb.

Briet stood and lit a fresh cigarette. As long as Trixim stayed in the car, she would know its every move. She dropped a five-dollar note on the bar and smiled as she left the hotel.

Chandigarh, in northern India, was not what Anja had expected. When it had been nothing more than a name on a map, she had thought to find a glorified town deserted and quiet after dark. Riding through its broad streets as a passenger in a pedicab, she found herself surrounded by a burgeoning city whose streetlamps and construction floodlights had been visible from kilometers away. Despite the hour, the city sounded busy. Jackhammers rattled and engines roared, and metallic bangs of collision alternated with distant booms of impact and collapse.

All she had wanted was to go north, but to her dismay India's rail system had no more direct routes northward from Chandigarh. There were alternatives that involved heading east or west, skirting the coastline, and then transferring near the Indian border to inland-bound trains, but those routes would take her far out of her way and only increase the risk of being intercepted again by more agents from the KGB, or maybe the Chinese, or who knew who else.

No, she had decided, *the most direct route is the best, even if I have to go on foot.*

Her pedicab driver pulled over on a poorly lit side street and stopped. "Here," he said, pointing at a door next to a shop that was closed and dark. "This is the place."

Anja climbed out of the pedicab and made sure to take her rucksack and tool roll. She dug into her pocket, pulled out a wad of Indian currency she had pilfered from her victims inside the Russian embassy, and pressed a five-hundred-rupee banknote into the pedicab driver's hand. "Wait for me," she said. "If your tip pans out, I will need a ride to the edge of town. If not, I will need you to take me some place where I can spend the night."

The driver pocketed the banknote and nodded. "Kunil will help you. And I will wait."

She hoped he was right. There weren't many options available to her at this time of night. She walked to the door and knocked on it with two hard raps of her knuckles.

The heavy door muffled a string of vulgarities and loud coughs. Through the door's small opaque window she saw the glow of house lamps being switched on. Then came a shadow that turned the window dark again, followed by an even darker voice. "Who're you? What do you want?"

"Are you Kunil? Your friend Narinder said you could help me."

"Narinder is a pest, not a friend. Who are you?"

"My name is Anja. I need your help." Her request was met by a ponderous silence, and then a tired grunt. Sensing she was being tested and found wanting, she added, "I have money."

Behind the door, a shuffling of feet and a loud sniffle. "It's late. Come back tomorrow."

"I will pay double your normal price."

"I said it's—"

"Triple."

She could almost hear Kunil's mental gears turning as he calculated the potential profit she was offering. Locks and bolts were undone in a flurry of clacks, and the door opened a few inches—just enough to reveal a tall, broad-shouldered man with dark brown skin and black hair. Shirtless and barefoot, he looked down with suspicion upon Anja. "What happened to you?"

His question made her self-conscious about the swelling and bruises on the left side of her face. "Not important. I need camping equipment. Food. And a warm coat."

"Why now? Why not morning?"

"Because I am late," she said, not wanting to burden him with tales of spies, international bounties, and magickal vendettas. She held up a wad of large-denomination rupee notes. "Can you help me or not?"

"Triple, you said?" Kunil acknowledged her nod of confirmation by opening his door and stepping outside. Anja chose not to comment on the prominent rip in the knee of Kunil's loose-fitting blue trousers. He led her a few steps up the sidewalk to the next door, the one to his shop. It took him a moment to pull his ring of keys from his pants pocket. Fumbling and swearing under his breath, he opened the door and stepped inside. He switched on the shop's lights and beckoned Anja to join him. "You have ten minutes."

"I will be done in three."

True to her word, she moved with dispatch through the store, snagging anything she thought she might need without stopping to inspect anything. She wanted to be gone from Chandigarh before the sun caught up to her; she was in no mood to comparison-shop.

Kunil primed the cash register as Anja piled the front counter with her haul, a few items at a time. A down-filled parka. Gloves. Hiking boots. Long underwear. Large backpack. Pup tent. A large canteen. Waterproof matches. Six cans of beans. A compass. A toothbrush.

The owner didn't seem enthused, despite the windfall he was about to reap. "Is that all?"

"No." Anja pointed at items behind Kunil. "Give me that map of the Himalayan ranges. And a couple sticks of that dried meat." She perused the stacks of boxes tucked low on a shelf behind Kunil's legs. "And I need a box of three-eighty ACP ammunition."

Kunil added Anja's impulse purchases to the pile. "Done yet?"

"Yes. How much?"

He made a fast tally on a piece of scrap paper, then multiplied his total by three. "Nine thousand six hundred rupees."

He was ripping her off, but she didn't care. She counted out ten thousand rupees in banknotes and pushed them across the counter. "Keep the change—and forget you ever saw me."

"You were never here," Kunil said, collecting the cash. "Now get out."

She stuffed her haul into the backpack and toted it out to her waiting pedicab.

"I want to be gone before the sun rises," Anja said, pressing her remaining rupees into Narinder's hand. "Take the fastest way out of town."

Narinder set his feet on the cab's pedals as he asked, "What direction?"

"North," Anja said, settling in for the last easy ride she would know for a while. "North."

～～

The road heading north out of Santa Fe was nearly deserted. Just like the road into town from Albuquerque, it was flanked by wide dusty plains dotted with dark green scrub, backed by the pastel blue outlines of mountain ranges far beyond the desert's shimmering haze.

Briet gripped the steering wheel with both hands, more out of frustration than anxiety. The owner of the only car-rental agency in downtown Santa Fe had informed her that he had only three cars in his entire inventory, of which the best one was already rented and the second-best was currently up on a lift in his garage for repairs. Consequently, Briet had secured the agency's last re-maining vehicle, a 1950 Crosley station wagon.

The CD-Four station wagon was a slow and lumbering beast of a car. It struggled to climb even modest inclines, and when Briet heard the clattering of its engine she doubted it could hold speeds greater than thirty-five miles per hour without throwing a rod. Adding to her dissatisfaction, its radio didn't work, the window on the driver's door was stuck half open, and the inside of the vehicle stank of motor oil and stale vomitus. It was a car with a history, but not one that she or anyone else would want to know.

The town of Cuyamungue provided only a fleeting respite from the des-ert's monotony. A few low and lonely houses lay scattered in the sand and scrub. A gas station blurred past on the right shoulder. Briet sped past the town's lone stoplight, which shone green. Within minutes the town was just another speck in her rearview mirror.

She sensed Trixim a couple of miles ahead of her. Her bond with her fa-miliar was one that she had forged through long experience, since before the war. Even though Trixim was hidden under Sullivan's seat in the agents' car, without a clear view of its surroundings, its link to Briet remained strong enough that she could follow them. Then she felt its pull tacking in a new direction, diverging westward. She started to look for signs of an upcoming junction. Less than two minutes later she spied the sign for Route 502 West and followed it.

By the time she passed El Rancho, the landscape bordering the road became less flat. Squat hills dotted with trees hemmed her in as the mountains loomed larger on the horizon. The hills grew taller and the rock formations more dramatic as she passed the turn-off for Route 30. Trixim was still ahead of her somewhere, she was certain of it, but the distance between her and her loyal rat was increasing. Torn between the risk of losing contact with her familiar and blowing out the engine of the Crosley, she put her foot down on the gas pedal and prayed.

Ahead of her the highway forked. One road led to Route 4 South, into White Rock, and the other continued west. Briet slowed and reached out with her magickal senses to gauge in which direction Trixim had gone.

West, she deduced. *Definitely west.*

She accelerated past the Route 4 ramp and continued onward toward Los Alamos.

Sooner than she had expected, the town of Los Alamos took shape around her. A few outlying buildings at first. An airstrip. A cluster of buildings sequestered beyond twelve-foot-tall fences topped with barbed wire. Then she crested a rise in the road and on the other side she was greeted by a warren of quaint local streets and modern-looking buildings. Here there was at least a bit of traffic: a few cars, a handful of pedestrians. Everything was clean and orderly.

Exactly what I'd expect from the birthplace of the atom bomb, Briet mused.

The slower traffic on the edge of town came as a blessing. She reduced her car's speed and concentrated on Trixim. She sensed that the agents' car had come to a halt somewhere nearby. She pulled off the road into the lot of a small freestanding drugstore and parked behind the building. Then she shut off her engine and focused on Trixim's perceptions.

Inside the agents' car, Trixim emerged from under the driver's seat. The rat scurried up onto the front bench seat, and it jumped from there onto the car's front dash. Through the windshield it saw a cluster of nondescript buildings, most of them without windows or markings. Surrounding the buildings was a well-groomed campus—smoothly paved roads, traffic medians populated with succulent plants, parking lots with fresh blacktop housing scores of late-model luxury cars and sports coupes.

Near the car stood one building that compelled Briet's attention. It bore no signage, but one thing marked it as noteworthy, a detail that only a trained karcist would be able to perceive: It radiated with magickal energies. Sullivan and Lippoldt walked to a door on the south side of the building. Lippoldt pressed a button on an intercom panel mounted on the wall next to the door. He exchanged a few words with someone, and then Sullivan opened the door, which was thick with armor and soundproofing. The two men went inside and shut the door behind them.

Trixim, Briet commanded, *scout the building's perimeter. Do not let yourself be seen.*

Deploying her familiar in broad daylight was a risky tactic, one that Briet would normally have avoided, but she needed to know what was inside that building. Trixim climbed out of the still-open passenger-side window of the car and dropped to the hot pavement. It skittered under the car, then darted beneath the others parked between it and the building.

Once it ran out of cars, the familiar ducked under bits of scrub and worked its way closer to the building. Just shy of the sidewalk, a jolt like an electric shock halted its progress.

What in the name of Hell . . . ? Briet called upon the Sight to add her own magickal perception to Trixim's. A brilliant dome of energy became visible over the building.

As I feared, Briet realized. *It's warded.*

Strong warding of this kind meant that no familiars or yoked spirits could violate the exclusion zone, which had been cast to extend several yards beyond the building's wall.

Who could have made wards this powerful? Briet knew no one had consulted her about creating magickal defenses for Los Alamos Scientific Laboratory, even though such a project should have been conducted under her supervision, as the master karcist of the United States' Occult Defense Program. But this was not the work of a dabbler—no amateur magician could have established so powerful a warding. *Whoever did this had training.*

She wondered anew what had become of all her previous adepts. *Could one of them have accomplished this? And if they did, why are they being given tasks that should be mine? And why are my superiors lying to me about it?*

A spark of intuition told her that the answers to those questions lay inside that warded building. Something momentous—or perhaps calamitous—was afoot here. As long as Briet held yoked demons under her control she would not be able to set foot inside, but without the power of yoked spirits she would be all but defenseless.

I'll have to be cautious, she decided. *Think this through. Not act until I'm ready.* She projected her will to Trixim: *Conceal yourself until dark, little friend, and then return to me with all haste—we have a mission to plan.*

17

FEBRUARY 5

A freezing wind cut across the mountainside like God's vengeance. No stars shone in the sky above the snowcapped mountains, no moonlight kissed the slopes. What had been a dark gray blanket of cloud by day had after nightfall become an impenetrable ceiling of darkness, one that dusted the earth with steady flurries of snow. Huddled alone against the elements, Luis could only retreat deeper inside his cassock and shiver while he prayed for deliverance.

About a kilometer ahead of him, nestled deep in a mountain pass, a small fire danced. Its licks of flame were the only light in the endless swath of black that had swallowed the world, and they teased him with memories of warmth now denied. That was not his comfort to claim; it was a spark struck by the woman known as Anja Kernova, who rested in the shelter of a pup tent, her body wrapped in warm clothes, her stomach at least partially sated by a small meal.

Luis exposed his forearm to scoop up a handful of snow and push it into his mouth. He pulled his arm back inside his robe while the snow melted. He knew that he could survive several days without food, so long as he didn't dehydrate or succumb to hypothermia, though only the latter was of real concern to him. His desire not to lose track of the Russian woman had forced him to take risks that he normally would never have accepted. Where she had been able to equip and provision herself for a trek into the Himalayas, he had been forced to pursue her with nothing but his cassock, a thin pair of hard-worn leather shoes he had purchased in a village the day before with the airline refund he had held in reserve since Rome, and a courage born of faith.

If only I could light a fire without betraying my presence, he lamented.

He knew better than to risk lighting a campfire, even though he was more than capable of making one. This far from civilization, the faintest glow could be seen from miles away. Even the red dot at the end of a cigarette could attract attention from a great distance. Any kind of flame would alert Anja to the fact that she was being followed, and there was no telling what she might do then. Flee? Attack? Luis couldn't risk either outcome.

And so he hunkered into a fetal position inside his robe and pulled its generous pointed hood down over his face. It was almost like having a tent—one full of holes and soaking wet.

The wind howled in minor chords while snow accumulated on top of him. Submerged in his litany of prayers and meditations, he lost track of time, but when he shuddered to consciousness he felt as if the world were far away. Sounds were muffled, and the wind's cutting edge no longer seemed to find its way into his robe.

I'm covered in snow, he realized. It was a weak layer of protection, but it hadn't come without a cost: a numbing cold had found its way into every inch of Luis's body. *This is how I'll be found someday,* he thought with mounting pessimism. *On my knees, frozen solid. An icy monument to faith. Or stubbornness. Or maybe stupidity.*

His mental acuity began to dull. He felt the bitter cold sapping his strength, his edge. It would be only a matter of time before he hallucinated feelings of warmth and comfort. When he became cold enough, his mind would trick him into thinking he was burning up, and like so many victims of the mountains before him, he would strip away what little clothing he had and run naked to his cruel fate. *If only I could have the blessings of fire without the liabilities,* Luis thought, *the heat without the light—*

As soon as he asked the question of himself, he felt a nudge of angelic intuition from DAROCHIEL, and he remembered the gift of BENOHAM: the ability to "conjure, shape, and wield angelic fire for a variety of purposes," Father D'Odorico had said.

He was about to summon an invisible bonfire to thaw his flesh and dry his cassock when he heard voices grumbling under the wind. *Men, at least two of them,* he concluded. *Getting closer.* He heard the crunches of their feet breaking through snow. The labors of their breathing. As they drew near, he realized they were speaking German. It wasn't a language in which he had great fluency, but he recognized enough of it to get the gist of what the men were saying.

"Down there," said one man. "A fire."

Another said, "Wait. The footprints split up." His footfalls became louder and clearer to Luis. "They end over here."

Luis crouched, still and silent as the night, a coiled spring under a paper-thin shroud.

Something hard poked him in the ribs.

He snaked his arm around a walking stick and stole it from its owner.

Luis sprang to his feet, now armed. He faced two men dressed in parkas and winter climbing gear. Each man wore a backpack. The taller one, farther from Luis, still had his walking stick. The closer one had only his slack-jawed look of surprise. The taller German cast away his walking stick. "It's him," he said as lightning crackled in his hand. "The priest."

"Honor the Covenant," Luis said. "Address me as Father Pérez."

The German who had poked Luis conjured a fistful of emerald fire. "We won't have to call you anything once we kill you." He cocked his arm to throw magick—

Luis charged the two men and spun the walking stick. It clocked Lightning-thug's temple and sent the dabbler sprawling into the snow. Luis pivoted and jabbed the stick's other end into Fire-punk's gut. The second Nazi doubled over, and his paltry orb of fire fizzled out.

Fire-punk drew a hunting knife and lunged to attack. Luis deflected the stab by striking the German's wrist with the walking stick, which knocked the knife from the man's hand. Fire-punk threw a sloppy punch. Luis ducked it. Fire-punk tried to grapple for the stick, and Luis used the man's own efforts to flip him onto his back in the snow.

Lightning-thug threw himself at Luis from behind and tried to wrestle him to the ground. Luis dropped the walking stick, bent like a reed, and shifted the German off-balance. The German stumbled and fell to one knee. Luis seized the man's right arm and pulled it into a locking hold. The German reached with his left hand for a pistol holstered on his right hip. Twisting, Luis forced the man facedown into the snow, and then he pulled the Luger from the German's holster and tossed it down the mountainside.

Fire-punk pushed himself up onto his knees and fumbled to draw his own pistol.

Luis let go of Lightning-thug and rushed Fire-punk. The dabbler had barely freed his pistol from leather when Luis kneed him in his nose. Fire-punk landed on his back, out cold.

Turning, Luis saw the second German crawl toward his discarded walking stick.

Lightning-thug's hand landed on the stick. Luis stepped on the man's fingers.

"Your friend's tent—will it fit both of you?"

Confused, Lightning-thug squinted through the falling snow at Luis. "Why?"

"Because you'll have to share it if you want to get off this mountain alive."

Lightning-thug flashed a taunting grin. "You should kill me while you can."

"The commandments of the Lord Our God tell us, 'Thou shalt not murder.' Unfortunately for you and your friend, there is no commandment against breaking the legs of one's enemies." Luis kneeled and knocked Lightning-thug unconscious with a quick punch to the back of his skull. *Can't have him awake for this,* Luis reasoned. *One good scream and Anja would bolt for certain.* Then, with a quick, precise stomp, Luis snapped the German's right femur.

It took Luis only a few minutes to relieve the stunned and hobbled Lightning-thug of his backpack, parka, and snow boots. *Forgive me, Lord, for this act of theft. But I cannot serve Thy will if I do not survive, and it is said that you help those who first help themselves. For my acts of violence and my sins of pride, I beg Your forgiveness in the name of Your son, Jesus Christ, and through the grace of Your Holy Spirit. Amen.*

Armored now against the falling temperatures and rising winds, Luis raised one of the Germans' tents. After breaking Fire-punk's left femur, he bound and gagged the two men together, as much to keep them warm inside their tent as to slow their inevitable escape. For good measure, he took the added precaution of snapping their wands and dropping their rolls of karcist's tools down a nearby gorge. *It will not prevent them from working more evil in* SATAN's *name, but one can certainly hope that it will slow them down and mitigate their efficacy.*

His foes dealt with, Luis set up the Germans' other tent, making sure that it, like their shelter, would not be visible from Anja's campsite. After rummaging through the Germans' gear and pulling out some canned food and two canteens of water, Luis conjured an invisible blaze of angelic fire and retired inside his tent to enjoy some pork and beans before settling down for a desperately needed night of rest. As he drifted off to sleep, he heard the Germans' pained groans mingle with the mournful wails of the wind, and he smiled with humble gratitude.

Verily, the Lord works in mysterious ways.

―――⌇―――

This was no ordinary phone call. It was nearly cross-continental, had been placed with reversed charges, and now was in the process of being handed off from civilian operators to a military-secured switchboard inside the Pentagon. Under the circumstances, Briet was not surprised that it was taking upward of three minutes to be connected, but her impatience was about to boil over.

She passed the minutes staring out the window of her room in the St. Francis. Twilight had settled upon Santa Fe in rich tones of violet, and the streets were nearly empty. She had seen only one car drive past the hotel in the past ten minutes, and she had no reason to expect another any time soon. *It's a wonder they don't roll up the sidewalks at the stroke of nine,* she mused.

Frank Cioffi picked up on the other end of the line. His voice was rough and slow, and it sounded impossibly far away. *"This is Cioffi."*

A nasal female voice replied, *"Director Cioffi, this is Pentagon switchboard operator three-seven-one. You have an incoming call from Briet Segfrunsdóttir. This call has been secured from civilian monitoring and verified clear of wiretaps. Will you accept the call?"*

"Put her through," Frank grumped.

"Connecting your call and signing off." There was a barely audible *click* on the line.

Briet heard a soft crackle of static on the line. "Frank? Are you there?"

Over the line, a disgruntled sigh. *"Do you know what time it is?"*

"I know, it's late."

"Two hours ago would've been late. It's the middle of the goddamned night." His exhalation turned to static on the long-distance line. *"What do you want?"*

"I need intel, Frank. A top-level summary on the LASL."

"The what?" He sounded genuinely mystified.

She spelled it out with dramatic pauses. "The Los Alamos. Scientific. Laboratory."

The silence between them was instantly heavy with dread. *"Bree? That's where they make the nuclear weapons."*

"I know that, Frank. And just in case I didn't, the feds sent two of their trained monkeys to keep me away from it. But there's something hinky going on out there, I just know it."

Now there was fear in his voice. *"Whatever it is, it's above your pay grade. Walk away from there, right fucking now, and do not look back. Do you hear me?"*

"Frank, they've got major magickal wards on one of their buildings. Why?"

"I don't know," Frank said, sounding defensive. *"Maybe to keep the Chinks and the Russkies from snooping our secrets with their own voodoo-slingers?"*

Briet wasn't sure what she found most offensive, his racist slurs or his dismissal of the Goetic Art as "voodoo"—a description that she suspected would prove just as insulting to the adherents of the art of Voudun. "Fine," she said. "Put aside the question of *why* it's there and just tell me *who* signed off on it. Because I know that wasn't *my* work, Frank. So whose is it?"

"I don't know. This is the first I'm hearing of it."

"I've got Level Seven clearance, Frank. A warding field like the one I saw shouldn't exist on a government facility without my knowledge. So what else is the DOD hiding from me?"

"Bree, I have no fucking idea. But as long as I have you on the line, I ought to tell you we've got more pressing concerns."

"Really? Such as?"

"While you've been traipsing about on your desert vacation, our pals in the spook community picked up an old friend of yours in Los Angeles."

Searching her memory, Briet was at a loss to imagine anyone she would call an *old friend.* "Care to be a bit more specific?"

"Does the name Cade Martin ring any bells for you?"

Just the sound of his name put a chill down Briet's back. "He's in custody?"

"Locked down tighter than a preacher's daughter. The Hammers put him and his MI6 partner in a magick-proof safe house. So, if you want to do something useful for a change, maybe you could pay Mr. Martin a visit and find out why he tempted fate by setting foot on American soil again for the first time in seven years."

Briet set down the phone's cradle. "Where are they?"

"The Kingman safe house."

"Fuck. I'll be there first thing tomorrow morning." She added with deadly sincerity, "Make sure they don't liquidate him before I get there." Before Frank could reply, she hung up.

It wasn't the threat Briet had traveled west to unearth, but the return of Cade Martin was a danger she couldn't afford to ignore.

I'll need to drive through the night to reach Kingman by morning, she realized. She stewed in frustration as she rushed to pack her bags. *So much for my "vacation."*

FEBRUARY 6

Ice water and bright light hit Miles in the face. An agent with a flat Midwestern accent grumbled, "Welcome to day two of your captivity, you Limey prick."

Miles blinked and sputtered as runoff trickled down his face. "Really, mate? Is that any way to talk to an ally?" His eyes adjusted, and he saw the American interrogators he had secretly nicknamed Husker and Bubba looming on the other side of the table to which Miles was cuffed. The two men collectively had less charm than the gray cinder-block room in which they stood.

Husker, a lanky man with a shoddy comb-over and poor taste in men's suits, opened a manila folder he had been carrying. "Allies, eh? Is that what we are?" He flipped through some pages. "I must have been confused by the fact that you and your partner have no permission to operate in American territory."

"I didn't think you Yanks cared about technicalities like that."

Shorter, fatter, and even more slovenly in his attire, Bubba snuffed his stub of a cigarette on the concrete floor, and then he palmed sweat from the top of his beige bowling ball of a head. "Espionage ain't just some technicality, pal." His bluster sounded decidedly East Coast in origin. "Neither is grand theft auto."

At first Miles didn't understand Bubba's accusation, and then he realized that his captors must have exorcised Cade of his yoked demons. No demons meant no magick—which meant the illusions disguising their "borrowed" sports car were now vanished.

Ah, well, Miles lamented to himself. *Easy come, easy go.*

"Let's start from the top," Husker said. "Why were you and Martin in L.A.?"

What do they really think I'm going to tell them? Miles directed his answer to whoever was behind the room's two-way mirror. "We came to sell our memoirs to Hollywood."

"I doubt that," Husker said. "I seem to recall your government makes its agents sign something called the Official Secrets Act."

"Speaking of your government," Bubba added, "boy, were they surprised to hear you're in America."

Miles put on a grin. "So, you've called the British consulate?"

"We did," Husker said. "For some reason they think you're in French Indochina. So let's return to my question: If you're supposed to be in Laos, why were you in California?"

"Forgive me, but didn't I answer that for you gents yesterday?"

Husker crossed his arms. "You really expect us to believe that fugitive Nazi magicians have compromised a U.S. nuclear fusion bomb? The most heavily defended secret program in the world? Please. That lab's warded up so tight, Merlin himself couldn't break into it."

His partner leaned in. "And they don't exactly return phone calls, either. You gave us a cover story we can't possibly confirm or deny. Seems a bit *convenient* to me."

"I assure you," Miles said, "it's anything but." *Apparently, the truth isn't good enough for these chaps,* Miles realized. *That's going to make the rest of this encounter far more difficult.* He did his best to correct his posture in the too-small uncomfortable chair. "You have all of our evidence. You took it when you nicked us. Why don't you review it yourselves? Then we can put an end to this farce."

Bubba parked his oversized ass on the edge of the metal table. "We're just getting started, pal." He slapped down a file folder in front of Miles and opened it to reveal its top sheet. It was a dossier about Cade. "Tell us about your magician partner."

A glimpse at the top page of the dossier gave Miles a good idea of things they already knew, and that he could use to waste their time. "Not much to tell, really. We were chums at Oxford—Exeter College, to be specific. He lost his mum and dad when the Nazis sank the *Athenia*, and after a turn in the hospital he signed up for British SOE. I, on the other hand, joined the army, so we didn't see each other again until he came to Achnacarry for Ranger training in spring of forty-four. After the war, we both got tapped to serve MI6. And lo, all these years and many cases of gin later, here we are."

"We know all that," Husker said. "What we need to know is, where's he been since forty-five? Our sources say MI6 loses track of him, sometimes for weeks. Where does he go? Is he slinging spells for hire? Is he teaching his tricks to others? And if so, to whom?"

Miles shrugged. "Have to ask him, mate. I'm not my brother's keeper."

"Oh, but I think you are," Bubba said. "In fact, I think you've been Martin's minder ever since you recruited him into MI6. There are powerful people who would like to see him dead. But no one will tell us *why*—and I have to confess, that troubles me."

"Sounds like a personal problem," Miles said.

Husker planted himself on the other side of the desk, so that he and Bubba were like sweaty bookends pressing in upon Miles. "I don't think you appreciate the precarious nature of your circumstances, Mr. Franklin. Your partner is in this country with forged identity papers. Plus, we found in your shared possession a staggering quantity of narcotics, amphetamines, and hallucinogens—all of which we believe you smuggled into this country."

Bubba leaned in closer—near enough for Miles to wince at the man's rotten-salmon breath and trash-bin armpit odor. "Want to know what your consulate said when we asked about your partner? They disavowed him. Said they never heard of him. Know what that means, wise guy? If we want your buddy gone, he's history. We could have him hanged. Or shot."

"Or," Husker added, "since he legally doesn't exist, we could just make him *disappear.*"

Miles was out of patience. "What are you bastards playing at?"

"We know your secrets, too," Husker said. "We have a whole file on you."

A foul whisper from Bubba: "We know you're a *faggot,* Franklin."

Husker smirked. "If we told your people at MI6 what we know about your nocturnal hobbies, that would be a real career-ender for you, wouldn't it?" The agent pulled a pack of cigarettes from an inside pocket of his jacket, extracted one, and lit it. He puffed smoke into Miles's face. "Tell us everything you know about Martin's movements, and about MI6's operations inside the United States, and in any country where we have national-security interests, and maybe we'll consider losing a few pages from your file. As a professional courtesy."

He knew how much their promises were worth.

"Sod off, you cunts."

The men stood. Husker nodded at Bubba.

Bubba took off his jacket and hung it from a hook on the wall by the door. He plodded in heavy steps back to Miles's side, where he started to roll up his shirt sleeves.

"The locals 'round these parts," Bubba said, "they got cute traditions. Know what my favorite is? A kids' birthday treat called a piñata. Know what a piñata is, faggot?"

Miles maintained his pretense of British stoicism. "Can't say as I do."

The fat man cracked his meaty knuckles. "You're about to find out."

~∾~

Too nauseated to sleep, too tired to stay awake, Cade sat handcuffed on a metal chair in a cinder-block room, lingering in a fugue state of misery. Bullets of sweat rolled down his brow and stung his itching eyes. Chills cooled the per-spiration on his back, and sour bile crept up his esophagus. The aching in his brain was on the verge of cracking open his skull.

His gut roiled. *Any second now I'm either gonna puke or shit myself.*

Forty-eight hours of cold-turkey withdrawal. Not a drop a booze, not a puff of opium. A torture Cade wouldn't have inflicted on his worst enemy. His cap-tors wouldn't even let him have a fucking cigarette, a privation that he was almost certain constituted a war crime.

Every muscle in Cade's body ached. Including his fingers and toes. Even his face. The only glimmer of mercy in his forced sobriety was the fact that the assholes who had taken him and Miles had exorcised Cade's yoked de-mons. *At least I don't have to deal with* that *right now. Not that magick would be of any use in here. Place is warded up tighter than a nun's bunghole.*

Now the light from the naked bulb above his head seemed to shift colors. White became yellow, and then orange. His head swam and, in slow succes-sions, turned the room crimson, violet, and blue. When he concentrated, he was sure he could hear the two-way mirror breathing.

A deafening clash of metal—the turning of a doorknob. Cade winced as the door opened. He looked up and registered the return of his interrogator from the previous day, a tall man of lean build and hawkish features who dressed himself like a mortician: a plain black suit, a crisp white shirt, a black tie, black sunglasses, and a black trilby. His hair was crew cut, his sideburns were short, his face was shaved. He sat down on the other side of the table, leaned forward, and folded his hands together, striking a thoughtful pose. A cold smile. "Good morning, Mr. Martin."

Cade's reply spilled out, a verbal slurry. "You call this good?"

The interrogator set his hat upon the table. "As we expected, after two days of incarceration, you're beginning to succumb to the effects of withdrawal. I've been told that opium withdrawal feels like the worst flu one can imagine—

and that alcohol withdrawal is far worse. Does that sound accurate to your current experience?"

"If you're asking if I'd rather be dead than feel like this, the answer's yes."

A nod. "Understandable." He stared at Cade, who looked at anything other than the stranger. After a pursing frown, the interrogator asked, "Do you know who I am, Mr. Martin?"

"Of course I do," Cade said. "You're a Hammer. Federal anti-magick squad."

"Correct. So what do you say we dispense with theatrics and mind games, and just speak to each other in plain and simple terms."

Suppressing an urge to vomit, Cade cocked an eyebrow at the Hammer. "I have to think there's a rule against that somewhere in your spook handbook."

"More than you can imagine. But forget the rules. I'm here to offer you a deal, Mr. Martin. One that would benefit both you *and* your country."

Cade huffed in derision. "I have no country."

"Not officially," the Hammer said. "But that can be fixed. Your death can be undone. Your fugitive status expunged. There might even be a way to restore your family's lost fortune."

"Seriously? Right now I'd sell my soul for a bucket and a roll of toilet paper."

"Ah, yes. I'd forgotten that opium constipates—and that the withdrawal process can reverse that state with peculiar urgency."

Cade feared his gut was ready to burst. "Get to the point, or get a mop."

"Today is your lucky day, Mr. Martin. I've been sent to offer you a job: master karcist of the American Occult Defense Program, operating out of the Pentagon."

"You mean Briet's job."

"Not if you want it. Say the word, and it's yours. A generous salary. Numerous perks. A stable lifestyle. Plus, if you sign our contract in the next ten minutes, I've been authorized to set you up with a kilo of premium Afghan opium, two cases of top-shelf Kentucky bourbon, and the key to a commode down the hall." He reached inside his jacket and pulled out a contract that had been folded into thirds, and a ballpoint pen. He flattened the contract onto the table and pushed it across for Cade's inspection. "What do you say, Mr. Martin?"

Cade shivered while he glared at the Hammer. "Doesn't sound like my kind of gig."

"What if we sweeten the offer? Take over at the Silo and we'll let you personally hand over Briet to the Israelis to stand trial for war crimes. We'll even get you a front-row seat for her hanging." The Hammer smirked. "This could be a win-win for both of us."

It was a tempting offer, Cade had to admit that much.

He stood. Turned his chair around. Unbuckled his belt. Then he dropped his pants, squatted while using the chair for support, and emptied his bowels onto the concrete floor, filling the interrogation room with his stink. Finished, he heaved a sigh of deep relief. The rest of him still felt abused and racked with nausea and aches, but at least this torment had been exorcised.

Cade told the disgusted Hammer, "You should've given me the bucket. And in case this wasn't clear?" He picked up the contract, wiped his ass with it, and threw the soiled pages back onto the table. "Go fuck yourself."

From the outside, the Kingman safe house looked like a long-neglected ranch house deteriorating in the Arizona desert. Twenty yards from its front porch Briet felt the first resistance of warding glyphs—a defensive measure that ensured no one with yoked demons could enter the house. She stopped her rented car ten yards from the shack and shut off the engine.

All warded up, just like Los Alamos. This is starting to piss me off.

A moment's concentration attuned her to the half dozen spirits she had yoked to her service. *I bid thee, one and all, to depart in peace, doing harm to none. Return at once to that place from which thou came; your service is discharged.*

She had no need to threaten or make demands. Free of her domination, the demons flew back to Hell, as if its fiery environs were somehow more welcoming than Briet's company. Their departure flooded her with a sense of relief. The crushing sensation she had come to take for granted in her chest abated, and the whispers of sinister voices in her head were gone, leaving only her own bitter musings to fill the void.

Two full days of yoking wasted. Still . . . free at last—but also defenseless.

She dug in her handbag to retrieve her credentials—and to confirm she had her Luger pistol. The weapon had earned her more than a few curious stares in the years since the war, but aside from its sentimental value it was a reliable firearm, and Briet saw no reason to part with it. She closed the handbag, tucked it to her side, and got out of the car.

The desert sun hit her like a fist. Everything was so bright that Briet could barely see. Using her hand as a visor helped a bit, but she was still plagued by the glare of sunlight off the sand. Eager to get inside before she went blind, she walked quickly toward the safe house.

The *ker-clack* of a shotgun being primed stopped her two paces shy of the porch. Standing in its shadows, a man asked in a deep rasp, "Whadda ya want?"

"I'm told you have something that belongs to me."

A man plucked from the pages of *The Grapes of Wrath* stepped off the porch into the daylight. The sun had baked his skin into brown leather and turned his thinning crown of hair bone white. Penury and misery had etched deep lines into his gaunt face, and his callused hands gripped his shotgun as if it were the only thing he trusted on God's forsaken earth.

He studied Briet with suspicious eyes. "Who the hell are you?"

She held up her Department of Defense identification. "DOD. Clearance Level Seven."

His eyes widened as he leaned in for a closer look. "Never seen a Level Seven before."

"Pray you never do again. Now let me in."

He waved her past. "Door's open."

Briet stepped around the sentry, climbed the steps to the porch, and continued through the front door. The inside of the ranch house was no better maintained than its exterior. Its main room was devoid of furniture, and its wooden floor was scuffed and in poor repair.

A boyish man in slacks and a loose white linen shirt emerged from a side room. "You must be Miss Segfrunsdóttir, from the DOD." He approached Briet and offered her his hand in greeting. "I'm Agent Burleigh. The house keeper."

"Good for you. Where's Cade Martin?"

A disarming smile. "You cut right to business, don't you?"

"I just drove ten hours through a desert. You think I'm here for small talk?"

"Point taken," he said with an abashed nod. "This way, please."

Burleigh led her down a corridor to a door. He unlocked it, then pushed it open. "Watch your step," he said, leading her down a flight of stairs.

The basement level was constructed of poured concrete. Overhead were exposed timbers and joists, the structure beneath the floor of the main room. Cheap folding tables and chairs stood scattered with affected randomness about the barren space. Tucked against a far wall was a long boxy structure of cinder blocks, complete with concrete ceilings. Three doors stood close together in the middle of the cinder-block wall.

Pointing at the door to the right, Burleigh said, "Your man is in there. His partner is in the left room. If you want to audit their interrogations—"

"Center door," Briet interrupted. "Two-way mirrors. I know the drill." She looked around and spotted a table piled with what looked to be personal effects. "Is that all they had?"

"As far as we know. Most of it was bagged in their hotel suite." Burleigh pointed to a second table in the corner. "That stuff we recovered when your boy Cade lost his porter demon, and half his shit landed in the dirt. It's the usual karcist's gear: tool roll, grimoire, et cetera."

He followed her to the tables. She ignored his probing stare as she pawed through Cade's equipment and other possessions. "Have they said why they came to Los Angeles?"

"They've told us a version of a story, but I think they're just fucking with—"

"Tell me," Briet insisted. "What did they say?"

Burleigh gestured for her to follow him behind a low partition. There, a pair of transcription clerks, both wearing headphones, typed reports of all that they heard from inside the interrogation rooms. Stacks of transcripts filled a table against the wall behind them.

The house keeper extracted a binder of transcripts from the bottom of one pile and handed it to Briet. "Read it yourself. Long story short: They say they got a book they call an 'Odessa journal' from a friend of theirs in South America. They claim it's full of diagrams and symbols that suggest someone is trying to merge a demon with an atom bomb, and that they were following a lead that suggested Odessa has a man in L.A."

Briet thumbed through the early pages of the transcript. "I've heard that name—Odessa."

"Yeah, we checked it out. A secret society of ex-Nazis. Rumor has it the Catholic Church helped a bunch of Krauts escape to South America after the war." Burleigh looked dubious. "We know a few of Hitler's goons made it to Argentina, but most of the brass thinks this Odessa thing's just a myth. Same goes for its mysterious leader, Dragan."

Hearing the name of her former adept, Briet looked up at Burleigh. "Dragan? Where did you see that name connected with Odessa?"

"In the journal." Burleigh opened a lockbox and pulled out a leather-bound notebook. He handed it to Briet. "One of the scraps your boy says he found says Odessa's 'man in L.A.' is linked to Dragan." He studied her with growing curiosity. "That mean something to you?"

She wasn't sure how much to trust a stranger with what she knew. It was better to err on the side of discretion, she decided. "I'm not sure," she lied. She perused the journal's contents. "Where are these diagrams?"

"Near the back," Burleigh said. "Nobody here can make heads or tails of 'em. But a few experts we called in said some of the equations are cutting-edge stuff. As in, atomic. Classified."

Looking at the fusion of occult glyphs and physics equations, Briet recognized strings of mathematics she had glimpsed in the perimeter laboratories of the Silo. Was their top-secret research part of this? And if so, did that mean the Silo's security was compromised?

She pulled a scrap of paper from the back of the journal and stared at its German sentence fragments. The one at the bottom commanded her attention. "*Dragan braucht unseren Mann in L.A.*," she said, reading it aloud. *Dragan needs our man in L.A.* A troubling notion came to her. *What if L.A. isn't Los Angeles? What if L.A. is Los Alamos?*

All at once, ASTAROTH's warning felt more dire than ever.

And somehow, Cade Martin and his MI6 partner-in-mischief had stumbled onto the same path as Briet. She had seen too much of magick to believe in coincidences; the tapestry of fate had intersected her thread with Cade's for a reason. *If I'm going to get inside LASL and find out what's really going on,* Briet mused, *I'm going to need professional help. The kind that trained MI6 field agents could provide. But first I'll have to get them out of here.*

She faced Burleigh. "I need Martin and his partner released, immediately."

"I can't do that," he said. "The only people who can authorize their release are the president, the secretary of defense, or the director of the CIA."

Briet's temper simmered. "Agent Burleigh, need I remind you that those men are agents of our strongest ally? And that, as a karcist, Martin is subject to my particular authority?"

"You can remind me of anything you want, but unless you come back with an order signed by President Eisenhower, Secretary Wilson, or Director Dulles, those two clowns are staying locked up tight." He noted the slight creep of Briet's hand toward her purse. "And before you do something foolish—like trying to pull that Luger out of your bag—you ought to know there are men armed with shotguns and rifles in concealed positions all around you."

Briet concealed her frustration with a cold smile. "A threat, Agent Bur-leigh?"

"Friendly advice. Hate to see a pretty lady like you end up in a ditch." He took back the journal and then nodded toward the piles of transcripts. "Now, if you want to stay and keep reading—"

"No, thank you." Briet walked toward the stairs. "I've seen enough."

As she climbed the steps out of the basement, Burleigh said, "I thought you were here to advise us on how to handle Cade Martin."

"You seem to have him well in hand." At the top of the stairs she paused and looked down at Burleigh. "Just make sure he and his partner don't die or go missing. Because I promise you, I *will* return. And the next time I leave this place, those men *will* be going with me." She walked out of the ranch house, leaving the last part of her vow unspoken:

Even if I have to kill everyone else in this house to make it happen.

19

FEBRUARY 8

The old woman's face was so wrinkled that Anja was certain it must be physically impossible for the crone to open her eyes beyond a squint. Nonetheless, the elderly Indian woman filled Anja's canteen with clean water from a glazed ceramic jug, spilling not so much as a drop while she poured. Just as surprising to Anja, the woman's hands, though they looked bony and arthritic, did not shake or tremble as she filled the canteen.

"Long trip ahead of you?" the old woman asked in a Hindustani dialect.

Anja feared to share her plans with strangers. "Long enough," she said, their conversation instantly translated by the demonic gifts of LIOBOR, with the old lady none the wiser.

A sage nod from the water crone. "Going north? Mind the borders. Always changing."

The genuine concern in the woman's voice snared Anja's interest. "What borders?"

"All of them." The woman finished filling Anja's canteen and set aside her jug. "Nepal, Jammu-Kashmir, Tibet, China—every day they move." She twisted the canteen's cap into place. "No one knows where one land ends and the next begins." She passed the canteen to Anja. "Some days I wake to five countries claiming the Spiti. Others, only three." She waved her hands in disgust, as if shooing flies. "No one knows anything anymore."

Anja handed the woman a ten-rupee note. "Thank you."

"Too kind," the old woman said. She pressed her palms together and honored Anja with a half bow. "Safe travels, young one."

Anja returned the gesture of respect, and then the old woman retreated into her hut.

Alone on a snow-covered dirt road in northern India, Anja stowed her canteen, and then she checked her map to confirm where she was and to satisfy her curiosity. Something the old woman had said had triggered Anja's memory of Khalîl's riddle: "Follow the needle true, and thread your way to the Key, on the bank of the river, where five lands meet as three."

Where five lands meet as three. Anja recognized the echo of Khalîl's words in the water woman's advisory: Mind the borders of Jammu-Kashmir, Nepal, Tibet, and China. *Add India to that mix,* Anja reasoned, *and that's five lands.* Then she recalled that India and Pakistan each asserted a claim to Jammu-Kashmir, and that China insisted Tibet was actually its sovereign possession. *Depending on one's point of view,* she realized, *this is either the meeting point of five lands—or of three.*

Retracing her route north from Chandigarh, she deduced that she must be in the town of Pangan, not far from the boulder-strewn banks of the Beas River. Her eyes started to search the parts of the map that detailed the lands to the north. *What was that name the old lady mentioned?* Skimming from one detail to the next, Anja quickly found the name she sought: the Spiti River. Its westernmost end lay roughly forty miles northeast of Pangan. She traced its route with her finger, curious to see where it led. And then her index finger halted upon a point of interest: the village of Key. And, on the north bank of the Spiti River, the Key Gompa monastery.

Thread your way to the Key, on the bank of the river. . . .

Yes, Anja realized, *that must be it. That's where I'll find Khalîl.*

She contemplated whether to follow the roads or if it might make more sense to yoke a demon so she could transform herself and fly to Key Gompa. As a straight flight it would be only a fifty-mile journey over the mountains. On foot, sticking to the roads, it would be a longer journey—more than eighty-five miles, at least three days of walking. Then she realized she would need at least that much time to make the preparations for more magick. *I can walk there in less time than it would take to work the magick for a flight. Might as well walk, then.*

That left just one detail to address before she began the last leg of her hike.

Except for her Makarov and her wand, Anja remanded her pack and other gear to her demonic porter, one of only four spirits she had felt strong enough to yoke. Then she detoured off the town's main road into an alley that had been cleared of snow. Mindful of her breathing, she calmed her nerves and became as one with the long morning shadows. Then she waited.

Several minutes passed before her prey showed himself.

He plodded along, heavy-footed and careless. Too confident by half.

Somehow he had draped his cassock over a pair of insulated hiking pants. Over the cassock he wore a parka, and his robe's hood was bunched up between his neck and his awkwardly stuffed backpack. He looked as if one misstep, or maybe just one unkind nudge, might land him flat on his face.

Anja gave him that nudge.

She focused her attack with her wand, directing the fist of BAEL as it tripped the monk, and then she restrained the demon's impulse to cause grievous harm as she used its invisible hands to drag her confused pursuer into the alley for a reckoning. As the man slid across the muddy ground to a halt in front of Anja, she used BAEL's power to flip him onto his back.

He raised his empty hands in front of him, a gesture of abject surrender. "Please," he begged, "don't kill me. I'm not armed."

"You have no weapons," Anja said. "But you lie when you say you are not armed. You know how to fight."

Rapid nods of agreement. "I'm trained to defend myself. That's all."

"No, it is not." She studied him with the Sight. "You burn with magickal power." After another moment of scrutiny, she recognized the particular radiance that seemed to infuse him from toe to crown. "*Angelic* power. You have yoked angels."

More nods. "Yes. My name is Father Luis Roderigo Pérez. I'm a Pauline magician."

"You have followed me since New Delhi," Anja said. "You also beat up a pair of Black Sun dabblers, in the mountains outside Chandigarh."

Luis started to get up. "You saw that?"

Anja forced him back to the ground with a swat of BAEL's hand. "You made enough noise to be heard in Pakistan. Now you are here. Why do you follow me?"

"I'm on a holy mission," Luis said. "The Holy See asked me to persuade you to return a piece of Church property currently in your possession."

She laughed, and not in a kind way. "The Vatican sent you to steal the Iron Codex."

Luis raised his hands again, though he hadn't been threatened or told to do so. "Please, Miss Kernova, if we could just sit and discuss this, I'm sure we could—"

She backhanded Luis with BAEL's fist—not hard enough to kill him, but with sufficient force to make certain he would be unconscious for a long while.

At least, for long enough to let her get out of town and begin her trek to Key Gompa without a White shadow.

But precautions were in order. She stripped Luis of his boots, parka, and camping gear, set them all aside, and then lit them on fire with a spark from HABORYM. Out of respect she left his karcist's tools untouched, and she spared the cheap shoes in his pack. Without gear Luis would be unable to follow her. At least here, in a village, the priest might find help and shelter.

Stepping over Luis on her way out of the alley, Anja almost felt a twinge of pity. The monk clearly had not been trained as a battle karcist. "Go home, little man," she said as she left him sprawled unconscious in the mud. "My path will bring you nothing but blood and pain."

20

FEBRUARY 10

Alarms yanked Cade from an anxious slumber. Armed men dragged him from his cell.

Smoke watered his eyes. He was being pulled one way, but the room spun in two other directions. Vomitus crept up his throat, looking for an exit. A firm hand on his neck pushed him toward a raging wall of fire. He tried to resist, but vertigo left him no idea where the smoke ended and darkness began, and the growl of flames competed with hoarse commands, leaving him lost in a maze of fire. A burning timber as thick as his torso crashed onto the concrete floor and kicked up a cloud of sparks. Fiery embers struck Cade's shirt and set it to smoldering, and scorched ragged paths through his brown hair. The ones that reached his scalp stung like a motherfucker. He swatted with cuffed hands at his head, desperate to rid it of fiery motes.

The Hammer and an older man who looked like a walking scrotum with a shotgun dragged Cade up a rickety flight of stairs toward an even wilder inferno. Cade hacked out a lungful of smoke, and then he looked back to see two other men, one skinny and one fat, hauling the handcuffed Miles toward the stairs as more timbers collapsed around them. Waving them onward was a young man with fair hair; he held a semiautomatic pistol in his other hand. He pointed it at one of his subordinates, a military-looking fellow toting a shotgun.

"Get the journal!" the younger man shouted over the fire.

Cade tripped on the stairs. Rough wood bit into his knee, and he felt his dead weight test the strength and patience of his handlers. Beneath them, the wooden staircase groaned.

"Move your ass!" the walking ballsack shouted at Cade.

At the top of the stairs they passed through a doorway and turned left. All Cade saw was the yellow glare of a fire spreading out of control. Ceiling timbers split with cracks like gunshots. He looked left and saw most of a large room's floor collapse and plunge into the basement from which he had just been evacuated. Behind him, tongues of red flame licked at him and the men dragging him, as if the fire were a predator sizing them up.

Something at the far end of the house exploded. A rush of warm oxygen goaded all of the flames higher. Cade looked back as he was muscled through the building's front door. Miles and his minders were just a few paces behind him. Then, without warning, Cade was airborne. After the blaze of the fire, he saw nothing outside the house but an expanse of black.

His face hit the pebble-rich dirt. He groaned and rolled. Only after he came to a stop did he realize how much pain he was in. He was still in the miserable throes of alcohol and heroin withdrawal, and now he had a body covered in second-degree burns, old bruises, and fresh lacerations. As he spat salty blood, he noted that a few of his teeth felt loose.

Miles crashed to the ground a few feet away from Cade. The normally dapper and collected Brit looked as battered and broken as Cade felt. He coughed, and then signaled Cade with a small lift of his chin that he was all right and hadn't broken. Cade returned the signal.

Their captors milled about in a loose cluster. Cade counted eleven men, including his interrogator. One of the military-looking brutes, who had been scorched black with soot, handed the young blond man the Odessa journal. All he got for his heroic effort was a curt nod.

Towers of flame rose from the low ranch house in which Cade and Miles had been held. Watching the place burn and slowly implode, all Cade could do was wonder how long it would take his confiscated karcist's tools to melt in the inferno. As for his grimoire—its wards of protection would save it from the fire, but he dreaded having to dig it out of the ashes.

"We should fall back a few more yards," the blond man said to his colleagues. "Get away from the heat before it cooks us." The other men nodded. The same ones who had been responsible for pulling Cade and Miles from the conflagration dragged them again by their cuffed wrists. Cade said nothing as he watched his heels cut twin trails through the rocky dirt.

Electric crackling sounds were followed by thunderclaps.

The hands holding Cade's wrists slipped away. Two unconscious men dropped into the dirt on either side of him, tendrils of smoke snaking out from under their shirts.

He rolled over and looked into the night just in time to see indigo pulses of light lash out and swat aside the men holding Miles. The tall man and his portly counterpart were launched backward into the darkness. Where they landed, Cade had no idea.

The other men from the ranch house hefted shotguns and pistols. They formed a circle and peered into the night, struggling to sight their opponent.

Their weapons came apart in their hands.

Wooden grips splintered. Metal components fused and twisted into steel pretzels.

A tempest of wind and sand sprang up in their midst and engulfed them. Within seconds they were blind, suffocating, and twenty feet off the ground. It ceased as abruptly as it had begun, and it dropped them all in a heap. None of them stirred.

From out of the night, a figure approached. Cade saw that it was a woman, and for a moment he hoped it might be Anja—and then the firelight revealed the woman's red hair, and he knew who he had to thank for his emancipation. "Hello, Briet."

"Hello, Cade." She flicked her hand one way and the cuffs fell from Cade's wrists. When she snapped her hand in the opposite direction, she freed Miles from his bonds. Then she smirked at Cade. "Looks like you need the hair of the dog." She extended an open hand, and in it appeared a flask, which she lobbed to Cade. "To take the edge off."

He opened the flask and inhaled its familiar, comforting scent. "Is this—?"

"Laudanum," Briet said as Cade drank. "I know your habits better than you do." She looked up. A shimmering in the air preceded the appearance of a briefcase, a leather tool roll, and a large leather-bound tome. The latter two fell to the ground in front of Cade. "Your grimoire and tools. A tad blackened, but neither the worse for wear." The briefcase dropped in front of Miles. "Your equipment case from Q Branch. Also fireproof, no doubt."

Miles stood and massaged his wrists. Gesturing toward the burning building, he asked Briet, "Your work?" When she nodded, he asked, "How did you get past the wards?"

"Wards against magick have little effect on gasoline."

"But you used magick out here," Miles said, "inside the warded area."

Cade paused his imbibing. "The wards were imprinted on the house, Miles. Burn down the house . . ." He let his partner finish the syllogism on his own and directed his next words to Briet. "Crude, but effective. That always was your trademark."

"Says the man getting well on *my* laudanum."

Cade got to his feet, but just as quickly wished he hadn't. Still, he refused to show weakness in front of Briet. "I'm guessing this flask full of get-well isn't charity."

"Of course not," Briet said. She extended her right hand. The Odessa journal dislodged itself from the fist of the unconscious blond man and flew into Briet's palm. She held the book toward Cade. "I want to know what *this* is about, just as badly as you do."

Miles did not sound persuaded. "Why should we trust you? You were a Nazi."

"I was never a party member," Briet said. "I wore their uniform during the war as a disguise, and because it helped me get things done. But I never cared about the Nazis or their war. I was loyal to my master—until I realized he'd gone insane."

"You mean until you realized he was gonna lose," Cade said. "Nice excuse for abandoning your master in the middle of a war."

"Call it what you want," Briet said. "I serve America now."

"Sure you do," Cade said. "I bet you're a real fuckin' patriot."

The Icelandic woman opened the Odessa journal and dropped it so that it landed open in front of Cade. "Have you seen what's in this book? Fusions of magick and science."

"We've seen it," Miles said. "Are you saying you know what that is?"

"I might," Briet said. "My patron warned me about one of my former adepts, a karcist named Dragan Dalca. A man whose name is in this journal. And I think you misread a clue. Dragan's 'man in L.A.'? I don't think he's in Los Angeles. I think he's in Los Alamos, New Mexico, at the facility that conducts the majority of America's atomic-weapons research."

All of Cade's experience told him not to trust Briet—*once a Nazi, always a Nazi,* Cade had long believed—but his gut told him that she might be on to something big.

"All right," Cade said. "Let's say we believe you. What's our next move?"

"We need to get away from here." She pointed into the night. "I have a car parked a hundred yards down the road. Come with me to Los Alamos. I need your spy gear and training to break into a magickally secured building on the

LASL campus. I think that once we get inside, we'll be able to figure out who we're dealing with, and what they're up to."

Miles picked up his briefcase. "I'm game." He shot a look at Cade. "What do you say, mate? Up for a road trip?"

It was a mad gamble—but what hadn't been since the war? Cade slung his tools across his back and picked up his grimoire. "Fuck it," he said, marching past Briet. "I call shotgun."

She followed him, her brow knit with confusion. "What does that mean?"

"It means I ride up front."

She shook her head. "No, Trixim is up front. You two ride in back."

Bringing up the rear, Miles asked, "Who the hell is Trixim?"

"Her rat," Cade said. "Yeah . . . this trip's gonna be a hoot."

FEBRUARY 11

It had been days since Anja had seen the road beneath her feet. Her world had been painted white by an unceasing fall of snow, a slow but steady accumulation that had followed her since her departure from Pangan. Powdery and light, it nonetheless had become an impediment after it rose higher than her knees. In spite of her preparations against the cold, her feet had gone numb many hours earlier. With her provisions exhausted and her canteen emptied, she hoped to reach her destination soon, before the dusk turned to starless night.

At least I know I'm not lost, she consoled herself. She had kept the wavy line of the Spiti River in view on her right since leaving the main road to cross a bridge to the river's north bank.

Shadows gathered around her with every step she took. The gentle storm encircled her, a white dervish with no beginning or end, and blocked her view of the ragged Himalayas and the half-frozen river. Encompassed by the blizzard, Anja found herself in the midst of an eerie silence. Beneath a blanket of fresh-fallen snow the world grew still. Muted. Peaceful.

The cynic in Anja wanted to call the placid winterscape a lie. She knew that Man and Nature both lay in ambush somewhere beneath that pale shroud, their appetites never sated, their mutual bloodthirst forever unslaked. But a spark of hope deep within her wanted to believe that there were still good people and places in the world. She wanted a reason to believe that Good might be just as durable an entity as Evil.

She wanted a reason to love.

A blade of wind parted the storm's blank curtain.

Less than half a mile ahead of Anja, a pyramidal cluster of boxlike white buildings with red roofs stood on a rocky mound high upon a snow-covered slope, beneath majestic cliffs crowned by ragged fangs of brown rock.

A winding road led up the slope to the buildings, which reminded Anja of a child's toy blocks stacked with abandon as high as they could go. A dozen meters downslope from the bottom layer of buildings rose a three-meter-high stone wall. On top of that were three-meter-tall stone pillars spaced roughly five meters apart; connecting the pillars were sections of taut chicken-wire fencing.

There was no sign outside its open gateway. No markings on its walls. But the moment that Anja saw the place, she knew that it had to be the Key Gompa monastery.

Elation banished the weight from her steps. She climbed the winding road lined with prayer flags, no longer minding the falling snow but reveling in its kiss as flakes melted against her face. The gateway of the monastery called to her. She had solved the master's riddle at last.

From the last bend in the road before reaching the monastery's entrance, Anja saw three figures approach the colorful gateway from the other side. Two wore the tangerine-colored robes of Buddhist monks, and they walked shoulder-to-shoulder. Behind them followed a man in dishwater-dull gray robes. All three had pulled their hoods low in front of their faces, and their folded hands were concealed by their robes' deep and overlapping sleeves.

She met the trio a dozen yards outside the gateway.

Face-to-face, she saw that one of the monks looked to be of Tibetan or maybe Nepalese heritage, though she couldn't tell for certain; the other had a deep brown complexion and facial features that suggested he was of Southeast Asian ancestry. Both appeared to be in their thirties, but their shaved heads and absence of facial hair made it hard for Anja to be certain of their age.

Each monk pressed his palms together in front of his chest. Together they bowed to Anja. Then the Tibetan man said to her, "Welcome to Key Gompa, Sister Anja. Shed your darkness and be welcome."

She didn't try to hide her confusion. "Shed my darkness?"

The man behind them stepped forward. The monks parted to let him pass. In front of Anja, the man in gray pulled back his hood. It was Khalîl. He smiled at Anja. "What Brother Tenzin means is, if you wish to enter, release any demons you have yoked."

Anja froze with indecision. It was a reasonable request, on its face. And it would not have been the first time she had agreed to divest herself of magick in order to enter a sacred space. But after all the recent attempts on her life, and the Black Sun's apparent renewed interest in the Iron Codex, she was reluctant to leave herself defenseless. But what could she tell Khalîl?

"I have many enemies, Master Khalîl. Some have followed me here."

Her warning didn't seem to trouble the old man. "They will be of no concern to you once you enter. You will find no safer place than here inside these walls. You have my word."

His assurance left her little room for debate.

She turned her back on her anxiety. *I did not come this far just to lose my nerve at the threshold. My journey was an act of faith—so let faith win the day.*

To the two monks she said, "I will need help taking my things inside."

She mentally commanded DANOCHAR, her demon of burden, *Return to me now all those items that I have remanded to thy care, and restore them in good repair and in an orderly manner.* In an eyeblink all of her many possessions that she had entrusted to the demon over the past several months appeared beside her and the monks. As she had instructed, all of her goods were neatly stacked and undamaged. The monks, clearly not strangers to magick, said nothing as they gathered up Anja's effects and then carried them up the serpentine path to the monastery.

Anja drew a deep breath and finished her leap of faith.

All of my spirits in thrall, I dismiss and discharge thee. Depart at once, returning without delay or detour to thy places of Infernal repose; do no harm on thy journey; and return when, and only when, I summon thee. You are released. By the holy names of ADONAY, ELOHIM, JEHOVAM, *and* TETRAGRAMMATON, *I command thee, begone!*

The exorcism of her yoked spirits was like a flood of ice water through her veins, extinguishing the heat of power and drowning the embers of demonic hatred that had fueled it. When the chilling sensation abated, Anja felt empty. Hollow. Forsaken.

Perhaps sensing Anja's dismay, Khalîl put his hand on her shoulder. "I know it can't have been easy, to let go of so much strength at once. But it will be worth it. I promise."

She nodded. "I am ready."

He ushered her through the gateway and led her up the path to the monastery.

Her mind was aflutter with questions.

"Where do we begin?" she asked. "Do I need to learn more of the Goetic Art? Or can you teach me the Pauline Art? And if I am *nikraim,* how do I—?"

The master raised one weathered hand to request silence. "All in good time. You've had a long journey, and you're more weary than you know. First you will bathe. Then you will eat. After that, you will rest. And when I judge you ready . . . we shall begin your training anew."

She suppressed her burgeoning curiosity—for the time being. "Very well, Master. I shall do as you command." With a mischievous gleam in her eye she added, "Unless you tell me to wear one of those robes. That I will not do. Orange is not my color."

The master cracked a sly smile. "Your objection is noted."

❧

"All these streets look the same," Briet said. She steered her rented car up one street and down the next, over and over, in the residential section of Los Alamos.

Hunkered low in the backseat, which reeked of puke and Pennzoil, Cade and Miles did their best not to be seen. "Just keep looking for a 'for sale' sign," Cade said. "A street with lots of them will be best. We need someplace empty, away from nosy neighbors."

Miles twisted and grimaced in discomfort. "And be quick about it," he said. "If anyone sees us looping around block to block, they might think we're casing the neighborhood to rob it."

"Not a problem," Briet said. "I'll just explain we've come to trespass, not to steal."

Cade's impatience felt like a ferret squirming in his gut. "Just relax, both of you. No one robs houses in broad daylight. And if anybody asks, just say you're house-hunting."

Briet threw a sour look over her shoulder. "A single woman looking for a house here? In a one-industry town full of scientists? When I'm obviously not? How do I explain that?"

Miles said, "You don't. If anyone asks what you do, flash those DOD credentials of yours and tell them your work's classified. Which happens to be true."

Briet halted the car at a stop sign, and then she turned right. "The street looks promising. Lots of signs and the houses look new. Most have dirt front yards."

"Jackpot," Cade said. "Pick one that has the most empty houses between it and the next neighbor, then park in back of it." Briet didn't reply, but Cade could tell she was doing as he'd asked. Part of him still felt queasy at the idea of trusting her, but at the moment he and Miles had no real allies, and also no easy way out of the country now that MI6 and the British government had disavowed them in the name of political expediency.

Briet stopped the car and turned off the engine. The trio clambered out. The house was tiny and low to the ground. Cade wondered if Miles would have to stoop to get through its back door. Looking around, he saw nothing but desert scrub behind the house, and nothing behind any of the others on either side of it. Not one sign of human habitation: no outdoor furniture, no children's toys or bicycles left in the sun, no vehicles parked beside or behind them. He nodded. "This'll do."

He helped Miles and Briet unload the car's trunk. Before starting their search for an empty house, he had sent Briet into town to procure supplies. In addition to a case of hard liquor, a carton of Lucky Strikes, and a gram of shitty heroin, she had purchased safety pins, white linen bedsheets, eight heavy blankets, fifty feet of hemp rope, a box of large nails, and a hammer.

It took them two trips to move everything inside the house. Then Cade went to work. "Miles, we need to cover the front door and all the windows in the living room with the blankets. Nail them into place—they have to hold against a storm-force wind."

Miles gathered up the hammer and nails, and then he grabbed the first blanket and headed toward the front door. "On it, mate."

Turning to Briet, Cade said, "I presume you have a demon of burden toting the gear you need for experiments. Candles, camphor, brandy, all that stuff?"

She stroked her pet rat and regarded him warily. "Are you saying you don't?"

"Half my stuff got flushed to Hell when those goons in Arizona exorcised my yoked spirits. The other half went up in the fire you set. All I've got now are my tools and my working clothes—and if I hadn't tossed my magick pajamas in with my gear out of laziness back in Bangkok, I'd be completely fucked right now."

Briet sighed. "Very well. I can provide the rest of the essentials."

"Thanks." He opened the package of white bedsheets. "Now help me cut this and mark it up for Miles. We'll need him as a tanist to close the circle, and he can't do it in street clothes."

Acting in concert, Cade and Briet made quick work of crafting a set of ceremonial garb for Miles. They made a few slices in the flat sheet with their bolines, and then Cade cut a hole in its center for his friend's head. Once the slicing and dicing was done, Cade folded the sheet in half along the neck hole, and then he pieced the sleeves together with the safety pins. "That should do it," he said. He handed the jury-rigged garment to Briet. "Can you turn the pillowcases into shoes and a miter? And then mark them up?"

"And what will you be doing?"

"Preparing the room," Cade said. "Which means I need your expendables now."

"You forgot to say 'please.'"

Cade felt his gorge rise at being upbraided by Briet. "Please, Miss Former Nazi Stooge, may I borrow your consecrated equipment to prepare the room so that I can help you finish your mission and save all of our goddamned lives?"

"Since you asked so *nicely*?" With an unspoken command to her demon of burden, Briet delivered all of the necessary provisions, neatly arranged at Cade's feet. "You're welcome."

⁓

Two hours later the room was ready. It was the fastest Cade had ever prepared a room for a magickal experiment, working entirely from memory. The house's living room was barely large enough to contain the grand circle of protection that would safeguard him, Miles, and Briet, and the outer triangle of containment, into which summoned entities would be corralled.

Miles tugged at the awkward folds of his bedsheet robe, which had been tied snug around his waist with a length of the hemp rope. He frowned at its crudely drawn symbols and the safety pins dangling from the undersides of its sleeves. "Not quite as fancy as yours, is it?"

"Buck up," Cade said as he straightened the cloth miter atop Miles's head. "You're just a tanist. Hell doesn't give a fuck what you wear, as long as you keep your mouth shut."

"He is not joking," Briet added. "Do not speak during the experiment, or by the rules of the Covenant the demon will be free to devour you and kill us."

Miles raised a two-finger V-salute at Briet. "I know the bloody rules."

Cade stepped into the operator's circle. With the tip of his sword he pulled a bit of chalk dust across a gap to close the circle. "We've begun. Both of you shut the fuck up until we're done. Light your braziers, then your candles." Cade ignited the brass vessel of consecrated charcoal at his feet. Bright green flames leapt from the coals. With care he laid his sword across the tops of his white leather slippers.

He rushed through the customary preamble, omitting nothing but not bothering to treat it with his usual grim reverence. He had places to be and scores to settle.

Within minutes the room was choked with foul vapors and dolorous noises from the Abyss, and the air in the room became as cold as a grave.

"I adjure thee, great SEIR, as the agent of the Emperor LUCIFER, and of his beloved son LUCIFUGE ROFOCALE, by the power of the pact I have with thee, and by the names ADONAY, ELOIM, JEHOVAM, TAGLA, MATHON, ALMOUZIN, ARIOS, PITHONA, SYLPHAE, SALAMANDRAE, GNOMUS, TERRAE, COELÙS, GODENS, AQUA, and by the whole hierarchy of superior intelligences who shall constrain thee against thy will, *venité, venité, submirillitor* SEIR!"

Cade thrust his wand into the burning coals, and was rewarded by a horrific roar of agony. The demon was close at hand but refusing to appear.

"I adjure thee, SEIR, by the pact, and by the names, appear instanter!"

The bounding triangle remained empty.

"Now I adjure—!" Frustrated and sick of Hell's predictable games, Cade shook his head. "Fuck this. I know you can fucking hear me, SEIR! And you know what'll happen if you make me call up LUCIFUGE ROFOCALE. So unless you're itching to learn new kinds of pain from the Prime Minister of Hell himself, I suggest you fucking show yourself. *Now.*"

A swirl of purple smoke coalesced into a beast with the head of a bison atop a man's black and muscular torso, and the body of a stallion. Blue flames and sparks danced under its shuffling hooves, and behind its haunches a leathery tail tipped with a scorpion's stinger twitched to and fro. The demon huffed blue smoke from its bovine nostrils, filling the room with a stench of rotting meat and scorched hair. Its voice shook dust from the room's ceiling.

CEASE YOUR THREATS, EVE-SPAWN. I AM HERE. WHAT WOULDST THOU HAVE OF ME?

"Fuck you, SEIR. You know exactly what I want."

YOU DENY ME YOUR THOUGHTS, SO YOU MUST SPEAK YOUR DESIRE.

Cade's temper, already frayed, was ready to snap. "When you were forced from my yoke six days ago, you were holding many of my personal effects in your care."

AND NOW THEY ARE MY PROPERTY IN HELL, AS PER THE TERMS OF OUR COMPACT.

It took all of Cade's willpower not to start torturing the beast. "I know what the compact says. And as far as I'm concerned, you can keep all those things you claimed—all save one. A jacket. Made of brown leather, with a silk lining on which was scribed a map of Europe."

WHAT OF IT?

"I earned that in battle. And I want it back. Now."

YOU CANNOT HAVE IT. THE TERMS OF OUR COMPACT ARE CLEAR AND INFLEXIBLE.

Out of the corner of his eye, Cade could see the incredulous looks transpiring between Miles and Briet. He put them out of his mind and focused on SEIR. "I have much to do today ere the sun sets and the stars wheel forth from darkness. But I will sunder all my plans from now until Judgment Day so that I may torture thee without respite—until you return that jacket."

I CANNOT COMPLY WITH THY DEMAND. ONCE TAKEN—

Cade jabbed his wand into the coals. Then he repeated the gesture, stabbing over and over, forcing sparks from the coals and anguished wails from the demon.

"You listen to me, you hellspawn motherfucker. You know who I am, and you know what I can do. So when I tell you that I will make it my fucking mission in life to devise torments worse than any ever inflicted on your kind by a mortal, you had best believe I will fucking do it. To the best of my knowledge, no karcist has ever torn a demon to shreds using just magick, but I vow in the name of thy eternal and most unforgiving father, the Emperor SATAN MEKRATRIG, that I *will* find a way. Do you fucking *hear* me, SEIR?"

Another thrust of Cade's wand into the coals put the beast on its front knees and left it baying like a gutshot wolf under a full moon. When at last Cade pulled back his wand, the demon glared at him with eyes that brimmed with cold hatred and unspeakable suffering.

IF I RETURN THY PRECIOUS JACKET, WILL YOU CEASE THIS TORMENT?

"Verily, I pledge it. But only if thou complies instanter."

The demon's tail thrashed up and over its back—and from the scorpion-stinger flew Cade's beloved bomber jacket, the one given to him by the crew of the *Silver Sadie* as thanks for saving their lives after their B-17 was shot down over enemy territory. The jacket landed just outside the circle, intact and unblemished. "I thank thee for thy compliance, great SEIR. And now I compel thee, as per our compact, back under my yoke."

Before the demon could protest, Cade drew its essence out of the bounding triangle and pulled it inside himself. The infusion of demonic power was almost narcotic in its thrill. Even knowing the pains it would bring, Cade still welcomed its return.

Outside the circle, the swirl of noxious fumes melted away, and the room went quiet.

Briet glared at Cade with horror and fury. "You risked violating a demonic compact over a *jacket*? Are you out of your fucking mind?"

"What can I say?" He shrugged at her. "I love only three things in this world. Miles and that jacket are two of them."

She looked flabbergasted but intrigued. "And the third?"

He didn't want to bare his soul to Briet, but the truth was too painful to hold inside.

"I didn't know I loved it 'til it was gone."

<hr />

A decent meal and a hot bath had worked wonders for Anja's frazzled nerves. She'd had no idea how much stress and anxiety she had been harboring until the ministrations of the monks coaxed it from her. In their care she had felt safe and yet somehow anonymous. Not one of the orange-robed members of the brotherhood had spoken to her since her arrival. The most involved interaction she had enjoyed after passing through the front gate had been warm smiles coupled with bows of polite greeting at dinner, and more of the same after she had been shown to the baths and then granted sole access to them.

After she had left the baths, she had been met by Brother Tenzin. "This way, Sister," was all he had said while beckoning her to follow him, and yet those three simple words had made Anja feel respected and welcomed. She felt as if she belonged in Key Gompa.

He escorted her to a small but comfortably appointed room in one of the monastery's uppermost buildings. It was small and sparsely furnished. A narrow pine-frame bed had a thin, firm mattress. An old but beautiful handmade

Persian rug covered the middle of the rosewood floor. There was no art on the walls of white plaster. A single window looked north toward the snow-dusted Himalayas. Opposite the bed was a freestanding cedar wardrobe for her things.

Anja considered introducing her head to the twin pillows on top of her mattress when she was startled back to full alertness by a knock at her door. She straightened her back and put on a proud air. "Yes?"

The oaken door opened with a squeak. Khalîl peeked past it. "May I come in?"

"Please," Anja said. She stepped aside for the white-haired master karcist. He shuffled into her room, closed the door behind him, and then cast approving looks in several directions. "Yes," he muttered. "Good, good." He faced Anja. "Settling in, I see."

"I have no complaints," Anja said, intending it as high praise.

Khalîl sat on the bed. He looked into Anja's eyes. "The Iron Codex," he said.

"What of it?" She hesitated to say too much about the precious grimoire.

"You've brought it this far," he said. "Show it to me."

She shook her head. "I keep it hidden," she lied. "In case I am ever captured."

The elderly Arabic man cracked a knowing smirk. "Anja—who do you think gave that tome to Adair? You really think I can't sense its presence?" In spite of a rheumy quality to his eyes, his gaze remained incisive. "It's the key to your future. Show it to me."

Can I trust him? she wondered. *At this point, can I afford not to?*

Perhaps reading Anja's reluctance, Khalîl adopted a gentler tone. "Let me guess: You've had trouble translating the parts of the book that are written in proto-Enochian." It was a correct deduction, and he seemed to react to some tell that Anja hadn't realized she possessed. "It's a common problem among karcists," the master continued. "No demon can help you learn proto-Enochian. It's the kind of knowledge that must be passed on from master to disciple."

"Cade seemed to learn it easily enough," Anja said.

Khalîl nodded. "Likely one of his gifts as a *nikraim*."

Just being able to talk about the codex after keeping it a secret for so long brought Anja a feeling of great relief. The master's easygoing manner helped to set her at ease; somehow, she knew that it would be all right for her to confide in him. "You are correct." She undid the clasp on her necklace. After she removed it from her neck, she set it on the bed beside Khalîl and opened the cover of her cameo. "Sit back," she advised the old man.

In her mind she recited the charm of reversal to undo the enchantment she had placed upon the codex, and then she snapped her fingers.

With a blink and a flash, the Iron Codex appeared on the bed in front of Khalîl. Though he must have been expecting it, the abrupt manifestation still made him whoop and recoil. Then he smiled and laughed warmly as he touched the tome of iron-bound leather. "Marvelous! You shrank it and hid it in a cameo all this time? How?"

"One of the talents of TAQLATH," Anja said. "A spirit from the Arabic texts."

"I know of that demon. How did you know its gift would work on the codex?"

"The adept who tutored me," Anja said. She recalled the gentle soul she had loved like an older brother—and whose vitality she had been forced by Master Adair to steal in order to save Cade Martin's life. "Stefan Van Ausdall. He used that charm during the war to sneak the codex back to us from enemy territory."

An approving nod from the old master. "Most clever!" He whispered charms of protection under his breath while he unfastened the clasps on the tome and opened it. He spread it open on the bed between himself and Anja. "It's been centuries since last I saw this book." His mood turned wistful as he looked up at Anja. "I entrusted it to Adair because I knew better than to let it fall into the hands of Kein Engel." He flipped the pages with slow care. Then he stopped and let his fingertips caress a vellum page. "Have you ever used this book for magick?"

"I have," Anja confessed. She reached down and turned pages until she arrived at the one and only spell in the book that she had ever executed. "I used it to bring Cade back from the Abyss after he sacrificed himself to close the hellmouth in Dresden." Feeling self-conscious, as if Khalîl might accuse her of boasting, she added, "Master Adair had to walk me through most of it. But once he helped me translate the text, I was able to draw the glyphs myself."

"Splendid," Khalîl said. "This gives us a foundation on which to build. Using this as our touchstone, I will teach you all that I know about proto-Enochian. Once you master the basics of the old angelic language, the rest of this book will reveal itself to you."

Anja found that a tempting notion but also a frightening one. "And once it does," she asked, "what will I find?"

"The power that you were born to wield. Your *birthright*."

His promise filled her head with questions and her heart with hope. Before she could decide which side of her nature to indulge, their conversation was interrupted by a clanging of bells from somewhere outside. She looked toward the window. "What is that?"

"The bell for the front gate." Khalîl stood. Mustering a beatific smile, he added, "It seems that Key Gompa welcomes another honored guest this day."

Trudging in knee-high snow and delirious with hunger, Luis stood shivering outside the gateway. He had no idea where he was, only that he had followed a woman here by tracking her footprints down deserted roads. Icicles clung to his hair and eyebrows, and to the scruff that had grown on his face since his journey had begun nearly two weeks earlier.

Winter had done its best to abuse him. Days of sunlight on snow had nearly blinded him; nights of frozen wind numbed his bare hands and thinly shod feet and left him all but insensate. He had a faded recollection of cloaking himself in holy invisible fire—but that gift had left him somewhere along his path. Now he stood alone in the darkness, his strength spent.

The canvas strap of his tool roll bit into his shoulder and stretched taut against his chest. Shivering and empty in front of the gateway, he couldn't remember why he was here. Behind him was a road flanked by prayer flags; his footprints formed a drunkenly weaving trail that disappeared beyond billowing curtains of snow and ice.

But I must go forward, he told himself. *Always forward.*

Out of the white chaos there appeared figures in robes of orange. They met him at the gateway, looked him over, and then they bowed to him. He returned the courtesy and nearly fell over. The two men helped Luis forward. Within a few paces they had stretched his arms across their shoulders so that they could carry him up the road to the great hill of houses beyond.

He wanted to thank them, but his throat was dry, his voice lost.

The closer they brought him to light and warmth, the more tenuous his hold on consciousness became. He had found sanctuary. Salvation. Refuge. Now he wanted nothing more than to surrender himself to it, for as long as it would harbor him.

A doorway filled with light loomed large directly ahead.

Luis looked up at the cluster of buildings. Gazing down at him from a high window was the Russian karcist.

His last thought as he lost his hold on the waking world was to wonder why the dark-haired woman with the facial scar looked so unhappy to see him.

FEBRUARY 11, PART II

Slashes of light and pools of shadow—the natural habitats of spies. Miles Franklin moved through the night like a ghost, his Walther carried low, safety off, held in both hands. Its balance felt off kilter because of the silencer attached to its muzzle. He hoped he didn't need to use the pistol tonight. He wouldn't have hesitated to pull the trigger in enemy territory, but on allied soil deadly force was not only a last resort, it was a tactic reserved for moments of true desperation.

His insulated wire cutters had made quick work of the electric fence along the perimeter of the Los Alamos Scientific Laboratory campus. Once inside, he had kept to the darkness between buildings as much as possible, while making his way toward the building that Briet had marked on a hand-drawn map.

Near a road that threaded through most of the campus, he was forced to hunker into the scrub as a patrol jeep cruised toward him. Miles planted his face in the dirt and put his trust in his desert camouflage fatigues and matte-black boots and cap. He caught the bluish-white glare of a searchlight as it swept over his position. There was no change in the humming of the jeep's engine as it passed by, no whine of brakes. Within seconds the vehicle was twenty meters away and receding into the night.

Too close, he confessed to himself as he got up.

Parked cars, trash cans, and clusters of shrubbery gave Miles cover the rest of the way to the rear entrance of the building that Briet insisted was proofed against demon-toting magicians such as herself and Cade. *I bet they yoked spirits today just to get out of this op,* Miles brooded.

He unfastened a clasp that held shut a panel of black cloth on his flank. Attached to its underside was an assortment of high-tech tools developed by

MI6's Q Branch. This particular set was intended for defeating and bypassing locks and alarms.

Miles studied the door and its frame. The lock on the knob was simple enough, but a keyhole on a pad beside the door indicated that the door had a secondary alarm system, one that required a separate access. Miles checked the side of the aluminum shell that enclosed the key port, and he found a brand logo: Black Diamond Security.

Ah, yes. He recalled this model from his training. *The PS-900, I believe.*

He selected a steel skeleton key from his gear set, wired it to a small portable battery, and inserted it into the auxiliary keyhole. Sparks shot from a pair of contact pads above the door, and then came a small puff of smoke. *One down, one to go.*

Picking the door's regular lock was child's play.

He opened the door with care and let his pistol lead the way inside.

The lights were low. Most of the facility appeared to be dark and quiet. Miles eased the door closed behind him and then he prowled forward, his Walther steadied with both hands at eye level. He followed the corridor around a turn, and then down another long passage to a four-way intersection. He noted the signage around him. Back the way from which he had come lay the facilities and engineering section. Straight ahead of him was the exit. To his left were secured laboratories. To his right were the administrative offices.

Footsteps approached from the corridor on his right.

Miles slowed and shallowed his breathing. He listened. There was only a single set of footfalls. Just one guard. *If I'm quick,* he told himself, *this doesn't have to end badly for anyone.*

He put his back to the wall and raised his hand to striking position.

The guard turned the corner. Miles backhanded the man in the nose, a clean hard shot. The guard's eyes watered, and he staggered half a step, stunned. Miles seized the man's arm and judo-flipped him onto his back. With a quick palm strike Miles slammed the back of the guard's skull against the tiled floor. The guard sank like a stone into unconsciousness.

He'll have a wicked headache tomorrow, Miles consoled himself as he dragged the unconscious man into the shadows, *but he'll live.*

A quick check of all the corridors satisfied Miles that he was alone inside the building. He dug his walkie-talkie from a pocket on his fatigues and switched on the two-way radio. Pressing the transmit switch, he said, "Blue Jay, this is Sparrow. Am in the nest. Over."

He released the switch and awaited the planned reply.

Cade answered over the radio, *"Copy that, Sparrow. Stand by for Starling."* A moment later, Briet's voice issued from the walkie-talkie. *"Sparrow, this is Starling. Report. Over."*

"Sky's the limit, Starling. Going to the Castle to find a Wolf. Over."

It was a simplistic code, but it got the job done. Miles knew he was looking for any files about Project Castle or a scientist named Wolfgang Krueger.

He moved down the hallway, noting the signs beside the closed doors. He stopped next to one that was labeled simply ADMINISTRATION. It was locked.

Not for long, Miles gloated as he reached for his lock-picking tools.

Fifteen seconds later he was inside the office and rooting through its file cabinets. Most of them were stuffed with banal paperwork—requisitions for office supplies, reimbursement reports for travel expenses, and authorizations for overtime compensation for teamsters and other unionized personnel. Then Miles set his sights on a separate office at the back of the room.

The director's office. Miles let himself in. Its furniture was just as ugly and utilitarian as that in the outer office, and the cramped workspace had no window, but at least it had a door and a frosted window, and therefore privacy.

It also had a touch of decorative flair: on the wall hung a print of a Renaissance painting in an oddly bulky frame. *How bloody conspicuous,* Miles mused as he pulled the picture's frame away from the wall. As he'd expected, one side of the thick frame was attached to the wall by hinges, and it swung outward to reveal a combination-lock safe nested in the concrete wall.

Q Branch to the rescue once more, Miles imagined he heard his quartermaster crowing. Sorting through some of the specialized gear he had brought for this op, he selected an enhanced stethoscope with an adhesive cup, which he affixed to the safe's door. Listening with great care as he turned the dial on the door, he heard the clicking of the tumblers in motion behind the steel, and the gentle *clack* of contact as the gears found the locking mechanisms and guided them into the open position. In just under half a minute, the safe's door was open.

The first file he pulled off the stack was labeled PROJECT CASTLE.

He thumbed his radio's transmitter. "Starling, I've found the Castle. Over."

"Good work, Sparrow. Keep an eye open for the Wolf. Over."

"Roger, Starling." He laid the open file folder on the office's desk and snapped photos of every pair of pages with his miniaturized camera. In between shots he pushed the halves of the camera together, and the internal spring advanced the embedded roll of film by one frame.

Even as he documented the file's contents, he skimmed the pages, looking for any sign of the name Wolfgang Krueger. It was nowhere to be found. There were dozens of other scientists attached to Project Castle, but none whose names seemed even remotely similar to the one about which Briet had asked. After he photographed the last two pages in the file, he put it back in the safe, and then he checked to see what else there might be of interest.

Most of the other files seemed irrelevant to Miles's investigation. Until he arrived at one marked PERSONNEL RECORDS—CONFIDENTIAL.

This sounds promising.

He pulled it from the stack and laid it open on the desk.

It was a thin file with only a few scientists' dossiers inside. As soon as Miles saw them, however, he understood why they had been segregated from the lab's main files. All of the profiles and curricula vitae inside this folder had been acquired from Operation Paperclip, an American intelligence initiative conducted in the aftermath of the Second World War. Its purpose had been to recruit top scientists in various fields from the collapsed Nazi regime and bring them to the United States, so that they could continue their work on its behalf.

The second-most racist nation on earth stole the greatest minds of the most racist nation on earth, Miles noted glumly, *and no one thought it might be a problem someday. God help us.*

There were only a few scientists in the program who had been attached to it through Operation Paperclip, and of those only one had changed his name as part of his immigration to the United States: nuclear physicist Dr. Wolfgang Krueger had embarked upon his new life under the desert sun wrapped in the squeaky-clean persona of Dr. Aaron Rosenberg, Ph.D.

Miles photographed Krueger's top-secret dossier, and then he put away the file and closed the safe—but not before he jotted down Rosenberg's local address in Los Alamos.

Making his way out of the building, he keyed his radio's transmitter.

"Sparrow to Blue Jay. Have the motor running when I land. Over."

Cade answered, *"What's the word, Sparrow? Coming in hot? Over."*

"Negative," Miles said. "I have a fix on the Wolf—and its lair is local."

Self-exile was proving more palatable than Dragan had expected. He had thought he would miss daily interactions, the distractions of a social life, but the more time he spent away from society, away from so-called civilization, the more he came to appreciate solitude. Isolated as he was, he finally had time to read, think, and just exist without the imposition of others' needs upon his time and consciousness. Casting himself out of the modern world had proved a blessing.

The day's work on the bunker was completed, and outside his quarters the compound was quiet. Inside his sanctum, he sat in a careworn vintage armchair and propped up his feet on a mismatched but still welcome ottoman. Outside his window a tempest howled, but the fire crackling in his hearth filled his residence with pleasant fragrances of woodsmoke and promised him comfort through the night.

He savored a mouthful of lush red wine from the Languedoc and considered embarking on a new reading of Milton's *Paradise Lost* to quiet his mind before retiring for the evening.

Then the voice inside his head came alive.

As it spoke to him, the flames inside the fireplace danced in wild sympathy. «*Our lab in Los Alamos is breached,*» it declared. «*Our asset is exposed.*»

At once all thoughts of respite fled from Dragan's mind. *Who did this?*

«*A British spy. The one who watches over the American mage.*»

The ones who escaped, Dragan realized. He sprang from his chair and put on his suit coat. *Someone is helping them. Someone who knows our methods.*

«*Indubitably. All that we have worked for is at risk.*»

Dragan moved quickly, abandoning his wine and invoking the clarity-enhancing talents of PELIZAR to clear his head in preparation for imminent magickal labors. He left his sitting room, and in the foyer he lifted his phone's receiver from its cradle. He tapped the cradle's bars repeatedly until he heard the operator's voice.

"*Switchboard,*" a man said.

"This is Dragan. Wake my tanists and tell them to come at once."

"*Understood.*"

Outside, the storm's ferocity worsened. Dragan was thankful that he didn't need to brave the weather to reach his conjuring room in the bunker. Instead he walked to the back of his residence, opened a door, and descended a flight of concrete stairs to the basement, which was connected to the warren of underground tunnels that linked all of the structures in the compound.

He arrived outside his conjuring room only moments ahead of his senior tanist, the ever-reliable Juliana Hess. The blond woman's features, severe under the best of circumstances, appeared downright intimidating as she approached in response to an emergency summons. In front of Dragan she snapped to attention. "Orders, sir?"

"Prepare the room," Dragan said. "Our man in Los Alamos has been compromised."

Hess nodded. "Yes, Master." After a brief moment of consideration, she asked, "Shall I prepare the room for an extraction? Or a neutralization?"

"The latter," Dragan said. "If our enemies have found Wolfgang . . . none of them can be allowed to see another dawn."

⁓

The house sat at the terminus of a dead-end street. Its yard was fenced, its front gate locked. Even from the street Cade could see that its windows and front door were protected by glyphs and wards of PAIMON, the demonic patron spirit to whom his late master Adair had been pledged. The home of Dr. Wolfgang Krueger, aka Dr. Aaron Rosenberg, was not a soft target.

Cade exorcised the ward on the gate with a wave of his wand. Banished the invisible hellhound prowling the grounds inside the fence with a thrust from ARMAEL's spectral blade. And the ward of protection on the door? He blew it and the door to bits with one bolt of lightning.

A magickal barrage struck Cade's shield as soon as he entered the house. Cade deflected a crackling stream of electricity that ripped smoking wounds in the living room's walls, sofa, and ceiling. Next came a jet of green flames that Cade absorbed through AZAEL's versatile shield.

Krueger vomited a cloud of hornets. Cade engulfed the swarm with his own fire, filling the living room with the horrid stench of burnt bugs. Then he used the hand of JEPHISTO to snap Krueger's wand in half before locking the unseen demon's claws around the Nazi's throat.

The Nazi broke free of the demon's hold, and with a wave of his hand he brought down part of the ceiling on top of Cade, who dodged the debris by pressing himself against a wall. He looked for Krueger. The man was retreating through the kitchen, heading for the back door—

A flash of indigo light and numbing cold splintered the back door, which blew inward and knocked Krueger onto his back. He scuttled backward like a frightened crab as Briet strode into his house through the broken rear doorway, a dark nimbus twisting around her own wand. Her rat familiar scurried in behind her and bounded up onto the kitchen countertop.

Briet smirked at Krueger. "And where do you think you're going?" She pointed her wand at him, and with a flick of her wrist she pinned the slight, balding man to the kitchen ceiling.

"Fancy," Cade said, admiring her handiwork.

"I have my moments," she said. Turning her attention to Krueger, she asked, "You're no dabbler. Who trained you?"

Krueger spat at Briet. She pointed a finger, and Cade could almost feel the demonic jab she landed on the uncooperative German. A subsequent blow from an unseen fist broke Krueger's nose and shattered the lenses of his wireframe glasses. He spat out blood.

"Who trained you?" Briet asked again.

"OTO," Krueger said.

"Pfft," Cade snorted in derision. "*Ordo Templi Orientis?* Not a chance. They aren't even dabblers. Just a bunch of hacks who bought Aleister Crowley's bullshit. Try again, moron."

Krueger ignored Cade and instead cast an imploring look at Briet. "Why are you doing this? We're on the same side, you and I."

"Whatever gave you that mistaken idea?"

"Because you know my true master's name," Krueger said. "Just as he told me yours, and that of the master who trained you. You are Briet, the last disciple of the great Kein Engel—"

Briet tormented Krueger with a dramatic twist of her wand. "Don't ever speak that name to me again," she commanded the man writhing on the ceiling. "Or I will pull every organ from your body and show them all to you, one by one, before I let you die."

"There's the Nazi bitch I remember from the war," Cade snarked.

Briet shot Cade an ugly look, then put her focus back on her captive. "Your master's name. Tell me, or this *will* get worse, I promise you."

"I serve the Master of the Black Sun," Krueger said. "Herr Dragan Dalca."

Cade joined the interrogation. "What does the Black Sun want with atomic research?"

Krueger flashed a bloody smile as he looked at Briet. "*She* knows. Magick . . . science. Both are part of the spectrum of knowledge. One day, the twain shall meet. With my help, Herr Dalca and the Black Sun have taken steps to engineer that meeting sooner rather than later." His smile became a mad grin. "*Much* sooner."

The ominous implications of Krueger's boast put a chill down Cade's spine. He detached his walkie-talkie from his belt and pressed the transmitter. "Miles, get in here. Bring the journal."

Seconds later Miles hurried inside the house through the open back door. He carried the Odessa journal under his arm. "Best step it up, mate," he said. "I think a neighbor called in the law to sort out the ruckus you two kicked up." He handed the journal to Cade.

Cade opened the leather-bound tome to a page filled with arcane fusions of magickal glyphs and scientific notations. He held it up toward Krueger. "Is this your work?"

"Not just my *work*," Krueger said, full of pride. "My *masterpiece*."

"Some masterpiece," Cade said. "It's gibberish."

"So is magick to those who don't understand it," Krueger said. "But when my work blooms, the world will know what the marriage of science and magick can achieve."

Cade attuned his thoughts to his cadre of yoked demons and singled out a finder of treasures and secrets. HECATOR, *I think Krueger is hiding documentation of his plans somewhere in this house. Search it, and bring his secrets to me with all haste.*

AS THOU COMMANDS.

Raising his wand to get Krueger's attention, Cade said, "Tell us all about this grand masterwork. Right here, right now. Because if you don't, we'll take you into the desert and continue this for as long as—"

"All you need to know," Krueger said from the ceiling, "is that I was the architect of the approaching black dawn." His last two words provoked a wince from Briet—a reaction that troubled Cade, though he was at first uncertain why. Then HECATOR returned like a chill gust of fetid air, and it deposited at Cade's feet a yard-long cardboard tube stuffed with rolled-up papers.

Miles scooped up the tube and pulled out its contents. He spread the poster-sized blueprints on the kitchen table. "These are copies of the plans for an atomic device," he said.

"Correction," Krueger said. "Plans for a hydrogen bomb. The most powerful ever made."

Briet asked, "You stole these for Dragan?"

Krueger looked offended. "I am no thief. I am a physicist. And the architect of doom."

There was fear in Miles's voice as he called out, "Cade? You should see this."

Cade hurried to Miles's side and studied the schematics. At the top of the sheet was a project code name: CASTLE BRAVO. Most of the mathematics and physics notations he saw made no sense to him, but he recognized passages from the Odessa journal—and saw that they had been superimposed onto the schematics of the Castle Bravo device, and into the blueprints for some kind of structure described as a "shot cab."

"He's right," Cade said to Briet. "He hasn't just been *building* Castle Bravo for the Black Sun—he's been *sabotaging* it."

Briet's horror became rage. She gave her wand a fresh twist, and on the ceiling Krueger yowled and groaned in agony. "What kind of sabotage?" she demanded. "To what end?" She filled Krueger's gut with white-hot lightning and shouted, "What have you done?"

The mad physicist laughed in spite of her torture.

Only after she relented did he reply, "I don't want to spoil the surprise."

Sensing that they were now officially in over their heads, Cade turned to Miles. "We've got to find that bomb and undo whatever the fuck he did to it."

Krueger's laugh turned maniacal. "Too late, Boy Scout. Castle Bravo is *long* gone. It left the country a *month* ago." Another grin of bloodstained teeth. "From now until it detonates, the instrument of Armageddon is safely under the protection of the United States military."

"Pack up the blueprints," Cade said to Miles. "We'll need to study them if we want to undo whatever he's done." To Briet he added, "Let the shitbag down and get him ready to travel. I'm not done with his dumb ass by a country mile."

Briet nodded. Krueger fell to the linoleum floor and hit with a loud smack. She was pulling out a length of rope to bind the man when an icy gust blew through the house, and all the lights went out. The air turned sharp with the bite of sulfur.

Hairs stood tall on the nape of Cade's neck. A prickling sensation raised gooseflesh on his arms. He tensed for battle. "We have company. The demonic kind."

Lying trussed on the floor, Krueger said, "My master approaches." With a vacant smile of true insanity he added, "I hope you all came prepared to die."

❧

Fear and loathing washed over Briet in cold, putrid waves, as tangible as if she stood chest-deep in an oily sea. A deathly silence pervaded the house. As she put her back toward Cade's, she saw veils of frost creep swiftly across the windows and the glass in Krueger's framed photos. "This is bad," she whispered to the American. "It's all around us."

"I feel it," Cade said. He drew his wand and searched high and low for the coming attack. "Miles, watch Krueger. Keep him between me and Briet."

"Right," Miles said, kneeling to press his Walther into Krueger's back.

All the glass in the room had gone opaque with frost. A soft creaking that seemed to come from all directions at once became louder. Fissures spread up and down the walls, branching off and expanding, and then they traversed the hardwood floor. As the fissures began to bleed, Briet heard the buzzing of flies close overhead. "Cade—?"

"I know," he said. He was about to say more when the screaming started.

Bloodcurdling wails filled the room as luminous horrors appeared, swirling like a vortex around the trio and their prisoner. Cade hurled lightning at a serpentine apparition, but the bolt sliced through it without effect and lit one wall of the room on fire. Briet tried to snare a lizardlike specter with Kushiel's burning whip, but the demonic weapon found nothing to hold.

Even Miles could tell something was wrong. "Talk to me, mate!"

"Demons," Cade said. "Loose and hunting." His ghost-serpent foe lunged at him, and he narrowly blocked it with his magickal shield. "We're not dueling a karcist—"

"We're the targets of a sending," Briet said, finishing Cade's explanation as she deflected a lunge from the spirit-reptile with her own shield. "We need—"

A great cloud of fog blossomed beneath Krueger and resolved into a misty maw surrounded by flailing tentacles. One suckered limb swatted Cade across the room; he hit the wall and made a ragged crater in the drywall. Another tentacle snaked around Briet's ankles and yanked her off her feet. She landed on her back and lay stunned with the wind knocked out of her. Miles unloaded his Walther into the center of the vaporous abomination, to no effect.

The great maw of smoke slammed shut, at once solid. Miles and Krueger both roared in pain and terror, and in a matter of seconds they stood in a widening pool of their own blood.

A tentacle above Briet turned corporeal. She conjured the scimitar of Lepidaros and slashed at the snaking limb, only to have it revert to mist as the demonic blade made contact.

This was the old-school way of magick—dispatching demons to do one's dirty work while remaining safe, hidden, possibly on the far side of the world. Despite all the times Briet had employed such tactics, she had never considered she might end up the target of a sending.

As she tried to stand, a terrible weight slammed into her from behind. The force of the blow knocked her face-first onto the blood-slicked floor. Then a scale-covered muscle coiled around her throat and began to squeeze with lethal force.

A black blur leapt from the shadows. Trixim landed on Briet's shoulder and sank its prominent incisors into the tentacle that was choking her. The familiar's red eyes blazed bright as its tiny paws clawed through the tentacle's scales and ripped into the flesh beneath. Black demon blood oozed from the limb as it went slack and released Briet—and then another one lashed out and snagged Trixim in a crushing grip. The familiar let out a pitiful squeak, and then the demon hurled the broken rat into a brutal collision with a wall.

Tears burned in Briet's eyes. "Trixim!"

Her familiar lay on the floor, not moving.

Briet wheeled toward the monstrosity in the middle of the room. Blue fire and lightning leapt from the crack of the demonic whip in her left hand; needles dripping with poison brewed in Hell's deepest pit flew from her right palm. Black rays of pain and paralysis shot from her eyes, and a cone of freezing vapor geysered from her screaming mouth.

All of it ripped into the tempest of demons circling the three men.

The spirits recoiled and then faltered, their assault disrupted just long enough for Cade to recover his bearings and finish them, with white light pouring from his hand as he bellowed, "By the holy names ADONAI, ELOHIM, and JEHOVAM, I banish thee! I adjure thee by name: ORCUS, SYNAPHAEL, and TAMALION, begone! I command thee by the names most blessed, MICHAEL, GABRIEL, and TETRAGRAMMATON, diminish as the wax melts before the flame, scatter as smoke before a gale, and be vanquished, wicked spirits, before the might of JEHOVAH!"

The demons howled, and in a flash of hellfire they vanished, leaving a cloud of black ash to disperse into the room and settle upon everyone and everything in it.

Cade fell to his knees beside his friend. "Miles! Are you okay? Talk to me, Miles!"

The handsome Brit didn't stir, not even when Cade shook him.

Lying on the floor, drenched in blood from countless open wounds, Krueger snickered. "You will never stop what is coming." His words gurgled through a mouth filled with red foamy spittle. "You are too late." With a horrible rattling gasp, Krueger went limp, and the malevolent gleam in his eyes faded.

Outside the house, sirens wailed in the distance.

Briet kneeled by the back wall of the living room, hunched over Trixim. The rat's body was limp, his fragile spine broken. Gone was the red fire in his eyes; silenced was his heart. Briet picked him up, cradled him against her chest, and stroked his black fur. Her tears cut trails through the fresh blood coating her cheeks.

No more sneaking you treats under the table.

No more toting you in my pockets to matinee movies.

You deserved better than this.

The sirens grew closer.

Cade's hand arrived gently on Briet's shoulder. "We need to go."

She didn't want to look up. Didn't want to give him the satisfaction of seeing her tearstained eyes. "Let them come."

"I'm not getting into a fight with police, and neither should you." He squatted beside her. "Krueger's dead, and Miles is too badly hurt for us to treat. We'll have to go without them."

"You'd abandon your friend?"

"Letting the cops take him to a hospital is his best chance for survival," Cade said. Then he adopted a gentler tone. "If you want to bring Trixim, bring him. We'll honor him properly once we're away from here. But we need to go, Briet. *Now.*"

Looking past her grief, she knew he was right. She held Trixim to her bosom as she stood. "The car's out back."

"If you don't mind," Cade said, "I'll drive."

"I don't care."

He led her out of the wrecked house. They got into her car, which Cade concealed with charms of invisibility and silence. Moving at a slow roll they slipped past an arriving parade of cherry-top police cruisers. It all felt unreal to Briet.

She watched in the side-view mirror as the police cars screeched to a halt outside Krueger's house, and a swarm of cops charged inside through the blasted-open front door. Then Cade turned a corner, and there was nothing left to see in the mirror but the black of night.

The road unwound ahead of them, a mystery revealed in motion by their headlights. Succumbing to shock and exhaustion, Briet let the blur of the center line and the hum of tires on asphalt hypnotize her.

Closing her eyes to hide more tears, she asked Cade, "Where are we going?"

Darkness drank her in as she heard him say, "Anywhere but here."

FEBRUARY 12

Iron chains pulled Anja's limbs apart spread-eagle on the hot tropical sand, a human X-marks-the-spot. She had been staked to the end of a sandbar with nothing but ocean on three sides of her and above her only sky. Resting on her belly was an hourglass, the final grains of sand in its upper chamber on the verge of tumbling through its neck to join all that had gone before.

The rising sun hung low in the sky, barely kissing the horizon.

Time slowed as Anja watched the last grain of sand inside the hourglass pass its point of no return and plummet through the neck—and then she was a second sun, a nova born of science and darkness. She cooked the beach into glass, transformed seawater into vapor, reduced coral reefs to superheated dust. Fire incarnate, she embodied the unity of creation and destruction.

Her crown of smoke and flame towered over the earth, and her feet broke through the foundations of this world into another, into the uncreated womb of night mortals knew as Hell, Sheol, or Hades. Its gates, so long invincible, buckled before her might, and its innumerable horde of the unclean, its legions of the Fallen, ascended once more, free at last to slake their eternal thirst for blood and chaos—

Anja woke with a gasp of terror and sat up in her bed.

There was a damp chill in the air. Her hearth's fire had dwindled in the hours since she had gone to bed. Outside her window the blizzard continued to mourn with atonal howls, and fat snowflakes cast out of a black heaven piled themselves high on the stone ledge, against the glass.

Key Gompa was cloaked in silence and serenity.

And then she heard it: an unearthly music, as if a drunkard were playing a flute.

The song was faint and intermittent but haunting. Somehow its erratic,

bizarre melody repeated itself, at least in part, which suggested that its ato-
nality and chaotic tempo were deliberate.

Too shaken to return to sleep but afraid to brave the cold beyond her bed,
Anja reached under the blankets to find the clothes she had tucked there, so
that they would be warm from her body heat when she needed them. She
pulled on trousers and a long-sleeved shirt, then cast aside her bedcovers and
swung her legs out of bed. Her stocking feet found the boots she had left at
her bedside, and she laced them up. She pulled her tousled hair into a pony-
tail as she got up and walked to the door.

For a moment she wondered whether her door would be locked. It wasn't.

She opened it and skulked down a short corridor to the staircase. There she
stopped and listened. The music that taunted her echoed from somewhere far
below. Drawn by its delicate dissonance she descended one staircase after another, followed the sound down deserted corridors and through dark passages, aware that with each step the air grew colder and smelled more richly
of turned earth, of moss and mildew, of decay and renewal.

To wander without knowing why—it felt to Anja as if she had risen from
one dream into another, as if it might be that none of this were anything
but a phantasm from her subconscious. Soon she found herself underground,
exploring paths hewn through bedrock, delving deep into tunnels beneath
the monastery that seemed, based on the lack of footprints in their carpets of
dust, to have been rarely visited. Down here the music was everywhere, resounding off the stone walls. Anja wondered if it might be a siren song, a
temptation for the unwary. If it was one she was meant to resist, it was proving
to be a test she seemed destined to fail.

When there seemed no deeper roads to follow, she arrived at the music's
source.

The expansive chamber was a tall dome. Its walls were tiled with a geometric mosaic that had been crafted from numerous hues of white marble. Except
for a short walkway that led from the entrance to a wide circular platform in
the center of the space, there was no floor, only a pool of water. All the light
in the chamber came from floating, shifting bands of radiance beneath the
water's surface, yet the pool's cloudy murk made it impossible for Anja to gauge
its depth.

Upon the platform was a bamboo and rattan papasan chair whose generous cushion was the same deep orange as the robes Anja had seen on the
monks when she had arrived.

On the chair, garbed in robes of white, was a woman who looked impossibly ancient yet timeless. Her hair was silver, and her eyes seemed to drill through Anja's façade of courage. She beckoned Anja with a curl of withered fingers.

"Come closer," she said, her voice a whisper amplified by the dome.

As Anja crossed the threshold and set foot on the walkway, the atonal music ceased and the colors of the light shimmering up from the pool changed from amber to emerald.

She halted when she reached the center platform.

The crone studied her with naked curiosity. "You are all that Khalîl promised."

"Who are you?" The question landed with more hostility than Anja had intended.

The old woman seemed not to mind. "I am the Vate Pythia." She let her answer stand on its own, as if it were supposed to clarify matters for Anja.

"I do not know what that means," Anja confessed.

An enigmatic smile of brown and yellow teeth. "It means I am an Oracle. Or, if one wanted to be more truthful, or even just more precise . . . I am the *last* Oracle."

"You speak prophecies?"

"I grant guidance to those who seek me out, and who are deserving of my aid."

"Is that supposed to be me?"

The old woman tilted her head in an almost birdlike manner. "You *are* here, yes?"

"With that crazy music of yours echoing through the monastery, it is a wonder you didn't summon everyone on the hill."

The crone waggled a bony index finger. "Only those for whom I hold a prophecy can hear the Cry of the Fates." She pointed at Anja. "And only the worthy can follow it to me."

She has an answer for everything, Anja observed. *Of course, she would not be much of an Oracle if she did not.* Willing to play along, Anja asked, "What is your prophecy for me?"

"You will be the one to rise where others have fallen," the Vate Pythia said. "You will be the shadow on the sun, and the flame in the darkness. Not for you the shackles of the Covenant. You shall seize the great Art with both hands and make *all* its secrets thine." Her countenance darkened. "Or . . . you will turn away from the Art. Turn your back on the world. And the world you deny will burn in flames everlasting, and all its souls will be delivered into Oblivion, their collective promise extinguished, their futures betrayed." After a breath, she concluded, "Which of these futures comes to pass depends upon what you choose."

Anja stepped backward, at once reminded of the nightmare from which the Oracle's music had saved her. *A world ablaze in flames everlasting. . . .*

"I do not understand," Anja protested. "What choice? When? How will I know?"

"That is for Chronos to reveal. No more can I tell thee. Our audience is done."

The waters began to boil and filled the chamber with steam that reeked of chlorine and stung Anja's eyes. The fumes burned her sinuses, and within seconds she was coughing with such violence she half expected to vomit vital organs.

There was nothing she could do but run.

Anja turned and staggered back across the narrow bridge. She stumbled out of the chamber, back into the bedrock tunnel. Awash in cool, clean air, she fell to her knees and gasped until the burning in her nose and throat abated. She wiped tears from her eyes, looked over her shoulder—and found nothing but a wall of stone.

She forced her hands against it. Searched it for seams, hidden levers, or any sign of the doorway through which she had just passed. If the wall had secrets, it gave up none of them.

Spooked, she stood and backed away from the wall.

What just happened? Did I hallucinate all of that?

She reflected on her meeting with the Vate Pythia. The encounter was oddly lucid in her memory. Every word the Oracle had said, Anja recalled with perfect clarity. She still had no idea what any of it meant, or how she would recognize the pivotal moment of choice that lay ahead of her. All she knew for certain was that she wanted to get away from this place.

Anja turned back the way she had come. Not caring who saw her or what they'd think if they did, she ran as fast as she could, back up countless flights of stairs, until she left the tunnels of Key Gompa and the prophecies of the Vate Pythia far behind.

⌁

Roaming like a ghost in the small hours of the morning, Luis felt lost in the maze of Key Gompa's intersecting corridors. Some stood half exposed to the elements as they stretched between buildings on the hill. Others were nestled well behind and below the monastery's buildings. None of them bore any markings that he could discern, nor did any of the staircases.

Each time he passed a set of stairs, he had to ask himself: *Do I climb, descend, or walk in circles?* Though he recalled that Anja had been housed in one of the upper structures, he couldn't tell from inside whether he was close to her lodgings. So he drifted, pulled onward by insomnia coupled with a sense of mission, until he arrived at a staircase that seemed to lead up to a dead end. He had no way to establish his bearings, but something about the angles of the walls reminded him of the vantage from which Anja had observed his arrival.

A nudge of intuition infected his thoughts. *This way.*

He had taken just two steps up the stairs when Anja asked from behind him, "Where are you going?"

Luis turned and did his best to affect a gentle presence. "I was looking for you."

"Doubtful." She edged toward him. "You were looking for the codex."

"I admit that I wish to speak with you about the codex." He hoped that not trying to deny the obvious might allay some of her hostility. It did not seem to work.

Her fingers curled, testing their strength to make fists. "You came to *steal* the codex."

"Stealing is a sin," he said.

She narrowed her eyes. "So is lying."

So much for deflecting her accusation. He raised his hands beside his chest, a pose of surrender. "I swear before God and His son Jesus Christ, and on the sanctity of my holy vow, that I have come only to speak with you, and not to burgle or do battle with you."

Anja paced toward him, her manner radiating danger. Luis backed away from her. She stopped once she had placed herself between him and the stairway to the upper vantage. "Talk."

He took a moment to consider his rhetorical strategy. "You know, probably better than most, how powerful an artifact the Iron Codex is. Items of such great potential inevitably attract the ambitions of the cruel and the selfish."

"This I know," Anja said.

"Of course you do," Luis said. "You've made many powerful enemies since the end of the war. And that's what concerns the Church: the risk that one of those unscrupulous powers might capture the codex."

"Only the Black Sun has tried to take it," Anja said. "I doubt the Red Star knows of it."

"Not yet, but that's only a matter of time, Miss Kernova." Luis put his hands together in a sign of supplication. "Please think about the risk you take, keeping the codex to yourself when you have such potent foes. Is the risk to innocent souls, perhaps to the entire world, worth whatever advantage you've gleaned from the codex's pages?" He dared to take a half step toward her. "Surely you can see the codex would be safer inside the Vatican?"

Her suspicion soured into contempt. "Safer for who? For me? No. For those I defend? No. For the Nazi dabblers I hunt? Yes, *much* better for them." She stepped to Luis, and her intensity made him flinch. "Always the same sad cry from your kind: 'What if the codex is used for evil?' You never think that in my hands it is used for good. But if I give it to you? Your Church locks it away and never uses it at all. Not for evil, not for *good*. But not fighting for good is the same as surrender." She backed him against a wall. "Why does the Church want the codex *now*? They have not seen it in centuries, but *now* its return is urgent? Why?" She drove home her final words by poking his chest with surprising strength and ferocity. "Maybe because the evil I hunt hits them a bit *close to home*?"

He crossed his arms over his chest to defend himself. "I don't understand."

"I hunt Nazis in South America. How did so many get there? They had *help*. Now I know that help came from *your* church."

Luis shook his head. "No, that's not possible."

"It is *fact*. Your church helped *thousands* of Nazis get fake papers. Helped create the ratlines that took them out of Europe."

"That goes against the official stance of the Roman Catholic Church."

She spit on his feet. "*Lies*. Your church is full of *fascists*." She backed up, perhaps satisfied that Luis was now in too deep a state of dismay to follow her. "You want to keep the codex from falling into the hands of evil?" She turned and said over her shoulder as she vanished up the stairs, "Do not take it back to Rome."

FEBRUARY 13

Cade leaned against the flat front of the Crosley station wagon and warmed his hands over a red-hot anvil. His breath turned to ghosts when he exhaled, thanks to the abandoned barn's damaged roof and rotting walls, which did little to keep out the knifing cold of a Colorado winter.

He felt lucky to have found the barn the night before, after nearly twenty-four hours of driving with stops only for fuel, water, and oversalted snack foods. He had spotted the broken-down structure and its half-collapsed companion farmhouse from the main road. In a rare stroke of good luck, no sooner had he closed the barn doors behind the Crosley than it had begun to snow. The accumulation was wet and heavy, and it had fallen quickly, covering their tracks more thoroughly than even magick could have done.

Briet had spent their shared drive asleep. Cade had seen no point to waking her. Once they were sheltered inside the barn, he'd set himself to work. He had compelled SEIR, his demon of burden, to move the anvil closer to the car. Then he'd employed the fires of XAPHAN to imbue the hunk of iron with Infernal heat, enough to keep him and Briet warm for most of the day. The rest of his labors he had seen to himself: using scrap wood, stones, and packed dirt to patch gaps in the walls, and bundles of straw to fill as many holes in the roof as he could reach.

Now if only we had brought something decent to eat, he lamented.

He heard Briet stir inside the car. She sat up in the backseat, pushing aside the extra layer of his bomber jacket, which he had placed over her the night before. She blinked and looked around, bleary-eyed and drowsy. "Where are we?"

"Southeast Colorado," Cade said. "Middle of fuckin' nowhere."

She turned frantically to and fro, searching the car. "Trixim—?"

"He's out back," Cade said, wreathing himself in a short-lived halo of breath.

Briet clambered out of the car and rushed to Cade's side, incensed. "You buried him?"

"Of course not. It's ten below zero and there's three feet of snow on the ground." He stood and walked around Briet to the open car door. He reached in and pulled out their coats. He handed Briet her trench coat, and then he shrugged into his bomber jacket.

"Come on," he said.

He led her to the barn's back door, which hung at an angle from its rusted but still working hinges. It scraped and squeaked as the pair walked outside, into a path that Cade had shoveled a few hours earlier, after the snowfall had petered out. At the end of the path, in a small circular clearing, stood a two-foot-tall funeral pyre of twigs, kindling, and straw. Atop it, swaddled in a piece of floral-print cloth topped with pink silk roses, was the body of Trixim.

Briet stepped past Cade and stood beside the tiny pyre. She pressed her gloved fingertips to her lips and spent a moment looking verklempt.

Feeling awkward about the silence between them, Cade said, "The wood was easy to find. Most of it was in the barn, so it's dry. Should light pretty easy." Sensing that Briet still wasn't up to speaking, he continued, "I checked what was left of the farmhouse. Found part of a window curtain. Used that for the shroud. Got the fake roses from a linen closet."

Briet palmed a tear from her cheek. "You did all this for a rat?"

"Figured you'd want to say good-bye." He reached inside his jacket's front right pocket, pulled out his Zippo, and handed it to her. "When you're ready."

She declined his offer with a wave of her hand. "Thanks. Don't need it."

She faced the pyre and snapped her fingers. Fire sprang into being from its center. In a matter of seconds the wood and Trixim were consumed in tall orange flames.

They stood and watched it burn. Then she regarded him with more vulnerability than he had seen in another person since the death of his master Adair. "Thank you," she said.

"Seemed like the right thing to do."

The fire crackled and launched sparks into the gray morning sky.

Cade lit a cigarette he had doctored with heroin. Feeling the need for a subject change, he said, "I spent part of last night looking over those crazy blueprints we took from Krueger."

Briet seemed eager to take his conversational bait. "And?"

"It's half genius, half insane."

She arched a reddish eyebrow. "Because?"

"First, he made sure we couldn't find the 'Castle Bravo' device in transit, by putting a glyph of concealment inside its warhead casing. Get that? The glyph is *inside* the bomb. So no one else even knows it's there. And since we don't know what ship it's on, we can't even try to defuse it until it gets to the Marshall Islands. Which means we need to find the *other* elements of Dragan's plan—the ones marked 'Bikini Site 20' and 'the bunker.'"

"I know where Site 20 is," Briet said. "A few weeks ago I saw a story in the paper about new atomic tests at the Pacific Proving Grounds. They plan to test a bigger, more powerful device than ever before on Bikini Atoll at the end of the month."

That made sense to Cade. "Okay. That tracks with the next thing I noticed. Castle Bravo, the bomb with the demon bonded to it—it's just *the fuel* for whatever Dragan is cooking up. The glyphs that they've hidden inside the shot cab on Bikini Atoll function as a *magickal lens,* to magnify the power released by the demon-bomb."

"Magnify it? To what end?"

Cade frowned. "That's the hidden part of the equation. The demon-bomb plus the hidden lens will release more raw energy than I can calculate, and more *types* of energy than I know how to describe. But if I were trying to harness that for a magickal experiment, I wouldn't want to be within a thousand miles of it when it goes off."

"Well, from what we saw in Los Alamos, striking from a distance is Dragan's MO. But if you're right, that means he could orchestrate this experiment from anywhere on earth."

"Maybe not." From the left pocket of his bomber jacket he pulled out the Odessa journal. Holding it toward Briet, he flipped to a page in the back of the book. On it was drawn a classic astrological horoscope chart labeled simply BUNKER. "I've been staring at this for days, trying to make sense of it. It's a full chart, with the major celestial objects tracked down to the arc second, and the zodiac signs on the house cusps precise to minutes of a degree. But there's no date, no name, no map coordinates. Someone drew this chart to check it against something—"

"Probably another chart," Briet said.

"That's my guess. I'm betting it was made to make sure the bunker would work as the anchor for the Castle Bravo experiment." He closed the book.

"Problem is, reverse-engineering a location from a horoscope without any of the other data used to create it is next to impossible."

"Nothing's impossible," Briet said. "But say we can't find that place. What about stopping the other two parts of Dragan's plan?"

"If we exorcise the bomb but can't neutralize the magickal lens, it could ramp up the blast way beyond what the military is expecting. Same goes for erasing the lens but leaving the demon in the bomb—there's no telling *what* happens when you atomize a demon."

"So dealing with those two threats is the imperative," Briet said. "The good news is, before the end of this month, they'll both be on the same atoll in the Pacific."

"Which gives us that long to figure out why Dragan is doing this, where his bunker is, and how to stop him. And all we need to do in the meantime is not get caught by the police, the FBI, or the CIA, and somehow make it out of the United States alive." Cade sighed and gave in to his need for sarcasm. "How hard can *that* be?"

———— ❧ ————

The monks of Key Gompa weren't much for idle chitchat, but this morning they had been more than willing to help Anja find her way to Khalîl.

Following their terse but cheerful directions, she found the ancient master alone in a large rectangular room near the top of the monastery. It had polished stone floors, and its walls of hewn rock were adorned by a mural rendered in vivid colors over a base coat of titanium white. There were tall windows on each wall, giving the room an airy quality as well as views of the entire valley, flanked on both sides by the jagged peaks of the Himalayas.

Khalîl sat cross-legged upon a thick, cherry-red velvet cushion. The Iron Codex was spread open across his lap. There were several such cushions scattered about. He looked up as Anja entered, and he greeted her with a smile. "Good morning. Did you sleep well?"

She withheld her answer until after she had crossed the room to stand over him. "No. I did not." She folded her arms. "Did you know she would call for me?"

His eyebrows lifted. "So soon?" He nodded, as if any part of this oddity into which he had lured her made the least bit of sense. "I knew the Vate Pythia had taken an interest in you. I didn't think she would summon you with such urgency."

"She spoke in riddles," Anja said.

"Of course she did," Khalîl said. "She *is* an Oracle."

"You spoke in riddles, too." Anja trained an accusatory stare at Khalîl. "Why did you not simply tell me to come here?"

"A test of your intuition," the master said. "And your patience."

Anja shook her head and almost had to laugh. "When Adair told me stories of the Oracles and their riddles, I thought they were just writers' gimmicks. They are quite annoying."

"As are so many things, once translated from fiction into reality." He closed the codex and set it aside. "I gather from your manner that you're in no frame of mind to begin your study of proto-Enochian." He gestured toward another nearby cushion. "Sit. Join me."

She pulled a turquoise-colored pad over to Khalîl and planted herself in front of him. "Did you know what she would say to me?"

"Oracles keep their own counsel," Khalîl said.

"She told me I would 'be the one to rise where others have fallen.' Then she said I would become 'the shadow on the sun, and the flame in the darkness.' Not for me the 'shackles of the Covenant,' she said, and then she told me I would 'seize the great Art with both hands and make *all* its secrets' mine."

Khalîl tugged at his bearded chin in slow, pensive strokes. "Or . . . ?" He took note of her surprised and defensive reaction to his prompt, and then he added, "With Oracles, there's always an 'or.' It's how they hedge their bets. So, what was yours?"

"*Or*," Anja said, abandoning her pretense, "she said I would 'turn away from the Art,' from the world, and everything would 'burn in flames everlasting.' She said my choices would decide which of those futures becomes real."

The old master let out a soft harrumph of amusement. "Pythia never does bother with the trivial. She's always had a flair for the apocalyptic." Turning more serious, he continued, "What can I do to help?"

Anja was desperate for real answers. "Tell me what her riddle means."

"I can try. The most obvious part . . . well, I'm sure you've figured that out. The world is facing a pivotal moment, one that might spell its destruction. And like it or not, Pythia believes that it's up to you to save the world—or to condemn it."

She suspected the master of stalling. "What about the rest? Her talk of 'shadows on the sun' and 'shackles of the Covenant'?"

He took a deep breath. "A shadow on the sun, a flame in the darkness." He pointed toward a symbol embedded in the mural: a circle divided into two equal and symmetrical halves shaped like curving teardrops—one black, one white, and within the larger portion of each, a dot of the contrasting color. "I think that is a reference to the concepts of yin and yang. Though they appear to be opposites, each contains a seed of the other. A symbol of balance and harmony."

"That does not sound like me," Anja said.

"Maybe not yet. But the reference to you breaking free of the 'shackles of the Covenant' suggests what Pythia sees in store for you: a new approach to magick, one that merges the dominant scholia. That might explain her comment about you 'seizing the Art with both hands.' She's predicting you will become proficient in both the Right-hand and Left-hand ways. A master of both the Goetic and the Pauline arts."

His interpretation struck her as implausible. "Is that even possible? Can one wield both White and Black magick?"

"At the same time? So far as I know, it's never been done. Not successfully, at any rate." A mischievous smile. "Then again, Pythia did say you would 'rise where others have fallen.'" He picked up the Iron Codex. "Which makes me think it can't be a mere coincidence that you've come here in possession of one of the greatest tomes of White magick ever created." Opening the book, he asked, "Ready to learn the secrets of Heaven?"

His words were encouraging, a friendly invitation, but the thought of being handed so much power, of being entrusted with so great a responsibility, shook Anja to her core. She raised one hand in refusal. "I cannot. Forgive me." She stood and backed away from him.

"Stop," Khalîl said, his voice sounding like a proclamation of law. "The Vate Pythia has told you the costs of failure. Of sloth. You no longer have the luxury of deciding can or cannot, will or will not. What needs be done will be, and if it is yours to finish, then you *will* finish it."

Anja refused to believe him. "I do not *want* this," she said. "I never asked for this."

"No, it is what is being *asked of you,* by a power far beyond our ken. You know the world will burn if you turn away—so why are you doing this?"

"You said it, when we first met in a dream: I am just a peasant. I can barely read."

Khalîl stood and confronted Anja up close. "I said you were *born* a peasant in a Russian logging town. I never said that you were nothing more than that, or that it was what you had to remain." He placed his hands on her shoulders. "I think I know what is holding you back, and it is not a dearth of book learning." His kindly smile returned. "Give me two days to prepare, and I will show you how to break the chains that bind your soul."

⁂

There was no reason for Cade to think she would answer or that she would hear him out if she did. But he had no one else to turn to. No one else he could trust. So he paced in the knee-deep snow a few dozen meters from the barn, and he waited.

The swirl of fog in the handheld rectangular steel mirror dissipated to reveal Anja's face. She scowled at the sight of Cade. *"What do you want?"*

He tried to keep his teeth from chattering as he said, "I need your help."

"It is not a good time." She looked away, as if she meant to break contact.

"Wait," Cade pleaded. "I know we didn't leave things on a good note, and I'm sorry. But I wouldn't bother you unless it was serious."

When she looked back at him, he saw years of mistrust reflected in her eyes. *"How serious? La Paz serious?"*

"More like Armageddon serious." From her resigned pause he inferred that she was willing to let him explain. "Miles and I followed some of the leads in the Odessa journal. And I think we're on to something huge."

"Good for you."

"But it's gotten ugly. Miles got wounded in the field and I had to leave him behind. Now I'm on the run in Colorado and—"

"Where?" she cut in, with sincere confusion.

"The western United States," Cade explained. "Near the Rocky Mountains."

Anja prompted him with a nod and a rolling hand gesture. *"Continue."*

He pulled his arms to his torso as the sun dipped behind the mountains, filling the valley with cold blue shadows. "Everybody and their cousins are hunting us out here, and we—"

"Us? I thought you left Miles behind."

He dreaded her reaction to the next piece of information he had to share. "I'm working with Briet for now."

Just as he'd feared, Anja's expression hardened with hate and resentment. *"You are* in league *with that Nazi bitch?"*

"I wouldn't go that far," Cade said. "We have common interests and a shared enemy. So for the moment, our interests align."

"If you trust her for even a second, you are a fool," Anja said. *"She will put a knife in your back the moment it suits her needs, and she will leave you to die, like an animal."*

He saw nothing to be gained from arguing with Anja. No point to telling her that he was having misgivings about his long-standing hatred of Briet—the woman who had maimed their friend and fellow magician Niko, who'd sent Niko's sister and countless others to die in the Nazi concentration camp known as Auschwitz, and who had murdered dozens of Adair's other adepts in the early years of the Second World War. He still had doubts about the woman, but Cade had to concede it was possible that she, like so much else since the war's end, might have changed.

He brushed off Anja's advice with a half truth. "I'll keep an eye on her."

Anja sighed. *"What do you need from me?"*

"A place to lie low and regroup," Cade said. "Where are you now?"

"India. Studying with Adair's mentor, Master Khalîl el-Sahir."

Her revelation widened Cade's eyes. "Master Khalîl is *alive?*"

"He summoned me. That is why I gave you the journal."

"I see." Cade's mind raced at the possibilities this new information provided. "Briet and I need the help of skilled karcists. And the guidance of a master—"

"I will not bring you here." Anja's declaration was coldly final.

Cade ceased his pacing in the snow, shocked by her stern refusal. "Why not?"

"This is not the kind of place where you would be welcome. Either of you."

It took Cade a moment to unpack that hint. "You're on consecrated ground of some kind. A church? No, they'd never tolerate our kind." Inspiration struck. "A monastery!"

"Clever, but I am still not telling you where." Something beyond the mirror's field of view distracted her. She looked up and away, and Cade was unable to tell what the other person in the room with Anja was saying to her. When she looked back at him, she wore the cheerless expression of one who had been overruled. *"My master bids you and Briet to come at once to Key Gompa monastery, on the north bank of the Spiti River."*

"We'll be there as soon as magickally possible," Cade said. "And please convey our thanks to—"

"He knows. Anything else?"

"Only that I'd rather be observing this anniversary with you than with Briet."

Anja seemed perplexed by his remark. *"What anniversary?"*

"Lost track of time over there? It's February thirteenth."

At first, her expression was blank, uncomprehending. Then Cade saw remembrance take hold, and a shadow fell upon Anja's empty countenance, bringing with it sorrow and regret. *"Dresden,"* she said. *"The day you threw yourself into the hellmouth."*

"One and the same." Cade shivered, but this time not from the cold that surrounded him, but because of his memory of the endless chill of emerging from oblivion into the forsaken darkness of Hell. "Not a day goes by I'm not grateful you pulled me out of there."

"You never told me what you saw there. What it was like."

"Pray you never find out."

"He said, to the woman who sold her soul to Hell nearly twenty years ago." After a heavy silence, she added, *"You remember where I told you to go?"*

"Key Gompa, India," Cade said. "Spiti River, north bank."

"Safe travels. Velarium."

Her visage faded from the mirror, leaving Cade to contend with his own melancholy reflection. He tucked the mirror back inside his bomber jacket and eyed the walk back to the barn. He thought of Anja . . . of his sojourn in Hell . . . of the sterile shores of an empty Heaven. Then he cleared the snow off the top of a wide stump, sat down, and lit a cigarette.

The enemy was close. Soon it would be time to run.

But for now he just wanted to savor a small taste of death, to remind himself of how good it felt to be alive. With each passing day, he was starting to forget—

No, he corrected himself. *I haven't forgotten. I've just stopped caring.*

He filled his chest with smoke. Enjoyed the silence. Exhaled.

Then he repeated his mantra of denial until his mind fixed itself upon some notion other than oblivion. Willful self-delusion accomplished, he enjoyed the rest of his Lucky in peace.

Unlike wine, which benefited from being served in the correct shape and size of stemware, whiskey was just as good straight from the bottle as it was from any glass. At least, that was the conclusion that Briet formed as she forced down several swigs of Jim Beam in between drags from her cigarette. Seated on the hood of her rented station wagon—which was now a day overdue for return and likely had been reported stolen—she stretched her feet toward the radiant warmth of the anvil that Cade had minutes earlier reheated to a bright crimson glow.

What the old barn lacked in dignity it made up for in obscurity, always a desirable quality in a hideout. In truth, however, there was nothing safe about the barn. It might hide them from the local authorities—avoiding smoke from a fire had been part of Cade's rationale for firing up the anvil—but the barn had no glyphs or wards of protection. No matter how well concealed she and Cade might be individually, the real enemy was bound to find—

Her prediction was fulfilled before she finished the thought.

Flames sprang up and danced from the top of the anvil, three feet tall and scintillating with colors like a kaleidoscope. Inside the twisting tongues of flame appeared the face of man who Briet had not seen in years: Dragan Dalca.

"Ave, *Briet*," he said, favoring the archaic form of greeting. His lean features smiled wickedly through the fire, a mannerism that reminded Briet of her late master, Kein Engel.

She slid off the car's hood and took a stand in front of Dragan's fire shade. "Dragan Dalca. Mr. Doomsday himself."

"*Please,*" he said, "*let's not stoop to melodrama. I'm not some mad agent of chaos.*"

"Then why did you fuse a demon to a hydrogen bomb?"

A broad grin. "*For science, of course. And also for insurance.*"

She side-eyed his fiery avatar. "Insurance? Against what?"

He chided her with a waggled index finger. "*Now now. It's too soon for us to start sharing* all *of our secrets, Mistress Briet.*"

"Don't call me that. I'm not some K Street dominatrix. How did you find me?"

"*No tattooed glyph of concealment is infallible, my dear. Not even yours.*"

"What do you want?"

His faux joviality vanished. "*To business, then. It's wasteful for us to treat each other as foes. After all, we both pledged to serve the same cause. When you swore your oath, we were the Thule Society. Today we are the Black Sun. But our mission remains the same.*"

"Yes, I trained half the Thule Society, but I never gave a damn about its members or its mission. To me and my master they were nothing more than a means to an end—a band of dabblers who were never meant to survive the war."

That did not seem to sit well with Dragan. *"I don't believe you."*

"Then believe this," Briet said. "Had I known you were part of Odessa, I would *never* have trained you. Or I would have made certain you died in the circle, by a demon's hand."

"The lady doth protest too much, methinks. You make a show of your moral probity—the classic defense of the hypocrite. You wore the uniform of the Reich—"

"I was never a party member. I—"

"It makes no difference," Dragan said. *"It would be so easy for me to make your whole life a matter of public record. And then what would you do? You'd be an embarrassment. The Americans would turn their backs on you. The Israelis would hunt you. You'd never know another day of peace, for as long as you live."* Beneath his narrow mustache he flashed an evil grin, like that of a predator poised to strike. *"Some sins can never be washed away."*

"What would you know of atonement?"

"I know it isn't given to traitors. Or to those who abandon their people."

Dragan's choice of words left Briet wondering what he knew. She had told very few souls—and none of her adepts—about her abandonment of Kein Engel in the closing days of the war. Her decision to flee, to turn her back on the war effort and the Thule Society, would have marked her as their enemy had anyone ever learned of her actions. But the only person who might have suspected her was Kein, and he perished in Dresden—

Nine years ago today, Briet realized. Was that timing a coincidence?

She looked into the burning eyes of Dragan's fire shade. "Do you have something you want to say to me, Dragan? Some gauntlet you want to throw down?"

"Why? Have you done something for which you need to answer?"

It was clear to Briet that he was mocking her. "I will not answer to you."

"No. Not today." An insincere smile. *"Last chance: End this feud. Join me."*

"The only oath I ever swore before coming to America was to Kein, and my vow died with him. Now I serve and defend *this* country—and I'll see you burn for trying to corrupt it."

"So mote it be." His manner remained impeccably polite. *"If you change your mind, of course, you know what to do—scribe the circle of* PERAGO, *offer the*

proper sacrifice to the blaze, and think of me as you say 'Exaudi' *three times.*"
His infuriating smile returned. "*I shall look forward to your inevitable supplication. Farewell.*"

The flames jetting from the anvil flared white and climbed higher as they
twisted in upon themselves. They vanished in a flash, leaving not so much as
a wisp of smoke or a flake of ash—just a faint but lingering bite of sulfur in
the air.

Briet climbed back on top of the Crosley's hood.

Downed another mouthful of Jim Beam to mute her demons.

And wondered what, if anything, she would tell Cade.

The less he knows about this conversation, she decided, *the happier we'll
all be.*

A long pour of brandy quenched the flames in Dragan's brazier and filled his
conjuring room with a most decadent brand of vapor. As the last flame died,
he lifted his sword from atop his shoes and used its tip to sever the line of chalk
to his right and open the circle of protection.

It had been nearly a year since he'd last run a solo experiment. Most of
his labors since then had been complex and dangerous enough that they had
required the assistance of tanists. Reaching out to Briet Segfrunsdóttir, however, had been a task better handled with discretion.

Or so his inner critic had told him.

Dragan stripped off his ceremonial garments as he walked to his worktable. "I told you that courting her would be a waste of time."

«*It is far too early to say that with confidence,*» the voice replied.

"She has tied her fate to Cade Martin. She's with the enemy now."

He felt his rider's doubt even before its voice echoed in his thoughts. «*Theirs
is an alliance of necessity. Neither cares for the other. Test them and they will
betray each other.*»

Dragan folded his miter and set it to one side of the table. "And what if they
do? Why do we need Briet?" He undid the lion-skin belt around his waist as
he continued. "Her time in America has corrupted her. She fornicates with a
male Jew and a female Oriental. She is a hedonist, a sybarite, a tribadist, and
an addict."

«*It is her weaknesses that make her valuable to us, Herr Dalca. They make
her malleable. Controllable. And while I agree that she is not to be trusted, it*

would be better to have her with us rather than against us in the battle to come. *Disparage her lifestyle all you like; it will not alter the fact that she is a skilled and dangerous magician.*»

After he removed his robe, Dragan folded it with care atop the worktable. "I do not share your interest in Briet, or your appraisal of her worth." He pulled off his white leather slippers and set them atop the rest of his garments. "I also have more pressing matters to attend. This bunker is provisioned for the ordeal to come, but I've yet to entrench its defenses."

The dark voice turned churlish. «*Very well. See to your petty details. As for the Icelandic woman? If she can be turned, do so. If not . . . I will bring her to justice soon enough.*»

FEBRUARY 14

Most karcists learned early in their practice of the Art that the most arduous—and painful—tricks to perform were those connected to teleportation, and the most excruciating of those were the ones predicated on moving through fire. The least painful variants were those that hinged on using water as a medium, but those were also the most restrictive in their rules and the most difficult to learn. Teleportation through air was nearly as hard to master as moving through water, and almost as painful as using flames. And with the exception of portal mirrors, which had to be manufactured to order from Hell at great expense and with lengthy waiting times, there were no popular charms for teleportation in elemental earth magick.

Consequently it came as no surprise to Briet that Cade chose to effect their jaunt from Colorado to India by way of a fire gate. Less expected had been his insistence that they flip a coin to see which of them would bear the responsibility for yoking the requisite spirits and managing the jump. Briet had provided the coin for the toss, an ordinary quarter.

Satisfied that it was not a trick coin, Cade had made the toss.

Briet had called heads, and it landed tails.

So it was that she had assumed the burden of their magickal flight from America.

It had taken her five hours to yoke the right spirits, and a few hours more to prepare the circle of teleportation inside the run-down old barn. Her reserves of several esoteric items common to Goetic rituals were being rapidly depleted. *I'll have to hope I can find replacements for some of these in India,* she mused as she finished the glyphs inside the circle's outer ring.

Now that it was ready just past midnight, she and Cade stood facing each other inside the innermost circle. "It might be safer if you held on to me," she told him.

He seemed put off by the idea. "Is that really necessary?"

"Makes no difference to me. You want to risk us being separated in transit? And find yourself stranded in Limbo or someplace worse? Be my guest."

He put his arms around her as if he were embracing a roll of barbed wire. "Okay."

Annoyed, she looked him in the eye. "Cade. This is no time for schoolboy stupidity."

"Sorry," he said, taking firm hold of her upper arms. "Ready."

Briet closed her eyes and focused the will of her yoked demons.

"*Ignis est portam*," Briet declared in a loud voice. "*Ignis est ponte!*"

A twisting funnel of violet fire sprang into being around her and Cade. Its heat stung her face and stole her breath as it spun and bent like a tornado, but it remained anchored around her and Cade's feet. Amid the snap and crackle of the flames, she heard faint echoes of the lamentations that wafted up from the Abyss whenever she summoned her patron, ASTAROTH.

The burning funnel consumed itself from the bottom upward, lashing Briet with strokes of white agony as it went. It spun itself out of existence several feet above her head—revealing that she and Cade were no longer inside the barn, but standing in harsh midafternoon daylight, on a snow-covered road at the foot of a jagged row of stone formations. The valley behind them was flanked by the majesty of the Himalayas. A dark and narrow river cut a snakelike path through the snow-frosted plain. Ahead of them rose a cluster of simple white buildings constructed on and around a rocky outcropping.

As Cade let go of Briet, she said, "Welcome to Key Gompa."

"Great." He brushed ash from the shoulders and sleeves of his bomber jacket and swatted burning motes from his hair.

They stood a dozen yards from the temple's open gateway. Briet walked toward it—and was rebuffed by an unseen force.

She recoiled. "It's warded. This is as close as we get with yoked spirits."

"That figures." Cade adjusted the strap of his tool roll, and then he froze as he clocked movement behind the gateway. "Someone's watching us."

A lone figure, a man in a deep-hooded cloak of dark gray, stepped out of the gateway's shadow and moved toward them. "I've been expecting you two," he said.

Briet felt exposed and off-guard. "And you are?"

The mysterious figure pulled back his deep hood to reveal a handsome face the color of oak, its lines flattered by a distinguished white beard that matched his thatch of close-shorn hair.

The moment Briet saw him, she remembered: he was the man she had seen in the jazz club weeks earlier, in Washington. The one who had warned her to flee the city.

Cade seemed more curious than suspicious. "You must be Khalîl el-Sahir."

"I am. I taught both your masters the ways of magick." Khalîl spread his arms in a welcoming gesture. "Shed your darkness, and you may enter." He noted looks of confusion on Briet's and Cade's faces. "Release your yoked demons if you want come in. The monks don't like them inside the temple."

Defenseless yet again, Briet lamented to herself, but she had trusted Cade to lead her to the far side of the world in search of sanctuary and allies. She shut her eyes and dismissed her demons. Their exit from her body felt like fresh spring water washing away the syrupy poison she had called blood.

When she opened her eyes, Cade was looking at her. His weary, deflated presence betrayed his own banishment of the demons whose powers he had arrogated. Without their strength, the tolls taken by his addictions were plain to see on his sallow face.

She gestured toward the gate. "Shall we?"

"We just bought the ticket." Cade trudged toward the monastery. "Let's take the ride."

───※───

The monks offered Anja the place of her choosing for her reunion with Cade. She chose the spacious room where she had met with Khalîl the day before. Daylight streamed in through the tall windows, and the bright surfaces inside the room glowed with reflected luminance.

I should have met him in the Oracle's cave, she thought with sardonic regret.

Her back was to the door when it opened. She turned and saw Brother Tenzin usher Cade into the prayer room. She was taken aback by the sight of her old comrade-in-arms: his hair was a mess, and his face was scruffy, bruised, scarred, and pale. Just as quickly as she'd felt a twinge of sympathy for him she masked it with indifference. "Been making friends again, I see."

He forced a smile. "I owe them all to you." He unshouldered his roll of karcist's tools and set it against the wall by the door. Then he pulled a pack of Luckies and his Zippo from inside his bomber jacket and lit one. He extended the pack toward Anja.

She gestured at the pristine room. "The monks would not approve."

"Fuck 'em, they can light some more incense." He exhaled plumes of thick smoke from his nose as he walked the room's perimeter and gazed out the windows. "Hell of a view."

Anja crossed her arms. "You did not come for the scenery."

"I came for the hospitality." He looked at her as he added, "I was misinformed."

"You said you needed sanctuary, and my help. With what?"

He puffed on his cigarette. "Nazis bent on global destruction. Matter of fact, I think all Hell's about to break loose. Literally." He stopped and leaned his back against a wall. "But before we drag Khalîl and your new monk buddies into a shooting war, I thought it might be a good idea for you and me to clear the air."

Anja cocked an eyebrow. "We said all we had to say a long time ago."

"Maybe you did. And at the time, maybe I thought I had, too. Now I'm not so sure."

This boded ill. Whenever Anja had imagined such a conversation between herself and Cade, it had never ended well, no matter how hard she had tried to pretend it might. "If you have sins to confess, I will introduce you to my latest human barnacle, Father Luis Pérez. Perhaps he can grant you absolution."

"I never said I had anything to apologize for. Or that you did."

"Then there is nothing else—"

"Yes, there is," he cut in. "We treated our romance like a game, like we—"

"*Romance?* You exaggerate, as always. It was a fling, maybe." Fighting not to recall the way she once had let herself feel about him, she added, "Or a distraction."

Her refusal to play along stoked Cade's frustration. "Let's just call it our *relationship.* That word covers a myriad of sins."

"Sins? Are you sure you do not need the priest?"

"Positive. Look, you want to fight me on every little thing? Fine. We can stay in here all goddamn day, goin' 'round in circles while the Nazis get closer to ending the world. Or you can just let me have my say, and we can be done with this."

This was not ground that Anja wanted to cover again, not after all the pain it had brought them the last time they had bared their souls to each other. But given a choice between a quick spike in the heart or the slow twist of a screw, she knew better than to prolong the pain.

"You speak your mind, and then we put this behind us, yes?"

"If that's what you really want," Cade said.

She surrendered with a wave of both hands. "Fine. Speak."

He stepped away from the wall and began to pace. He held his palms to-gether as if in prayer, the tops of his fingers pressed to his lips, as if he were gearing up to argue for the life of an innocent man condemned to die, or to propose the founding of a new nation. Anja found his affected solemnity al-most comical. How could he be so distraught over what had amounted to little more than a few months—*all right, half a year*—of casual sex?

"What we had," Cade began, choosing his words with excruciating delib-eration, "for the brief time that it lasted . . . meant more to me than just a bit of fun. We shared more than a bed, Anja. For seven months—"

"Six months and one week," she corrected.

He continued without acknowledging her fact-check. "We were together. Not just physically, but in every way that matters. We were friends. We were lovers. We were allies." A deep breath. "I don't know why we treated it like it was no big deal. Maybe I just took us for granted, and that was wrong. But I know this: Since we split, I've never been that happy again. Matter of fact, I feel like I've been circling the drain for a long time. I'm not trying to blame that on you, or on us. I'm just saying that when I look back, I see now that the way I felt when we were together was the best I've been since the end of the war."

"Of course it was," Anja said. "I have never seen you more drunk or more high. It must have felt *amazing*—for *you*." She stepped in front of him to halt his pacing, plucked his Lucky from his fingers, and took a drag from it. "But watching you stew in heroin in Kabul, or stagger through Manila after drink-ing all the rum on the waterfront"—she blew smoke in his face—"was not what I call a good time." The nicotine's effects hit her quickly, thanks to her being in the middle of her second day of preparatory fasting.

Cade nodded, clearly ashamed. "You're right. There were bad times, lots of 'em, and some"—he caught her look of reproach—"okay, *most* were my fault. But we had good times, too. You really expect me to believe you don't remem-ber swimming between the rock towers in the South China Sea? Or the long weekend we spent in Havana, learning to salsa?"

"Or the cabaret in Melbourne," Anja said, realizing only after the words had left her mouth that Cade's enthusiasm and affection were contagious. She forced herself to shift gears. "Or that coven of blood-drinkers we tore to shreds in Pankara."

A broad smile lit up Cade's face. "That's what I'm saying. Good things happen when we're together. We're good for each other." After a pause he added, "Mostly."

Anja backed away from Cade, and then she stepped around him on her way to the door. "The past is gone. Let it die."

"Wait," he said, his tone desperate.

Against her better judgment, she stopped and turned back. "Why?"

"Because there was one thing I know for a fact I did wrong when we were together. Something I should've done but didn't."

She knew what he was building toward, and it was the last thing in the world she wanted to hear. She pointed at him. "Shut up." She grabbed his roll of tools. "One more word and I will gut you with your own sword. You want sanctuary? The monks gave it to you. You want help against the Black Sun? When I finish what I came here to do, I might join your fight. But if you bring up our 'relationship' ever again? I will kill you in your sleep. Do you understand?"

Cade bowed his head and let his open palms fall to his sides. Anja tossed him his tool roll, and it hit him hard in his chest. He caught it and said nothing as she backed away from him. He just wore a hangdog look on his abused face as he watched her go.

His dejected expression haunted her thoughts as she turned her back on him and walked away down the countless stairs, in search of any place within the walls of Key Gompa where she could be well and truly alone.

─────※─────

The voice inside Dragan's head was as smug as ever. *«I told you Briet would be of use to us.»*

The heat from the shallow six-foot-wide copper basin was intense. Its bottom was covered in white-hot coals, and the bluish flames that rose from them had coalesced into the weltering image of a pyramid of buildings on a desolate rocky slope. Dragan saw a shimmering orb of protection surrounding the entire cluster. "You know this place?"

«The Key Gompa monastery in northern India. A place to which Briet would never go of her own accord. She jaunted there with Cade Martin. But he also

shouldn't know of it. If he led Briet there, it can be for only one reason: That's where Anja Kernova has taken refuge.»

"And if we find Anja—"

«We find the Iron Codex.»

Dragan sleeved sweat from his forehead. This room, like most others in the bunker complex, had been designed to retain heat—a quality that made pyromancy an uncomfortable form of divination. "And then what?"

«We take it by force.»

Dragan circled the basin to study the monastery from all sides. "Key Gompa's wards are too strong. No demon we could send could breach them, and a direct attack on our part would be a calamity."

«No fortress is impregnable. A proper assault could be readied inside of a week.»

"Too risky. If we fail, we would spook Anja. She would flee with the codex, and then we would need to find her again. Thankfully, a subtler alternative is now open to us."

«What alternative?»

"Not every problem is best solved with violence. Now that we know where to find Miss Kernova, we have a rare opportunity to resolve this matter through diplomacy."

«Do you really think she can be persuaded to give up the codex?»

"We would be remiss if we failed to try. If we can acquire the codex without bloodshed, we could abort this calamitous Castle Bravo experiment."

«A noble sentiment.» In the deepest shadows of Dragan's psyche, the voice turned sharp with cynicism. *«But mark my words: when she rejects your overture, you will understand why we have spent so much time and treasure developing our "Plan B."»*

FEBRUARY 15

Deep below the Key Gompa monastery, even farther beneath its foundation than Anja had ventured for her meeting with the Oracle, a natural hot spring lay hidden. According to Khalîl, the monks of Key Gompa had centuries earlier reinforced the chamber around the warm, saline pool in order to preserve it, and they had kept its existence a secret ever since then so that it would not be desecrated by tourists or the well-meaning but unreliable agents of academia.

"You should feel privileged," he told Anja as he guided her inside the chamber. Its floor, walls, and ceiling all had been tiled with obsidian that matched the ink-black water, and which cast dim reflections of the yellow light from the kerosene lantern in Khalîl's hand. "Only a handful of the lamas who train here ever see this room."

"A shame," she deadpanned. "It is so beautiful."

Whatever heat source warmed the pool in the room's center and filled the room with vapor had also taken the chill out of the tiled floor, which made it all the more hospitable to Anja's bare feet. Even so, she hugged her silk robe tighter against her thin frame as she neared the pool's edge. She tested the water with the toes of her left foot. It felt like bathwater—not too hot, but warm enough to be both soothing and welcoming.

She threw an anxious look at Khalîl. "You are certain I will float?"

"Absolutely. This water is denser than even the Dead Sea."

Her doubts came to the fore. "And how will floating in a warm salt bath help me?"

"You won't just be floating. You will be on a journey. One directed inward. This place—the Pool of True Reflection—is merely a tool to help you on your way."

"I do not understand."

"Once you're afloat," Khalîl said, "I will close the door. There will be no light. No sound but that which comes from within you. You will lose all sense of your physical self—"

"Astral projection," she cut in. "Soul travel."

He shook his head. "It might feel similar, but it will be something quite different." He fished deep inside a pocket of his robe and pulled out four small, leathery stalks with tiny pale caps and blue bruises at the bases of their stems. He pressed them into Anja's palm. "Eat these, one or two at a time. They will take some chewing. Once they're soft, swallow them."

"Mushrooms?"

"A special variety I found in northern California," Khalîl said.

Her enthusiasm waned. "You want me to hallucinate while floating in the dark?"

"It's nothing the native peoples of America and Australia haven't done for thousands of years." He tapped gently on her forehead. "*This* is a hard nut to crack. The mushrooms soften the shell." He gestured toward the pool. "Shall we begin?"

She pushed the first two mushrooms into her mouth.

Their flavor and texture both disgusted her. Rubbery and tough, they tasted to her like freshly fertilized dirt mixed with scorched peanut shells, with extra bitterness in their caps. Through the half-chewed mess she mumbled, "These taste terrible."

Khalîl nodded. "Yes, that sounds about right. The sooner you swallow them, the sooner this part of the experience will be over."

She choked down her first mouthful of mushrooms, perhaps a few chews too soon. "Do I need to eat all four of these?"

"Put the last two in your mouth and finish them in the water."

Only now at the edge of the pool did Anja become self-conscious at the prospect of disrobing in front of Khalîl. She was still trying to find a way to express her reticence when he intuited the cause of her awkwardness. "I see. Forgive me. I did not take you for a modest woman." He padded out of the chamber, into the tunnel outside its entrance, but held the kerosene lantern in the doorway. "Tell me when you're in the pool, and I will close the portal."

She put the last two mushrooms into her mouth. "Still chewing."

"Take your time. It's not as if the world is in peril and waiting upon you."

"If you were in a hurry, you should have hidden these in chocolate."

"Hm. A splendid idea. I'll have to try that next time."

Sickened and fighting to suppress her gag reflex, Anja swallowed the last two mushrooms. Only then did she slip off her robe, fold it, and put it on the floor beside the pool. Naked, she sat on the edge of the pool and put her legs in first. The warmth of the water was pleasing, but its viscosity and buoyancy felt peculiar. Unsure how deep it might be, she eased herself in. Her feet touched bottom and the water in the pool's center came to an inch above her navel. She took a deep breath and let herself sink and lean backward into the black.

"All right," she called to Khalîl. "I am in."

"May the darkness bring you enlightenment." The master withdrew the lantern.

Anja heard a soft grinding of rocks as the chamber's round stone door was rolled into place. After it covered the portalway, the room was filled with a darkness and a silence both more perfect and absolute than any Anja had ever known.

Alone in the dark, Anja soon became aware of the tides of her own breathing . . . the gradual slowing of her heartbeat . . . its echoes in the rhythm of her pulse . . . and then she was certain she witnessed light and motion, a macabre dance of spectral shapes and a sensation of falling, of hurtling through time and space . . . and soon she had no idea where her visions ended and she began . . . or where they began and she ended . . . or if she had ever been real at all.

Key Gompa was not an especially large place, at least not in terms of its circumference or its population. One could walk its perimeter in a matter of minutes when the ground was dry, and in less than half an hour through even a modest depth of snow. It housed fewer than three hundred people most of the time, the majority of them new monks and nuns in training to be clergy for adherents of Tibetan Buddhism. But once one submerged into the warren of narrow staircases and twisting underground paths, it was easy to become disoriented and lost.

Losing one's way was even easier, Cade discovered, when one was shunned by all of the temple's regular inhabitants. In the course of roaming its stone passages he had paused three times to ask directions to the monastery's library, twice from monks and once from a nun. Each time he had been silently chastised with cold scowls and waves of dismissal. After an hour of wordless rejections, he had started to wonder whether Key Gompa even had a library.

Turning a corner at the bottom of a staircase, he saw an open doorway that led to what he was sure must be the library. Stretched across the doorway was a wide strip of what appeared to be off-white translucent silk. Then he saw two hand-printed signs above the door. One read in block letters GHONKHANG. The other said ONLY MONKS ENTER.

Not much of a barrier, Cade thought as he approached the doorway.

Before he was close enough to touch the band of silk, an old Tibetan monk with sunken eyes and cheekbones fit for cutting glass appeared on the other side. The elderly man's presence radiated authority, and his unblinking stare at Cade was gravid with contempt and refusal.

Cade did his best to defuse the moment with pleasantries. "Hi, there. My name's Cade Martin. I'm a guest of Master Khalîl." The old monk was as expressive as a stone. Feeling exposed, Cade pressed onward. "I was hoping I could use your library for a—"

"No," said the monk. "Library not for you."

At least I know he speaks English and I'm not just talking to myself. Cade held up the Odessa journal, which he had been toting at the small of his back, tucked behind his belt. "I just need an ephemeris and some guides to calculating house cusps, so I can—"

"No books for you."

The monk's declaration had left little room to haggle, but Cade was not ready to surrender. "Please, there's a horoscope in the back of this book. If I can figure out its place and time, I might be able to stop a terrible—"

"No." The monk crossed his arms—an arthritic gesture that took many seconds to finish. Through it all his expression never changed, and his eyes never left Cade. "Leave this place."

"Is this how you treat all your guests? Or just the ones trying to stop Armageddon?"

He wondered whether he could force his way past the old monk. The wizened Tibetan didn't look imposing, and Cade doubted the man could outrun cold molasses. *It's not as if I don't have combat training,* Cade reasoned. *Even without magick, I could probably—*

"Do not," the old monk said, as if he'd been reading Cade's thoughts.

For all I know, he is.

"Look, I get the whole White magick–Black magick grudge. You don't want me inside your library, fine. I can't say as I blame you. But if I could just borrow a few books—"

"No borrowing," the monk said. "Not for you."

"Look, mac. I'm trying to be patient, but you're not makin' this easy. I'm not just asking for some light bedtime reading. I need these books to stop a genocidal Nazi Black magician from possibly destroying the world. Believe it or not, I *think* we're on the same side here. And if we aren't, I'm pretty sure we *ought to be*. So can we put aside whatever differences you think we—"

"No." If nothing else, the monk was consistent.

Cade stewed while considering his few remaining options for dealing with the monk—fire, bribery, or a broken nose—when a strong hand clasped his shoulder. He turned to see one of the monks who had met him and Briet at the gateway the day before. Searching his memory from the brief introductions that had taken place on the walk from the gateway to the ground floor's visitor's hall, Cade recalled the man's name. "Brother Tenzin?"

"Yes." Tenzin studied Cade with a peculiar intensity, as if he could look through Cade's eyes to discern something hidden deep within his nature. "May I be of help, Mr. Martin?"

"Maybe. Your librarian refuses to let me borrow a book or two."

Tenzin folded his hands in front of his chest. "Do you require specific tomes?"

"An ephemeris, and a guide to calculating zodiac house cusps."

"What system? Campanus? Equal House? Placidus? Koch?"

Cade felt swamped by Tenzin's banquet of options. "Um . . . Placidus, I guess."

"I trust you know that Placidus can't factor house cusps for locations with latitudes greater than sixty-six degrees and thirty-three minutes."

"I don't think I'll find what I'm looking for in the Arctic Circle," Cade said. "And it's still a damn sight more accurate than Koch."

Tenzin nodded. "Very well." He spoke in rapid-fire Tibetan to the librarian, who shuffled away while grumbling under his breath. The younger monk favored Cade with a beatific smile. "Brother Sangyal will return with your books in a moment."

"Thank you," Cade said. He wondered if it would be rude to indulge his curiosity, and then decided the risk was worth the potential insight. "Your fellow monks all seem to think I'm an irredeemable piece of shit. Most of them won't even speak to me. The ones who do"—he nodded at Sangyal—"haven't put out the welcome mat. So why are *you* helping me?"

After a moment of consideration, Tenzin said, "Master Khalil promised me that if I was willing to let myself see the *real* you, I would know you are not an enemy." He summoned a wan smile. "I am pleased to see that he spoke truly."

Brother Sangyal returned to the doorway carrying two large, dusty books. Tenzin relieved the old monk of his burden and handed the books to Cade. "That should get you started. Let me know if there is anything else you require."

"Thank you, I will." Cade honored Tenzin with a small bow, and then he repeated the gesture to Sangyal. Of the two monks, only Tenzin returned the courtesy.

Cade toted the books up several narrow flights of stone steps to his cell-like accommodations, his mind full of questions. *I wonder if Tenzin actually saw the angel bonded to my soul. Is that crazy? Could he really do that? And why would Khalil tell him to do that? Is that what it takes to get these guys to forgive me for being a Black magician? And if it is, what does that mean for Briet? Or for Anja?* Trudging up the last flight of stairs between him and his cell, he fixated on the most pressing questions of all. *Where the hell do I get breakfast around here? And what are the odds these guys have ever fucking heard of coffee?*

***

From the first moments of Briet's waking, the sound was there. Faint, lost behind the business of the day, but as stubborn as it was erratic. When she tried to listen for it, the sound faded into the background and eluded her. But when her mind was idle, when she was still, it crept into her thoughts.

While she ate breakfast, her imagination turned nostalgic. She found herself recalling her childhood in Iceland: sailing from the northern city of Akureyri on fishing expeditions with her father, or traveling south with her mother to visit the Svartifoss waterfall. With its fjords and volcanoes, Iceland had filled young Briet with an appreciation of nature's harshest beauties and a reverence for its random and all-conquering violence. Now she understood that all she had loved about nature—its power, its chaos, its ability to create and destroy at the same time with one impartial stroke—was what had drawn her to the Goetic Art.

Life and Death. Creation and Oblivion. All are One and One is All.

Once again the sound intruded on Briet's reflections. It made her think of a small rock being hammered against a larger one. There was no pattern to its percussion, no music in its tone, just a dry *plink* of impact, like that of a hammer striking a xylophone muted by a wet wool blanket. It sounded the same to her no matter what direction she turned, and no matter where in the monastery's de facto dining hall she stood. The few monks and nuns who were still enjoying the last morsels of their breakfasts did their best to ignore Briet as she explored the room in search of a sound that, apparently, none of them could hear.

She left the dining hall and headed back upstairs to her cell. Along the way she passed Brother Tenzin, the only one of the monks who had shown her even the smallest degree of courtesy. "Excuse me," she said, grabbing the sleeve of his robe. She pointed at her ear, and then she pointed upward and motioned around them. "Do you hear that?"

Tenzin looked and sounded genuinely perplexed. "Hear what?"

"That banging sound. Like someone hitting stones together."

The monk listened, raised his eyebrows, and shook his head. Then he walked away.

Briet scrounged a warm coat and went in search of the chaotic banging. The longer she looked for it, the more it vexed her. Most of the morning had expired by the time she was certain she had searched every building, staircase, and nook inside Key Gompa. Whatever was making that infernal racket, it was not inside the walls of the sanctuary.

At high noon the snow-covered hillside was blinding. Briet took some ash from the pit of an extinguished cooking fire and smeared it under and around her eyes to dull the sun's glare. Then she wandered down the snaking road and passed through the open gateway before doubling back, this time outside the monastery's walls of stone topped with fencing and barbed wire.

The sound grew louder and clearer as she climbed the hillside.

Now we're getting somewhere.

Every breath she drew was a struggle. The air was thin at this altitude, and bitterly cold. Pulling in what she needed made her lungs feel as if she had set them aflame.

Briet trudged upward, cutting a path with her body through waist-deep snow. All around her the world was blank and white, robbed of its details. She wondered if she had gone snow-blind, and if it might be permanent.

Her only beacon was the irregular beating of stones. It pulled her forward through the white void, until her feet touched bare rock and she found herself gazing into a cave as dark as the sun-washed slope around her was bright.

The sound emanated from inside. She was sure of it. Echoes resounded from somewhere deep beyond its shadows.

The black rocks were treacherous with snowmelt. Briet fought for balance as she made her way into the cave and navigated its steep downward grade. Water trickled through cracks in the rock above her head, anointing her with a near-freezing baptism.

She pressed into the underdark. The echoes grew shorter; the source was close now.

Quick bends in the tunnel cut her off from the ambient glow of daylight. Where she expected to find absolute darkness she was met instead by a surreal glow: moss coating the walls, floor, and ceiling shone with a pale green phosphorescence, giving the rough-hewn downward staircase ahead of her an otherworldly quality.

The stony percussion became alarmingly present as she descended the stairs—and it ceased when she reached the bottom and passed through an open doorway into a large cavern. The chamber was circular and had a dome-shaped roof. Spectral lights of many hues swirled and danced beneath the floor, which was made entirely of ice.

In the center of the room stood a crone stirring the contents of a large cauldron. There was no flame beneath the cast-iron pot, yet thick vapors rose from its interior. The old woman looked up from her alchemy and beckoned Briet with a crooked finger. "Come closer."

Briet hesitated to cross the ice. She tested it with one foot, adding weight slowly to see whether it would crack. When it showed no sign of stress, she risked setting her other foot farther out. The ice was slick and made for slow going, but it seemed thick and strong. As she made her way to the crone, the lights beneath the ice followed her and made a point of circling her feet.

She stopped just beyond the crone's reach. "Were you the one making that noise?"

The crone flashed a yellowed grin riddled with missing teeth. "The Cry of the Fates is different for everyone. Some call it the saddest, most beautiful song they've ever heard."

"I heard rocks being pounded together. And not in a pleasing way."

The crone cackled. "Curious." She lifted her long spoon from the cauldron and used it to point at Briet. "You always were the *contrary* one." She went back to her stirring.

"What does that mean?" Briet asked.

"You like to defy expectations. Confound those who dare to think they know you."

"I don't—"

"You are one of the few souls who has ever thwarted one of my prophecies."

In a flash, Briet assembled fragments of lore imparted to her decades earlier by her master, Kein. *The Cry of the Fates. A chamber underground.*

She gaped at the old woman. "You're an Oracle."

"The *last* Oracle. I am Vate Pythia—and you, Briet Segfrunsdóttir, are an enigma."

Briet felt both praised and accused. "What do you mean?"

"Twenty years ago," Pythia said, "when you began your studies as Kein's apprentice, I told Khalîl that one day you would betray your master."

The Oracle's words made Briet remember her desperate flight from Germany in the autumn of 1943. "And so I did."

"No," Pythia replied. "You *abandoned* your master. You did not turn *against* him. Those are very different outcomes."

Briet suppressed a bitter huff. "I'm sure Kein would disagree."

"So now you walk your own path. But tell me, Child of Fire—will you continue to stand alone? Or will you align yourself with the one called Dragan, who so recently tried to seduce you into his service? Which path truly calls to you?"

Striking a haughty pose, Briet replied, "You're the Oracle. You tell me."

"As I said before"—another yellow grin full of gaps—"you're an *enigma.*"

This time Briet was sure the woman's tone was accusatory. "Why do you care what I choose? What difference would it make?"

"Only the difference between redemption and damnation."

The crone snapped her fingers.

The ice under Briet's feet shattered. She plunged straight down and tensed to face the shock of immersion in freezing-cold water—

—and she bolted upright out of the snow on the hillside, gazing into the searing orb of the sun. She was facing downhill, looking at her own ragged path through the snow, and at the clustered buildings of Key Gompa a hundred yards below.

When she turned and looked for the cave, she was unsurprised to find no trace of it—just the virgin canvas of a wintry mountainside.

I just met an Oracle, she mused with wonderment. Then her cynicism re-asserted itself. *And somehow, despite meeting a person whose claim to fame is doling out prophecies, all I have to show for the experience is more questions.* She frowned at her snow-covered self. *Typical.*

FEBRUARY 15, PART II

It was cold the night Piotr died.

Anja watched her memories through the eyes of her twelve-year-old self. She could not change what happened. A visitor in her own past, all she could do was be her own witness.

Her nine-year-old brother had taken off like a shot at the first sight of what they'd both thought were fireworks. Now she could barely see him in the dark as she chased him through the forest a few miles outside their village of Topo-rok. Their booted feet churned through knee-deep snow as they ran. Branches pushed aside by Piotr snapped back like whips into Anja's face. Each one that struck put her another half step behind him.

Of course he has the rifle, young Anja fumed. She would catch hell from their mother if anything happened to her father's Mosin-Nagant M91/30, a weapon he'd taught her to use since she was old enough to remember.

Unearthly thunder shook the ground as Piotr broke from the woods into a small clearing. Anja stumbled into the glade seconds later. She froze at the chilling spectacle before her.

A wizards' duel. The older mage—Adair—was gray and bearded; the younger one—Kein—was clean-shaven and golden-haired. Fire and lightning flew in wild torrents between them. A bruise-colored maelstrom swirled above the clearing and flashed with eldritch light.

Kein coiled a smoky tendril around Adair's throat.

Gasping for air, the Scotsman cast a desperate look at Anja and Piotr.

His eyes were full of fear as he croaked out, ". . . help."

Piotr aimed the rifle at Kein. "Let him go!"

The German karcist pointed a manicured index finger at Piotr. A ghostly blade of green fire appeared in front of the boy. It fell in a swift and terrible arc.

Time slowed for Anja. Flames streaked behind the falling sword. She seized

Piotr by his shoulders and pulled him toward her. Through his body she felt a tremor of contact. She fell on her back in the snow, holding him on top of her. Their hard landing knocked the breath out of her, but for an instant she dared to think they had dodged the blade.

Then she blinked and realized she was holding only the top half of Piotr's body. His legs lay in the red-spattered snow. His warm blood drenched the front of her coat and pants. Revolted and terrified, she pushed his torso away. It landed in the snow with a dull *thump*.

She sprang to her feet and turned to confront Piotr's killer, only to see Kein lash out at her with a spectral whip whose end split into three hissing serpents. The snake-whip struck the left side of her face with the bite of a razor's edge soaked in grain alcohol.

Her anguished scream and tears made Kein laugh—and distracted him just long enough for Adair to rip the smoky tentacle from his throat. The grizzled Scot hurled a fistful of lightning at Kein, who deflected it with a flick of his hand and a muttered curse.

Back and forth the wizards fought, trading salvos of ghostly light, Anja's presence all but forgotten. Driven to panic by the pain inflicted by the serpent-whip, she tensed to run. Then she saw Piotr's lifeless eyes staring at the sky.

Rage devoured her fear, dulled her pain, and made her turn back.

Kein hit Adair with a surge of indigo light that brought the older man to his knees. The murderer raised his left hand and conjured his blade of fire for another killing stroke.

Anja plucked her father's rifle from the bloodied snow.

Her aim was true, and she fired without hesitation or remorse.

The rifle's *crack* echoed through the forest as her shot ripped through Kein's chest. She pulled the bolt, chambered a new round, and fired again before the casing of her first shot vanished into the snow. Her second shot tore through Kein's ribs and erupted from his back in a red spray. Anja chambered the last round in the rifle's magazine, intending to finish Kein with a headshot. She never got the chance.

A tempest of demons rose from the ground, a cloud of noxious vapors filled with gruesome phantasms: specters in the shape of rotting corpses, perverse chimeras with beastly heads atop misshapen human bodies, a great swarm of flies, and others so bizarre and grotesque that Anja had no words for them.

The dark cyclone enveloped Kein. With a sonorous boom, it swallowed itself.

Where the wounded karcist had stood there now rose a plume of black smoke that was torn asunder by an icy wind.

Silence fell on the glade. Anja pressed a dirty palm to her bleeding left cheek and staggered back the way she had come. She halted between the orphaned halves of Piotr's body.

This, she realized, was the moment of her life that she knew better than any other. This was the one in which her soul had lived, mired in guilt and regret, every day since Piotr died.

This is my prison, Anja realized, outside her theater of memory. *And these are my chains.*

<hr>

The onyx dagger in Anja's hand was as cold as the hatred in her heart, and it was as sharp as her will to vengeance when she stabbed it into Kein's back.

Oily black smoke filled the Zwinger grounds, while beyond the walls of the fortress the city of Dresden vanished beneath a carpet-bombing raid more brutal and thorough than any Anja had ever seen, even during her time with the Red Army in Stalingrad. But all she cared about now was twisting the onyx blade inside Kein's torso—making him feel all the teeth in its serrated edge as they shredded his left lung and the muscles in his back and chest.

One savage turn of the blade made Kein drop his quartz dagger.

Anja pulled her blade free of Kein's back. She seized him by his hair; then she stabbed him in his ribs and flanks, over and over, growling like an animal, her eyes wide with rage.

Just a few yards in front of them, a hellmouth conjured by Kein's dark sorcery churned with the fires of Hell and groaned with the lamentations of the damned.

Kein was bloody and listless when Anja spun him at last to face her.

"For my brother," she rasped. She plunged her dagger into his gut.

She gave him a push toward the edge of the fiery vortex behind him.

He staggered backward. One of his feet slipped over the crumbling edge, and he began to succumb to gravity's embrace.

From behind Anja, Adair's hoarse cry came too late: "Stop! Don't—!"

Kein spread his arms and smiled as he fell: "It is finished."

He vanished into the pit, unleashing a crash of thunder that buried Adair's plaintive shout of "No!" A geyser of fire and shadow shot up from the bottom of the vortex, cutting through the smoke that now crowned all of Dresden.

Anja and Cade rushed to Adair's side and helped him sit up. "Master," Cade said, "are you all right?"

"Of course not!" Adair pointed at Anja. "The fuck were you thinking?"

She recoiled, offended. "I killed him. We won."

Her master shook his head, furious. "You finished his spell!" He nodded at the hellfire geyser searing the sky. "Hell's rising, and there's fuck all we can do to stop it!"

Cade said, "There's got to be a way to close it!"

"It's too late. She locked it open when she sacrificed Kein. It would take—" He stopped in midsentence, horrified by whatever notion had occurred to him.

Anja shook Adair by his shoulders. "Take what?"

"Another sacrifice," Adair said, crestfallen. "One of equal measure."

It was obvious to Anja what she needed to do.

"My mistake," she said. She stood. "I will pay the price."

Adair caught her leg. "No—" He coughed up blood and gasped for breath. "Not how it works. Kein was a *nadach*. You sacrificed a man bonded to a demon. Closing the gate . . . requires an equal sacrifice. A man—" More blood-soaked coughs.

Cade finished Adair's thought: "Bonded to an angel."

Sorrow filled Adair's eyes. "Aye. . . . It's the only way."

Bombs rocked the burning city. Charred ghosts staggered in its avenues turned funeral pyres. Behind Cade, the host of Hell began its ascent.

He stood to face the inferno. . . .

Standing outside of her memory, Anja couldn't bear to watch Cade cast himself down again. Nor could she stand to witness the pain and guilt so evident on her face. Instead she looked at Adair . . . and for the first time, she saw that in the moment when Cade took his selfless step over the edge into the darkness below, Adair's sorrowful gaze had been directed at *her*.

He knew I could have been the one to go. Instead he let Cade pay for my revenge. I knew Adair loved me, but until now I did not realize how much.

But that does not erase my debt to Cade.

It should have been me *who fell. I should have faced the Devil's wrath.*

Cade was ready to die for us. For me.

I owe him nothing less than that.

～✧～

Anja stood apart from her own memory and watched as Adair planted her younger self in the middle of his conjuring room at Eilean Donan Castle, on the day that Kein had abducted Cade.

"Stand here," Adair said. "Don't move."

He walked a few paces more, then took from his pocket a large pearl and lifted it over his head. "*Eripe me Angeli Dómini a malo!*" He smashed the pearl on the stone floor.

It exploded with a flash that forced younger Anja to shut her eyes. When the glare abated, an eldritch fog rolled around her and Adair. They both had been changed—they were attired in their ceremonial robes. Around their feet, circles of magickal protection had appeared. Beyond them had been described a thaumaturgic triangle inside a grand double circle, but the glyphs and symbols that populated its spaces were ones Anja had not seen before that day. A gleaming golden sword was balanced on Adair's feet, and the Iron Codex sat upon his lectern.

"Stay still," he cautioned. "Don't speak. I'm going to yoke spirits to you like you've never felt. It'll burn in ways that words don't do justice. But it has to be done."

Anja remembered the fear she had felt as her younger self said, "Master? I do not recognize these symbols. What demon are you conjuring?"

He looked over his shoulder at her. "Demons won't cut it if we want to see Cade alive again." He opened the Iron Codex. "You might want to close your eyes."

Younger Anja did as the master said. His voice filled the conjuring room. Then came a light so powerful that Anja knew it could not have been spawned in Hell. Somehow, Adair had done what all the scriptures and grimoires ever written had sworn could never be done.

He had called down the arsenal of Heaven.

He had yoked angels.

Watching her memory of those moments when Adair had summoned angels and bound them to her flesh, yoking their boundless reservoirs of power to her mortal frame, Anja reflected on the terrible toll that angelic magick had extracted from her and Adair. It had left them both spent and ravaged, bloodied and soul-scorched. But not once had she objected to what Adair did. Not for a second had she paused to ask whether it was possible, or what the price might be. There had been no time then for the luxury of questions, not in the heat of battle and crisis.

Now she stared, mesmerized at the sight of her memory viewed from the outside. Her eyes widened as she bore witness to Adair's mad act of impulse, as he bound not one but three angels to Anja in quick succession, in order to prepare her for the battle royale with Kein and his adepts that was soon to follow. Only now, viewing the moment in hindsight, did Anja see the shocking truth that had eluded her notice that day.

Though Adair had shed all his demons before daring to yoke angels, he had taken no such precaution with Anja. He had given her no such command.

Instead he had acted without delay, joining her to angels one after another—all while she still had more than half a dozen demons already bound to her.

That should have been impossible, she realized as she bore witness to her past. *The spirits should have clashed and torn me to pieces. To hold angels and demons in the same yoke—*

The parallel hit her with stunning clarity.

—would be to practice White magick and Black magick at the same time.

She watched her younger self do exactly that.

I had the power of the Left-hand Path and the Right-hand Path at the same time. I seized the power of magick . . . with both hands.

<hr />

Anja bolted upright in the Pool of True Reflection, her dreamlike revelation still fresh in her mind. She felt exhilarated, enlightened, energized with a fresh spark of hope.

For years I have chained myself with lies, she realized. *I denied the truth of my own power. Refused to see I could be more. That I could be greater.*

The chamber remained as dark as the grave. She had no sense of direction; there was no way for her to know whether she was facing toward the door or away from it. Then she remembered where she had placed her folded robe. She walked to the pool's edge and then paced the pool's perimeter, with her right arm outstretched and her hand on the tiled floor. After she had walked seventeen paces, her hand landed upon the folded robe.

She positioned herself behind the robe, which she had placed between the pool and the door, and climbed out of the water. She could taste the brine that had built up at the corners of her mouth, and when she touched her fingertips together she felt that her skin had pruned from its long immersion. The tiles, thankfully, were still warm, and the comforting humidity that lingered inside the chamber made the transition from pool to air easier for Anja to endure.

Her wet feet slipped a bit as she stood and put on her robe. She took care to recover her balance as she tied the robe shut, and then she padded in cautious steps to the great stone that barred the chamber's only path of egress. She knocked on it three times.

Seconds of silence . . . and then the soft gritty music of stone moving against stone. A sliver of light appeared, and then it grew. The circular rock rolled away to reveal Khalîl, waiting alone in the passage outside the chamber, the flame in his kerosene lantern dim and faltering.

He held up the lantern so he could see Anja's face. "Did you find what you needed?"

"Yes," she said, almost breathless before her new world of possibilities.

"Good," Khalîl said. The old master took her hand and led her out of the chamber to begin their long trek back to the world above. "Now your true work begins."

FEBRUARY 18

There were many things worth hating about the protocols of ceremonial magick, but the one that Anja despised most was fasting.

It was one of the most common prescriptions in the process known within the Art as "the preparation of the operator." The duration of one's fast varied from one conjuration to another, but in all cases it was intended as a step in the physical purification of the karcist, one that would enable one's body to purge itself. Renaissance-era magickal philosophy held that this ritual cleansing was essential to the fostering of a properly reverent state of mind for the magician, but in Anja's experience the primary effects tended to be light-headedness and irritability.

Another side effect of deliberate starvation, she had found, was a tendency to slip into a waking dream state, one in which the gnawing of one's empty belly was forgotten, along with many related discomforts. That was where she found herself now, on the third day of her fast.

Halfway there, she reassured herself.

Six days of fasting was one of the preparatory demands of the ritual Khalîl was preparing for her. She had entrusted the Iron Codex to his care so that he could prepare the monastery's prayer room to host their experiment—one that would be unlike any Anja had ever performed.

It was a proposition that the monks of Key Gompa had opposed with great vigor, for one simple reason: It would mean admitting a demon inside the walls of the monastery. They were not mollified by Khalîl's promise that any spirits' powers would be constrained within the walls of the temple. It was the mere notion of letting such monsters inside that offended the monks.

Anja understood their objections. To a degree, she shared them. A demon's presence would sully consecrated ground inside the monastery, and one of the risks Khalîl would need to take to bring it here involved engineering a tem-

porary ingress through Key Gompa's wards of defense. All so that Anja could
fulfill a prophecy about which none of the monks cared, and expand her rep-
ertoire of powers, which they considered diabolical at best.

After a lengthy argument, all of which had been conducted in whispers,
Khalîl had taken aside the monastery's elder lamas to speak in private. When
they returned a short time later, the lamas announced that the matter had been
decided: the experiment would proceed under Master Khalîl's supervision, and
none of the monastery's monks or nuns would interfere in any way.

That left Anja's fast as the only hurdle left to be cleared.

The hardest part is done, she told herself. *Soon the fatigue will fade away. . . .*

She closed her eyes and slipped into a daze. Then, drifting as a disembodied psyche in the void of the astral plane, she realized she was not alone.
Extending her senses, she reached out and manifested herself in a soul-
projection—and then she saw him.

The astral projection of a man in his thirties. His complexion was pale; dark
hair showed beneath his trilby. His face had handsome qualities—a strong
chin, dramatic cheekbones, a thin mustache—but his overall affect was cheerless and severe. He wore a dark three-piece suit but did not look at ease in it.
On him, tailored clothes and bespoke shoes looked like a costume rather than
a statement of wealth or class. He waited until she made eye contact.

"Anja Kernova." His accent was Slavic, with perhaps a touch of German.
He lifted his hat in a momentary gesture of courtesy. "Dragan Dalca. I've
waited *so* long to meet you."

Her good mood turned defensive. "The feeling is not mutual."

He circled her; in the astral plane, her projection sat in a Lotus pose, just
as she did inside Key Gompa. She willed her perspective to rotate so that she
could keep Dragan fully in her perception. His smile broadened, as if he found
their situation funny.

"You're quite the harridan. Hunting my adepts all over South America. I
thought you would tire of it after the first year or two." His mirth soured. "But
you didn't."

"I was enjoying myself," she said.

He studied her with an appraising eye. "I know you took König's journal.
I also know you have the Iron Codex with you at Key Gompa."

"I do not care what you know," Anja lied.

Dragan ceased his roaming and faced her. "You should. I have all the man-
power, capital, and time that I need to hunt you down." He shifted his stance

to spread his arms, palms up—a supplicant's pose. "But why should we waste resources on a pointless conflict?"

"I do not find killing Nazis to be pointless."

"This war of ours has been limited in scope, Miss Kernova, but it can't remain that way for long, not with the way the world is changing. If our kind are going to survive in the world of tomorrow, we must learn to resolve our conflicts in a more reasonable manner."

Anja's hard-won inner peace crumbled as her instinct for violence came to the fore. "There is no reasoning with Nazis. Not then. Not now. Not ever."

"I would beg to differ," Dragan said. "You've killed dozens of my adepts over the last several years. But I'm willing to put that behind us and forswear revenge—on the condition that you surrender the Iron Codex to me."

She let slip a derisive snort. "Go fuck a wheat thresher."

He folded his hands, as if mimicking the act of prayer would make him look or sound more reasonable. "There will be dire consequences if you refuse to cooperate. Not just for you and your friends, but for every soul on earth, and for every living thing on its surface."

"Scary. Too bad I do not believe you."

"Miss Kernova, let me be truthful with you. I have urgent need of the Iron Codex, and I have, for some time, done all that I could to take it from you by force or by deception. Clearly, my minions have failed. But my patience is finite, and I have prepared a contingency that will achieve my needs without the codex—but only at a terrible price for the earth and all mankind. I would prefer not to be pushed to such an extreme solution, but that now depends upon you. Unless you give me the codex, I will have no choice but to shatter the foundations of the earth and break open the gates of Hell itself. And when I do, my master LUCIFUGE ROFOCALE and all his legions will be loosed upon the earth without charge or constraint."

At once Anja recalled the nightmare she had suffered during her first night in Key Gompa: a vision of the world in flames, a rising cloud of fire—and, flowing from it, a seemingly endless river of demons to wreak destruction upon mankind.

It was too horrific a possibility for her to accept. "You lie," she said to Dragan. "No ritual ever devised in the Art can do that."

Dragan chortled, his laughter full of malice. "Why would I limit myself to magick when I have access to the horrors of science?" He checked his watch. "You have until precisely six thirty P.M. Key Gompa local time on February twenty-eighth to comply with my request. If you elect to refuse me, your self-ishness will condemn humanity to a most gruesome conclusion." He lifted his hat once again. "*Auf wiedersehn,* Miss Kernova."

His astral projection vanished like a sculpture of dust scattered by a gale.

Anja opened her eyes. The confines of her prayer cell in Key Gompa remained quiet and inviolate, but all of her hard-won serenity was now gone, replaced by terror and anxiety.

If Dragan was telling the truth, she realized, *I may have no choice but to surrender.*

In a place as sacred as Key Gompa, one demon was all it took to foul the air for miles. Luis lay awake in his prayer cell, preoccupied with the stench of evil that had permeated the monastery, and he simmered with resentment toward whomever had brought it there.

The odor likely emanated from a yoked spirit in the service of a Black Sun amateur karcist lurking just outside the monastery. The presence of such profound evil this close to Key Gompa was like the putrid fumes of decay bedeviling a rose garden, or the miasma of an open sewer wafting through a bathhouse. It was all the more horrid for the contrast.

There was no clock in his cell and he had no watch, but he didn't need either to guess the time. A glance out his window at the moon, coupled with the Infernal odor that poisoned the local atmosphere, told him that it was sometime between the hours of three and four in the morning: the infamous witching hour, that time of night best suited to magickal operations of malice, cruelty, and violence. It was also the hour most conducive to the yoking of spirits, which suggested to Luis that their enemies were close and far from idle.

No point trying to get back to sleep, Luis decided. Even if he did succeed in returning to slumber, any dreams he might have under these conditions would certainly be unpleasant. He pushed off his bedcovers, sat up, and stretched. *Perhaps a walk will clear my head.* He stood, put on his cassock, and tied his rope belt loosely around his waist.

The hallway outside his cell was deserted and silent. The stone floors were frigid, but that was a discomfort to which he had adapted during his years of study at Monte Paterno. His ears soon found the sounds within the silence: the faint cries of the wind as it twisted through the monastery's passages, the rustlings of snowdrifts traversing slanted rooftops, the chaotic harmonies of chimes both wooden and metallic left out as playthings for the elements. . . .

And tainting it all, the stink of the Fallen, sharp and fetid in the winter air.

Seeking refuge from the cold and the pungency, Luis turned his steps toward the inner paths of the monastery, the protected corridors. They were no warmer and no less effluvial.

I will never understand why the monks permit this offense to continue, he brooded. He felt ready to give up his search for relief and return to his bed.

Then he turned a corner and saw a figure slumped in the shadows of an alcove. For a moment he feared he had stumbled upon a corpse, but then it shifted. He heard a sharp intake of breath, and the cherry-red tip of a cigarette brightened to reveal Cade's face. Luis recognized the American from a page he had seen in Anja's dossier—one labeled "known associates."

Luis stepped closer and saw that Cade held a mostly empty bottle of whiskey in his left hand, and the cigarette in his right. The youthful American exhaled twin plumes of smoke through his nose and grinned. "What's the matter, Padre? Lost?"

"Sleep eludes me when demons plague the sanctuary." Luis sat down cross-legged just out of Cade's reach, so as not to risk making him feel as if his personal space had been intruded upon. The acrid bite of the American's tobacco smoke almost blocked out the reek of nearby hellspawn. "What is it that troubles *you,* my son?"

Cade downed a mouthful of whiskey, and then he took a long drag from his cigarette. "Who says I'm troubled, Father?"

"You're sitting on the floor, in the dark, in the middle of the night, drinking alone from a fifth of whiskey. These don't appear to be the actions of a man at peace with himself."

The American mustered a smile that failed to conceal his distress. "You'd be surprised how much peace you can find in a bottle of Tennessee sour mash and a pack of Luckies."

"I suspect that to be less than the truth," Luis said.

Cade puffed a smoke ring at Luis. "Here to take my confession, Father?"

"Do you feel the need to confess?"

Cade looked Luis in the eye. "No."

"That's just as well. To tell the truth, I've never cared for the rituals of absolution." He extended a hand toward Cade. "Got enough left to share?"

The American wore a curious expression as he handed the whiskey to Luis. "You drink?"

"I took vows of celibacy and poverty." Luis sipped the whiskey and savored its sweet, smoky burn in his throat. He handed back the bottle. "I never promised anyone temperance." He watched Cade take another drink, and then he continued, "Forgive me if I'm overstepping the bounds of propriety, but yours seems to be a spirit in turmoil. I can respect that you have no desire to speak to me as a man of the cloth—but perhaps you could speak to me as a fellow student of magick. If you want to, that is."

Cade snuffed out the end of his cigarette on the floor. "Don't know what good it would do. Wouldn't change anything. Wouldn't fix what's broken."

"Is something broken?"

"*Everything* is broken," Cade said. "Me. You. Everyone who's ever lived, the entire world, the *whole fucking universe*." He lit a new Lucky. "It's all fucked."

The man's passion and desperation captivated Luis. "Can you be more specific?"

"None of it amounts to anything," Cade said. "There's no purpose to it. To us. We're all just sparks in the night, burning out on our way to nowhere. The whole universe is like this. Everything and everyone that's ever existed? We were all created just to die."

Luis thought it odd that a karcist of all people would be plagued by an existential crisis. "Death is nothing to be feared, my son. It's merely the—"

"Spare me the sermon," Cade cut in. "I've heard it, and you're wrong."

"Wrong about what?"

"Life, death, Heaven, Hell. You name it."

"A rather presumptuous assertion."

Cade sent a smoke ring wobbling toward Luis. "You speak from faith, Father. I speak from experience. And I'm telling you: You've got it wrong."

"Please, enlighten me. About what am I so mistaken?"

A swig and a drag preceded Cade's question. "What do you think happens when we die?"

"I believe that after our souls leave this life, we stand before God," Luis said. "If one has accepted the salvation and forgiveness of His son, Our Lord Jesus Christ, then one is welcomed into the Kingdom of Heaven. But if one perishes in sin, not having accepted Jesus Christ as Lord and Savior, then the eternal punishments of Hell become one's inheritance."

"A nice story," Cade said. "But it's all crap. Every word of it."

"And you know this how?"

"Because I've been there, Father. I've seen Heaven and Hell."

Luis wondered whether the dark magician was willfully deceiving him for sport. "Is that a fact? You've been to the life beyond this one and returned?"

"That's right. On D-day."

Driven by an impulse to be charitable, Luis chose to play devil's advocate. "You had a brush with death on D-day?" He pondered that for a second. "Are you sure you didn't simply suffer a hallucination? A delusion brought on by injury or fatigue?"

"I'm positive." Cade squinted at Luis. "Father . . . do you know what a *ni-kraim* is?"

The word jogged Luis's memory of an ancient grimoire he had read during the early years of his studies at Monte Paterno. "A human soul bonded with the spiritual essence of an angel?" Noting Cade's nod of confirmation, Luis said, "I thought they were just myths."

"You're looking at one, Padre. My bond-spirit is an angel named GESHURIEL."

Luis searched Cade's manner for any sign of jest or dissemblance. So far as he could tell, the American was completely serious. "How is that . . . ?"

"Never mind," Cade said. "What matters is, while my body lay half dead on Pointe du Hoc, GESHURIEL took my soul to Heaven and Hell. Neither was what I expected, but the biggest surprise was what *wasn't* there: not a single human soul. Not one. Anywhere." Cade took a long drag from his cigarette. "I gotta be honest, Father . . . it's haunted me every day since I saw it. I lie awake some nights thinking about all the lives I took during the war, and after it. All the people I wish I could've saved but didn't. None of them went on to Heaven's reward or Hell's justice. They just vanished. Disappeared forever. And now my best friend is lying in a hospital somewhere. Or maybe he's already gone. Because I wasn't strong enough, or fast enough, or smart enough. I got caught off-guard, and a man I love like a brother paid for it."

"Don't give up hoping for him, my son. If his fight was just, the Holy Spirit may yet protect him. As for your underlying premise, I find it both chilling and suspect. Just because you saw no human souls in those other realms, that doesn't mean they are not elsewhere."

"I had the same thought. Which is why I asked GESHURIEL where the human souls were. And both Above and Below, he told me the same thing—*that there were none.*"

"That's not as surprising as it might seem," Luis said. "When one considers the concepts of Limbo and Purgatory—"

"Both of which GESHURIEL told me are human fictions."

"Have you considered the possibility that GESHURIEL lied?"

"Why would an angel lie?" Cade asked.

Luis chewed on that and came up short of a satisfying answer. "Regardless, my son, just because you experienced a vision that challenges some of our conceptions of the afterlife—"

"*Some* of them? It blows them all out of the water. Heaven, Hell, resurrection, reincarnation—none of them make any sense once you realize our souls are mortal." He pointed his cigarette at Luis. "And that's the part I can't get my head around. If the universe is the result of God's will, why the fuck did He set it up like this? How am I supposed to believe in a loving God who would create intelligent life that has no other purpose than to die? How could a merciful God make a conscious soul whose fate is to be extinguished forever?" He exhaled a long flood of smoke and stared up at the ceiling, as if he could look through it into eternity. "How can I see God as anything but malign, and life as anything but malignantly useless?"

A silence freighted with despair lingered between them.

"Might I suggest," Luis said, "that we aren't meant to be able to understand God? Perhaps His motives are not ours to know, and never will be. But just because we don't understand His plan, that doesn't mean He is without one. By the same measure, just because you could not find human souls in Heaven or Hell, that does not mean they are mortal."

"But GESHURIEL said—"

"Angels are *not* omniscient. They are God's messengers and soldiers, but they are no more like unto the Divine than we are. It's possible your bondspirit believes what it told you. But it's equally possible that it's mistaken." He moved to sit beside Cade. "You spoke of our souls as 'sparks in the night.' I know that metaphor. It compares the Divine to a bonfire and posits that we are ephemeral motes launched from the blaze to expire in the cold and dark."

Luis rested a hand on Cade's shoulder. "But perhaps, when our lives end, our sparks return to the fire that made them. Maybe the reason there are no human souls in Heaven or Hell is because they have once again become part of God Himself."

"I'm not sure I believe that," Cade said. "But part of me wants to."

"Then perhaps there is still hope for your salvation, my son."

Cade passed the whiskey back to Luis, who drank while the American talked. "I don't know if I need saving so much as I want answers. I might even be able to accept this screwed-up universe the way it is, if only I fucking knew why God made it this way."

"Bargaining with the Almighty," Luis said. "You'll have to tell me how that works out for you."

This time when Cade chortled, he did so with genuine mirth. "You're all right, Father. Who knows? In another life, we could've been friends."

Luis arched an eyebrow. "Who says we can't be in this one?"

"There you go again," Cade said, "asking the tough questions. Shut up and drink."

"You're quite sure it was a genuine astral projection?" Khalîl's question sounded to Anja as if he were fishing for a reason not to believe her account of Dragan's ultimatum.

Standing in front of him atop the monastery's roof, Anja maintained an air of quiet certainty. "It was no delusion, Master. Even after three days of fasting, I can still tell the difference." She glanced up at the bright orb of the full moon. "As clearly as day from night."

"Yes, I'm sure you can." The old karcist scratched at his bearded chin, an affectation that reminded Anja of her late mentor Adair. "That being the case, we're in greater danger than I knew. This Dragan—how long do you think he's been practicing the Art?"

Anja shook her head. "No idea. He leads the Black Sun, so he might be ex-Thule."

"Which would mean he might have started in the midthirties." Khalîl frowned as an icy breeze fluttered his robes. "It still makes no sense. Even with twenty years of practice he shouldn't have been able to force an astral shade through Key Gompa's defenses."

"But he did," Anja said.

"Yes," Khalîl conceded. "He did. Which means either he has access to privileged information about this place, or he's one of the most talented magicians in the history of the Art. Whichever proves to be true, this place is no longer safe for you."

His snap judgment alarmed her. "What are you saying? I need to leave?"

"Soon, yes." He grimaced into a blast of wind. After it abated, he continued, "But first we need to finish your experiment. Only then will you be ready for what comes next."

"And what will that be?"

"Challenging," the master said, employing a cryptic reply to mask his obvious refusal to confide in her. Anja expressed her annoyance with a scowl, but Khalîl seemed not to care.

He walked toward the door that led back inside the monastery. "Come. You need to rest and meditate."

"And if I get another visit from Dragan?"

"I'll scribe new wards on your prayer cell," the master said. "Barriers the Devil himself couldn't break. Dragan won't bother you again."

She followed him inside and down a narrow flight of stairs, with winter's breath hard at their backs. "And what will you do while I rest?"

"Recruit you a second pair of tanists." Khalîl heaved a sigh. "You're about to take a leap into the unknown. You're going to need all the help you can get."

———— ⌇⌇ ————

"Absolutely not." Luis turned his back on the old man and retreated to the corner of his prayer cell. He felt trapped. "I won't be party to such an abomination."

If his refusal irked Khalîl, the master karcist hid it well. "I would prefer you rendered your aid freely," he said in a calm voice. "A willing tanist is more reliable than one coerced."

Luis faced Khalîl. "How can you be so brazen as to ask this of me?"

"You act as if I'm guilty of some malicious imposition. The fact, Father Pérez, is that I'm asking nothing of you that I wouldn't ask of any other qualified karcist. And if another of your stature but lacking your religious convictions were available, I should most certainly have sought that person's aid before yours. But I need a fourth tanist, and you are my last option."

The priest crossed his arms. "You can't really expect me to help you call up a demon."

"I can, and I do." The old man took a thoughtful pause. "Do you understand what it is that Miss Kernova is about to attempt?"

"Knowing the proclivities of Black magicians, I'd guess she's about to find the shortest of all shortcuts to Hell."

Khalîl shook his head. "No, Father. In three days' time she will summon one of the Fallen and call down one of the Elect—and then she will yoke them both at the same time."

The very notion of what Khalîl proposed sickened Luis. "You've lost your mind! Who would even *imagine* such a perversion? Much less attempt it?"

"I don't deny this experiment comes with risks," Khalîl said. "But the dangers to Anja as the operator, and to the world at large, become that much greater when one considers the threat posed by Dragan Dalca."

The name was unfamiliar to Luis. "Who?"

"A renegade karcist," Khalîl said. "Trained years ago by Briet, before she knew he was part of the Black Sun, a cabal of Black magicians formed from the survivors of the Thule Society. He's demanding that Anja give up the Iron Codex to him, or else he will carry out some kind of doomsday ritual that fuses magick and science to blast open the gates of Hell."

Luis remembered his nightmare encounter with the well-dressed man on the train to Rome, the one named Dragan who'd warned him not to pursue the codex. Recalling the pain of his heart being torn from his chest made Luis queasy. "Do you consider his threat credible?"

"Extremely. I also fear he might sabotage Anja's experiment."

The master's warning reminded Luis of the lecture he'd received from Father D'Odorico. "I know what a disrupted experiment means," Luis said. "Demons loose in the world. Death and destruction." He hardened his resistance. "All the more reason to cancel this experiment."

"No," Khalîl said. "Anja needs to do this in order to embrace her destiny and become the karcist she was always meant to be. But she needs our help to do it safely."

"You appeal to me in the name of protecting Anja and the world," Luis said. "If safety were truly your concern, you would not be attempting this." He picked up his roll of karcist's tools and tried to shoulder past Khalîl. "I'll have no part in it."

The old mage seized Luis's arm. "Hold! Your commission is *not* discharged, Father." He fixed Luis with a stern look. "But you already know that, don't you?"

"What are you going to do? Stake me to the floor inside your circle?"

Khalîl seemed amused by Luis's defiance. "I won't have to. Whatever holy mission brought you here, as a karcist of the Pauline Art you have a positive duty to your Church and to your Lord. You *cannot* refuse my request. Your service is part of your vow by stipulation, and included in the Covenant by implication."

Everything the ancient one had said was true, and Luis knew that continued debate would not be to his benefit. He relaxed and backed away from the door, and Khalîl released him. Luis set his tools by his cot. "What, precisely, do you ask of me?"

"Your unabridged advice in the preparations of the ritual. Your presence during the conjurations. And, should it be required in the event of calamity, your unwavering aid in helping me and the other tanists to abort the experiment."

Luis breathed a sigh of surrender. "Very well."

"Begin your fast now. I promise to return before sundown to review the details of the ritual, so that you might focus your mind upon the experiment in the days to come."

With a single nod, Luis said, "Understood." Khalîl turned to depart. Luis halted him by asking, "Wherever did you find this obscene ritual?"

A wide yellow smile. "In the Iron Codex, of course."

The master took his leave, and Luis stood alone inside his prayer cell, pinned between his guilt and his hypocrisy. *For all my protests, I would not miss this experiment for the world,* he admitted to himself. Something unprecedented in the history of the Art was in the works, and though he knew that helping to raise a demon would be a sin, part of him thought it might be worth risking the Church's ire not just to see the Iron Codex in action, but to be a part of it.

Forgive me, Lord. . . . But I need to know.

29

FEBRUARY 21

The great prayer room at the top of the monastery had been transformed, and not in a manner of which its regular stewards would have approved. Anja had scribed its floor with circles of protection and conjuration, and the perfume of incense had been supplanted by the fumes of smoldering charcoal, the mingled steams of camphor and brandy, and the purifying smoke of consecrated sage. Bright flames weltered atop dozens of candles cast from virgin wax. The air itself seemed to shimmer with electric potential.

She and her tanists all had donned their ceremonial garb: white cassocks of linen and paper miters inscribed with holy names of power. White leather slippers. Girdles of various animals' skins. Though Anja alone bore a sword and an athamé, her tanists all had taken the unusual precaution of bringing their wands, all of which were wrapped in colorful silks.

It is up to me to ensure they do not need them, she told herself.

Cade and Briet lingered in different corners at the south end of the chamber, each of them absorbed in their own pre-ritual thoughts and preparations. Khalîl and Father Pérez, the troublesome Jesuit who had dogged Anja halfway across the Indian subcontinent, conferred over the pages of the Iron Codex in between making tandem reviews of the room's details.

Anja had complained more than once to Khalîl that the priest should not be allowed near the codex, but the old master had assured her that Luis's aid and insight would be crucial to her safety and success. Grudgingly, she had acceded to the master's advice, but her temper still flared when she saw the Vatican's agent lay hands on the book that Adair had given her.

"It's almost time," Cade said, drawing the room's attention. "Are we ready or not?"

The question had been directed at Khalîl, who looked at the priest. "Well?"

Luis walked at a casual pace around the scribed areas, making observations as he went. "The great circle is correct. The names inside its bounding rings are the most powerful known to the Art. And all the totems are in place: goat's horns, a wolf's hide, a horse's heart, the skull of an infant." He tapped a candle stand. "All the flames are lit." He lifted his chin toward the interior of the great circle. "The positions for the operator and the tanists are secure." He shifted his focus to the two outer circles. "To the northwest, a Solomonic double circle encompassing a triangle drawn in hematite. To the northeast, another double circle around a six-pointed star." He stopped and looked at Anja. "Are your sacrifices ready?"

"They are." She pointed at a lidded basket to the left of her operator's circle. "A live serpent for the demon." Then at another lidded basket to the right of her assigned position. "A live dove for the angel."

The priest nodded at Anja, and then he said to Khalîl, "The room is prepared."

"I concur," the master said. "Anja, the ritual is now in your hands."

Anja declared in a proud voice, "Tanists, take your places and light your vessels."

Cade, Briet, Khalîl, and Luis entered the great circle. Each of them took care not to disturb the numerous glyphs Anja had laid down as they made their way to their assigned places. Once in position, they ignited the coals inside the braziers at their respective stations.

With her tanists all in place, Anja entered the operator's circle, from which she used the tip of her sword to drag a small bit of lime chalk to fill the circle's final gap. "The circle is now closed. I know you are all veteran karcists, but decorum requires that I remind you all not to speak or to leave your circles once the experiment starts."

She balanced her sword across the tops of her toes. Then she struck a match on the side of her brazier, dropped it in, and stood as violet flames danced from the small vessel. She looked back and saw various hues of flame twist up from her tanist's braziers. The ritual was begun.

"Tonight we will do what no living karcist has done before," Anja said. "We will summon BAEL, a great king of Hell, and also HAMARIEL, an angel of the Order of Dominions. Once they both have been constrained and appeased . . . I will yoke them both at the same time."

Behind her she heard Luis mutter, "Or die trying."

"Silence!" Anja snapped. "If I fail to harness both spirits, I will die. If I do, both spirits will fly free. Then the four of you must contain them, banish them, and abort this experiment." She drew her wand from under her belt of lion skin, removed its shroud of red silk, and draped the long crimson band around her neck and let it hang down the front of her vestments. She heard her tanists prepare their own wands. When all had settled, she said, "Let us begin."

A flourish of her wand raised a jet of blue fire from her brazier.

She coarsened her voice and said: "Havoc. Havoc. Havoc."

Sparks in a thousand hues erupted from her brazier and bounded off the ceiling. Burning motes scattered across the floor around her. At once an impenetrable, putrid fog filled the room, and macabre lights danced outside the towering windows. Then came a chorus of unearthly wails that echoed as if they had risen from an inconceivable depth.

Over the clamor she shouted, "I invoke thee, great BAEL, King of the East, by the power of the pact I have with thee, and by the names ADONAI, EL, ELOHIM, ZABAOTH, ELION, ERETHAOL, TETRAGRAMMATON, RAMAEL, SHADDAI, and by the names ALPHA AND OMEGA, by which Daniel destroyed BEL and slew the Dragon; and by the whole hierarchy of superior intelligences, who shall constrain thee against thy will—*venité, venité, submirillitor*, BAEL!"

Putrescent gusts of hot air roared through the conjuring room, but no spirit appeared. In no mood to entertain the petulant whims of a demon, Anja skipped the customary warning and thrust her wand into her brazier. Flames and sparks shot out of it as monstrous howls shook the walls and spiderwebbed the ceiling with cracks. "I adjure thee, BAEL, by the pact and the names, appear, lest I summon our patron ASTAROTH!"

An answer came from the darkness in syllables of burning ash.

STAY THY ROD; I AM HERE. DISTURB NOT MY FATHER.

The beast appeared in its true form outside the great circle. It resembled an enormous toad, its glistening skin a mottling of green and brown.

"Hadst thou come when first I invoked thee," Anja said, "I should not have thought to rouse thy father. Defy me again and thou shalt feel my wrath."

Resentment and hatred radiated from the demon, both as tangible as the heat of a fire. Its inhuman voice was hoarse and full of contempt. WHAT DOST THOU DEMAND OF ME?

"Take thy place inside the triangle. I shall yoke thee into my service as I have done before, and you will comply, as our pact requires."

The spirit said nothing as it moved in a single hop to take its place inside the triangle to the northwest. Contained, it would be easier to control, but Anja knew never to take a demon's cooperation for granted. One mistake was all that any demon ever needed to put an end to a karcist's career in the Art. With a gesture of her left hand she removed the lid from the basket containing the serpent. The snake slithered out of the circle without disturbing its glyphs and proceeded directly to BAEL, who devoured the creature in a single wet gulp.

Now, she reflected with trepidation, *comes the hard part.*

As she began the second phase of the experiment, she abandoned the bellicose shouts that she used to bully Hell and adopted an almost musical cadence suited to entreating Heaven.

"O thou mighty and potent angel ABASDASHON, who rulest the fifth hour of the night, I, humble servant of the Lord thy God, do conjure and instruct thee in the name of the immortal host of hosts, JEHOVAH TETRAGRAMMATON, and by the seal to which you are sworn.

"By the seven angels that stand before the Throne of YAHWEH, and by the seven planets and their seals and characters, I beseech thee to be graciously pleased with my entreaty, and by Divine permission to come from whereso-ever you may be, show thyself visibly and plainly before this circle, and speak with a voice intelligible and to my understanding.

"O thou great and powerful angel ABASDASHON, I petition thee to come forth, to inform and direct us in all things good and lawful to the Creator, by the power of the holy names ADONAY, ELOHIM, ZEBAOTH, AMIORAM, HAGIOS AGLAON TETRAGRAMMATON, and by the name PRIMEUMATON, which com-mandeth the whole host of Heaven. Amen."

Thunder rolled outside the windows, and an earthquake trembled the room. Anja started to fear the walls might collapse and bury her and her tanists— and then a deafening shriek heralded a blast of light from above that left her squinting with her head turned toward the floor.

The unseen angel spoke with a majestic voice that resonated in Anja's bones.

AVE. THE BLESSINGS OF JEHOVAH BE UPON YOU. WHY HAVE YOU SUM-MONED ME?

"O great and terrible angel ABASDASHON," Anja said, "please accept my gratitude for thy presence. I seek thy aid, to arm myself with powers Divine so that I might oppose an agent of Hell, one who means to wreak great and lasting damage on the Lord YAHWEH's creation."

YOU WOULD DO BATTLE WITH THE ONE WHO MEANS TO BREACH HELL'S GATE.

"Yes. Please, take mercy upon me and my mission, O great angel ABAS-DASHON. Grant me the aid of one of thy dukes, so that I might smite the enemies of the Lord and succeed in this venture most sacred." With her right hand Anja took the lid off of the second basket. From it flew the sacrificial dove, which was absorbed with a flash into the angel's scintillating form.

WHICH OF MY DUKES DOST THOU HOPE TO PRESS INTO THY SERVICE?

"By the grace of JEHOVAH TETRAGRAMMATON, and by thy Divine and infinite patience," Anja said, following the script Khalîl had taught her, "I would beseech thee to intercede on my behalf to secure the willing services of HAMARIEL."

WISELY CHOSEN, the angel said. ARE YOU PREPARED?

"I am. Will your duke consent to be yoked to my will?"

IT BENDS TO THE WILL OF THE DIVINE, WHICH HAS GRANTED THY BOON.

"Please direct HAMARIEL to appear inside the bounded circle to the northeast."

A cloud of light like silver rain manifested above the six-pointed star. Inside of it appeared a towering figure with magnificent feathered wings folded behind its back. The robes that hung loosely about its torso undulated as if submerged in a strong but sluggish current. Where Anja might have thought to see its face, there was only a brilliance that hurt to behold.

Confronted by both light and darkness, Anja's nerve faltered, but only for a moment. *I must not wait,* she reminded herself. *Do it quickly.*

She tucked her wand under her belt and loosened the ties on two pouches she had slung at either hip. From the left she took a fistful of gold dust, and in her right she clutched a handful of powdered emerald. She cast them together into her brazier. "*Adiuro caro uires et animos concatenata animam meam!*"

Crimson flames spiraled upward from the brazier and kissed the ceiling. Anja raised and extended both arms—her left hand stretched toward the demon, her right toward the angel.

The two spirits started to fade, becoming translucent—and then, as Anja closed her hands into fists, they were pulled forward with great violence and absorbed into her.

Vertigo and delirium overwhelmed Anja. The dual yoking felt like a push of heroin in her left arm and a shot of methamphetamine in her right. The angel and the demon warred inside of her, battling for control of her heart. They were waging what to them was just the latest battle in a war older than time. Neither cared that Anja's body was their battlefield; to them she was just an ephemeral vessel, her life nothing more than a blink in the stare of eternity.

I must regain focus, she commanded herself. *Finish the ritual.*

She opened her eyes. The room was still as she remembered, but it felt distant, unreal. Her hands moved as she willed, but she could not feel them. Then the room seemed to tilt. Dissociated from her body, Anja feared she might fall or otherwise stumble out of the operator's circle—a mistake that would cost her life and possibly those of her tanists unless they could terminate her experiment. She wanted to cry out a warning, but her mouth was as dry as ash.

Finish the ritual, she commanded herself.

She focused her mind on the two spirits grappling inside of her. *Enough! You are both bound to my will, and I command thee both to end your strife and be silent!*

The din of spiritual combat faded from her thoughts.

An eerie silence settled over Anja and the conjuring room.

From outside of the great circle, the invisible Abasdashon said, It is done.

Her equilibrium restored, Anja drew her wand.

"I thank thee, O great angel Abasdashon, messenger of Jehovah Tetragrammaton, for delivering unto me this blessing most holy. May its use be lawful and good in thy sight, and pleasing to thee and to Yahweh, the Lord Almighty. Thy boon having been fulfilled, I dismiss thee, great Abasdashon, with the deepest gratitude, and I charge thee to depart directly, doing harm to none, and to return when, and only when, I shall call for thee. In the name of Adonay, Elohim, Ariel, and Jehovam, depart!"

The spirit wasted no time in making its exit. One stroke of thunder and the Celestial radiance was extinguished, followed by a tempest wind that cleared away the noxious fog left behind by the demon and blew out all of the ceremonial candles.

For several seconds, no one in the room spoke.

Then Khalîl said, "The ritual is finished."

Anja closed the Iron Codex.

Exhausted and relieved, she dropped to her knees. "I did it," she whispered. Then, for the first time in more years than she could remember, she let out a laugh of pure joy.

I did it—and I am still alive.

The ritual was over, but the room still stank of demons. With every breath, Luis felt oppressed by the taint of sulfur in the air. Even the presence of

Celestial powers had failed to negate the effect, the angels having left behind their own powerful scent of ozone. He stood as if rooted to the floor inside his tanist's circle, his wand back under his belt and his arms slack at his sides, and he stared at nothing.

Around him the others left their places and divested themselves of their cassocks and miters. Briet was the most efficient of the group. She doffed her ceremonial garments, folded them, and tucked them inside her tool roll. Then she left the conjuring room without saying a word to anyone. No one made any effort to waylay her for congratulations or farewells. Noting her expression as she left, Luis surmised that Briet had found the ritual unnerving.

Anja paced outside the grand circle as if she were in a giddy daze. Cade watched her while he shed his robe and other accouterments, his eyes full of curiosity and longing.

Khalîl was the busiest of them. He closed the Iron Codex and tied its cover shut, and then he did the same for Anja's grimoire. With the ritual's two key tomes secured, he walked the circle and removed candles from their stands, gathering them all into a silk-lined box. The master noted Anja's sudden departure from the room, as well as Cade's anxious move to follow her. Then Khalîl resumed his labors, policing up the totems and then dousing the braziers with holy water—an act for which Luis was silently thankful, as the vapors from the extinguished charcoal helped suppress the demon's lingering foulness.

Through it all, Luis remained where he had been all along. Alone in his circle, neither moving nor speaking. He clocked Khalîl's actions along the edges of his vision, and he tracked the master's movements behind him by the sounds of his feet treading softly on the floor.

The master set the boxed totems on a table at the end of the room, and then he turned back to survey what remained of the preparations. "I wish we hadn't needed hematite for the northwest circle," he said, as if talking to himself. "Getting those marks off this floor won't be easy." He inspected the floor near the operator's circle. "And the monks won't be happy when they see these burn marks." He looked up at the blackened ceiling. "Or those."

Luis said nothing. What was there to say?

The old master puttered briefly behind Luis. He returned with a mop and a bucket. "I'm going to wash the floor. You don't need to move, but it might make my job easier."

A small nod of affirmation was all that Luis could muster.

Khalîl set aside the mop and bucket. "Would you like to talk, Father?"

"I wouldn't know where to begin," Luis said.

"Is it about the ritual?" Luis nodded. Khalîl continued, "Rules were made to be broken."

"Not according to the Church," Luis said, his voice flat, like that of a person in shock. "This went against everything my superiors at Monte Paterno told me was possible."

"It would not be the first time the Church concealed the truth to serve its own ends—or to suppress someone else's." The master seemed amused. "Is that really a surprise to you?"

Dismay and confusion raised Luis's brow. "If people I trusted have lied to me about the true potential of magick . . . about what else might they have lied? How can I trust that anything they've ever told me is true?"

Now the master regarded Luis with genuine concern. "Forgive me for prying, but are you suffering a crisis of faith, Father?"

"In God? No. I can lose my faith in people. In the Church. Maybe even the Bible. But even then my heart would still be filled with the love of God."

"As it should be." Khalîl moved closer to Luis. "Do you really wish to know more about magick? About the Goetic Art as well as the Pauline?"

Luis replied as if by rote, "Practicing the Goetic Art is a sin."

"So you've been told. But you've started to learn that not everything we are told turns out to be true." Khalîl stood in front of Luis, close enough for them to speak in a more confidential tone of voice. "If you can bring yourself to renounce the Synod, I would be honored to be your mentor in the true Art. The kind the Church would never let you practice."

"I can't," Luis said, his protest lacking all conviction. "Black magick is an abomination."

"That's the Church talking. The Goetic Art is just a body of lore and technique, a set of tools for investigating and manipulating the fabric of God's creation. Its only major difference from the Pauline Art is the Persons whom it presses into service."

"The Pauline Art is never used for violence," Luis countered. "I consider that distinction more than trivial."

Mischief sparkled in Khalîl's ancient eyes. "Father, if you were a student of ancient coinage, but you only ever studied one face of each coin you encountered, how could you presume to understand the fullness of your subject?" He gestured toward the markings on the floor. "Think about what Anja accomplished here tonight. She performed a ritual that united the Goetic and Pauline traditions. Merged the Right- and Left-hand paths. She has taken the Art in a new direction, one that promises balance. Harmony. *Wisdom.* Let go of your dogma and your prejudice, and share this new age of discovery with us." He reached out and rested his right hand on Luis's left shoulder in a quasi-paternal gesture. "Let us help you."

Luis rested his right hand over Khalîl's, and he smiled warmly at the master.

"I assure you, Master Khalîl . . . you already have."

On any other night Cade would have expected Anja to retreat to her prayer cell, to bow to her instinct to hide from the world—but this night was not like any other. He had seen it in her eyes, heard it in her laugh. Something had changed. She had changed.

His intuition became fact as he followed her out of the conjuring room and up a narrow flight of stairs to the roof of the monastery's highest building. Cade made no secret of the fact that he was following her, but she either didn't mind or didn't notice. At the top of the stairs he found the roof's door ajar. He pushed it open and stepped outside into a clean and bracing cold that he found refreshing after the sultry atmosphere of the experiment.

Anja stood in the center of the roof, her head tilted back, her arms raised and wide as if to embrace the universe. Her black hair billowed in the wind, and once again she laughed like one set free after a lifetime in chains. As her mirth subsided she let her arms fall slowly to her sides, but she continued to gaze at the stars.

Her back was to Cade as she said, "I know why you followed me." She faced him. She was smiling as she palmed a tear from her cheek. "You want to know how I did this."

"For starters, yeah. What made you think it was even *possible*?"

"Because I am like you," Anja said. "A *nikraim.*"

Cade didn't know what to say. "How can you—? I mean, I don't—" He shook his head in confusion. "How long have you known?"

"Since La Paz. Khalîl told me. Adair hid the truth from me because he feared what I might do." A profound sadness overtook her. "I could have closed the hellmouth in Dresden. If I had known, I would have. I would not have let you—"

"Don't apologize. You did nothing wrong." He moved closer to her. "If anyone owes an apology it's me, for pushing you to give me something I never should've asked for."

"I had no clue what I was doing," Anja said. "Or what my feelings meant." She looked at her feet, and her shoulders slumped as if the weight of all their bitter years had just landed on her at once. "I told you our affair meant nothing. . . . I lied." She looked into his eyes, and in hers Cade saw remorse. "I knew the truth," Anja continued, "but I was scared. And then I saw how much being with me meant to you. How much you wanted me with you. But I thought I had to be alone. That I had a mission." Tears fell from her eyes; she let them meander down her face. "But my mission was another lie. An excuse to hide. To run from myself. So that I did not have to see that I was wasting my life, alone in the shadows."

Cade reached up with his thumb to wick the tears from Anja's face, but then he hesitated. Anja gently took his hand and guided it to her cheek. "I told myself the same lies you did," he said, "only I didn't know they were lies until it was too late." His fingertips caressed the edge of her jaw. "I didn't know I was in love with you 'til you were gone."

Anja pressed her palm against his chest. "Even then, you were in pain. I felt it. A great wound in your soul. It has been there since the war. Since the day I brought you back."

"I know." Cade struggled to bury his memories of D-day. To forget his visions of Heaven and Hell and his prolonged exile in the astral plane, from which he had escaped only thanks to Anja's magickal ministrations. "I never told you what I saw on the other side of death. What I learned."

"I never wanted to ask," Anja said. "Any secret that came with such sorrow—" A shift in her expression signaled a moment of insight. "That is why you were curious about the codex."

"I hoped it might tell me why things are the way they are. Or give me the tools to call down a spirit that could."

Shame darkened Anja's countenance. "I was afraid to share it. I feared you would unlock its secrets before I did and take it away"—she looked up at him, her eyes wet with tears—"the only thing Adair left to me."

"I would never do that," Cade said. "You have my word." Standing so close to her, he felt the heat of angelic power coursing within her.

She smiled at him. "So . . . now we are equals."

He smiled back. "I never thought otherwise. But now that you're ready to master proto-Enochian, maybe you can help me find some answers to my—"

From the monastery below came a frantic ringing of bells followed by shouting voices. Cries of alarm. Cade and Anja shared a worried look: *So much for our moment alone.*

Then they ran back downstairs to see what had gone wrong this time.

The door to the conjuring room was blocked by an orange gaggle of monks. In no mood to be polite, Anja elbowed her way through the group and pushed the last two out of her way. Cade forced his way through the cluster a few paces behind her, and he came to a halt at her side as they took in the details of the room. The chalk markings on the floor were a scuffed mess.

Khalîl lay on the floor, awake but dazed, his head cradled in Brother Tenzin's lap.

Inside the circle, the lectern that had held the Iron Codex stood empty.

No! Anja's heart sank—her most valued possession had been stolen. She ran to Khalîl's side and kneeled, desperate for an explanation. "What happened?"

"Father Pérez," Khalîl said. "We were talking. . . . Put my hand on his shoulder. He grabbed my arm. Pulled it behind me—" He coughed. "Then his arm—around my throat. I tried to fight, but everything went black." He fought for breath. "I was only out for a minute, but—"

The knot of monks in the doorway unraveled again as Briet shouldered her way into the room. "What the hell—" Her eyes widened, first at the sight of Khalîl, and then at the empty lectern. "Where's the codex?"

Irked at Briet's callousness, Anja replied, "Master Khalîl is *fine,* thank you for—"

"Moron!" Briet snapped. "The codex is gone. So are Father Pérez's tools." She turned and seized one of the monks by his robe. "Where is the priest?"

The one she held shook his head and said nothing, but another monk answered from the hallway outside: "I saw him run downstairs."

"He can't use magick inside the monastery," Cade said, looking at Anja.

She finished his thought. "He's heading for the gateway!"

The monks cleared the doorway well ahead of the running departure of Briet, Anja, and Cade, who scrambled out of the conjuring room and down a dozen narrow flights of uneven steps, all in a desperate bid to catch the escaping White magician while they still could.

Holy ground or not, Anja vowed, *if I catch that* skotolozhets *I will feed him his balls.*

Briet led the chase down one flight of steps after another, zigzagging through Key Gompa's vertical maze in pursuit of the fleeing priest.

Father Pérez's path was not hard to follow. There were only a handful of direct routes to the main road that led out of the compound, and the Jesuit thief's trail was littered with stunned and bruised Buddhist monks who had been unlucky enough to be in his way. One had been knocked down while carrying a basket filled with fruit now scattered on the ground; another had been pushed into a cart of silks, beneath which he now lay pinned.

Briet hurdled over the trapped monk and took the next descending flight two steps at a time. Cade was close behind her, matching her step for step, with Anja only a few strides behind him. Even in the middle of the night the pathways of Key Gompa were lit by the soft light of paper lanterns and glows of firelight beyond drawn curtains, but the shadows were deep and deceptive, especially in the stairways.

Above her, voices shouted out warnings and more bells rang. Monks populated the rooftops and leaned from windows, all curious to see the cause of the midnight commotion. Some pointed as they cried out, but most stared, jaws agape—in other words, useless.

Sprinting down the main road toward the monastery's main gateway, Briet passed more monks who had been felled by Father Pérez. One with a broken nose cried out to her as she ran past, "He hit me with a book!" Another lying on the side of the road just moaned pitiably while he cradled his broken left arm. An older monk lay sprawled in the center of the dirt road, spread-eagled and unconscious. Briet dodged around him and hugged the inside curve as she rounded the final bend toward the temple's main entrance.

Father Pérez was several dozen yards ahead of her, very nearly to the gateway. His leather roll of karcist's tools banged against his back in a steady rhythm as he ran, barefoot, while hugging the Iron Codex to his chest with both arms.

"Luis!" Cade called from a few yards behind Briet. "Stop!"

Cade's shouting only made the priest run faster.

If only I could put a lightning bolt up his ass, Briet lamented. But she had surrendered her yoked spirits in exchange for sanctuary inside Key Gompa, leaving her without magick. Even the Russian woman, despite having just yoked two spirits, couldn't exercise the powers of either one inside the heavily warded confines of the monastery. But was the priest really this foolhardy? Couldn't he smell the demons lurking just beyond Key Gompa's defenses?

The two advantages that Cade, Anja, and Briet had over Father Pérez were that they didn't have to lug a ponderous grimoire while making this mad run, and that they were wearing shoes. On the last downhill stretch toward the gate they nearly closed the distance to the errant priest, who passed through the open gateway and continued without stopping. Just a second behind him, the trio fanned out to flank him—

A burst of fire blocked the road ahead of Father Pérez.

The priest lifted the codex and used it to defend his face from the flames. All that Briet and Cade could do was stumble backward a few steps and raise their hands—and then Briet realized that Anja had manifested a shield around the three of them and Father Pérez.

As the flames dissipated, a trio clad in white parkas and other winter survival gear emerged from hiding along the road ahead of Luis. All three brandished wands of natural, twisted wood. One summoned a fistful of lightning, and another cocooned his hand in macabre indigo light. All of them focused their attention on Father Pérez.

The priest turned his back on his ambushers and smiled sadly at his pursuers.

"Forgive me." He closed his eyes—

A bolt of lightning shot down from above, accompanied by an earth-shaking stroke of thunder. In a flash Father Pérez was gone, and where he had stood nothing remained but a wild scar of scorched ground.

For an awkward second, the Black Sun ambushers and the trio of renegade karcists regarded each other with mute surprise across the expanse of suddenly empty space.

Then the dabbler with a handful of lightning raised his arm to throw it—

Anja lashed out with three attacks at once: a javelin of hellfire that skewered one dabbler, a spear of light that staked the second to the ground, and an invisible attack that wrenched the third into a bloody pretzel whose screams ended quickly—unlike the wet cracks of his splintering bones and shattering vertebrae, which went on for half a minute after he was dead.

Briet turned to congratulate Anja, only to find the dark-haired Russian on her knees, tears falling from her closed eyes. Cade took a knee beside her and tried to console her, but his words were of no help. Sorrow and rage poured from her in an unstoppable flood.

"Gone! . . . He took it. Stole it! The only . . . only thing . . ."

Cade wrapped Anja in an embrace that seemed only to amplify her grief.

Briet looked at the dead men lying in the road, and then at the weeping woman in Cade's arms. "I take it losing that book was a big deal."

Cade shot a poisonous look at Briet. "You have no idea."

"Then maybe it's time you made me understand." She moved closer and stood over them. "Whatever's going on, we're *all* part of it, whether we like it or not. So in the name of mutual survival, and maybe also saving the world, I suggest we go inside, sit down, and share what we all know, until we all get on *the same fucking page.*"

⚬⚬⚬

Moving with the speed of a thought and the grace of Heaven, Luis felt more alive than he ever had. He was the crash of thunder; he was the brilliance of lightning. In a glorious blaze that transformed him into living fire, he vanished from the mountainside in India—

—and in a flash he stood on a street of paved stones set diagonally, flanked by the familiar architecture of western Rome. Streetlamps set atop obelisks glowed with amber light, barely visible through the torrential downpour that scoured the Via della Conciliazione. It was late enough that the streets would have been sparsely populated under the best of conditions, but tonight the broad thoroughfare stood deserted, its usual complement of late-night pedestrians driven to shelter by the cold wind and rain.

He held the Iron Codex to his chest as he turned to see a welcoming shape through the storm: the dome of St. Peter's Basilica. The power of MALGARAS had delivered him to within mere meters of Vatican City, just outside the zone of its own formidable defenses against magickal intrusion.

Luis looked toward Heaven and let the rain fall upon him like a baptism.

Forgive me, Lord. I have borne false witness. I have stolen. I have raised my hands in violence. I have taken part in rituals unclean. For these and my sins of pride, I beg Your forgiveness. And I ask You to watch over the souls of Khalîl, Cade, Briet, and Anja. Amen.

Not minding the sting of the rain against his face or the slick chill of the wet cobblestones beneath his feet, Luis made his way west across the Piazza San Pietro, and then up the steps of the Basilica di San Pietro. His mission was very nearly at an end, his victory and vindication at hand. At the doors of the basilica, he stopped.

I should feel joy, he brooded, *or at the very least, relief. But all I feel . . . is shame.*

Part of him wondered whether he had made a mistake—but then he recalled his training. *I was executing papal orders. It is not for me to question the wisdom of the Pontiff, or the holy mission of the Church. I must have faith that my cause is noble and my actions just.*

Hope and regret warred for his heart as he opened the door and went inside.

30

FEBRUARY 21, PART II

A surfeit of conversation had thickened the air inside the monastery's library. Taking turns around the long reading table at which they sat, Anja, Cade, Khalil, and Briet had passed the night sharing one revelation after another. Dawn had come and gone while the four magicians had laid bare every secret that they thought might be relevant to the crisis at hand.

Now, as the sun neared its apex above Key Gompa, all four of them possessed a much clearer picture of the threat: The link between Dragan and the Black Sun. The warnings Briet had received from her patron about a "black dawn." And the ultimatum that Dragan had given to Anja, that he would turn an imminent atomic-weapons test in the Marshall Islands into a breach of Hell's gate unless she gave him the Iron Codex.

It was a recipe for an apocalypse, of that much Anja was certain.

"Now that we see the danger," Khalil said, "we must decide how to stop it."

Anja pushed back her chair from the table and stood. "There is no stopping it. Not without the codex." She walked to the library's only window, which was behind Khalil's chair at the head of the narrow table. "We have lost our strongest weapon and our only bargaining chip."

Her protest drew a pensive look from Briet. "The weapon, yes. The bargaining chip? Maybe not. If Dragan doesn't know that Luis stole it, we might be able to bluff him."

Cade shook his head. "There's no way he doesn't know we've lost the codex. Hell, the Synod's probably throwing a party for its return even as we speak." A defeated sigh. "I'm sorry, but Anja's right. Without the codex, we're fucked."

"We might not be able to bargain," Briet said, "but we can still attack."

Cade answered her assertion with incredulity. "Attack who? Dragan? I'd love to, if I had the slightest fucking idea where he is." He grabbed a sheaf of papers filled with handwritten calculations and crushed them in his fist. "I've been running numbers for almost a week, trying to match the 'bunker' chart I found in the Odessa journal to a date and a place." He threw the pages back down onto the table. "So far I've only got the date and a range of longitude."

Briet signaled her doubts with a raised eyebrow. "Are you even sure you have *that*?"

"Positive." Cade plucked a sheet of paper from the bottom of the crumpled pile. "Whoever made this chart was precise. The positions of the sun and the inner celestial bodies are tracked to the arc second. I cross-checked the sun, Mercury, Venus, the moon, and Mars, and all of their positions are correct for precisely six forty-five P.M. Greenwich Mean Time on February twenty-eighth."

At the end of the table, Khalîl nodded. "That verifies the time."

"If I had to guess," Briet said, "I'd bet that's when Castle Bravo goes off."

Khalîl scrunched his brow. "Cade, you said you also had a longitude?"

"A *range* of longitude." Cade pointed at details on the bunker horoscope. "This chart has the sun, Mercury, and Venus in the Twelfth House, all sitting right on top of the First House cusp. That means this chart was drawn for a location that'll be seeing sunrise when it's almost seven o'clock at night in London. The only place on earth where that's possible is a narrow sliver of the Pacific Ocean, between one hundred seventy-three and one hundred seventy-five degrees of west longitude." He sighed. "That, unfortunately, is all I can tell you so far."

Briet's brow wrinkled with curiosity. She reached across the table and picked up one of the sheets of calculations. "Why can't you find the latitude?"

"Because shifting even a few arc seconds of latitude can change all the house cusps."

"Cade is correct," Khalîl interjected. "Even the smallest variations in latitude can alter the apparent relationships of celestial objects, constellations, and the zodiacal houses."

Their objections failed to diminish Briet's interest. "But you said this longitudinal line cuts through the Pacific Ocean. There can't be that many viable locations for Dragan's hideout."

"There are more than enough." Cade reached inside his bomber jacket, pulled out a map, and unfolded it flat on the table. With one finger he traced a line from north to south through the central Pacific. "This longitude misses the Pacific Proving Grounds, so we know it's not for the atomic test site. It's close to a few of these tropical islands, but they're so small and populated that there's no way Dragan could base himself there without drawing attention."

Briet asked, "Could the coordinates be at sea? What if Dragan's on a boat?"

"Most grimoires warn against conducting experiments at sea," Khalîl said. "Magick is meant to be practiced on solid ground, and with good reason."

Cade continued, "As it happens, there's only one significant landmass that falls along this longitude." His finger stopped in the South Pacific. "New Zealand."

The master rose from his chair as Briet circled the table. From the window, Anja watched them huddle behind Cade and look over his shoulders as they studied the map.

Khalîl pointed at the tiny island nation. "Why would he be there?"

"For one thing," Cade said, "it's a safe distance from the atomic test."

Briet nodded. "And sparsely populated in certain areas. Good for privacy."

The old master stroked his beard. "Yes, I see. Perhaps we should assume Dragan would avoid cities and choose to make his stand in a remote area. Away from the eyes of the curious."

Anger born of frustration darkened Cade's expression. "I've run the numbers for half a dozen sites all over New Zealand. Each time it takes me nearly a full day to compute all the variants on the house cusps, and each time I'm wrong is another day wasted." He shuffled through pages of equations and set one on top of the map. "The closest I've come to matching the chart with a New Zealand location is Tangiwai. And get this: A rail bridge collapsed there on Christmas Eve. Sent a train full of people into a river. The news said there were no survivors."

A grim nod from Briet. "That *sounds* like something Dragan might do. But why?"

"No idea," Cade said.

Anja was tired of listening to her peers prattle without purpose. "It makes no difference." She waited until the other karcists looked at her, and then she continued. "Even if you find Dragan, how can I fight him without the codex? Without it I cannot even beg for peace."

The old master stood straight, no doubt in a bid to make himself look taller and more commanding. "There is always a way forward."

"Not against Dragan. Not without the codex." Anja fixed her stare upon

Cade. "The plan you found, the one that fuses a demon to a bomb and turns its shelter into a magickal lens. I command no spirits who can undo those charms. Do you?" She pointed at Briet. "Do you?" She felt satisfied that she had made her point. "Without the codex this war is lost. If you still wish to fight, the first thing we must do is take back the codex."

Briet almost laughed. "You want to break into Vatican City? One of the most heavily defended places on earth. A place where you can't bring yoked demons. And you think you're just going to walk in, evade the Swiss Guard, breach the Pope's secret archives, find your codex inside one of the largest libraries in the world, *steal it,* and somehow escape with it *and* your life?" Her voice rose in pitch and volume as she added, "Are you *insane*?"

"This. Or nothing." Anja spread her arms. "Who is with me?"

An awkward silence. Then Briet shook her head. "No. There are ways I can help you"—she shot a cryptic look at Cade—"but dying at the hands of the Swiss Guard isn't one of them." As she exited the library she added, "If you live through this, I'll be in touch." Her footsteps echoed and faded as she retreated through an outer passage and then down the nearest stairs.

Khalîl wore a look of regret. "Forgive me, Anja. I am far too old to risk such peril without the defenses of magick." His countenance turned mischievous. "However . . . I've been inside the Vatican's archives more than once. I might not be able to join you in this heist, but I can tell you how to get inside—and where to look once you're there."

"Thank you, Master Khalîl." That left only one person to answer, the one whose aid Anja most feared to solicit, never mind accept. But she would need all the help she could get if she truly meant to recover the codex. She faced Cade. "And you?"

"Apparently, the Church no longer considers 'Thou Shalt Not Steal' to be a binding commandment." His face, as youthful and as handsome as ever, brightened with a roguish smile. "Let's go where *they* live and do unto them as they've done unto us."

⁓

Ever a fan of symmetry, Briet appreciated her circumstances for nothing if not their balance: she had come to Key Gompa all but empty-handed, and now she was taking her leave of the ancient temple in the same state. Aside from some winter clothes she had begged from the monks, all she was toting out of the monastery was her karcist's tools and a small battered rucksack into which she had packed some food and water—and one sheet of paper.

A copy of the bunker horoscope from the Odessa journal.

Something about the horoscope Cade had obsessed over for the past week now had snared Briet's interest. She had watched with curiosity and amusement as the American had struggled in vain to deduce the location indicated by the chart. His was a task she did not envy. Trying to reverse-engineer the chart's initial data set using only manual calculations was, at best, a fool's errand. All the same, she had a hunch that Cade was right about its importance and that unlocking its elusive mathematical secret might be the key to staving off a global disaster.

Or maybe it's a diversion, she worried. *A ruse to waste our time.*

She had a plan to find the answer—but first she needed to get home.

The brick of American cash she had brought with her would buy airline tickets back to the United States once she reached New Delhi, but in rural India foreign currency was all but useless. Here she would have to rely on barter. She always traveled with a hidden pouch of small uncut gemstones and a few nuggets of gold and silver. Those, she hoped, would help her secure a ride or maybe buy her a horse that would take her back to the edge of modern civilization.

None of the Buddhist monks spoke to her as she made her way to the main road that encircled the monastery. She tried to avoid meeting their stares, but even with her eyes averted she felt the weight of their contempt.

Leaving this place would be a relief, she was certain of it.

The long shadows of late afternoon stretched across the dirt road, deepening winter's chill. Briet did her best not to fixate upon the cold, or the wind, or the long empty miles that stretched out ahead of her. It would be a long hike to New Delhi, and a dangerous one unless she secured some kind of transportation.

The KGB almost certainly knows I'm here, she brooded. *The last thing I need is—*

She halted in the middle of the road.

A lone figure stood under the open gateway, facing her. Briet squinted against the glare of sunlight off the snow until she recognized Khalîl. *What does he want now?*

She resumed walking. As she neared the gateway, he shifted his position to bar her exit. A gust of wind billowed his robe around his wiry frame. He held up a hand. "Briet."

Briet stopped. "You can't keep me here."

"I don't intend to." Khalîl brought his sleeves together to shelter his hands from the cold. "But I will speak my mind before you go."

Her patience waned. "Be quick about it, then."

"Your meeting with the Vate Pythia. She told you that your path is not yet set."

"She said I'd broken her prophecy. Which I guess means she isn't much of an Oracle."

The master shook his head. "Far from it. And I doubt that you've defied her prognostication. At best, I would say you might have deferred it."

"Get to the point, old man. It's freezing out here."

"You can still claim the destiny you abandoned during the war."

"I never wanted that destiny. I'll do without it." She tried to step around him, but he was quicker and more agile than he seemed. "Let me go."

He parted his sleeves and reached out with his crooked right hand to hold hers. "You knew what you needed to do, but you ran away. You knew what road led to redemption, but you did not take it. Now the paths you've followed have led you back to that crossroads."

His words chilled her deeper than winter ever could.

She was struck by memories of her decision to abandon Kein Engel, to disguise herself and flee Nazi-occupied Europe in the hope that she could shield herself from the consequences of his escalating madness. Suddenly, the truth spilled from her unbidden.

"I knew I should have killed him . . . but I didn't think I was strong enough. How do you stab the Devil in the back? If you fail, you don't get a second chance."

Khalîl closed both his hands around Briet's. "There are no second chances. Just moments islanded in the river of time. But hear me, Briet: You can do better than you have—you can *be* better. You command powers that can shape the fabric of the universe—or rend it. Will you be an agent of light, or of darkness?"

"I've tried to serve the light."

"Is that what you told yourself last summer? When you helped the Americans topple the elected government of Iran, all so the British and the Americans could go on plundering Iran's oil?" His tone darkened. "Such actions always come with unintended consequences. Even now there are cells of Islamic dark magicians uniting to act in concert against the powers of the West. They've started to call America 'the Great Satan.' Ask yourself, Briet: Is that really who you want to be? Is that what you want to serve?"

Briet freed her hand from Khalîl's gentle grasp. "I can't change the past. I can't refight the war, or untrain Dragan, or put Iran back together again." She shouldered past him, this time refusing to bend to his passive obstruction. "It's too late for me. Just let me go."

She walked away from Key Gompa. Part of her hoped that Khalîl might call out to her, try to bargain with her, give her a reason not to embrace the nomad's path. But as she plodded down the dirt road, there was nothing at her back but wind and silence.

Melting wax and smoldering incense. Old leather. Ancient wood polished with lemon oil—the office of Cardinal Lombardi was a feast for the olfactory sense. Luis stood in front of the cardinal's desk, reverently silent while the Synod leader examined the Iron Codex. It took effort for Luis not to stare in wonder as Lombardi pored over the tome. Instead, Luis turned his eyes away—to the towering walls of shelves that were filled with books obscure and arcane, curios and artifacts older than most of Western civilization, and objets d'art worth more than the gross domestic product of most countries in the developing world.

"You've done well, Father," the cardinal said, studying the fine details of a page through an antique gold jeweler's loupe. "The codex is intact and undamaged. Most remarkable."

Luis bowed his head in a gesture of humility. "I am relieved to hear it, Eminence."

The window blind behind Lombardi was closed, but intense morning light bled past its edges, casting the older man in a partial silhouette as he closed and sealed the codex. "You have done the Church a great service by returning this to our care." He looked up wearing a smile that struck Luis as less than genuine. "As a token of thanks from His Holiness, you have been forgiven for defying our explicit orders to return from New Delhi."

"Too kind, Your Eminence." Luis watched the cardinal sheath the codex in a bag of midnight-blue crushed velvet trimmed with golden thread. "Might I be permitted to inquire about opportunities for research?"

A quizzical look from Lombardi. "I've recommended to His Holiness that he should renew Monte Paterno's charter for another half century. You and your brothers will be free to continue your studies through the end of the millennium."

At the risk of angering the cardinal, Luis chose to clarify his point. "Your Eminence, I speak with regard to the Iron Codex. It is an essential guide to the Celestial—"

"The codex will remain *here*," Lombardi interrupted. "This book is too valuable to be entrusted to anything but the Vatican's secret archives."

Luis felt the cardinal's unspoken contempt and condescension for him as a practitioner of the Pauline Art. "A sensible precaution, Your Eminence. That said, my peers and I would be willing to conduct our studies of the codex here—under proper supervision, of course."

His suggestion left Lombardi red in the face. "Absolutely not! Neither I nor His Holiness will ever permit the abominations of sorcery to be committed within the walls of Vatican City."

It took effort for Luis to constrain his temper. "I never implied any such thing, Your Eminence, nor would I. But if my brothers and I could consult the codex here and then conduct our experiments back at Monte Paterno—"

"Experiments," Lombardi cut in. "Such a sanitized term for an abomination." He removed the codex from his broad desk and tucked it out of sight. "The Church did not send you to recover this book only to see you unleash its heresies upon the world."

"Your Eminence, please! The codex must be studied! It holds secrets to—"

"Enough! The decision has been *made*, Father, and it is not subject to further debate. Learn to accept that you will never again see or lay hands upon the Iron Codex. And while you're expurgating yourself of contaminating influences, I recommend you abandon all thought of ever again taking part in the horrid practice of yoking spirits." Lombardi's rebuke took on an edge of intimidation as he asked, "Do I make myself perfectly clear, Father Pérez?"

Luis lowered his head. "Most clear, Eminence."

"Good. Show yourself out."

Wearing a mask of obedience, Luis seethed as he stood, turned, and walked out of the cardinal's office, leaving behind the most powerful artifact of White magick he had ever seen. He knew that he had no avenue of appeal for Lombardi's decision. The argument was lost, and the codex with it; consequently,

Luis had no reason to stay in Rome. But DAROCHIEL, the angel whose gift of intuition Luis had not yet released, urged him to stay.

Dismayed but not defeated, Luis returned to his guest quarters in the Apostolic Palace to see what the future might yet bring.

FEBRUARY 23

Opening a portal from one place on earth to another was the simplest thing in the world, or so the voice had explained to Dragan. All one really had to do was use the gift of SITRAX to fold together two disparate points in the fabric of reality and then cut open a path between them using an athamé whose edge had been refined on the Infernal anvil of OROCHEL. It couldn't be easier.

The transition from a dry and bracing chill to the sweltering embrace of the tropics hit Dragan like a damp blanket thrown in his face. All at once the air became so thick that breathing in became a labor; each breath felt as if it were more water vapor than air.

His stylish shoes sank into the warm, wet sand. A frothy wave lapped at the shore and kissed his heels, prompting him to dance a few steps forward onto dry ground. He had left his suit jacket behind, knowing what awaited him, but now that he had arrived on the northwest shore of Bikini Atoll's Namu Island, he wished he had come au naturel.

How can anybody breathe in this soup?

The voice in his head replied, «*Save your complaints for those who care. We came here to set our endgame in motion.*»

I am well aware of the reason for our visit. I only wish it weren't necessary. Dragan trudged down the beach, displeased by the sensation of sand creeping into his shoes with every step he took. He looked up at the stars. Here, close to the equator, he expected them to shine with extra brilliance. Instead, they looked dulled by the humidity, and they flickered more violently than he had ever seen before.

But the atoll itself—it was beautiful. White sand. Clear water in its lagoon, even at night. A dense jungle covered Namu Island, whose primeval beauty resounded with the whoops of birds and the sawing music of insects. Bikini Atoll was nothing short of a paradise.

«*So naturally, mankind has come to destroy it.*»

Man did not destroy Eden, Dragan reminded his soul rider. *We were exiled from it.*

«*And have borne it a grudge ever since,*» the voice retorted. «*Hence humanity's singular passion for laying waste the very orb that sustains it.*»

In no mood to revisit old arguments, Dragan sequestered his thoughts as he walked the beach toward the causeway. The man-made sandbar stretched more than 2,900 feet southwest from Namu's western shore. Its broad, smooth surface was occupied mostly by a stacked cluster of pipes in a rigid framework. Those pipes linked a bunker full of protected recording devices to a suite of sensors inside the shot cab, a concrete building at the far end of the causeway. The official purpose of the shot cab was to protect those sensors so that the scientists could gather uncorrupted data about the impending detonation of their latest hydrogen device, which the Americans had code-named Castle Bravo.

Dragan, of course, had other plans for both the shot cab and the atomic device. Plans that he had to be certain would not be interrupted by those who lacked his clarity of vision.

A squad of American soldiers stood between him and the entrance to the causeway. He had been told that they preferred to be called marines, not that he cared. Dragan wrapped himself in silence and invisibility before he emerged from the darkness, and with the wiles of PALOCHEL he passed by them without leaving so much as a single footprint in the wet sand.

He quickened his pace across the causeway. Holding so many spirits yoked at once was taxing his strength, and he couldn't risk being spotted before he reached the shot cab.

By the time he reached it he was almost jogging, and his shirt and hair both were drenched in sweat. He palmed bullets of perspiration from his forehead and swept his hair back from his face. *I was not meant for such sultry conditions,* he lamented.

«*Then I suspect you will not find Hell much to your taste,*» his rider teased.

Two more marines blocked the entrance to the shot cab, a drab and boxlike structure of pale gray concrete three stories tall. Dragan put both men to sleep with a wave of his hand and the gift of BAETHUS. They slumped unconscious to the ground as he walked past them, opening the locked door with the power of PERFIDEX, almost as if by reflex.

The interior of the shot cab was not much more impressive than its banal exterior. On one side, a riot of pipes intruded through the wall, their ends open to reveal lenses and other sensory devices, all of them trained upon one thing built into a housing of metal along the opposite wall:

The Castle Bravo device.

Installed only three days earlier, it looked nothing like a bomb; it was just an ordinary cylinder with no obvious openings or panels, like an oversized water heater on iron stilts. It had been sealed in Los Alamos, New Mexico. Only a handful of souls on earth knew that the device hid a demonic stowaway, one whose Infernal essence would be ripped apart by the hydrogen blast, unleashing a fury of energy far beyond human comprehension.

«*And the inscriptions we are about to place will focus and amplify that energy toward a single purpose,*» the voice said to Dragan. «*The sundering of Hell's gates.*»

Dragan took the enchanted black pearl from his trouser pocket. Holding the tiny orb of darkness between his thumb and forefinger, he hesitated to do his rider's bidding. *Are we sure about this? Once it's done, there is no turning back.*

His rider was adamant. «*We no longer have a choice. The girl lost the codex to the Vatican. This is the only way.*»

But are you sure this will work? Never in the history of the Art has a conjuring circle been situated so far across the world from the operator.

«*Then this will be one for the record books.*»

But how can we monitor the experiment if we—?

«*I will see to it. Do what needs to be done.*»

Dragan raised the black pearl above his head. "*Et non abscondam a praesidio cum circulo inscribi meo obumbratio!*" He threw the pearl at the concrete floor. It shattered and released a flurry of green and indigo smoke flickering with spectral light, and the raging wind assailed Dragan with odors of sulfur and sandalwood. When the Infernal tempest abated, he saw that a thaumaturgic circle had been scribed into the concrete, and glyphs of warding and focus covered the walls and ceiling. All of the magickal inscriptions glowed for a moment, as if they had been cast from molten metal—and then they all faded from sight, masked by an illusion.

«*Well done,*» the soul rider said as Dragan walked out of the shot cab, back into the smothering embrace of the tropical night. Using the Sight of RAUM, he beheld the enormous dome of protection they had erected. It stretched for more than a mile in every direction around the shot cab, reached hundreds of feet into the air, and extended beneath the waves. Within it swarmed a small army of demons tasked with keeping any karcist but Dragan from getting anywhere near the Castle Bravo device.

"It's done," Dragan said under his breath. "In five days, Armageddon begins."

«Don't be so melodramatic,» the voice chided. «This is not the end. Just a new beginning. Now, let us return to safety—and ready ourselves to usher in a new age.»

FEBRUARY 25

Short of blackouts, perfect darkness was nowhere to be found in modern cities. On overcast nights the reflected street light of Washington, D.C., tinted the clouds with pastel hues of peach and tangerine. Neither was there any true silence on the streets of the capital. Even in the small hours of the morning, the distant drone of traffic and the cries of the wind as it passed beneath the elevated highways suffused the city with soft white noise.

New York isn't the only city that never sleeps, Briet mused. She made the turn onto the Georgetown block she called home. *All our cities have become insomniacs.*

She stopped at the bottom of the steps to her brownstone's front door. Even from the street she could see that it had been damaged. The knob and front plate were new, and fresh wood in the door's jamb had not yet been stained to match the older pieces.

Briet scowled. Someone had forced open the front door of her home, and she had a reasonably good idea who might be to blame. Her anger festered as she climbed the steps, but she tried to let it go, to purge herself of poisonous feelings before she faced her lovers.

At the top of the steps she tried to push her key into the lock. When it didn't fit, her confusion was brief. *They had to change the lock when they fixed the door,* she realized.

Feeling like a visitor to her own home, she knocked on the front door.

At once there came sounds of activity from inside the house. Hyun and Alton conferred in hushed voices tinged with concern. Dim lamps snapped on behind pale draperies as they neared the front door. Then came the *clacks* of bolts and locks being undone.

It was Alton who opened the door and first saw Briet, but Hyun darted past him to wrap herself around Briet and pepper her face with kisses, all without saying a word. Then Alton enfolded them both in his embrace, and Briet knew that she was home.

After several seconds Hyun paused in her affectionate assault, long enough for Briet to suggest, "We should go inside." Alton nodded and helped Briet free herself from Hyun, whom she led to the front room. Alton closed the front door behind them.

At a glance Briet knew the room had been ransacked. The furniture was in all the right places, but the contents of the shelves and end tables were in chaos, as if they had been scattered by violence and then grudgingly restored to a semblance of their proper place. Hyun's favorite lamp stood dark in the corner; its bulb had been shattered, and its stained-glass shade now was marred by chips and fissures. Everywhere that Briet looked she found more proof that her home had been violated. A rude homecoming after five long flights and four days in transit.

She faced her lovers. "We've had visitors while I was away."

"They had a search warrant," Alton said. "It felt like Nazi Germany."

His unknowing invocation of Briet's hidden past filled her with shame, but she did her best not to let it show. She looked at sweet, fragile Hyun. "Did they hurt you?"

"No," she said. She tried to project confidence, but her eyes were full of fear.

"They asked us lots of questions about you," Alton said. "They wanted to know where you'd gone. What you'd taken with you." He leaned in and lowered his voice, as if they might be under surveillance. "Are you in some kind of trouble? What's going on?"

"I'm fine," she lied. "It's all going to be okay."

She climbed the stairs to the second floor. There, too, she found signs of government intrusion. Framed photos had been knocked askew, their panes cracked. Was nothing sacred?

Then she arrived at the door to her study. It listed at an angle. Whoever had kicked it open had ripped its top hinge from the door's frame. She nudged it open, dreading what she knew would await her on the other side. It was every bit as bad as she had feared.

Her desk had been smashed into kindling, her shelves torn down. The agents who had done this clearly had come with an intent to terrorize Briet's loved ones. All of her reference books had been torn apart, their pages scattered. *Some of those were first editions,* she thought with equal parts rage and sorrow. The contents of her desk's drawers had been spilled across the floor.

Mementos of her life in the Art—none of them commercially valuable but all of them irreplaceable—had obviously been crushed underfoot with malice aforethought.

It was infuriating, but Briet had endured worse offenses.

Then her eyes found the wreckage of Trixim's cage.

Its metal frame had been kicked to pieces; his glass water bottle was smashed, and his comfortable bed of straw had been used as an ashtray before it was pissed upon.

Briet's eyes filled with hot, rageful tears. She gritted her teeth to stop herself from sobbing. Gazing upon the remains of Trixim's cage reopened the wound left by his loss, and it rekindled the fury she had unleashed on the demon that had killed her beloved familiar.

Behind her a dry scuffle of shoes on hardwood. Briet palmed the tears from her eyes and turned to face Alton. "I guess I have some cleaning to do."

"This was McCarthy, wasn't it?"

"I don't know, love. Maybe."

Alton shrank his voice to a fearful whisper. "Hyun is scared, Briet. She's talking about going back to South Korea." He stuffed his hands into his cardigan's pockets and stared at his shoes. "I can't say as I'd blame her."

Briet put aside her feelings of violation and summoned her courage. "No one is going anywhere." She stepped out of her study and curled her arm around Alton's so that he would walk with her. "Go downstairs. Mix her a gin and tonic. Tell her I'm going to fix this."

"And how do you mean to do that?"

"Just mix the drinks, Alton. Leave the rest to me."

He stopped her at the top of the stairs. There was real worry in his voice as he said, "You're not just a research assistant at the DOD . . . are you?"

She kissed him, then caressed his stubbled cheek. "I'm many things, my love. More than I can name. But as of now, I am first and foremost an agent of *vengeance*—and when I find the men who did this to you and Hyun, I give you my solemn vow: I will *make them pay.*"

Though it called itself a city, the Vatican in many ways better resembled a small town. Insular, suspicious of outsiders, and jealous in the defense of its privacy, it conversely made a habit of intruding upon the personal sanctity of its denizens. Even in its most secluded gardens and remotest pathways, true isolation was difficult to come by.

Luis had resigned himself to Vatican City's impositions, but he still did his best to keep to himself and avoid unnecessary contact with others. As a general rule that had meant staying away from the parts of the city most prone to tourism: the museum, the Sistine Chapel, the Basilica of St. Peter, and St. Peter's Square. Even once he spared himself those interactions, however, he still had to contend with the full-time residents of Vatican City, many of whom evinced either disgust or an unhealthy inquisitiveness upon learning the nature of his studies at Monte Paterno. For his own peace of mind, he had made a habit of conducting his morning meditations at a different location each day, to make himself harder to find.

Today he had secreted himself on the marble bench built into the wall of the Oval Courtyard of Casina Pio IV, a sixteenth-century villa adorned with frescoes and sculptures. Its courtyard was a work of art unto itself, with a geometric mosaic of gray and white marble tiles, and its central fountain of black marble topped with a pair of mirror-image cherubs astride leaping dolphins. Luis found the music of water splashing into its basin restful enough that he was able to block out the occasional footsteps of scholars coming and going from the Pontifical Academy of Sciences, which were housed within the former papal residence.

He had very nearly achieved a state of clear-minded bliss when he heard someone sit down beside him. He suspected he knew who it was.

Maybe if I remain still and say nothing, he will leave me in—

"Father Pérez," said Cardinal Lombardi. "I'm surprised you're still here."

Luis opened his eyes. "My ordeal in India was quite taxing, Eminence."

"So I'd gathered from your request for prolonged sanctuary." Lombardi and Luis watched a scholar walk past on his way out of the villa, and then the cardinal said, "I also learned this morning that you've submitted a request for access to the secret archives."

There was no point in denying what was already a matter of record. "I did."

"To what end, Father?"

"May I speak plainly, Eminence?" Encouraged by a nod from Lombardi, Luis continued. "I know you can't be so obtuse that you don't see what's at hand. Dragan Dalca means to blast open the gates of Hell and unleash untold horrors upon the earth."

The cardinal appeared unmoved. "I have my doubts about that. But even if you're correct, Father, the Covenant forbids us from interfering with his experiment. We are barred even from praying for its failure. So what would be gained by letting you access the codex?"

"If nothing else, it might give me and my brothers at Monte Paterno a chance to contain the damage after the fact. Perhaps even to close the gates and seal the breach."

A disapproving glare telegraphed Lombardi's objection. "That is not your decision to make, Father. If such a calamity should manifest, it will fall to His Holiness to make—"

"By then it will be too late, Eminence. Once billions have died and the world is laid waste, what will be the value of all our thoughts and prayers? The time for action is now."

"You forget yourself, my son." Lombardi stood and smoothed the front of his cassock. "I suspect the atmosphere of Vatican City disagrees with you. Perhaps you might be happier if you returned north, to your cloister."

Luis rose and took a confrontational stand in front of the cardinal. "You want me to turn away from evil? Abet the Devil's ill works by omission, in the name of the Covenant?" When the cardinal tried to step around him, Luis blocked his escape. "I wonder: Was the Covenant our excuse when the Church decided to help Nazi war criminals escape Europe for South America?"

Lombardi thrust his index finger like a stiletto at Luis's face. "Do not *ever* speak of that again. Not to me. Not to anyone. Do you understand, Father?"

"I understand all too well, Eminence."

The cardinal shook his head in disappointment. "You are too old to be so naïve, Father. By now you should have learned that in the real world, good and evil are far from absolutes."

"As it happens, I have learned the opposite. I've looked both pure good and true evil in the eye, and now I can tell the difference between them." He added with a touch of menace, "I also know which one I'm looking at right now."

"May that gift serve you well." Lombardi forced his way past Luis and walked toward the courtyard's exit.

Luis called after him, "I'm not leaving until I've reviewed the codex."

The cardinal stopped at the gate and looked back at Luis. "Then you'll be here a very long time, Father. Because I've made it clear to Cardinal Archivist Mercati that under absolutely no circumstances should you or any member of your order ever see the Iron Codex again."

33

FEBRUARY 26

At half past five P.M., Cade and Anja stood on the north side of Rome's Viale Vaticano, at the top of the staircase to Via Sebastio Veniero, opposite the entrance to the Musei Vaticani. She wondered if he was as uncomfortable in his disguise as she was in hers; somehow she doubted it. A stiff breeze pushed her wimple into her face and nearly stole the black padre hat off of Cade's buzz-cut head. As they struggled to hold themselves together, waves of pedestrian traffic coursed past them in several directions, defying lanes of traffic populated by madmen in Fiats.

Cade straightened his cassock to hide the bulges of assorted pieces of MI6 spy gear hidden underneath. "I still say we should've stopped on Via Leone for a *gelato*."

"I barely fit into this thing now." Anja shifted beneath her habit to make her concealed Makarov stop chafing her thigh. "One *straciatella* and I will have to drop my ammo."

The wind started to pick up. Cade rubbed his hands together. "You've shed your demons, right? Can't have you bursting into flames when we cross the street."

"My demons are banished, yes." The light for the crosswalk changed. Anja nudged Cade and started across the street toward the imposing barrier of the Vatican's outer wall and the impressive arched entrance to its official museum. Cade walked at her side. As they merged into the crowd of tourists heading for the museum, she was amused by the deference shown them by strangers when they noticed that she and Cade were dressed as Catholic clergy. It was a painfully obvious choice of cover, but she had to admit that it seemed to be working.

As they reached the steps to the entrance, Cade held Anja's arm. "Wait."

"Why?"

His manner turned serious. "There's something I want to say."

Anticipating yet another of Cade's heartfelt confessions filled Anja with dread. She frowned. "What?"

"Before we pass the point of no return, I just want you to know . . . that this is, by far, the *dumbest* fucking thing we've ever done."

"And?"

"That's it. That's my whole thought. I just wanted it on the record before we die."

Museum visitors detoured around Cade and Anja as they stood looking at each other at the bottom of the stairs. Anja blinked. "So . . . are we still doing this?"

"What? Yeah." Cade started up the stairs. "Absolutely we're doing this."

They climbed the steps and waited in the shortest line they could find for a ticket window. When their turn came, the young woman behind the counter struck an apologetic tone. "*Mi dispiace, padre, ma il museo si chiude alle sei.*"

"*Sì, lo so,*" Cade replied, pushing his lira notes across the counter. "*Grazie.*"

The clerk nodded, and then she exchanged the bills for tickets, which she delivered to Cade and Anja with a smile. "*Padre. Sorella. Benvenuti al museo.*"

"*Grazie,*" Anja said, forcing a polite smile before she left the counter.

She and Cade followed the slow-moving river of humanity into the museum. In a whisper, she asked him, "How long do we need to pretend to be tourists?"

"Until it gets dark." He nodded at a map of the museum's exhibits on the wall. "Once we're past the Cortile della Pigna, we can head upstairs and find an open window."

"A pity there are no doors connecting the museum and the archives."

"I suspect that's by design." He pointed her toward a passage to a large courtyard. "This way." They passed through the crowd quickly but without contact, drawing no attention, and arrived at the north end of the Cortile della Pigna. Behind them, a thirteen-foot-tall bronze sculpture of a fir cone stood inside a towering hemispherical niche. At the far end of the courtyard stood an edifice defined by eight classical columns. Beyond that stood the transverse wing of the Braccio Nuovo and, behind and parallel to that, the wing devoted to the Vatican's secret archives.

Naturally, the plan called for Anja and Cade to head in the opposite direction.

"This way," he said, leading her toward the northeast corner of the courtyard. "We can cut through the Egyptian exhibit and take the stairs up to the Etruscan wing. From there—"

"—we double back," she cut in, "and head south through the Galleria dei Candelabri, to the Galleria degli Arazzi, and force open one of the windows. Without getting caught."

"Preferably, yes."

They let themselves disappear into the crowd, in spite of the fact that it was thinning as the museum's closing time approached. As Cade had predicted, there was a late surge of visitors who had deluded themselves that they could see the entire contents of the museum in under an hour, and those frantic tourists, with their nervous chattering and snapping photos, provided Anja and Cade with ample cover as they followed their planned route to the tapestries exhibit.

As beautiful as the tapestries were, the visitors whom Cade and Anja had followed seemed more interested in the Galleria delle Carte Geografiche, which tended to inspire awe by virtue of its great length and the gilded murals of illustrated maps that adorned its walls and arched ceiling. The group around Cade and Anja hurried through the tapestries exhibit, all of them eager to reach the other side of the next doorway.

Cade and Anja stepped to the side of the corridor and pretended to absorb themselves in the details of a tapestry featuring a character whose eyes seemed to follow the spectator. To their left was a window that faced west, toward the parking lot adjacent to the museum's wing and, beyond that, the Pontifical Academy of Sciences and, even farther away, the Vatican gardens.

Within half a minute, Cade and Anja were alone in the tapestries hall.

"Clear," Anja whispered. Cade sidestepped to the tall window and tested its handle. It wasn't locked. He stopped short of opening the window until Anja said, "Go."

He moved quickly, decisively. A push and the window was open. Cold air rushed inside as Cade stepped up and out onto the ledge, and then he gently closed the window. Anja pivoted slowly, with her hands folded as if in prayer, and looked to see if anyone had taken notice of Cade's exit. The rest of the tapestries gallery was empty, and all of the visitors to the maps gallery were too engrossed by the ceiling to pay any mind to what was behind them.

Anja looked back once more to make sure no one else had entered the tapestries gallery behind her. Seeing no one there, she removed the lower half of her nun's habit, which had been designed as a breakaway dress, then tore off her wimple. She threw the unneeded disguise pieces behind a statue's pedestal, opened the window, and followed Cade out onto the ledge.

It was nearly two feet wide, more than broad enough for them both to find footing. Its biggest hazard was that the façade of the building was illuminated, and the longer they remained on the ledge, the more likely it was that they would be seen.

Cade had removed and pocketed the white tab of his priest's collar, donned a pair of black leather gloves, and traded his padre hat for a black wool stocking cap. Anja pulled on her own gloves, which she had kept tucked under the waistband of her loose-fitting trousers. The two of them had become dark specters haunting a ledge outside the Musei Vaticani's western wing.

"What now?" Anja asked in a hushed voice.

"Climb," Cade said, pointing at a cluster of thick, well-anchored pipes that hugged the wall from the ground two stories below, to the roof one story above. Taking his own advice, Cade used the pipes for leverage and scaled the wall with the speed of a monkey in the jungle. Clambering awkwardly up the pipes behind him, Anja felt a pang of envy for the training Cade had received from the U.S. Army Rangers.

As she neared the tiled roof, Cade was already there. He reached down and helped her up onto the terra-cotta tiles. "Watch your step," he said, pointing at the tiles. "Don't kick any loose." He led her toward and then over the roof's peak. As they descended the other side, they were in deep shadow. They scuttled down onto the roof of the transverse wing that linked the museum's eastern and western wings, and which also housed the offices of the secret archives.

On their left, beyond the edge of the roof lay a long drop into the Cortile della Biblioteca. On their right was a narrow dormer housing a single-paned window. Cade approached it from above its peak, which extended from the wing's pitched roof. Lying atop it, he retrieved a flat instrument that he'd kept concealed beneath his priestly garb. He slipped the tool—which he'd borrowed without permission from an MI6 cache in Rome, just like the rest of their equipment and their disguises—between the window and its frame and probed with it. "The window's rigged with an alarm," he said, feeling his way along its top edge. "I should be able to bypass it."

He drew another tool from his hidden kit and snaked its wiry extension into the gap behind his probe. Seconds later came a soft electric crackling. A wisp of smoke that stank of burnt wiring emerged from the cracks between the window's hinges.

Cade started to put away his tools. "That should do it."

Anja wasn't so certain. "Are you sure? This is the secret archives, yes?"

"Yeah, but it was built in the Renaissance." Cade pushed open the window. It swung inward with nary a squeak from its hinges. "Fort Knox it ain't."

He climbed inside, and then he helped Anja through the narrow window. They found themselves in a dark alcove off of an equally dark hallway. Cade moved to the corner and tilted his head forward while he listened. His shoulders relaxed and he started to move forward, out of the alcove. Anja caught his arm and pulled him back. "Wait."

"What?"

"Before we go any farther, there is something I must say." It was difficult for her to be honest with him. Then she let go of her pride, and the words came freely: "Thank you, Cade."

He showed her a roguish smile. "Thank me when we're far from here, *with* the codex."

Cade checked the corner again, but this time he motioned for Anja to move back. As she pressed herself deeper into the darkness, a pair of Swiss Guards armed with semiautomatic carbines ambled past in the corridor. Cade let them pass—and then he stepped out, directly behind them, as silent as a shadow.

With a brutal right-hand palm strike Cade slammed the left guard's head against the stone wall. The man collapsed in a limp heap as Cade's right elbow snapped back to strike the jaw of his comrade, who staggered half a step until Cade's left palm introduced his noggin to the opposite wall with a dull *smack*. In a blink, both men were on the floor, unconscious. Cade kneeled and checked their pulses. "They'll live. Help me put 'em in the alcove."

Anja and Cade piled the stunned guards atop each other inside the alcove. For good measure, Cade bound each man's wrists to the other's ankles, and he secured them both to a radiator before he gagged them. "That ought to buy us about twenty minutes," he said, standing over the trussed guards. "Let's go find the codex and get outta here."

They moved with caution as they left the alcove. Though the museum was now closed, the secret archives technically were open and operational twenty-four hours a day from Monday through Friday, for the sake of academic research. Depending upon who was in its many reading rooms downstairs and what items they were asking to review, archive personnel might come poking through the vast stacks at any moment.

The pair moved west along the transverse passageway, down a flight of stairs, and then south as they entered the Soffittoni—the floor of the western wing directly above the Galleria delle Carte Geografiche. They turned the corner to find the way blocked by a gate worthy of a bank vault or a maximum-security prison. Standing behind it were two men, a Catholic priest and a Swiss Guard.

Both men stood at attention, alarmed by the sight of Anja and Cade.

The guard said in a brusque voice, "Halt! Identi—"

A drugged dart flung by Cade struck the guard in his throat. Before the shocked priest could cry out in fear or protest, Cade lodged a dart into his carotid, as well. Both the cleric and the soldier collapsed against the bars, drooling as they slipped into oblivion. Cade approached the barrier, reached through its bars, and stole the keys from the guard's belt.

He unlocked the gate, opened it, and ushered Anja into the Soffittoni. "After you."

"Leave it open behind us." She stepped through the gateway into the archives. "I get the feeling we'll be making a fast exit."

Anja took the lead as they walked down a narrow aisle between seemingly endless stacks of leather-bound indexes, wood-bound codices, tubed scrolls, and boxed sheaves. The metal shelves reached from floor to ceiling on either side of Cade and Anja and were flanked by barred windows covered with translucent brown paper. Between the windows and partially hidden by the crammed shelves were ornate frescoes depicting the shipwreck of Saint Paul in Malta, and the ceiling was decorated with a mural of glittering stars in a black sky.

Beneath their feet, names had been etched into the marble floor: *Tramontana, Sirocco, Ostro*—the Names of the Wind. Odors of must and leather, perfumes of incense and old paper . . . they combined with the vast wing's eerie half-light and a lingering haze of dust to give the archives the atmosphere of a medieval alchemist's laboratory, or a mad wizard's sanctum.

The march through the west wing of the archive seemed endless, not just because of the great length of the wing but because Anja's fear had slowed time to a crawl, and with each step all she could focus upon was the frenzied beating of her heart and the fat beads of sweat tracing crazy paths down the back of her neck.

At last they reached the far end of the wing and the final barrier that separated them from the secure vault, in which Khalîl had predicted the Synod would hide the Iron Codex.

A solid wall stretched across the wing before Anja and Cade. Its outer surface appeared to be composed of brick, but Khalîl had warned them that it was more than it seemed. Powerful glyphs of protection had been etched into the Roman concrete underneath, to prevent magicians from traveling or teleporting into or out of the vault through its walls, floors, or ceiling. The only safe way in or out was through its heavy steel door—one thicker, heavier, and more complex than any used in any bank in the world. It was a marvel of both science and magick, one that delivered a clear message to would-be plunderers: *Thou shalt not pass.*

Cade regarded the vault's door with clear respect. "Well, here we are." He turned a sly look at Anja. "Ready to show off?"

"I will do what needs to be done." Anja cracked her knuckles. "And no more."

A mortal safecracker could have spent a month trying in vain to defeat that door.

A Black magician would never have made it inside Vatican City in the first place.

But Anja had not come to the vault fortified with the powers of a demon. She had come armed with the gifts of an angel—an advantage which she had no qualms exercising.

She set her hands on the dials of the door's combination locks and let Heavenly intuition guide her hands. Each tumbler locked into place with a tangible, audible click, one digit at a time, until she felt the great mechanisms within the five-ton door shift to grant her entry.

"We're in."

Anja turned the master wheel on the vault door, and then she pulled it toward her.

It made no sound as it swung open on massive hinges. It turned with the easy grace of a ballet dancer, and it slowed and stopped before it made contact with the wall.

On the other side stood the interior of the vault. The most secure repository of religious arcana on the face of the earth. All of it now exposed and open to Cade and Anja's inspection.

She motioned for Cade to enter. "After you."

He smiled. "I thought you'd never ask."

Cade stepped inside the vault.

Alarms wailed and red lights nested in the archive's wall sconces flashed. Cade looked back at Anja, and in unison they voiced the same thought: "Shit."

～～

Cade and Anja rushed toward the back of the windowless vault, all notions of subtlety abandoned. The alarms echoing inside the archives were almost loud enough to swallow Cade's ongoing mantra of "Fuck fuck fuck fuck fuck fuck. . . ."

Though the vault represented only a small fraction of the Soffittoni, it was over twenty meters long and crammed with four parallel rows of shelves that had barely a shoulders' width of space between them. Even stronger than the scents of leather and paper here were the smells of dust, stone, and copper. The air inside the vault was colder and drier than it had been in the rest of the Soffittoni, a fact that Cade chalked up to the archives' efforts at conservation.

He didn't indulge his urge to peruse the contents of every shelf. There were so many occult artifacts and lost secrets of the ancient world sealed inside glass boxes that he knew that to stop and examine one would paralyze him with wonder, and that was a mistake neither he nor Anja could afford. They needed to lay hands on the Iron Codex as quickly as possible, and then they'd have to improvise a new exit strategy, all before the Swiss Guard came to—

The shelves on his right ended abruptly, giving Cade a clear view of a collection of large stone tablets and irregular slabs, all of them either engraved or illuminated with text in various ancient languages; several also bore breathtaking painted illustrations. The pieces were assembled in what seemed like a random order against the vault's western wall.

Cade stopped in midstride, mesmerized by the peculiar array.

Anja continued to the end of the vault and wasted no time using her yoked angelic talents to shatter the steel bands that held the codex prisoner on a marble shelf like a bibliographic Prometheus chained to a stone. She pulled the codex free and clutched it to her chest as she faced Cade. "Got it! How do we get out?"

He was too enthralled to reply. Staring at the illustrated stones, he felt as if he were standing at the precipice of discovery. "Anja, do you know what this is?"

"The lost commandments? Who cares?"

He raised his hand to halt her retreat. "Wait! It's a creation myth." He moved closer to it. "It's not like anything I've ever seen before."

She tensed to flee, but his obsession with the mural left her stuck but straining like a thoroughbred that couldn't wait for the bang of the starter's pistol. "So what? Time to go!"

Cade couldn't believe that Anja didn't see the tablets' importance. "Dammit, Anja! Just *look* at them. This wasn't *one* work. It was compiled from half a dozen different sources." Her exasperated glare told him she still wasn't seeing his point. "Look at each one. They're not just in different languages—they're from different *civilizations*. The Babylonians. The Chinese. The Maya. The Hebrews. The ancient Greeks. The Egyptians. All telling different parts of the same story. They overlap in a few spots, but they've definitely been arranged like this to tell *one* myth. I'll bet some of these pieces were created centuries or even millennia apart."

"Incredible," Anja deadpanned. "*Now* can we go?"

The anger behind her question freed Cade of the tablets' spell. "What? Yes." He dug a small spy camera out of his pocket. "Just let me photograph them."

"No time!" Anja grabbed his sleeve. "Cade!"

He resisted her and kept snapping pictures. "Almost done." He shot quickly, pumping the tiny box camera like a shotgun to advance each frame between exposures. After he got two shots of each stone in the collection, he stuffed the camera into his pocket. "All right, let's—"

Anja glared toward the vault's entrance with her hands raised to shoulder level.

Slowed by caution and regret, Cade made a gradual pivot until he too faced the vault's entrance—and saw the platoon of Swiss Guards aiming carbine rifles at him and Anja.

At a glance Cade noted the special insignia worn on the uniforms of the secret archive guards. The symbols would likely mean nothing to a layman, but Cade recognized them instantly: glyphs of protection against both angels and demons.

So much for fighting our way out.

"Turn around," the guard captain said, his harsh command clearly brooking no argument or resistance. "Down on your knees! Hands on your heads! Do it now!"

Anja reproached Cade with a scathing look as she complied with the captain's order. Cade could only grimace in shame as he did likewise.

An icy steel handcuff snapped pinch-tight around Cade's right wrist, and he winced as his right arm was yanked behind him, followed by the other, and his wrists were cuffed together. Beside him, a guard sergeant did the same to Anja, and then the duo were pulled to their feet.

"Take them to the inquisitor," the captain told his sergeant. "But keep this out of the logs." The sergeant saluted, and then he and the rest of his platoon escorted Cade and Anja out of the vault, back through the Soffittoni, and then down a dark spiral staircase that seemed to drill into the bowels of the earth.

As darkness enveloped them, Anja whispered to Cade, "Was it worth it?"

He whispered back, "I had no choice."

"Why? What does it say that is so important?"

There was a good chance they both were about to suffer anonymous deaths underneath the Apostolic Palace, so Cade decided to stop protecting Anja from the truth that had haunted him for the past nine years. "All six pieces start with the same sentence." He looked at her as he quoted from the mural, "*The universe exists because God wanted to die.*"

34

FEBRUARY 26, PART II

"Are you quite comfortable, *Signor* Martin?" The voice—deep, rough-edged, with an Italian accent—roused Cade from his painful state of twilight consciousness.

At first the room was too dark for Cade to make out much detail. There was a dull orange glow from an oil lamp with a tarnished glass chimney in the corner of the room, several yards away from him; a man wearing cardinal's robes stood silhouetted between Cade and the light. So far as Cade could tell, they were the only two people in the room.

The cardinal slapped Cade's cheek just hard enough to ensure Cade was awake. "This is no time for sleep. You and I have much to discuss."

"I doubt that." As wakefulness returned, Cade became aware of the fact that he was naked, spread-eagled with his wrists and ankles bound by iron manacles. Under his back he felt wooden planks. Almost by reflex he tested his bonds. They did not yield in the slightest.

His captor circled to Cade's left, permitting the lamp's glow to illuminate his face. The man looked to be in his sixties, judging from the creases in his features and the wisps of thinning white hair that poked out from beneath his scarlet skullcap. "Do you know who I am?"

"The ghost of Bernardo Gui?"

"In a sense, yes. My name is Cardinal Umberto Lombardi—"

"—and you're the Vatican inquisitor. As well as the director of the Pauline Synod." Cade smirked before he added, "I should have known it would be you. It makes sense."

Lombardi seemed intrigued. "And why would that be?"

"Because according to the Church, neither of your jobs actually exists."

The cardinal's lips thinned along with his patience. "You like to parade your wit. Almost as much as you enjoy showing off your Oxford education. Take a moment to acquaint yourself with your predicament."

It was hard for Cade to turn his head, but he didn't need to look far to see that he was strapped to a variation on a medieval stretching rack, one that would pull his limbs toward its corners. Though the room looked like a holdover from the medieval era, he couldn't help but notice that the bloodstains on the stone floor looked and smelled fresh.

Lombardi folded his hands and leaned in. "Tell me what you see."

"You've gone to a lot of trouble to help me get a crick out of my back."

"You are most droll, *signore*. I wonder if you'll be so glib after I dislocate your shoulders? Or your knees?" He seized Cade by the throat. "Will your japes come so easily after I break your spine?"

Cade met the cardinal's mad stare with one of practiced calm. Then he croaked out, "Aren't you skipping a step?" When Lombardi loosened his grip on Cade's throat, he continued, "You haven't asked me any questions. I thought the point of torture was to make people talk."

His observation appeared to amuse Lombardi. "I'm afraid you are misinformed. The purpose of torture is not to extract information, or even to compel submission. As anyone truly experienced in the art will tell you, the only true purpose of torture . . . is torture." He shrugged. "But you raise a valid point. There *are* questions I would like to put to you, and I suspect I'll find your answers more cogent *before* this procedure than I will after it."

"How very post-Enlightenment of you."

"Let's begin with a simple query. Why did you photograph the mural?"

"Why do you think? So I could study it later."

Lombardi adopted a pretense of gentle concern. "To what end? What do you think the mural represents?"

"Considering where I found it, and what it says, I'd guess it represents a truth the Church doesn't want people to know."

A disingenuous smile. "Nonsense. It is a collection of heresies. Nothing more."

"Then why not just destroy it?"

"Because its pieces are works of great antiquity, with incalculable archeological value. And contrary to what you might believe, the Church is not an organization of barbarians."

"Said the inquisitor to the man about to be stretched on a medieval torture device." Even in the half-light, Cade could see that Lombardi looked troubled. "Your scholars have already translated the murals, haven't they? They know what it says."

The cardinal nodded. "I'm certain they do." He stepped away and retrieved Cade's miniaturized camera from a side table. "Just as I am certain that you never will." He dropped the tiny camera on the floor and crushed it under his heel. He stomped it a few times more for good measure, no doubt so Cade could hear it being ground into fragments. Then the older man leaned down and spoke to Cade in an almost conspiratorial tone, so close that Cade felt Lombardi's breath on the side of his face. "Your existence represents an existential threat to the Church, *Signor* Martin. Do you know why?" Cade remained silent. Lombardi asked, "Shall I tell you?"

"I'm not really in a position to stop you."

"No, you're not." Lombardi rested a hand on Cade's bare chest. "I'm given to understand that you endured the torments of Hell *in the flesh*—and returned alive to tell the tale. This makes you privy to certain truths that the Church cannot allow to propagate."

"In case you haven't noticed, I don't really talk about my time in Hell. If all of this is because you're afraid of a public-relations problem with your flock—"

"It isn't." Lombardi straightened and loomed over Cade. "The faithful will never believe you, nor will most of the heathens. But others like yourself—and *la Signorina* Kernova—very well might. And if your strain of heresy were to infect the White orders of the Church—"

"You're afraid of losing control over your own people," Cade realized. "The Church barely tolerates the Pauline Art as it is. So if its adepts decided to break away—"

Lombardi took hold of the table's main wheel and gave it a single turn. The bonds around Cade's ankles and wrists tightened and spread apart. It had been a shift of barely an inch in each direction, but that was enough to make him feel as if his skin were about to rip apart, and his joints burned with pain as muscles, ligaments, and cartilage all frayed from the strain.

Cade clenched his teeth and struggled to deny Lombardi the satisfaction of hearing him scream. "That all you got?" he said between desperate gasps. "I spent six months as SATAN's chew toy, asshole. You want to break *me*, you gotta do better than *that*."

"Oh, I intend to. But not all at once, and not without the introduction of some truly excruciating variations. So take a deep breath and make yourself comfortable—because I promise you, your torments have only just begun."

———※———

In all of Vatican City, despite the countless wonders housed within the Musei Vaticani and the many priceless paintings and sculptures that graced its basilica, chapels, and gardens, there was only one work of art that could bring a measure of calm to Luis's unquiet mind: Michelangelo's *Pietà*. A masterpiece in marble, the image of Mary holding in her lap the body of Jesus after the Crucifixion stirred profound emotions in Luis's heart while at the same time bringing him peace.

Maybe it was the countenance of an ever-young Mary, her purity unblemished, her love both saintly and maternal, that soothed Luis's troubled soul. Or perhaps it was the way in which Michelangelo had captured a moment of great sorrow with supreme dignity; he had minimized the wounds to Christ's hands and ribs and omitted any evidence of the Passion from the Savior's face, rendering his visage serene. This was not an image that glorified death. It enshrined the moment in which God's promise to Man was at last fulfilled.

Grant me peace, Lord. Help me set aside my doubts and live in true faith.

It was a blessing, Luis knew, that as a member of the clergy he had access to the *Pietà* after hours. It was the sculpture closest to the main entrance of St. Peter's Basilica, and often the last one to be liberated of tourists before the basilica closed its doors each evening. But he was free to remain here for hours if the spirit moved him, admiring its beauty in solitude.

He was working his way through the Hail Mary beads in the first decade of his rosary when a clamor of shouting and running steps disturbed his meditation. He turned toward the commotion. A young priest and a custodian scampered to and fro, both of them agitated. The priest swung and snapped his sash in the air as if it were a whip, and the custodian thrust a broom at the air above them. And then Luis saw the cause of their alarm: a raven was inside the basilica.

The great black bird flapped and squawked, clearly no less upset about the situation than were its human pursuers. It was almost comical to Luis, watching the two men struggle to chase and direct the swooping bird without accidentally striking any of the priceless works of art and architecture that surrounded them, their every stumbling miss the epitome of slapstick.

Observing the spectacle with a calm heart, Luis moved away from the *Pietà,* took a few steps toward the frantic chase, and extended his left arm as a perch. Channeling the grace of the two angels that still resided within him, he summoned the bird with a short whistling call. As if it had been trained, the raven dived toward Luis and alighted upon his forearm without sound or struggle.

The two men who had hectored the bird stopped and stared. Lowering his broom, the custodian asked in a bewildered voice, "How . . . how did you—?"

"All things are possible through Christ Our Lord," Luis said with a smile. He nodded toward the nearest door and prompted the young priest, "If you'd be so kind, Father?"

"Of course." The young priest hurried to the door and pushed it open as Luis strolled over a few paces behind him.

Stretching his arm through the doorway, Luis whispered to the bird, "*Vuela, sé libre.*" The raven launched itself upward and vanished into the night. "*Ve con Dios, mi amigo.*"

It had felt like such a simple, easy thing, and yet the young priest gazed upon Luis with awe. "That was amazing, *signore.* How did you do it?"

"I didn't," Luis said. "The Holy Spirit did. I was just a conduit."

The younger man shook his head. "This is shaping up to be a night of oddities."

Luis felt out of touch. "What do you mean, Father?"

"The break-in, of course."

"Break-in?"

"You haven't heard? The Swiss Guard arrested two intruders in the secret archives. A man and a woman." The young priest dropped his voice to a conspiratorial whisper. "I hear they made it inside the vault before they were captured."

A sick feeling stirred deep inside Luis—a mingling of regret and shame. He did his best to hide his burgeoning nausea as he asked, "Where are the prisoners now?"

An exaggerated shrug. "Who knows? No one's seen them at the palace lockup, so. . . ."

The lilt in the young priest's voice seemed to imply that Luis should have known how to finish that thought, but the White magician found himself at a loss. "So? What does that mean?"

Now the other man's voice shrank further, this time out of fear. "It means they've been given to the inquisitor." He pulled the door closed. "God keep you safe, Father," he said in valediction, making the sign of the cross as he departed from Luis.

Alone in the yawning splendor of the basilica, Luis was haunted by guilt and sorrow. *It can't be a coincidence that it was a man and a woman who broke into the vault. It has to be Cade and Anja. They came for the Iron Codex.* He tried to purge his mounting anguish with a deep breath, but the sense that he had led two people to their doom by robbing them weighed like a mountain upon his conscience. *I can't blame them for trying to take it back. It belongs in the hands of those who will study it. Who will try to use it to do good works. Not hidden away, buried and forgotten.*

He walked slowly up the center aisle of the basilica, lost in his thoughts. It felt too early to turn in for the night, but he was scheduled to leave before dawn the next day, to catch a train that would take him back to Monte Paterno. To his abode of isolation.

To his exile from everything that really mattered.

To his refuge from everything except his conscience.

Lombardi will torture Cade and Anja for sport. All because they had the courage to attempt what I should already have done. To undo what I should have never let happen.

He reflected upon the sparks of Heavenly grace that still smoldered within him and realized he had never felt less worthy of them than he did at that very moment. He wiped tears from his eyes as his shame threatened to overwhelm him.

"Forgive me, Lord," he prayed, "for my trespasses against others."

———

The inquisitor's bastinado cracked against the soles of Anja's bare feet, sending jolts of white agony up her legs. Enraged, she screamed and swore in Russian, and then she spat at Lombardi and growled like a feral beast. "*Mudak!* I will eat your heart!"

The cardinal's smile was mirthless, the taunt of a sociopath. "I really don't see why you're so upset. This entire debacle is your fault. You disguised yourself as a nun—" He nodded at a pile of clothes on the floor. "Yes, we found the rest of your costume in the tapestries hall. And you broke into the Pope's private archives. Did you really expect to get away with this?"

Anja struggled in vain against the ropes that bound her to the raised bench, with her wrists secured underneath it and her ankles locked in place at its end. Adding to her indignity, she had been stripped to her undergarments. "I will cut off your balls and feed them to you."

Her threat failed to disturb him. "Oh, how I do enjoy your empty postur-ing. But my time is valuable, so let's return to the matter at hand." He turned toward a lectern he'd had brought into the shadowy underground torture chamber. Upon it sat the Iron Codex, its front cover open. "You took a terri-ble risk to steal this book. It's not hard to guess why." He flipped with aplomb through its pages. "On which page would I find the ritual that you employed to free your friend Cade from the clutches of Hell?"

She savored the taste of her own blood as she licked her punch-loosened teeth. "I will use your eyeballs to make soup."

His smile widened into a predator's grin. "You truly are a delight."

He picked up a scalpel from a tray of torture implements on a stand beside her head, inserted its blade into her right nostril, and sliced it in twain with a flick of his wrist. It was a small wound, far from lethal, but the pain was hot and terrible. Anja shuddered as she watched a steady rush of warm blood spill from the wound and dribble onto the floor beneath her.

"Are you familiar with the concept of 'death by a thousand cuts'?" His breath was warm in her ear as he leaned in to add, "If you don't start answer-ing my questions, you soon will be." He put down the scalpel and picked up a ring-shaped iron clamp. With almost tender care he fit it around the top of Anja's head and turned its screw until its hold was snug. "I want to know how many of the codex's rituals you've performed, and to what result."

"And I want to cut off your head and shit down your neck. It is good to want things."

He gave the clamp's main screw a half turn. The pressure against Anja's skull was firm enough to be uncomfortable—obviously just a warning of what was in store. Lombardi drummed his manicured fingernails once across Anja's forehead. "Have you ever heard a skull crack under pressure? It's a sound one never forgets—unless it's one's own, of course." He gripped the screw's handle. "Give me anything, *signorina*. Even the smallest morsel of information, and I'll ease the pressure. Just tell me this: the ritual that freed Mr. Martin from Hell—what page of the codex is it on? That's not so much to ask, is it? A page number?"

"And what would you do with it?"

"Study it, of course. Knowing where to begin our research would be of tre-mendous help to our scholars in the archive."

She wanted to believe him, but something about his words rang hollow. *If only he hadn't exorcised my yoked angel, maybe I could tell for sure if he's lying.* With only her instincts to rely upon, Anja fixed Lombardi with a hateful look. "I do not believe you."

Her refusal garnered only mild surprise. "Why not?"

"If you wanted to study the codex, you would not have locked it away." She regarded him with disgust. "You don't want to study it. You want to *bury* it."

He chuckled. "I must say—you're quite astute. For a woman, that is."

"This palace has many rooms. When I am free, you will be found dead in *all* of them."

Lombardi turned the screw. Crushing force from every direction filled Anja's head with inescapable pain. Panic sent her heart racing, and her eyes felt ready to pop from their sockets. She gasped for air between guttural howls, hoping to drown out the sickly crunch that would signal the fracturing of her skull.

After minutes that felt like forever, she was too spent to scream, too exhausted to fight. All she could do was lie on the bench and wait for the next turn of the screw.

Standing beside her with a spike in his hand, Lombardi shook his head in dismay. "Are you really so stubborn that you won't cooperate, even now? Or just so foolish?"

"You and your church helped Nazi war criminals escape justice. Helped them run to South America. First you refused to fight them, then you took their side. Fuck you all."

He absorbed her tirade with professorial calm. "I see. I should have realized sooner. Nothing gives one strength under duress like the fury of a noble cause." He set down the spike in his hand and used his index finger to trace the Y-shaped scar on Anja's left cheek. "In your mind, you've cast yourself as some kind of righteous avenger, yes? You think that you can expiate your sins by hunting Nazis. You hope to cleanse your soul by turning your body into a vessel for demons and using their powers to commit murder. Do you really think that you can wash yourself clean of all your evils . . . by bathing yourself in blood?"

His smug attitude melted away, only to be replaced by one of condescension and pity. "Foolish child. There is no act of contrition that can remove the tarnish from your soul. You surrendered any hope of salvation the moment you signed your pact with the Devil." With a mad gleam he added, "And when I am done with you, it is to the Devil himself you will go."

Cade's whole world had been transformed into pain. The rack had been left in a state of tension, just taut enough to distend his naked body in four directions at once, leaving his shoulders and hips half out of their sockets and the ligaments around them in prolonged distress. There was no point to struggling. Even the smallest effort of resistance redoubled his agony. All that he could do was lie in the dark, do his best not to move, and focus on slowing his breathing.

Shallow and easy, he counseled himself. *Let it go slowly.*

Drawing too deep a breath had expanded his chest and aggravated the rack's pull on his shoulders, so he had been forced to persevere on small breaths. It was just as well. The beating he'd received from the Swiss Guards during his capture had left his nostrils caked with blood, forcing him to breathe through his mouth, which had long since gone dry as a result.

Relax, he told himself. *Go limp. Be like water, and let the pain wash away.*

It was easier advice to give than to follow. The more he thought about not resisting his bonds, the more his muscles wanted to tug and jerk—until the pain hit, and he let go again.

The door creaked open just outside of Cade's angle of view. He listened for the measured strides of Cardinal Lombardi—but instead of the click of heeled shoes against stone, he heard the soft padding of bare feet. An assistant torturer, perhaps?

Hands grasped the wheel of the rack.

Cade mentally steeled himself for the moment in which he would be literally torn apart—and then the tension in his bonds relaxed, and his arms and legs fell limp upon the slatted table. Confused but too desperate for air to talk, he took deep breaths and filled his lungs, hoping to clear his head while the pain in his muscles and joints abated. Then the shackle on his left wrist was undone. He wanted to pull his arm to his side, but he could barely move it.

His right wrist was freed next, and then his liberator stepped into view, his face only half lit by the kerosene lamp on the wall: it was Father Luis Pérez. "*Buona sera, Signor Martin.*"

"Are you fucking kidding me?"

The priest put his index finger to his lips and shushed Cade. Then, speaking sotto voce, he warned him, "The inquisitor is just next door with your friend. We must be quick." He moved to the end of the table and freed Cade's ankles. "Can you stand?"

"I can barely fucking breathe."

Luis slipped one hand behind Cade's back and eased him up to a sitting position. "Lean on me. I will help you off the table." Cade leaned into Luis, who caught him and pulled him off of the rack. The monk eased Cade down onto the cold, rough stone floor. "Catch your breath, my friend. Your clothes are over here. I'll bring them to you."

Cade watched, all but dumbfounded, as Luis gathered his shoes and phony clerical vestments from the far corner of the torture room, and then dropped them in front of him.

"Get dressed," Luis said. "We need to go."

"Not without Anja."

The priest nodded. "We'll get her next."

Cade struggled to resume his disguise. Every muscle, tendon, and joint in his body burned with protest. "Fuck."

"Hold still." Without a glimmer of awkwardness or embarrassment, Luis dressed Cade, and then he helped him put on socks. "Can you finish up while I put your shoes on?" He noted Cade's nod, and then he proceeded to push shoes onto Cade's feet and tie the laces while Cade's half-numb fingers fumbled to straighten his costume's notched collar.

"Thank you," Cade said, feeling abashed.

"Thank me after we escape." He lifted Cade to his feet and held him until he was sure he was steady. "Can you walk?"

"I'll fucking well walk outta here," Cade said, meaning every word of it.

Luis moved to the door and listened. Then he whispered to Cade, "Stay close." He opened the door and slipped into the corridor outside. Like the torture room, it was lit only by weak kerosene lamps with glass chimneys tarnished over many decades to a dark amber. Their footfalls, in spite of being slow and soft, scraped across the gritty stone floor.

Every step left Cade feeling dizzy, and the spasms in his muscles made him fear that at any second he might collapse and be unable to get back up.

Several strides down the narrow passageway, Luis halted at the entrance to another torture chamber. Its heavy wooden door was ajar, and from the other side of it came muted sounds of feral growling interspersed with Russian profanities.

Cade leaned close to ask Luis in a hushed voice, "What's your plan?"

"I think a direct approach is best." He put his hand to Cade's chest to steady him. "Stay here. I shall return directly."

Luis pushed the door open and strode inside the chamber.

Cade leaned forward to peek around the corner—just in time to see the inquisitor rise up with imperious anger at the sight of Luis. "Father Pérez, what do you think you're—!"

Luis's fist slammed into Lombardi's nose.

As the cardinal crumpled toward the floor, his chin met Luis's knee.

Lombardi landed on his back, out cold, bleeding from his nose and mouth. His zucchetto lay on the floor, halfway across the room from his bald head.

The monk wasted no time binding the inquisitor's wrists and ankles with rope from the table of torture implements, and then he gagged the older man, all in the space of a minute.

Not bad for a man of the cloth, Cade mused with quiet respect.

Anja wore an iron clamp on her brow like a crown of pain, and she was bleeding from more tiny incisions than Cade could count. Lombardi's scalpel had nicked her face, her arms and legs, her torso, the sides of her neck, between her fingers—and now she was drenched from head to toe in crimson.

Luis removed the monstrous-looking clamp from Anja's head. He used a blade from the tray beside her bench to cut her bonds before draping her with a threadbare blanket. "Get dressed. It won't be long before the Swiss Guard comes back."

Anja regarded Luis with suspicion as she climbed off the bench and gathered her nun's disguise. Seeing Cade in the doorway, she threw him a questioning look, to which his only answer was a befuddled shrug. He was grateful at least that she was able to dress herself, despite the fact that she was coated in her own blood and could barely walk on her savaged feet.

After she pulled on her shoes, she hobbled to the tray of torture implements and grabbed a small cleaver. Luis, who had bundled the Iron Codex inside its silken shroud, stepped between Anja and Lombardi. "Stop. We need to leave."

"Not until I keep my promise." Her knuckles went white around the cleaver's handle. "And I made him *many* promises."

"We don't have time," Luis said, his tone insistent. "But even if we did, I would not let you do this. I will not be a party to murder."

Cade nodded. "He's right, Anja. We have to go." He caught Luis's attention. "How close are we to the secret archives?"

The priest looked confused. "Why?"

"We need to go back. I need to record those tablets I found."

"Blessed Mary, you're *both* mad!" Luis wrested the cleaver from Anja's hand and flung it across the room. "We are *not* killing the cardinal!" He clutched the Iron Codex to his chest and walked toward Cade. "And we are *not* going back to the archives. If I'm right, we have about fifteen minutes and one chance to get out of Vatican City alive." He shouldered past Cade on his way to the corridor. "If the two of you value your lives, follow me. If not"—he walked away, muttering as he went—"to Hell with both of you."

Anja limped to the doorway and stood beside Cade. "Do we trust him?"

"Do we have a choice? He's got the codex."

"Then we go." She draped Cade's left arm across her shoulders, and together they shuffled in a stiff and agonized pursuit of the confounding priest.

<hr />

There were many paths out of the dungeons beneath the Apostolic Palace. Luis knew none of them, but he had the intuitive guidance of the yoked angel DA-ROCHIEL and the kind of courage that came from not knowing what was or wasn't possible. Trusting his eyes and ears, he led the pair of limping, bruised, and bloodied karcists down long-deserted corridors, up cobwebbed stairways, and through forgotten connecting passages until they reached a ground-level exit that led into a small private courtyard at the southeast corner of the palace.

It was pitch dark in the courtyard. The only light came from a small guard's station beside a locked gate at the top of a steep and narrow flight of stairs.

Cade regarded the scene with a disgruntled frown. "It's a dead end."

"No, it's not." Luis turned toward the stairway. "Wait here." He put on his bravest face and jogged forward, affecting a stumble as he cried out, "Help! Guard! Help us!"

Inside the hut someone stirred. A single Swiss Guard poked his head out. "Who's there?"

"Down here!" Luis waved one hand frantically as he fell to one knee. "Help us!"

"Hang on," the guard shouted back. "I'll call the sergeant."

"There's no time! Can't you see she's bleeding?" He pointed at Anja, who to her credit took his cue in stride and feigned a collapse into Cade's arms—

nearly taking him down with her. Playing on the pathos of the moment, Luis pleaded, "There's a madman in the palace! Save us!"

The guard hesitated for a second, but then he scrambled down the steps and ran to Luis's side. "Are you hurt, Father?"

"Yes, but my wounds are slight. The maniac—he slashed that poor nun half to death!"

Cade joined in the ruse. "Do you know how to tie a tourniquet? We're losing her!"

"Lay her down," the guard said as he undid his belt. "I can use this to—"

Luis hit the guard in the back of his head with the full weight of the Iron Codex. The young corporal fell like a cut tree and landed facedown in the dead grass, unconscious. Cade and Anja got up and shambled to join Luis as he kneeled beside the fallen guard and stole the ring of keys from his belt. Holding them up, he explained to Cade and Anja, "This man is the sentry to the Passetto di Borgo." Pointing to the top of the stairs he added, "And that's the entrance."

He raced up to the gate while Cade and Anja labored up the steep stairs behind him. By the time they reached him, he had found the key to unlock the gate. Its rusted hinges scraped as he pushed it open to reveal a dark and debris-strewn passage barely wide enough for two persons to walk abreast. Its only illumination came from ambient street light slipping through its many narrow windows. He ushered Cade and Anja in ahead of him. "Hurry. The guards could find Cardinal Lombardi at any moment."

Shuffling into the shadowy tunnel hidden inside an ancient wall, Cade asked over his shoulder, "I've read about the Passetto. How far to the Castel Sant'Angelo?"

"About a kilometer," Luis said, closing the gate behind him. "But we only need to make it past the perimeter of Vatican City. Then I can use magick to take us out of here."

Anja asked, "How far to the perimeter?"

"About a hundred meters."

Cade seemed encouraged. "That doesn't sound so—"

He was cut off by the shrill whooping of alarms from inside the palace.

"They found the cardinal," Luis said. "Quickly!"

Despite his urging, Cade and Anja continued to hobble at a maddeningly slow pace. "Sorry, Padre," Cade said, "but this is as fast as we go right now."

"Please, you must try to hurry." Panic flooded Luis's thoughts. "The guards will be requesting updates from their sentries. When the Passetto sentry fails to answer—"

"We understand," Anja said with a snarl. "But my feet are bleeding and he is broken."

There was nothing for Luis to do but herd them forward and steal glimpses out of the narrow windows facing the Piazza San Pietro, so that he could try to gauge when they were past the boundary of the Vatican's ring of magickal defense.

They were about sixty-five meters into the Passetto when they heard the grinding scrape of the gate opening behind them, followed by hoarse shouts of orders to advance and search.

Luis felt compelled to state the obvious. "The guards are coming."

Cade glowered. "I'm crippled, not deaf." Running footsteps grew louder by the second. "Fuck me. Didn't you bring a weapon?"

"Into a house of God?"

"Forget I asked."

Driven by fear and adrenaline, Cade and Anja quickened their steps. Luis could see the strain on their faces: they both were in hideous pain but desperate to survive. He felt the same urge, the compulsion to run and leave them behind, to save himself—but that was not an option.

A long stretch of the wall on his left was without windows, but they were quickly drawing near to one on that side. Driven by hope he sprinted to it and looked outside—below the window stretched the Via di Porta Angelica, a road that ran parallel to the Vatican's eastern wall.

"This is it," he said. "You're almost out!"

The drumbeat of running feet on stone thundered in the passage behind Cade and Anja. There was no longer any point to silence. Luis stretched out his hand toward the pair and said, "Think of a safe place you want to go and hold it in your mind!"

Without missing a step, Anja blurted out, "Done!"

Cade and Anja were only a few steps away from him.

A squad of Swiss Guards toting carbines rounded the corner ten meters behind them.

Luis shouted at Cade, "Take her hand!"

Cade grabbed Anja's hand. She held it with all her might as she lunged toward Luis, pulling Cade with her. Behind them, the guards raised their rifles and aimed.

Anja's hand clasped Luis's.

The squad leader gave the order to fire.

In the moment between the order and the action, Luis channeled the power of MALGARAS.

A bullet slammed into Luis's shoulder, followed by another in his thigh.

Thunder rocked the Passetto as a stroke of lightning bent in through one narrow window.

In a flash of light and fury, the escaping trio vanished—

—and when the disorientation of being teleported wore off, and Luis could see and hear once more, he, Cade, and Anja stood together in a large empty room in a rustic house filled with dust and not much else. Outside its many windows sprawled a mountain range bathed in pink twilight.

In agony from the bullets lodged inside him, Luis let go of Anja's hand, and then she let go of Cade's. The pair collapsed onto the floor, both of them battered and spent—just like Luis, who felt his yoked angels depart his ravaged form in a cold rush as he succumbed to the swift vertigo of blood loss. Suddenly bereft of the angels' power, Luis felt hollowed out.

Awed by the natural beauty of the high mountain terrain, but also dismayed by their desolation, Luis asked though his haze of pain, "Where are we?"

Anja replied as she and Cade rushed to bind Luis's wounds, "Welcome to Argentina, Father. Land of exiles and fugitives—of which you are now both."

FEBRUARY 27

No matter how inconspicuous Luis tried to be, he felt like an unwelcome guest in Anja's safe house. She and Cade had retired to opposite ends of the villa the night before, and both had woken early that morning. Despite having spent the first part of the day in a hushed war council to plan their action against Dragan, neither of them had made any effort to engage with Luis, who was amazed that either of them was moving at all. The punishments they had endured would have left most people incapacitated. But somehow these two soldiered on.

It wasn't magick that drove them, Luis realized. It was courage.

Anja had taken over a large empty room on the south side of the villa's ground floor, and Cade had isolated himself upstairs in the villa's equally capacious and long-empty library. They both were drawing from a cache of magickal supplies—candles, blessed chalk, and assorted occult components—that Anja kept stored in the villa's cellar alongside a reserve of canned food, opium, and liquor, to which Cade had all but beaten a path shortly after their arrival the night before. They each were preparing a room for a magickal experiment, both intent on conjuring and yoking a slew of demons. And now that Anja once again had the Iron Codex, there was a distinct possibility that she had designs on enlisting angelic support, as well.

Luis had tried to watch Anja's preparations, but she had scared him off by promising to vivisect him. Nothing about her threat had struck him as empty, so now he found himself upstairs, watching Cade struggle against a litany of aches and pains to draw glyphs and sigils. The American had not acknowledged Luis's presence, so the priest cleared his throat.

The simple half cough, half grunt was enough to raise Cade's head. Without looking back at Luis, he asked with obvious irritation, "What?"

"Do forgive me." Luis waited until Cade looked at him before he continued. "I know that I am far from an expert in the minutiae of the Goetic Art—"

"No shit."

"—but I notice that both you and Miss Kernova have included in your preparations sigils for demons whose prescribed days and hours are vastly different. But your circles, as drawn, imply that you mean to conjure them all in sequence during the same experiment."

Cade sighed and sat back from the circle he was scribing. "Yes. I know."

Luis wondered if the implication of his question had been lost on the karcist. "Isn't that a recipe for disaster? What will happen when you conjure spirits on unfavorable days?"

"Not much. A few complaints, which I'll silence by stabbing my wand into my brazier." Cade looked up and noted Luis's surprise. "You're used to the old ways. One experiment, one spirit." Cade rubbed his eyes. "That's the safest way of doing it. But not the only way."

This was the first time Luis had ever heard anyone suggest such a thing. "Are you telling me that the old grimoires lied? Or were mistaken?"

"More like they were redacted for our safety." Cade picked up his chalk and resumed working on the glyphs between the outer concentric rings of his circle. "During the war, there were times when necessity trumped caution. We learned through trial and error which demons could be forced to obey on our schedules, and which couldn't."

"So it doesn't always work."

A small shake of Cade's head. "No. But it worked enough. And that kept us armed, even on short notice, or when we got stuck in enemy territory."

A look around the room revealed another glaring omission to Luis. "Where are your tools? Surely you can't conduct magickal experiments without them."

"Of course not," Cade said, inscribing the last character in the Latin spelling of the holy name JEHOVAM. "Anja's got a spare set of tools here. She'll conduct her experiment first, yoke a few spirits, and then send a demon to fetch our tools and grimoires from the train station locker they currently share in Rome. After that, we'll patch up our wounds, and then we'll each run parallel experiments overnight to finish arming ourselves to deal with Dragan."

The American's confidence struck Luis as misplaced. "Dragan the Black Sun leader? Are you saying you know where he is?"

"No. But Briet's looking into it."

"I see. But why the hurry? Why not give yourselves time to heal properly?"

Cade paused in his meticulous scribing of Greek characters to check his watch. "Because in roughly thirty-two hours, if we don't deliver the Iron Codex to Dragan, he's going to blast open the gates of Hell and usher in some kind of postmodern apocalypse."

"What does this madman Dragan want with the codex?"

"Fucked if I know, Padre. But if we don't come up with a working plan before ten o'clock tomorrow morning, we might have to hand it over to save the world."

"And if giving him the codex only makes matters worse . . . ?"

Cade looked incredulous. "Worse than Armageddon?" A shrug. "I guess we'll punt."

"And how does Miss Kernova feel about surrendering the codex?"

"She says she'll die first."

All at once Luis understood the gravity of their predicament. "I see."

"A pity we can't ask your brothers at Monte Paterno for help—not that they'd get their hands dirty." Cade's lament turned snide as he added, "Mustn't violate the fucking Covenant."

"The Covenant exists for a reason," Luis protested, almost as if by rote.

Cade stink-eyed him. "Whoever cooked it up had one agenda: cutting off the balls of White magicians. And the only reason it still exists is that your kind are too fucking scared to fight back." Continuing his meticulous preparations, Cade added, "Bitch about unintended consequences all you want, but the simple fact, Father, is that all it takes for evil to succeed in this world is for good men to do nothing. And that's *exactly* the result your Covenant ensures."

A thousand feet deep and as black as the center of a fist, the Silo stood empty and silent. Through the windows of its control suite there was nothing to see but darkness, and not much more than that inside its deserted confines. Briet stood alone amid the banks of computers that ringed the level, confounded by their control interface on the elevated director's platform.

I can shape reality, transform matter . . . but I can't figure out how to turn on these fucking machines. For over an hour she had poked at buttons, flipped toggles, and adjusted dials and sliders, but nothing seemed to snap the Silo's army of computers to attention.

Then she heard a single set of footsteps approaching in the shadows.

Briet considered raising her wand but thought better of it. *I can kill him with a thought,* she reminded herself. *Why give him an ounce of warning?*

When her visitor was still a few yards shy of the platform, she switched on its overhead lights, illuminating them both, and then she flashed an evil smile. "Hello, Frank."

"Bree." Frank Cioffi was as big of a sartorial mess as ever. His belly hung over his belt, his shirt was so wrinkled that it looked like a topographical map of the Badlands, and sweat glistened atop his melon of a head. He took a step toward her. "When the silent alarm on my console was tripped, I assumed it was you." He waved toward the Silo. "You're the only person I can think of who could get in here while the place is locked down."

She gestured at the master control console. "Why won't it start up?"

From his pants pocket he fished out a key. "Because you don't have this."

Briet extended her hand as a request. "If you would."

"Not so fast." He tucked the key back into his pocket. "What are you doing here? You know we need to lie low while—"

"Spare me the McCarthy bullshit." She picked up a satchel she had brought with her and set it on the console. From it she pulled a folder tied shut with ribbon. She tossed it at Frank. It struck the floor at his feet with a loud *slap* that echoed in the empty spaces of the observation ring. "I just spent the last two days making my own inquiries into McCarthy's witch hunt. Want to know what I found, Frank?"

He warily eyed the folder in front of his feet. "I'll admit to a passing interest."

"McCarthy *never* investigated us. He and his office know nothing about us. They don't even know we *exist.*" With a tiny flick of one finger, she untied the folder's ribbon and flipped open its cover to reveal its ream of contents. "Whoever told you we were being targeted by McCarthy *lied* to you." She decided not to tell him what Infernal horrors she had visited upon the trio of FBI agents who had violated her home during her absence.

Frank squatted over the folder and pawed through its pages. He looked bewildered. "Are you telling me that McCarthyism is just a red herring?"

"Worse: it's a cover-up." She retrieved a second, slimmer file from her satchel and tossed it on top of the McCarthy report. "I traced the orders that shut us down. They came from a handful of senators and congressmen who sit on key committees. People who had just the right kind of influence to bully the

Department of Defense." She waited until Frank opened the second file, and then she continued. "Here's what troubles me, Frank. None of those officials are supposed to know about us. So who told them? And why?"

She watched Frank with the emotional sight of MEVAKOS. Shades of confusion and fear were bright in Frank's aura, but it was untainted by hues of deception. "I don't know," he said, turning pages and looking stunned anew each time. "I wasn't part of this, I swear."

"I believe you. Truth be told, I have a pretty good idea who's to blame." Noting Frank's suddenly keen interest, she added, "My former adept, Dragan Dalca. You told me he was being transferred to a new ODP unit on the West Coast."

"That's what I was told. That's what his paperwork said."

"He never got there, Frank. After he left the Silo, he vanished into the private sector. Along with all of my other former students, most of whom are now unaccounted for."

Her revelation put a look of horror on Frank's face. "They're missing?"

"If we're lucky, they're dead. But I suspect that's not the case. More likely they've all turned mercenary. Which means we have many new threats to assess when we finish dealing with our current crisis." She pulled the last folder from her satchel and lobbed it on top of the others. "The Castle Bravo atomic test scheduled for tomorrow on Bikini Atoll. Dragan's sabotaged it using magick far beyond anything I've ever taught him. But whatever he's up to, he'll be doing it from a distance." She reached inside her jacket and pulled out the copy she had made of the horoscope in the Odessa journal. "I think this chart indicates the location Dragan chose for his base of operations. If we can figure out what location corresponds to this chart, there might be a chance to put an end to his plan before it gets started."

She held out the paper to Frank, who stood, stepped forward, and took it.

He adjusted his glasses as he studied the chart. "This is why you were trying to start up the computers." He waited for Briet's nod of confirmation. "It wouldn't have helped. They aren't programmed to run these calculations in reverse."

"How long would it take you to teach them to do that?"

He rolled his round shoulders. "It's not as easy as it looks. Lotta variables. Some heavy-duty math. Calculus, trigonometry. And don't get me started on the precession correction and—" He stopped when he became aware of

Briet's piercing stare. "I might be able to do it, but we'd have to pull an all-nighter. At least."

That wasn't the answer Briet had hoped for, but it was better than what she had feared. "All right. Is there anything I can do to help you?"

"Yeah, you can go to the kitchenette and start a pot of coffee." Once again he belatedly caught Briet's murderous glare, and he shifted gears into apology mode: "If you would be so kind, Miss Segfrunsdóttir. Please."

"Work quickly." Briet abandoned the control panel's dais and passed Frank on her way to the kitchenette. "The fate of the world depends on it."

FEBRUARY 28 / MARCH 1

Flush with newly yoked demons, Anja emerged from her conjuring room feeling both energized and nauseated. More work lay ahead of her before sunup, but she had earned an hour of rest.

The ritual had gone smoothly in spite of its dangerously truncated prep time. For that much she was thankful. As soon as she had left the circle she had used BUER's talents to heal the dozens of wounds Lombardi had inflicted upon her. Then she had picked up Cade's tool roll and grimoire from the outer circle, to which her dispatched-and-returned spirit PELFAGOR had delivered it, along with her own primary set of tools and book of pacts.

As planned, Cade met Anja outside the conjuring room. He reached for his tools. "You're an angel." He took the roll by its strap and slung it over his shoulder, and then he accepted his grimoire from Anja. "Too kind." He turned and walked toward the stairs.

Anja followed him. "We need to talk strategy."

"I'm short on time." His strides quickened. "Talk on the move."

She hurried to keep pace with him. "Do we have a target for Dragan?"

"No. So we focus everything on Bikini Atoll."

"Are you sure that is wise?"

"If we can only deal with one half of this nightmare, it's gotta be the bomb." He noted her concern. "Think about it. If we take out Dragan but don't separate the demon from the bomb, that plus his magickal lens could turn a small test explosion into a world-breaker. But if we neutralize his superbomb, what happens when he tries to run his experiment? Nothing."

Cade climbed the stairs two steps at a time. Anja stayed close behind him, and the steps creaked under their combined weight. She asked, "Can you live with that?" Her ceremonial garb made the steps hard to climb quickly. "If we let him run, we might never find him again."

Cade side-eyed her. "I wouldn't worry about that. I get the feeling he'll find us."

At the top of the stairs, Cade turned toward the villa's library. Anja jogged to catch up to him. "Can I ask you a question?"

He slowed to let her walk at his side. "Shoot."

"Are we doing the right thing?"

He seemed confused. "By going after the sabotaged bomb?"

"No. By not giving Dragan the codex."

They stopped outside the library's door. "There's no other choice," Cade said. "He's ready to end the world if he doesn't get this book. Any time a Nazi wants something *that* badly, you can bet there's damned good reason not to give it to them." He offered her his hand. "Dragan gets that book only over my dead body."

She clasped Cade's hand. "And mine."

While their hands were joined, she channeled the healing powers of BUER and restored all of the rips and sprains Lombardi's yoke had caused to Cade. He blinked, drew a long deep breath through his nose, and took an awkward half step backward. "Whoa. That felt good."

"I would not send you to war with only half your strength."

A grateful smile. "I've done worse—but thank you." He checked his watch. "It's almost four. I'd better get started. See you in a few hours."

"Be safe." Anja watched Cade enter the library and close the door.

When she turned back toward the stairs, she saw Luis standing there. He looked haggard and pale. Anja approached him. "Are you all right, Father?"

He dismissed her concern with a small gesture. "Fine." As she neared him, he asked, "Is Cade calling up another legion of the Fallen? The house already stinks of brimstone."

"Learn to love that stench. Without it, we die."

"Pragmatic. But not comforting."

Upon closer inspection she saw how pale he was. "You lost much blood when we took the bullets out of you." She rested her hands upon his shoulders and invoked BUER's healing gift once more. The priest tensed, likely in aversion to the notion of being made whole by demonic power, but after a few seconds his face regained a healthful color, and he stood straighter.

"Thank you," he said, unable to look her in the eye.

Too busy and tired to waste energy easing the priest's ethical misgivings, Anja passed him and descended the stairs. To her surprise he trailed anxiously half a step behind her. Without looking back, she said more than she asked, "You want something, Father."

"I—" His reply seemed caught in his throat. "That is to say—" Another strained, throttled pause. "Yes, but—" Again he lost his rhetorical way.

"Father, the world is ending in a few hours. Will you finish your thought by then?"

He nodded, duly chastised. "Sorry. I guess all I really want to say is . . . good luck."

"I do not need luck. I need *firepower.* I need *allies.*" She stopped and grabbed Luis by the front of his robe. "We have the Iron Codex. I can show you how to use it."

Luis shook his head. "No. I can't."

"You can. If Dragan wins, we all die. Even now, Khalîl readies his circle at Key Gompa. Briet makes hers in the Silo. If Cade and I fail, they will try to close the gates of Hell, to save the world from Dragan. Why should you do any less?"

The priest's denial grew more defiant. "I'm a scholar, not a soldier."

Fury welled up inside Anja. "Meaning what?"

"I can't use the codex alone. If I had the help of my brothers—"

She let him go. "They are not here. You are."

He seemed to be grappling with a painful truth. "I won't deny the book's power tempts me. But that's exactly why I must *not* use it alone. In the hands of a novice operator, the codex could unleash an even greater disaster than the one we hope to prevent!"

"Or, it could save the world. But left unopened, the codex is *useless.* Just like you." Sick of his excuses, she marched back to her conjuring room.

Luis followed her to its door. "Please! It's not that I don't want to help. I *do.* But my vows compel me not to gamble madly with the lives and safety of others."

Anja stopped to confront him. "Your vows were the chains that made you a slave. But you broke them when you saved me and Cade. You are a free man. Act like it."

He stood tall in the face of her challenge. "I saved you to prevent a greater evil. One act of defiance does not vitiate all of my oaths. I will not let it."

She saw the problem in his face. He had never fought in a war. Never shed blood in anger or taken a life. He could not understand what Cade and Anja knew all too well. All that she could do as she regarded his naïveté was shake her head in pity and disgust.

"If your vows do not allow you to fight evil . . . then what *good* are you?"

Tears welling in Luis's eyes told Anja that her double entendre had cut him deeply. She turned her back on him and abandoned him on the other side of a closed door.

Let him wrestle with his conscience. I must make ready for war.

The final minute preceding the deadline of his ultimatum brought Dragan a strange cocktail of emotions. Optimism. Despair. Irritation. Vindication. Disappointment.

In his palm lay his pocket watch, its hands ticking and creeping with inexorable precision around its face. In forty-nine seconds it would be one second past midnight in the Pacific Proving Grounds. When that moment arrived and found him still without possession of the Iron Codex, he would have no choice but to make good on his threat to the Russian woman.

He would have to shatter the world.

The voice in his head grew impatient. *«She will never give up the book.»*

"She still has a few seconds left, and our word is bond." He stared at the longest hand of the watch, tracking its march toward the face's apex.

Outside of the office he had appropriated as his study, the rest of the house was quiet except for the cries of the wind. His cohorts all were down in the bunker. Though it was the middle of the night and the final experiment was still more than six hours away, he knew they would be awake, awaiting his declaration. They had labored for years and spent millions of dollars to set this in motion. He couldn't blame any of them for being unable to sleep.

"Twenty seconds. What if, by some miracle, she hands over the codex?"

«We proceed with the experiment.»

"But once we have the codex—"

«There is no guarantee it will deliver the remedy we seek in a timely manner. The experiment indubitably will. Not that it matters, because she will never give you the book.»

The last seconds ticked away as Dragan bore witness.

"The deadline is passed." He tucked away the pocket watch and left his study.

The voice fell uncharacteristically silent while Dragan made his way downstairs and through the tunnels to the bunker whose magickal defenses he had spent the last two weeks crafting. The corridor ended at a T-junction. His conjuring theater lay at the end of the short hall on the left. The recreation room lined the longer hallway to his right. He homed in on the sound of voices in the rec room.

As soon as he stepped through the open doorway, his tanists' conversation fell away. The four karcists faced him, their eyes wide with hopeful expectation. At the front of the group was Ulrich Schlesinger. Dragan stepped up to him and took him by the shoulders. "It's time."

Schlesinger's manner was calm but grave. "Tell us truthfully, Herr Dalca: Are we about to end the world?" He shared a look with the three magicians behind him. "We have a right to know if we're being asked to serve as the agents of Armageddon."

Dragan swallowed his misgivings and put on his most reassuring smile. "Not at all, Ulrich. I won't lie to you"—he let go of Schlesinger and stood beside him as he addressed the others—"for a time it might *feel* like the end of the world. But that's why we built this fortress. This place can sustain us and our garrison for up to three years—but I doubt we'll be here more than a few months."

He detected flashes of doubt in the faces of his tanists; he needed to bolster their morale. "Trust me, friends. I did not bring you this far only to fail you at the end." Dragan looked each one of them in the eye as he said their name. "Juliana. Dieter. Erik. Just like Ulrich, the three of you have proved yourselves to be skilled, reliable karcists, as well as loyal soldiers of the Black Sun during its long years in South American exile. Six hours from now, we will bring the Americans to their knees and change the face of the earth forever. From those bitter ashes the Fourth Reich will rise, and all of my master's promises will be fulfilled."

He saw that they had left glasses of half-consumed Riesling on the table. He poured himself a glass, then gestured for his four associates to raise theirs as he lifted his own. "Be of good cheer, *meine Freunde!* Tomorrow the Black Sun will rise—and our black dawn will last a thousand years, with us as the new lords of the earth."

———

Heavy curtains tied shut kept the inside of Anja's villa cold and gloomy even at midday, and that was the way she liked it. She felt jittery enough with angels and demons clashing inside her psyche; she had no need to be blinded by sunlight blazing through clear alpine air.

Her yokings were finished, but Cade had yet to emerge from his conjuring room. Anja had passed the time in her bedroom taking inventory of her gear: a hunting knife, a compass, her wand, and a lock-picking set—just in case. After doing that twice, she had elected to calm her mind by sitting outside Cade's door and sharpening her blade with a whetstone. The repetition of the movement, the slow steady pulls of the edge across the oiled surface, became a mantra for her, an action that she could perform by muscle memory while she blanked her thoughts.

Then the door of the upstairs conjuring room opened, releasing a billow of greenish fog that reeked of rotting flesh and skunk spray. Cade emerged from the funky cloud with his wand in hand, and he pulled off his miter as he walked past Anja. "Of all the days for MARCHOSIAS to be a prick about the rules, it had to choose *today*. . . ."

Falling in behind him, Anja asked, "Are you ready? We have less than eighty minutes before the bomb goes off."

He sounded irked. "I didn't get what I *wanted,* but I got what I needed." Descending the steps to the first floor, he pulled off his ceremonial robe and draped it over the banister at the end of the staircase. "What about you? Get what you need?"

"I am ready, yes."

Cade stopped at the bottom of the stairs, kicked off his white leather slippers, and sat down to pull on a well-worn pair of combat boots. He tucked a dagger into the right boot before he laced it up. "Remember: Don't hurt any troops or civilians. They're victims, not the enemy."

"I remember. Can you tie your shoes any faster?"

"Not without wasting a demon." He pulled his trousers over the tops of his boots, picked up his wand, and stood. "How do we get to Bikini?"

She led him toward the front room, where they could at least enjoy some warmth from a banked fire in the hearth. "I yoked an angel named ATHIEL. It will thunder-jump us there, much like Luis's angel did when we left Rome." As they turned the corner into the front room, they saw the priest leaning against the far wall and peeking past the curtain into the harsh light of day. When he looked their way he seemed to wear his shame like a crown of shadow.

"Speak of the Devil," Cade said. "If it ain't our own little conscientious objector."

Luis ignored the slight, but Anja had no doubt that he'd heard it. She let Cade's remark pass and returned to business. "ATHIEL is good for only one jaunt. Did you yoke a portal spirit?"

"GARAGOG. But it has the same limitation as ATHIEL—one trip and then it's gone."

"That should be all we need to—"

Two pillars of violet flame appeared in the center of the room. Anja, Cade, and Luis all turned toward them as the fires dissipated to reveal the ghostly images of Briet's and Khalil's astral projections. "Cade, Anja," Briet said. "I've found Dragan."

Eager to hear good news, Anja asked, "Where is he?"

"I used the Silo's computers to analyze the Odessa horoscope. Only one spot on earth could've yielded that chart: Shemya Island. West end of the Aleutian chain, in the Bering Sea."

Luis drifted closer. Cade sounded dubious. "How can you be sure he's there?"

"I did some digging," Briet said. "DOD files confirm that Shemya was an Air Force base until a few weeks ago. It was decommissioned and transferred to private control as part of a shady deal involving some highly placed congressmen and senators."

Anja nodded and looked at Cade. "Makes sense. A former military base would be defensible. And the Bering Sea is far enough to be safe from his superbomb."

Cade shook his head. "Might be old intel. How do we know he's there now?"

"I scried it through a bird's eye," Khalil said. "There is a company of armed men posted around a fortified bunker, and a glyph on the bunker's front door wards it and the island against unwelcome teleportation. Dragan is most assuredly there."

It was the best news Anja had heard in weeks. "Cade, this is our chance. We can hit Dragan on two fronts at once, take him by surprise."

"No way," Cade said. "We stick to the plan."

"We made that plan because we did not know where Dragan was. Now we do."

"It makes no difference, Anja. We coordinated our yokings for a joint attack on Bikini. If we split up, neither of us has an exit strategy. Which means whoever goes to Bikini ends up stranded next to an *atomic fucking bomb*."

He was absolutely correct, but Anja knew in her heart that this was the right choice. "We have a chance to stop the bomb *and* kill Dragan. We need to take it."

"No," Khalîl said. "You do not. Only stopping the bomb matters."

"Wrong. If we let Dragan escape, he will do this again. And next time we might not find out in time to stop him. We cannot let him hold the world hostage one more day, no matter the cost." Anja took Cade's hand. "You told me that you love me. If that is true, prove it by doing as I ask: Go to Shemya and kill Dragan, and let me go alone to Bikini."

⌁

Sorrow cast a pall over Cade's face. "If you do this . . . you'll die."

"If I die," Anja said, "it will be as I have lived: fighting for what I know is right."

He fought to resist his mounting grief as he looked to Khalîl. "The last place you belong is on a battlefield." He shot a look at Briet's specter. "Don't suppose you'd care to lend a hand?"

"Sorry, but I've already got my hands full preparing to turn back Armageddon. The fight on the ground is all you."

Cade aimed a scathing look at Luis. "I already know what *your* answer is." He clasped Anja's hand in both of his. "I guess it's just the two of us."

"*Da.* As always."

Cade let go of her hand and bowed his head in a failed bid to conceal his heartbreak. When he looked up again, he had put on the hard mask of a soldier. "Khalîl, did your recon suggest the best way to approach the island?"

"From the north," the master said. "But after you land upon the beach, you will need to scale a steep cliff."

"What about the other shores?"

"Easier landings," Briet said, "but the Shemya maps say they're all littered with land mines and covered by machine-gun nests. Only the north side is clear."

"And I can't portal onto the island, so I'll need to start at sea. That's just fucking great." Cade turned away from the group. "KERIGOS, front and center."

A monstrous shape of smoke coalesced as if from thin air and hovered in front of Cade, black and tenuous. It spoke in a voice as deep as time. WHAT IS THY COMMAND?

"Procure the following items and deliver them to me here in the next ten minutes. A seaworthy LCRS with a working outboard motor, fully fueled. My small-arms footlocker from my safe house in Kataragama. A Soviet winter-camouflage battle dress uniform in my size. A U.S. Army grapnel launcher, armed and ready, with a two-hundred-fifty-foot rope ladder. And a U.S. Army medical corps field surgery kit. That's all. Go."

He dismissed the demon with a wave, and it vanished in a swirl of vapors.

"Good luck," Khalîl said. "I must return now to my preparations."

"And I have to batten down the hatches here at the Silo," Briet said. "Give 'em Hell."

The master and the Icelandic woman bid each other farewell with small nods, and then their astral shades faded from sight, leaving Cade, Luis, and Anja alone once more.

Anja waited until Cade looked her way, and then she said softly, "Thank you."

For a moment he was at a loss for words. "We should finish getting ready. As soon as my demonic concierge gets back, we'll have to get this show on the road."

"Agreed."

Luis was aghast. "I can't believe the two of you. How can you be so calm?"

A shrug from Cade. "Why shouldn't we be?"

"For the love of God! This plan—it's a *suicide* mission."

Cade lit a cigarette and exhaled. "A suicide mission would have better odds."

FEBRUARY 28 / MARCH 1, PART II

Detonation minus 22 minutes

The portal opened beneath Cade's rubber landing boat. He and it dropped like a stone into the black churn of an angry sea. Frigid spray crashed over the sides and stung his face as he pulled the cord to start the outboard motor. It kicked on with a deep buzzing that came and went as the boat crashed through one ice-cold wave after another.

A fast check of his combat gear confirmed it was all still in place, lashed together beneath and secured to the boat's built-in bench seats. Then Cade noticed wild flurries of snow dancing around him in mad spirals, driven by a shriek of arctic wind. He had fallen smack into the middle of a blizzard. *Yeah, this op's off to a great fuckin' start.*

Steering the boat with one hand on the motor's handle, he used his free hand to check his compass. His heading was more than ten degrees off true. He adjusted course to due south.

Navigating to Shemya Island was going to be as much a test of his seamanship as of his faith, because he couldn't see any sign of it. Between the predawn darkness, the violent pitching of the sea, and the curtains of snow encircling his landing raft, he was charging headlong into an endless stretch of black and gray, with no safe harbor in sight.

D minus 22 minutes

Tropical wind filled Anja's wings. Wearing the form of a great frigate bird, she soared above the open ocean, approaching Bikini Atoll from the north. The sun peeked over the horizon, and the sea glittered like a fortune in gold coins.

Engaging the magickal sight of Vos Satria, she perceived a bright sphere of sorcerous protection that Dragan had raised over the sabotaged hydrogen bomb. The shimmering dome, which would be invisible to the unaided eye, was more than two miles in diameter.

At its center was the Castle Bravo device's concrete enclosing structure—its shot cab—standing on a constructed patch of sand at the end of a long man-made causeway that ran west-southwest from the side of Namu Island that was farthest from Anja. The nearest edge of the dome extended past the north-eastern shore of Namu, into the water.

Namu is the only way to the shot cab, Anja realized. *Unless I want to swim more than a mile through demon-infested waters.* She had come prepared for a fight, but not one that she would have to wage while swimming. She set her sights on the northern tip of Namu and dived.

Her wings flapped twice to slow her descent as she neared splashdown. It was almost low tide, and she could see Namu's wide leeward reef through the shallow, crystal-clear water. As soon as her feet touched the sea, she returned to her human shape. She sank thigh-deep into the cool water. Around her, sharks' fins broke the surface and then submerged. In the near-dawn twilight she tracked the sharks' deadly shadows as they circled her.

Remembering her newly discovered natural rapport with animals, she concentrated on transmitting a clear thought to all of the fish in her vicinity.

I am not food. I am not prey. I will kill you.

The circling fiends dispersed in a frenzy of retreat. Free to move, Anja pushed ahead, toward the luminous barrier. Up close she was able to see that it was composed of glyphs and sigils taken from both the Pauline and Goetic arts, symbols whose cumulative power had one clear purpose: to prevent demons from passing through in either direction.

To go ashore I must shed my demons, Anja realized. She peered beyond its glowing surface and discerned an army of the Fallen waiting for her on the other side, all of them trapped inside the barrier. *This was made to be a death trap for Black magicians.*

Resigned to the inevitable, she dismissed all of her yoked demons—and savored the moment of relief exuded by the handful of angels that remained bound to her will.

She took a confident step forward—and passed without resistance through the barrier.

As I thought. Just like Key Gompa, or the Vatican. Not made to exclude angels.

A cluster of demons on the beach raced toward Anja. She waded ashore as quickly as she could. The fiends rose like a tidal wave of black smoke and towered over her, poised to crash down with overwhelming force—

—and as they fell, Anja swung a sword of holy fire in a white-hot arc.

Not since the war in Heaven had spirits wailed with such pain and terror. The blade slashed through one demon after another, maiming them, shredding them, and hurling them backward as if they'd been fired from catapults. They dropped into the water ahead of her, and she finished each one with a death stroke on her way past, returning them to Hell.

Anja ran as she reached ankle-deep water, and sprinted faster than she had ever run in her life once her feet hit dry sand. Pushing herself harder than she would have thought possible, she followed the northern beach of the tiny island toward the causeway on the far side.

Behind her, ahead of her, and beside her, demons manifested on the beach and poured out of the jungle, all of them converging upon her. She smirked. *Do your worst.*

Wielding the sword of MICHAEL in her right hand and the shield of GABRIEL in her left, Anja feared no evil as she charged alone against an army of darkness.

D minus 17 minutes

Rocks scraped against the hardened bottom of Cade's landing boat. He'd made it to shore. He cut the outboard motor. *Showtime.*

The blizzard had worsened in the few minutes it had taken Cade to reach the island. Snow devils spun across the beach while he gathered his weapons and gear. From his cache he had armed himself with a fully automatic M3 carbine equipped with a scope and a flash suppressor. The leg pockets of his gray-and-white camouflage fatigues were packed with spare thirty-round magazines of .30-caliber ammunition for the rifle. On his right hip he carried a nine-millimeter Browning Hi-Power semiautomatic pistol. Spare fifteen-round magazines for the Browning lined his belt.

Completing his load-out was the portable grapnel launcher, a heavy piece of gear he had used at Pointe du Hoc on D-day. Though its rope bundle was awkward to handle, it promised to make his ascent of Shemya's nearly verti-cal, ice-covered cliffs at least nominally possible.

He slung the rifle across his back and lugged the grapnel launcher under his left arm while he dragged his LCRS across the beach with his right. It wasn't likely that anyone atop the cliff could see more than a half dozen yards through the storm, but he couldn't take a chance on his boat being spotted and giving away his presence. He hid it between two large stands of rocks at the base of the cliff wall. Then he stepped back from the cliff and looked up.

Fuck, that's high. Two hundred feet, at least. Twice as high as Pointe du Hoc.

Cade set up the launcher twenty feet from the base of the cliff, with a four-degree pitch to guide the rocket-propelled grapnel over the cliff's edge. It took him a few seconds to untangle its rope, which was slippery as fuck when wet. He crossed the fingers of his left hand as he primed the trigger. *Here goes nothing.* Wincing against the gale, he fired the grapnel.

Its bang of launch was swallowed by the storm. The grapnel disappeared into the whorls of white and gray overhead, trailed by its unspooling rope lad-der. Cade counted to ten. When the grapnel didn't come crashing back down beside him, he tested the ladder with a few firm tugs. It didn't slip or shift. Wherever the grapnel had landed, it was secure.

Time to climb, Ranger.

The wind threatened to blow him off the ladder several times each minute while he pulled himself upward. *Fuck me. I could start taking fire at any mo-ment. If anyone saw the grapnel, or heard it hit, they could have a platoon wait-ing to greet me at the top.* He forced himself to keep climbing and not look down, while his imagination concocted more dire scenarios. *Hell, why bring a platoon? If even one sentry spotted my grapnel, all he'd have to do is wait another minute and cut the rope. He gets a medal and I get an express eleva-tor to hell.*

He spotted the top of the cliff through the swirling snow. No one seemed to be looking back at him. His shoulders and hips ached, and the muscles in his arms and legs burned from the effort of his rapid ascent, but as he pulled himself over the top, he marveled at how much faster this climb had gone than the one he'd made on D-day.

Climbing's not so hard when no one's shooting at me.

He crawled forward through a knee-deep blanket of fresh-fallen snow and scouted the terrain. The rest of the island sloped downward from his position. To either side of him stood clifftop fortifications designed for large coastal-defense artillery. Neither emplacement had any guns installed, and both looked dark and deserted.

Guess no one expected an attack to come up the cliffs.

Cade unslung his rifle, opened the cap on the scope, and surveyed the landscape. Several pillboxes stood at regular intervals facing the southern and western shores.

He trained his scope on the men inside the pillboxes. They wore a wide assortment of uniforms. Some of the men were white; others were black, brown, or Asian. Their weapons displayed the same variety. In one sweep Cade spotted a Sterling submachine gun, an M1 Garand, a Zhongzheng rifle, a Mosin-Nagant rifle, and a Czechoslovak light machine gun.

Mercenaries. He felt relief. *No need to play nice.*

Cade considered using stealth tactics to infiltrate the command bunker while minimizing contact with the mercs. The bunker was much closer to him than it was to them. If he could penetrate its defenses without alerting the soldiers of fortune guarding the beach—

No, that's stupid, he decided. *One shot fired and I'll have a whole company of shooters charging up my six.* He turned his scope toward the bunker. Within seconds he saw more men huddled around a trash-can fire outside the main building, and two more on its roof. *No way I'm getting in there without a fight.*

He checked his watch. Twelve minutes to detonation. *No time to play it safe. Too bad I yoked up to fight demons, not mercs.* Regrets were unprofessional, but Cade always preferred to tailor his yokings to his tasks with as much precision as possible. *If only I'd had time to yoke* GADREEL, *or even* SABAOTH. *Being a ghost to bullets would be useful right now.*

Hands tight around his carbine, he pushed through his doubt. *Forget what you don't have. Make the most of what you've got. You're a goddamned Ranger and an MI6 agent. Act like it.* He surveyed the ground ahead and spotted a dip in the terrain that would provide him natural cover and put him within few dozen meters of the command bunker. *Here we go.*

He crouched and jogged forward in a serpentine manner through the raging snowstorm. At the depression in the ground he stopped and lay prone.

Another peek through his scope. The men on the roof continued to face south and west. The mercs on the ground remained in a tight huddle around their trash-can fire.

Cade lined up his first shot. Fired.

The closer of the two rooftop sentries collapsed and tumbled off the top of the building, landing behind it, out of the sight of his comrades.

On the ground, the men around the fire looked up and about, confused. Between the wind and the mild muffling effect of the suppressor on Cade's rifle, they seemed unable to tell from what direction the crack of gunfire had come.

The second man on the roof noticed he was alone just as Cade lined up his crosshairs on the man's throat and fired. Scarlet bloodmist filled the air, and the dead merc slumped out of view, swallowed by the gray howl of the storm.

One of the mercs at the trash fire pointed in Cade's direction. The man to his left pulled a walkie-talkie from his belt and lifted it toward his face.

Cade channeled the martial prowess of CASMIEL and put a single round through both the radio and the face of the man holding it. Bloody brains spattered his brothers-in-arms, who recoiled in surprise and disgust—giving Cade the extra half second he needed to use the incendiary gifts of XAPHAN to turn their trash fire into a bomb that engulfed them all.

Burning corpses thrown from the blast landed in smoking heaps.

Cade smirked. *Now it's a party.*

Across the compound, mercs deserted their patrols and ran for cover. Cade switched his M3 from single to full automatic and charged toward the command bunker while he swept the cluster of fleeing men with hails of lead. He made it halfway to his objective before his foes found cover behind a stack of snowcapped wooden crates and started to return fire.

Time for the hard part. Cade dived to the ground next to a jeep and put his back to its rear tire. Gunfire rent the air, and Cade's jeep pinged and pealed beneath a barrage of bullets.

Only another dozen yards to the bunker's entrance, Cade observed. He saw plenty of cover—more crates, a canvas-topped military surplus troop truck, corners galore on the surrounding buildings—but those would help the enemy as much as they'd benefit him.

He laid down a few bursts of suppressing fire at the mercs behind the nearby stack of crates, and then he ducked back behind the jeep, ejected his weapon's empty magazine, and slammed in a fresh one. Alarm sirens shrieked in the distance. Word of his attack was spreading.

Unleashing a fireball as he sprang from cover, he bounced the explosive sphere off of the building behind the crates. Its emerald flames swallowed the four men huddled there—and then it ignited the ammunition inside the boxes. An earsplitting bang, and then a shock wave knocked Cade onto his stomach.

The clamor of running steps and the angry stutters of automatic gunfire drove Cade back to his feet. He unleashed his own fusillade into the drifting smoke and snow. Halfway to cover his M3 clacked empty. He dropped another spent magazine and reached for a fresh one to reload on the move—and then, through the cold fog, he saw a merc step around a corner and target him with the nozzle of a flamethrower.

The nozzle flared as it spat fiery liquid at Cade.

He raised his fist, and with the will of XAPHAN he bent the cone of burning jellied gasoline back upon the man who'd fired it. In the space of a breath the merc was aflame from head to toe, screaming in agony as greasy black smoke cocooned him.

Cade ducked behind another stack of crates. The burning merc's fuel tanks exploded, trembling the ground, painting the narrow street and the buildings around the command bunker with flames, and choking the frigid air with noxious fumes.

Fuck that was close.

Cade magickally smothered patches of burning fuel on his fatigues and then he reloaded his M3. He shifted to get a better view south and west. The mercs who had manned the pillboxes facing the beach now were piled on top of each other in jeeps that were fishtailing their way up the icy roads to the command bunker. *They're almost a mile away,* Cade told himself. *Not a problem yet. Unlike these assholes behind the building on my left—*

A three-man squad advanced to the corner nearest Cade, who swiftly adjusted his cover—and then he used the demonic sight of SATHARIEL to peer through the crates he was using for protection. Two men took turns leaning out and peppering Cade's position with automatic fire. Just as he'd suspected, the men spraying bullets were just keeping Cade pinned while the third man in their team steadied a bazooka on his shoulder.

Cade used the telekinetic power of JEPHISTO to hurl his sheltering wall of seven crates like giant splintering dice at the rocket man and his gunmen. The three mercs dodged and split up in a mad scramble to avoid being bowled over or crushed—and then Cade hit all three of them with a triple fork of red lightning courtesy of ZOCAR. The mercs twitched as they dangled a few feet off the ground, trapped in the grip of the electric assault. Then Cade ended it and let their crisped bodies drop dead in the snow.

Having sacrificed his own cover, Cade made a run for the command bunker.

As soon as he crossed into its zone of magickal defense, a wave of nausea hit him along with a tightness in his chest. Vertigo struck him next. Sickened and spinning, he fought for balance—and then his demon sight revealed a pair of Infernal terrors bearing down upon him: one a lumbering biped with a head that opened like a flower whose petals were carpeted with spines and whose pistils were forked tongues dripping poison; the other a crablike horror with two tentacles sprouting from its back and a maw made of hellfire. Cade didn't know the demons' names, and he had no desire to make their acquaintance.

He fed petal-head a jet of white-hot fire and threw an Olympic bolt of lightning into the other's gaping mouth of flames and fangs. The crab snared Cade's left leg with one of its tentacles and broke his M3 in half with the other. The flap-faced nightmare trudged forward, undeterred even as Cade intensified his attack.

Both fiends drew close enough that he smelled the stench of the Pit on their breath. He coupled a glaive of VAELBOR with XAPHAN's hellfire and cut the open-faced freak in half. Then he wrapped ZOCAR's lightning around the barbed whip of VALAK and with three brutal snaps severed the crab's tentacles and tore off the lower part of its jaw. The beast turned to retreat, and Cade cut it in half with a final lash of the whip across its back.

A spray of machine-gun fire strafed the front of the bunker, narrowly missing Cade. He spotted the incoming jeep with a .50-caliber gun mounted in its rear and ran toward the nearby troop truck as bullets chewed up the snow and dirt behind his feet.

He slid across a patch of ice and shot under the parked truck. The jeep's sloppy assault ripped apart the canvas tent that covered the truck's flatbed as Cade grabbed the its rear tire to halt his slide and pull himself back to cover.

The jeep swerved. It passed the front of the truck, giving its gunner a clear shot at Cade—who flipped the speeding military car onto its side with help from JEPHISTO. The jeep tumbled in a symphony of crunching metal and breaking glass, crushing driver and passengers alike before it slammed into the front of a nearby building.

Cade felt his strength fading as a consequence of whatever invisible attack the bunker's sentinel demons had inflicted upon him. His hold on his yoked spirits was slipping. *That's what I get for yoking in a hurry,* he stewed.

Suspecting his yoked spirits might try to desert him at any moment, Cade set to work unraveling the normally invisible glyphs that protected the bunker's entrance. Once those wards were undone, he would be able to take his attack inside to Dragan and finish this fight.

He was only half finished fragging the wards when he heard more jeeps closing in behind him. Distracted for the briefest moment while he considered the best way to fight both battles at once, his focus on the glyphs slipped—

—and a spike of ice plunged into his ribs.

Fuck.

His erasure of the bunker's anti-teleportation glyph had freed an ice demon set to act as its guardian, and the second Cade had split his focus, it attacked.

He primal-shouted a jet of flames into the ice demon's face.

In half a second the fiend was melted and banished to Hell, but its damage was done. Cade fought for breath; his lung was collapsing. Blood sheeted down his right side. Ice-cold pain traveled inside him—part of the demon's frozen talon had broken off to tunnel though his guts.

As his pain grew and his strength diminished, his other yoked spirits struggled to break free of his control. Focusing all of his will, he tightened his grip on them.

You fuckers aren't going anywhere, he warned them. *Not 'til I say so.*

He staggered, stumbled, and then scuttled toward the bunker's entrance. Jeeps raced toward him from both sides. He used JEPHISTO's power to knock over the troop truck and drag it closer to himself. A few seconds from now he'd need all the cover he could get.

Exhausted and delirious with pain, Cade slumped against the undercarriage of the truck. He heard the jeeps skid to wild halts on the other side, followed by the patter of running feet and the clattering of weapons being brought to bear. He let the mercs have their moment while he used his field surgery kit to clean the wound in his ribs and then packed it with sterile gauze.

A man on the other side of the truck shouted in a Slavic accent, "We have you surrounded! Lay down your weapons and surrender!"

Two stiff shots of morphine dulled Cade's suffering. The drug flowed through him, its presence in his blood warm and soothing. It softened the rough edges of his pain and gave him back his calm. *That's better,* he thought with relief.

The merc leader bellowed, "Come out with your hands up!"

Cade ejected the magazine of his Browning. Confirmed it was full. Slammed it back into place. Pulled back the slide to load a round into the chamber.

I'm a master karcist.

"You behind the truck! This is your last warning—"

I'm an MI6 assassin.

"If you do not surrender by the time I count to ten—"

I'm an Army Ranger.

"—we will show you no mercy."

I won't surrender.

"One . . . two . . ."

Cade rose into the air brandishing his wand in one hand and his Browning in the other—"Ten!"—and flayed the island's remaining mercs with lead and lightning.

No mercy, motherfuckers.

D minus 11 minutes

The stone basin in Anja's conjuring room rippled as the spirit invoked by Luis transformed it into a scrying portal. The ritual had required no yoking, a simple charm he had learned during his tenure at Monte Paterno. Now he hunched over the basin and peered through its dark window to observe Anja's assault on the demon hordes that infested Namu Island.

He marveled at her courage. She moved forward, always forward. Never a look back. Never a moment of hesitation or doubt. Graced with the sword and shield of two of Heaven's greatest archangels, she blazed her way along the island's northern beach, cutting down demons with righteous fervor. Laying waste to Hell's legions, she was everything that Luis had ever dreamed a Pauline magician should and could be.

But she isn't one of us, he marveled. *She's a student of the Goetic Art. A disciple of the Left-hand Path. Yet she wields the arsenal of Heaven as if she were born to it.*

The longer he observed her, the deeper his guilt became.

With every step she takes, she races toward an appointment with Death. His shame was so strong that it made him feel sick. *I should be more than a spectator to this moment. How many times did I beg Father D'Odorico to let me stand and fight against evil? How many times did I argue that faith without works is empty?*

The spectacle on the other side of the scrying window was breathtaking. Holy fire leaped from Anja's blade, shot from her eyes, jetted from her open mouth—and every barrage tore demons to pieces and sent them back to their proper place in the Abyss. Imbued with angelic gifts, Anja had become a force of nature, a living weapon. Watching her filled Luis with awe—until he remembered that none of that power would save her from the atomic bomb.

Despite all of his protests and invocations of the Covenant, in his heart Luis knew that turning his back on Anja and Cade as they risked their lives for the good of the entire world was nothing less than a mortal sin of omission. *Standing here, I commit no explicit crime, but neither do I effect any tangible boon. What if Anja was right to doubt me? What good am I?*

A lifetime of training compelled him to reject his doubts. *I must have faith that my vow to the Church and the Covenant was neither misguided nor pointless. God will show me the way.*

Haunted by his refusal to act, all Luis could do was watch in amazement as Anja took the fight to their enemy while he counted down to Armageddon.

D minus 9 minutes

Past the edges of Briet's conjuring stage inside the Silo there was only darkness. Hovering perpendicular to the stage above its north side was a massive ring of blue fire, a scrying window through which Briet observed Cade's massacre of the Shemya mercenaries.

Despite being visibly injured, Cade levitated above the field of battle and wreaked havoc. Each sweep of his wand laid down blankets of flame, explosions of shredded steel, and storms of jagged ice. His foes' bodies were hurled aloft in a tempest of carnage that swirled around him as if he were the eye in a hurricane. Briet found the spectacle terrible and beautiful at the same time.

"I knew Cade was talented," she said, knowing that Khalîl was listening by means of clairaudience from his circle in Key Gompa, "but I had no idea he was *this* powerful."

"*This is only what he can do with a minimum of preparation,*" Khalîl replied, his voice disembodied in the Silo's black void. "*His true potential is far greater.*"

Six demons rose like ghosts from the bunker behind Cade and instantly were cut down by his barbed whip of lightning, which he cracked twice behind his back without so much as a glance in their direction.

"I was right not to go. I'd only have slowed him down."

"*Perhaps. But nobody is invincible. And no one is stronger alone. Not even him.*"

As Cade floated to the ground, all of the buildings around him were consumed by fire—all except the bunker, whose entrance stood revealed and stripped of magickal defenses. It was a door made to withstand bombs and artillery, a barrier designed to repel any force known to man.

Briet smirked as Cade pointed his wand at the door and blasted the five-ton portal off its hinges with a single burst of hellfire. There were armed guards in the passages beyond, but she knew they were no cause for alarm—just pity.

Even though she looked forward to seeing Cade tear Dragan to pieces, regrets festered in her heart. *Dragan was my adept. My failure. Letting Cade clean up my mistake is a coward's play.* She pushed her disappointments aside. *If I get involved, Frank will never let me hear the end of it. Have to leave the messy stuff to the rogues. Got to keep our hands clean. . . .*

As she watched Cade stride into the bunker, she doubted that vicarious revenge could ever be half as satisfying as the real thing—but this promised to be a battle for the ages, and she was determined to enjoy the show, honor be damned.

D minus 6 minutes

Freezing wind—thick with smoke and reeking of scorched metal and burnt flesh—followed Cade as he strode through the bunker's corridors and down the main stairway to its lowest level. Through the acrid tang of spent gunpowder he smelled the sweet perfume of fear.

Sacrificial lambs—cloaked in the shapes of three men toting submachine guns—rushed out to meet him. He blocked their salvos of bullets with a shield of demonic force and then he swatted them aside with the unseen hand of an Infernal giant. The trio of guards slammed against one concrete wall and then the other with sickening crunches of impact. By the time Cade reached the nearest of them, all three were on their knees, dazed and bleeding from their ears.

One shot from Cade's Browning Hi-Power removed the top half of one man's skull. The second man Cade shot in the throat, severing his spine from his brain. The third man's face vanished in a crimson splash that spattered the legs of Cade's gray-and-white camouflage.

Shield raised, Cade turned left at the top of the T-junction, drawn by the magickal power that radiated from the end of that short passageway. A sentry at the end raised a Chinese-made semiautomatic rifle, but an itch in Cade's mind—a demonic warning of danger—told him there was another threat behind his back. Cade pivoted to shoot the guard behind him while at the same time he thrust VAELBOR's sword through the first sentry's weapon and then through the man's chest. Both men dropped dead, and Cade found himself alone with the cries of the wind and the crackling of flames left in his wake.

Icy pain stabbed between his ribs as the loose demon's claw writhed deeper into his gut. He faced the warded double door at the end of the corridor. Its lock was adorned by a classic demonic guardian, the kind used by karcists to protect their labs from intrusion.

That has to be Dragan's conjuring room, Cade reasoned.

He paired TARANAT's gift for cowing other demons with ARIOSTO's knack for opening locks, and then he fused them both to VAELBOR's blade. With one stroke he sliced through the guardian and disintegrated the double door's locks, bolts, and bars.

Then he walked up and kicked the doors open to reveal the conjuring room beyond.

Inscribed in white on the painted-black floor was the most complex set of pentagrams, circles, and containment triangles Cade had ever seen. It was more elaborate than anything he'd wrought in his thirteen years of practicing the Art. Standing inside that collection of arcane weirdness were four tanists—three men and a woman, all paragons of the Nazi's "master race" template—and, in the operator's circle, an impeccably dressed man who matched the description of Briet's renegade adept Dragan Dalca.

Cade lifted his wand as a preface to his prepared threat, only to have Dragan cut him off.

"Herr Martin, I presume." Dragan picked up a pocket watch from the lectern in front of his circle and checked it. He smiled coldly at Cade. "Right on time."

A twitch of Dragan's hand knocked Cade's wand from his grasp, and a lightning-fast gesture slammed Cade against the corridor's ceiling. Cade tried to free himself, only to discover he was paralyzed and held fast.

Then he noticed that someone else was in the corridor behind him. A man, walking at a languid pace, as if he had all the time in the world. As he stepped into view, Cade felt a sick tide of horror move through him. It was Dragan—

or, to be more precise, a second iteration of the dark magician, because the first one was still safely inside the operator's circle.

Second Dragan smiled up at Cade. "Fascinating. Such power. Such training. And yet, once you saw my guardian, you never even thought to look for other defenses." He motioned toward the ceiling, revealing a hidden circle filled with a pentagram and a number of occult symbols. "A devil's trap, for instance." He *tsk*ed at Cade. "Thus ends your witless rampage."

Cade looked away from his interrogator and eyed the Dragan inside the conjuring room. That version of the man called up a large triangular window framed with red lightning, one that offered him a bird's-eye view of Anja's heroic run along the north beach of Namu Island. What Cade saw through the scrying portal that Anja couldn't was that there was a single figure waiting for her at the start of the causeway that led out to the Castle Bravo device.

A figure that wore the same ceremonial robes as Dragan and his doppelgänger.

"You're in three places at once," Cade said under his breath.

Dragan grinned at him. "*Yes*. You recognize me *now*, don't you? *Say my name.*"

He looked Dragan in the eye and beheld his inner demon. "Your name is LEGION."

D minus 6 minutes

The last of the demons fell away from Anja, leaving behind a pungent zing of ozone in the thick morning air. Waves lapped at her feet as she rounded the last turn of the shoreline before the man-made causeway that linked Namu to the shot cab's artificial islet.

As she came out of the turn, she saw a lone figure at the start of the causeway, blocking her path: Dragan, wearing the ceremonial robes of a karcist. His hands were empty, and he had no wand tucked into his belt, but he exuded danger. Behind him blazed a triangle limned with red lightning—a portal to some distant location, maybe?

His eyes followed Anja as she raced toward him.

Mere meters from the causeway, she raised her wand to attack. "*Effundet sanguinem—!*"

The rest of MARBAS's spell caught in Anja's throat as an unseen force swept her feet out from under her. She landed hard on her back and felt a rush of panic as she gasped in vain for breath. When she tried to sit up, she felt as if she had been welded to the ground. Even raising her head hurt—it felt as if it weighed a hundred pounds.

Dragan strolled over to Anja and towered above her.

"Sand is a remarkable canvas when one paints with hellfire." He waved his hand, and a stiff wind blew away all the loose sand around Anja—revealing a massive region of blackened glass inscribed with eldritch symbols. The few that she could see by turning her head were proto-Enochian in origin. Dragan smiled at her. "It's called an angel's snare. Much like the devil's trap that holds your accomplice Cade Martin, even as we speak."

A sweep of his arm directed Anja's attention toward his portal. Through it she saw two more of Dragan—one standing in an operator's circle, the other tormenting Cade, who was pinned against a corridor ceiling inside the bunker, just outside Dragan's conjuring room.

Anja remembered the last time she had seen a single karcist exist in three places at once. It had been over nine years since that terrible night, but its memory was one she would carry to her grave. She glared up at her captor. "You are not Dragan."

"Oh, I certainly am." He dropped to one knee beside Anja. "But I also happen to be much *more*." He drew his athamé and held it in front of Anja's face. "*Say my name.*"

She growled it at him like a curse. "*Kein Engel.*"

He stabbed his dagger deep into her gut and grinned. "In the flesh."

FEBRUARY 28 / MARCH 1, PART III

D minus 6 minutes

After so long in the shadows, revelation felt like liberation. Safe inside the operator's circle, Kein Engel controlled Dragan's body like a marionette, and he extended that privilege to both of the Dragan-doppelgängers he had spawned through the power of his bonded spirit, LEGION.

"Too long have I watched the world through these borrowed eyes. Too long have I needed another to speak for me. But now that time draws to an end."

In the corridor, a twist of his wand torqued vital organs and tender sinew inside Cade's wounded torso. "I must say, Herr Martin, I've missed your company since you were freed from the Pit. And in case you think I've forgotten that you pilfered and broke my wand, leaving me at the mercy of an army of the Fallen"—he threw another fiery jab into Cade's gut—"I have *not*."

D minus 6 minutes

Hearing Anja speak the Nazi magician's name filled Luis with cold terror. He stood inside her conjuring room, paralyzed with fear but shaking with anger as he heard the master dark magician taunt Anja on the beach and, through another portal, torture Cade inside the bunker.

Kein's doppelgänger on the beach stabbed Anja with his athamé. The savage thrust drenched her in her own blood. *"Does this hurt? I assure you, it's merely a taste of what you did to me. For more than nine years I've borne the wounds you gave me in Dresden."* He pushed his black-handled knife deep into her shoulder and smiled with malicious delight at her feral cry of pain. *"Did you know that wounds never heal in Hell? A lesson I learned at a terrible cost."*

Luis recalled the proof that Anja had shown him of the Church's complicity in the escape of Nazi war criminals from Europe. Now she lay at the mercy of the Nazis' former top sorcerer, a man whose reputation was so feared by the Pauline orders that the Church had declared neutrality during the Second World War rather than face his wrath.

He's evil incarnate, Luis raged. *If I don't oppose him now. . . .*

He hurried away from the stone scrying basin.

Opened his roll of karcist's tools. Drew his sword.

Then, in defiance of his vows and the Covenant, he entered the operator's circle that Anja had inscribed on the floor, closed its outer boundary with a draw of his sword's tip through the excess chalk, blessed himself with the sign of the Cross . . . and opened the Iron Codex.

D minus 5 minutes

Fury and guilt collided inside Briet as she heard Kein's voice issue from Dragan's mouth. Framed by her scrying circle's border of indigo flame, the original Dragan stood inside his operator's circle as Kein used him to issue orders to the Shemya tanists: *"Mind your places. In less than five minutes we begin the final ritual to break open Hell's gate."*

Briet shifted the focus of her scrying window to check on Cade. He remained stuck with his back pressed against the ceiling while one of Kein's Dragan-clones stood beneath him.

Cade gritted his teeth against the fiery twists that Kein drilled into him. *"Breaching the gate,"* Cade said. *"It was never about letting out the demons—it's about freeing you."*

"You always were a quick study." Kein's mirth soured. *"I never liked that about you."*

"The feeling's mutual."

Kein entangled Cade in a snaking ivy of electricity. Cade writhed and choked back howls of agony as the crackling tendrils blackened patches of his skin. Cade drew a deep breath with a hiss through clenched teeth. *"How'd you get out? Did you possess this sap?"*

"Herr Dalca volunteered *to be my avatar."* Kein gloated beneath his snared rival. *"Did you think you were the only one whose allies sought to rescue him from Hell?"*

Briet had heard enough.

With her sword she closed her operator's circle.

Frank's voice boomed from the Silo's loudspeakers: *"BREE? WHAT THE FUCK ARE YOU DOING? DON'T MAKE ME—"*

She lobbed a forked lightning bolt into the darkness and destroyed all the speakers.

Master Khalîl's voice resounded from the darkness, as if he were all around her, in every direction at once: *"Briet, you must stand fast! If Cade and Anja fall—"*

"If they fall, it's because I didn't step in." She opened her grimoire and drew her wand. "You wanted me to embrace my destiny. Well stand back, Master, because *this is it.*"

D minus 5 minutes

On the beach, Kein savored the resistance of flesh against steel as his second doppelgänger carved a mirror image of Anja's facial scar onto her right cheek. The scent of her blood was delicious.

"Regrettably, my allies lacked the Iron Codex, so I was forced to be more patient about my return from Hell than your friend Cade. I had to bide my time in a place never meant for mortal flesh. And when, at last, one of my disciples learned how to raise my spirit back to earth, all that remained was to teach my followers how to reunite my soul and my body: by breaking open Hell's gate so that my patron Lucifuge Rofocale may bear my flesh across its threshold, back into *this* world."

Kein shoved his blade between the lower ribs of Anja's left flank. "Of course, you could have averted the global catastrophe to come if only you had surrendered the codex when I asked. With it my disciples could have raised me as you did Cade." He looked toward the end of the causeway. "But you had to do this the hard way. Now, because you'd rather be stubborn than sensible, the world will burn." He gave his knife a twist and delighted in her shrieks and sobs. "I offered you a choice; you chose Armageddon. So mote it be. What is done cannot be undone."

He pulled his knife free and licked her blood from the blade. "My only regret is that I don't have time to repay you in kind for all the horrors you've inflicted on me. But I will take a measure of satisfaction from the knowledge that, in four minutes' time, every last particle of your being will be eradicated by the greatest burst of nuclear fire ever unleashed."

In the hallway, Kein's first doppelgänger smiled up at Cade, whose reaction to his twin's conversation with Anja was verging upon apoplexy. "Save your strength, Herr Martin. After I make you watch atomic fire consume Miss Kernova, I plan to feed you to our mutual patron, LUCIFUGE ROFOCALE—a reckoning that I assure you our lord most *anxiously* awaits."

To Kein's genuine surprise, Cade started to laugh.

"You find this amusing, Herr Martin?"

Reining in his mirth, Cade replied, "No. I'm just imagining the look on your face a few minutes from now when I fucking gut you like the pig you are."

He admired the American's relentless bravado. "What a peculiar thought in which to take solace. Tell me: What do you think this dying expression of mine looks like?"

The only response Cade offered was a cocked eyebrow.

Then from Kein's conjuring room came a roar like a typhoon. He spun to see a circular portal shred the air above his grand pentacle—and from it leapt his former adept Briet, throwing fire from one hand and snapping a whip laced with green fire in the other.

Explosions consumed Kein's tanists Dieter and Erik.

The whip tore off Ulrich's head.

Of the four, only Juliana got a shot off, a massive bolt of purple lightning that Briet bounced back at her with her demonic shield. The bolt launched Juliana out of the circle and deposited her smoking corpse at Kein's feet.

Briet landed with a crash of thunder, her stare full of hate and trained squarely upon her former master. For half a second Kein looked at her, his eyes wide and jaw agape.

Above him, Cade smirked. "*That's* the face! Just like that."

D minus 4 minutes

Standing outside of a grand circle felt wrong to Briet. Decades of training and experience had taught her that the spaces outside the warded double circle were nothing but a killing floor for demons. But the only monster she currently saw in the room was the one standing inside the operator's circle—and also in the corridor, thanks to his innate talent for self-duplication.

Dragan grinned, and then he spoke with Kein's voice. "Briet. How kind of you to deliver yourself to me. Especially since I would've hunted you down soon enough."

"I should've killed you long ago." Briet wreathed her left hand in fire as she raised her wand. "Should've struck you down the moment I realized you'd gone insane."

Her threat only seemed to amuse her former master. "You mean instead of running like a coward? Deserting me in the middle of a war?"

"Running was a mistake." Energy crackled around her wand. "One I've come to correct."

"No, my dear. You've come to *die.*"

Dragan-Kein in the circle and his twin in the corridor attacked in unison, bombarding Briet with fire, black energy, lightning, and thrusts from the fetid spear of SAVNOK. Their combined assault struck Briet's shields like a freight train. Its force knocked her backward, against the conjuring room's far wall, and trapped her there.

She forced the panic from her mind and concentrated on her shield demon, AMYNA. Let herself feel the brutal onslaught of Dragan-Kein's attacks. She reflected the pulses of black energy, which screamed between original Dragan and his twin but hit neither of them.

"Is that the best you can do?" teased Second Dragan. A wave of his hand fractured the floor under Briet's feet; from the fissures rose tendrils of black smoke that moved as if driven by a hideous intelligence. The original Dragan-Kein inside the operator's circle laughed as he bathed Briet's shield in fire. Even through the shield she felt the searing heat of the attack, and as her hold on AMYNA weakened the shield thinned and bent inward. . . .

From the corridor came a truncated scream, followed by a wet choking gurgle.

The black smoke-serpents under Briet's feet retreated into the floor, and the mad assault on her shield ceased long enough for her to see clearly to the far side of the room.

Cade drove his hunting knife deep into the back of Second Dragan, who spat up blood and then disintegrated into a cloud of ash and cinders.

Just as Briet had hoped, Dragan-Kein hadn't noticed that the energy she'd reflected past him and his twin had cut a smoking scar through the devil's trap in the corridor, freeing Cade.

Prowling forward with his blade's back edge braced against his forearm, Cade flashed a predator's grin at Dragan-Kein. "One down. Two to go."

Dragan-Kein pivoted inside the operator's circle to keep both Cade and Briet in sight. He hurled a flight of ghostly burning arrows at Cade, who scattered them with one wave of his hand; he shot a cascade of lightning at Briet, who used her shield to absorb its energy and turn it back at Dragan-Kein as a blast of lethal cold delivered with an inchoate shout of rage.

Kein's second duplicate from the beach leaped back to the conjuring room through the triangular scrying window, betraying its true nature as a fully operational portal. Third Dragan hectored Briet with a swarm of wasps, freeing the original Dragan-Kein to pummel Cade with a series of ever-shifting attacks: invisible fists rammed Cade's shield; spectral swords hacked at him from multiple directions at once; flying daggers made of mist penetrated Cade's shield and cut fierce gashes into his arms and legs.

Briet fried her harassing cloud of wasps by belching flames, and then she resorted to a beginner's trick, a simple attack for which there was no immediate defense: she enveloped Third Dragan-Kein in darkness.

It would take him only a second to dispel it, she knew, but that was all the time she needed. She hurled the javelin of MEZAMALETH through Kein's still-open portal. The ghostly weapon slammed down into the eastern glyph of the angel's snare holding Anja. The sigil's foundation of volcanic glass shattered as the javelin made impact.

"Anja, you're free!" Briet shouted through the portal. "You've got three minutes! Go!"

On the other side of the portal, the blood-soaked Anja struggled to sit up.

Inside the bunker's conjuring room, the Kein-twin scattered Briet's curtain of darkness. "Clever." He waved his hand and the portal vanished. "But it won't save you—or her."

Briet almost pitied her old master. "We aren't here to save *ourselves*." She smiled as Cade's thrown knife pierced the doppelgänger's neck and jutted out of its Adam's apple. Third Dragan-Kein fell to his knees and then scattered into cinders and ashes as it hit the floor.

Then there was only the original Dragan-Kein, alone in the operator's circle, with Cade to his right and Briet on his left. For a man outnumbered, he affected a strangely smug air. "You can't win, you know. Even if you kill this body, my spirit will simply return to Hell. And in three minutes' time, I and the rest of the Fallen will rise and claim this world as our own."

Briet raised her wand. "Every extra second you spend in Hell is worth the effort."

Cade filled his hands with fire. "And the only thing happening three minutes from now is your fucking funeral."

FEBRUARY 28 / MARCH 1, PART IV

D minus 3 minutes

Aching and bleeding, exhausted and racked by pain inside and out, Anja forced herself to sprint faster than she had ever run in her life. One of her yoked angels had mended her deepest wounds, but she was still bleeding and in agony with every step. Every inch of her felt raw.

To her left, on the other side of a massive steel-and-wood framework of pipes, the sun rose across the lagoon of Bikini Atoll. Loose sand shifted beneath her feet, slowing her down. She moved closer to the water, to run on the damp and more tightly packed portion of the sandbar. It improved her balance, but every part of her still hurt.

At the end of the causeway and its cluster of pipes lay the shot cab. It seemed so close and yet it grew so slowly. Racing toward it felt to Anja like the kind of futile run one makes in a dream. The harder she pushed ahead, the farther away her destination seemed to get.

She imagined the countdown ticking toward zero. Could she reach the shot cab in three minutes? If she did, would she have time to exorcise the demon from the bomb and eradicate the magickal lens from the shot cab?

I have no choice. She willed herself to run harder. *I am the only hope.*

She was exhilarated and terrified, euphoric and spiritually crushed all at once.

This would be the greatest thing she would ever do. It would also be the last.

Tears burned in her eyes as she summoned the strength to quicken her pace.

I chose this. Please let me be fast enough—and brave enough—one more time.

D minus 2 minutes

A flying rush of needles broke like a wave on the left side of Cade's magickal shield. Crimson lightning slammed against it from the right. Scorpions surged over Cade's boots as a blinding funnel cloud of toxic smoke surrounded him, blocking his view of Dragan-Kein.

A tide of brute force pushed Cade's back to a wall. It was all he could do to keep from being crushed. *Fucking hell—I forgot how hard it is to fight this bastard.*

He tried to conjure wind to disrupt the churning smoke, but he was too distracted by the scorpions crawling up his legs to control the currents. *If they reach bare skin, I'm fucked.* He purged the fear from his mind and remembered a lesson from his late master Adair: *To survive a storm, be the mountain or be the sky.*

Cade marshaled the gift of his yoked spirit VESTURIEL. *Sky it is.*

He dropped his shield as he transformed his body, clothing, and gear into a living shade, a ghost form untouchable and all but invisible in the material plane. Momentarily beyond the reach of needles and scorpions, he darted clear of Dragan-Kein's tornado of poisonous smoke.

Halfway across the conjuring room, Dragan-Kein answered Briet's salvos of flame with searing beams of indigo light shot from his eyes. She blocked his death stare and hurled a burning scimitar, which he batted aside. A broad sweep of his arm threw Briet across the room. She bounded hard off the concrete wall but landed on her feet—bruised, bloodied, and pissed off.

Dragan-Kein thrust one hand at Briet. With the Sight, Cade watched her raise a shield—only to see it shatter beneath a blow from a demonic fist. The spirit's battering-ram punch caught Briet by surprise. It knocked her against a wall with a loud *smack.* She stumbled forward, stunned but struggling to raise her wand. Dragan-Kein conjured a fistful of lightning—

As Cade threw a punch at Dragan-Kein he invoked the gift of ADAMASOR, abandoning his ghost form for stoneflesh, and he coupled it with the titanic strength of MEUS CALMIRON. His granite-hard fist slammed into the back of Dragan-Kein's head. Cade felt the man's skull dent as the blow landed. Now it was Dragan-Kein's turn to stagger like a drunkard. Weaving and spinning, he was off-kilter as he swung around to face Cade—

—who landed a jab onto Dragan-Kein's too-perfect nose, followed by a left cross to his square jaw and proud chin. The two punches left the dark mage reeling, but only for a moment. Then he unleashed a chaos of flies, fire, lightning, and shattered glass, all of it arcing and whipping madly around him, as if he could no longer choose targets and had resorted instead to destroying everything in his immediate vicinity.

The wild fusillade tore across Briet, who shrieked in pain—but then her cry became a growl. As the mad attack shifted off of her, she ducked through its inner spirals to kick Dragan-Kein squarely in his groin. That folded him over, and Briet kneed him in the forehead.

Dragan-Kein pitched backward—and landed squarely on Cade's knife.

Cade coiled his arm around the throat of his old nemesis. "I didn't give you the send-off you deserved last time." He pulled his knife from Dragan-Kein's back. Then he plunged it back in through the spine and twisted. "*That* was for my father. And *this*—" He yanked out the blade, flipped it to change his grip on its handle, and then plunged it into Dragan-Kein's gut just below the sternum. He drove the blade upward with a savage turn. "This is for my *mother.*"

He felt Dragan's body go limp in his grasp, and he heard the wet rasp of Dragan-Kein's dying breath. He pulled his knife from the dark mage's torso, and then he broke the dead man's neck with a sharp twist, just to be certain this death would take.

Briet sat on the floor, exhausted. Overcome by pain and fatigue, Cade did the same.

A ticking captured his attention, and he searched for its source. To his relief, it was only Dragan-Kein's pocket watch lying on the floor. He picked it up and checked the time.

His heart sank. "One minute to detonation."

Briet took his hand. "She'll make it. She'll get it done."

"I know. It's just—it all happened so fast, and . . ." His truth felt as if it were trapped in a jagged snare of emotion: "We never said good-bye."

D minus 1 minute

Anja's muscles felt ready to rip themselves to pieces with every running step. Each breath of sea air burned in her lungs, and she was drenched in her own blood, which spilled fresh and bright from Dragan-Kein's savage attacks on her body. She didn't know how much blood she had lost, only that she had left a scarlet trail across the causeway. Now, light-headed and awash in golden morning light, she charged toward the door of the shot cab.

There was no time for subtlety. She hurled a blade of angelic fire through the locks on the door, blasting it open ahead of her arrival. She had less than a minute before the device detonated. Every second mattered now.

Stumbling to a halt inside the stifling heat of the high-ceilinged building, Anja fought to catch her breath. One frantic gasp for air followed another. She forced her sore lungs to draw one deep breath; she would need it all for what came next.

Wand raised, she declared in a proud but trembling voice, "*Per virtutem sancti Domini et in robore* SOLARIEL, *ad quos eieci te, immunde spiritus, et conteram vobis vinculum fugere ad inferos!*"

A monstrous, ram-horned shadow arose from the fat cylinder mounted on stilts against the wall to Anja's right. It was the demon that Dragan's disciple had bound to the bomb in Los Alamos, the fiend Black Sun intended to sacrifice to the bomb. The spirit emerged and loomed over Anja, radiating hatred and contempt. Its smoky hands extended into talons.

Anja channeled the fire of her yoked angel and let it engulf the beast.

Its howl of agony fissured the floor and walls.

Anja conjured a palmful of holy fire and thrust the tip of her wand into it, as she would jab it into a brazier of burning coal to punish any uncooperative spirit. "By the holy names of ADONAI, ELOHIM, TETRAGRAMMATON, and JEHOVAM, I *banish* thee! Be gone!"

A circle opened in the floor beneath the demon, revealing a starless void from which issued inhuman wails of suffering and regret. The shadow-beast plunged through the aperture, which snapped shut as soon as the monster was gone.

Now to break Kein's lens.

She engaged the Sight and beheld the intricate pattern of occult designs and symbols that had been scribed on the walls, floor, ceiling, and outer casing of the bomb. It was a masterwork of Goetic magickal engineering, one that Anja wished she had time to study, but she had barely enough time for sabotage.

One last time she called upon her yoked angels to share their holy fire

as she raised her wand and concentrated upon the array of runes that surrounded her.

"*Marcas immunda sunt delere orbem rigidum!*"

Every symbol, character, and line that Kein had drawn inside the shot
cab sizzled and burned from underneath. Within seconds the entire occult formula of his diabolical lens had been obscured by charcoal scorch
marks.

Anja coughed. The air inside the shot cab was hazy with dust and smoke.

She staggered out the door into the dawning sun.

Plodded across the man-made beach.

Fell to her knees as she reached the sea.

From her pocket she took out a watch. Its second hand ticked past the 9.

Fifteen seconds to spare. To think about what's coming.

To think about Cade.

The touch of his hand on my cheek.

The way he looked at me like I was the only perfect woman.

The way he kissed me . . . like no one else ever has.

She closed her eyes and did her best to live again in those moments, one
last time.

Then came thunder, and a flare of white brighter than any she had ever
known.

Detonation

The blast was fifteen megatons, nearly three times what the atomic scientists
had expected.

It would be months before they learned why the Castle Bravo yield was so
much greater than they'd predicted—a mistaken assumption that only the
lithium-6 in its secondary assembly was active, and that its far larger quantity of lithium-7 was inert—but as the bloodred mushroom cloud climbed into
the sky and a black pall blotted out the Pacific dawn, all that mattered to the
men huddled inside the Enyu bunker on Bikini Atoll was whether they would
live long enough to find out what went wrong—and just how widespread the
damage would be.

They would soon learn that their misfired experiment had changed the
course of human history; they would never learn how close their project had
come to ending it.

D plus 5 seconds

The light faded, and the thunder with it. The beach was gone, and so were the sea, the sky, and the sun. All that Anja expected to find at the end of the light was darkness.

What she found was Cade. Burnt, bloodied, and weary, but alive.

She was inside Kein's smoky, carnage-filled conjuring room on Shemya Island.

The force that had held Anja immobile released her. She tumbled forward. Cade sprang up and caught her. Clutched in his arms, she had no words to encompass her joy.

He looked past her, and she turned her head. Behind her stood Father Pérez. An enormous pair of feathered angel's wings at his back evaporated into mist.

The priest offered her a bittersweet smile. "Good enough?"

She smiled back. "Good enough."

Out of the corner of her eye, she saw Briet acknowledge Father Pérez with a small bow of her head. On the other edge of her vision, she saw him return the gesture of respect in kind.

When she looked back at Cade, he looked like a man afraid to hope. His voice trembled as he touched her cheek and asked, "Is it really you?"

Tears welled in her eyes. "*Da,* my love. Is me."

He pulled her close, his hug firm and comforting. She buried her face in his shoulder and seized him in her own fierce embrace, determined never to let him go again.

MARCH 11

The world had gone gray. Rain tapped on the roof and ran in twisting paths across the windows of Anja's villa. Outside, the stark Andean mountainsides had been erased by low-flying clouds and lingering fog. Looking out a window with a tumbler of bourbon in one hand and a Lucky Strike in the other, Cade found the day's pale canvas restful.

In the middle of the first floor's great room, which Anja had continued to use as her conjuring laboratory, she and Luis had spent the morning sitting at a worktable and studying the Iron Codex. Her talent for medical magick had effaced the myriad wounds that Dragan-Kein and his minions had inflicted upon her, Cade, and Briet. That plus a week of rest after she, Cade, and Luis had returned to the villa had restored her youthful vigor.

Luis pointed at a character on a page of the codex. "Do you remember this one?"

Anja squinted at the page. "Is that *Phe*?"

"Note the clean vertical downstroke."

Comprehension banished the creases in Anja's forehead. "*Cadic*."

"Very good. Now translate that word, and the sentence around it."

She silently mouthed the words as she read the sentence to herself. After the second time through, she offered a halting interpretation: "Fumigate the room with an incense of cedar, alum, and newly consecrated charcoal made from the wood of a yew tree."

"Excellent. That's the last step in this ritual's preparation of the room. Do you feel up to starting on the components of the ritual?"

"I need a break," Anja said. "Maybe after lunch."

"Whenever you're ready." Luis stood as Anja rose and left the table.

On her way out she stopped to kiss Cade's cheek and favor him with a smile, and then she continued on her way to the kitchen, leaving Cade and Luis alone in the laboratory.

Cade watched the priest organize the papers on the worktable. "Sounds like she's getting the hang of proto-Enochian."

Luis replied with excitement, "She's making good progress."

"With your help, Padre."

The priest deflected the compliment with a shrug. "It was just a matter of bypassing John Dee's fraud and drawing from Pantheus's original *Voarchadumia Contra Alchimiam*." He turned a knowing look at Cade. "She tells me you've been lending a hand, as well."

"I've picked up my share of proto-Enochian. But I'm not as good a teacher."

"Too kind." Luis finished stacking the papers on the table. He put a stone on top of them and closed the codex. "Might I ask how your pet project is coming along?"

"Let me show you." Cade ditched his drink and snuffed his Lucky as he led Luis out of the lab and upstairs to one of the villa's spare rooms. He had chosen the room because it had only one window. That maximized its wall surface, upon which Cade had reproduced by hand the writings he had seen engraved on the tablets inside the vault of the Vatican's secret archives.

Luis circuited the room, awed by the level of detail Cade had put into his facsimile, which included both the text and the art of the ancient tablets. "Remarkable. How did you do it?"

"I yoked a demon named GURIOCH. It enables perfect recall, even for old memories." Noting Luis's lack of reaction, Cade added, "I half expected you to douse the room with holy water when I told you that."

"I think we're past that." Luis's mood turned pensive. "Anja's practicing a fusion of the Pauline and Goetic arts, and I imagine you're likely to do the same before long." He breathed a sigh that felt full of hidden meaning. "And I would be lying if I denied my curiosity about the Left-hand Path. But having seen what you did on Shemya . . . I have to conclude that the good or evil in magick isn't the product of its source but of its application."

"Not Black or White," Cade said, "neither the Left- nor Right-hand Path. Welcome to what my late friend Stefan once called the Middle Way—the path of the Gray magician."

Luis mulled that observation with stoic calm. "So it would seem, my friend." Forcing a brighter expression onto his careworn features, he gestured at the room's wraparound mural. "So tell me about this. Have you been able to trans-late any of it?"

"All of it, actually." Pointing at various bits around the room, he contin-ued, "Some of the words had no direct translation, so I went with the closest match I could think of. And some of them referred to events with ancient names that we know today by other terms. But I'm pretty sure I've nailed the gist of it."

An arched eyebrow hinted at Luis's intense interest. "And? What do they say?"

"They all say pretty much the same thing. None of them are complete, but each overlaps at least a few of the others. Together, they tell a full story.

"As I tried to tell Anja," he continued, "what makes this so impressive is that the various pieces hail from different civilizations around the world, and were created centuries or even millennia apart." Gesturing at one panel after another, he added, "This piece was made by the Maya in the third century BC. This one by the ancient Egyptians dates to nearly 3000 BC. This one, from China's Zhou dynasty, was made in 1000 BC. The Babylonian slab was cut out of a cave wall in Iraq, where it was carved in 1700 BC. The one written in Old Aramaic was found inside a cave in the Judean Desert, not far from where the Dead Sea Scrolls were unearthed a few years back; it dates to 800 BC. The pieces in ancient Greek were carved in the ninth century BC, and smuggled out of the ruins of the Sanctuary of Delphi."

"So, six accounts of the same creation myth, recorded by six different civi-lizations on three continents, over a period of three thousand years?" Luis looked gobsmacked. "Incredible." He leaned forward and asked with some urgency, "So what does it *say*?"

"It's called *The Mystery of the Dead God*." He moved in slow steps from one panel to another as he translated their contents for Luis. "It begins, 'The uni-verse exists because God wanted to die.' Each version uses different poetry to say why God couldn't die as He was. The gist of it is that God's wish to com-mit suicide was impossible so long as He existed as a unified entity outside of four-dimensional space-time." He pointed at the Chinese slab. "'Seeking to nullify His oneness so that He could be delivered into nothingness, God shattered Himself.' I'm reading that as an allegory for the Big Bang creation of the universe. This transformed Him into what the Egyptian murals called 'the time-bound fragments of the universe.'"

Luis nodded, his brow furrowed. "I see. So this myth's core postulate is that God changed Himself from existing in a state of superreality to one of non-being through the creation of a finite universe of multiformity."

"Exactly." Cade pivoted toward the Aramaic pieces. "From there, it goes on to say that God's act of Creation made the universe, and also the angels, in His image." Pointing at specific lines of the duplicated text, he added, "This part basically says that those angels who still resonate with the will of the Divine are the ones who continue to honor His true plan: a deliverance of all things, including themselves, into entropy."

Luis asked, "What about the Fallen?"

"That's where the Maya sections get really interesting. Their tablets are the only ones that have this bit of the story. Demons, it says, were severed from the Divine because they dared to suggest reuniting the mortal and the immortal, the Alpha and the Omega." He turned toward Luis. "This matches up with things I saw and heard during my six months in Hell. . . . Father, I think Lucifer wants to put God *back together again,* as He was in the beginning—and if it can't be done in this universe, then maybe in another one, perhaps one of Hell's own making."

"A chilling prospect." Looking around the room, Luis said, "I note that most of the tablets seem to end with a piece set apart from the main text. Is that significant?"

"I think so. Each final line translates the same way: 'God is dead . . . and His death was the life of the universe.'"

In the center of the room stood a lone chair. Cade sat on it facing rearward so that he could fold his arms atop the chair's back. "Think about it, Padre: Angels committed to entropy while demons live in the hope of putting God back together and avoiding death."

Luis pondered the notion. "That might explain why Lucifer would have wanted to help humanity become sentient."

"And why the demons taught us about magick," Cade said. "They need us to help them reassemble their Humpty-Dumpty God. But they use fear and lies to keep us in check because they're afraid that if we ever learn the real cosmic score, we'll abuse their gifts of power."

This time the priest appeared less convinced. "Perhaps. But it might be best not to leap to conclusions without corroborating evidence." Gesturing at the panels, he added, "For starters, as peculiar as this discovery might be, it hardly constitutes incontrovertible proof of the origin of the universe. For all we know, this is yet another ancient myth taken out of context."

"Except that it comports perfectly with everything I witnessed firsthand in Heaven and Hell, and corroborates things told to me by my bond-spirit, GESHURIEL."

"Which is another way of saying you found anecdotal material that reinforces your confirmation bias." He forestalled Cade's retort with a raised hand. "For the sake of discussion, let's assume this mysterious creation myth is true. What would that *mean* to you?"

It was a difficult question for Cade to answer. "I don't know. I guess it would come as a relief."

"Why?"

"Because I could finally stop hating God for making a universe in which everything is doomed to oblivion. Knowing He went down first somehow makes it . . . easier, I think."

"All right. Continue that thought. If this myth is true, what does it tell you about the universe and our place in it?"

"What, am I being tested for the seminary?"

"Humor me."

Cade cleared his throat. "Okay. It tells me the universe is made of death. And that the angels exist to uphold the natural order—which is death. And that the demons are more like us than we thought, because they're trying to beat death any way they can. But in the end it's all probably a losing proposition, because if the universe is made of death, then that's all we get."

Luis folded his hands in front of his chest, as if in prayer. "Which sounds not so different from what you believed *before* you found the tablets, am I right?"

"What's your point, Padre?"

"Let me offer you an alternative perspective. Even if we assume this tale of the Creation is true, its account of God's motivations might be mistaken. After all, Cade, how can any man ever know the mind of God? Even angels know only what they are told by the Divine." He squatted beside Cade's chair so as to look him in the eye. "Remember that night in Key Gompa, when I suggested to you that our souls reunite with the Divine? That possibility was right in front of you, and yet you'd never even considered it until I pointed it out. Now you find this myth that tells you our existence is a consequence of God's wish to destroy Himself." He rested one hand on Cade's shoulder. "But how do we know that God didn't shatter Himself because He so *loved* the idea of us and our universe that He couldn't bear *not* to create us? Why ascribe the Creation to despair rather than to love and joy? Both visions are equally valid, my son."

Cade's mind was a storm of questions that he didn't yet know how to ask. He reached inside his bomber jacket, pulled out his flask, opened it, and took a swig of bourbon. "You and your philosophy." He handed the flask to Luis with a smile. "Shut up and drink with me."

———

Propped up on pillows that could masquerade as pancakes and covered with sheets that could double as sandpaper, Miles Franklin sat in his hospital bed, grateful to be alive and holding the hand of his beloved Desmond Spencer. Tall and fair-haired, Desmond had lost weight in the months since Miles had last seen him. The wrinkles in his gray Savile Row three-piece suit betrayed the fact that he hadn't left Miles's hospital room for more than two days.

With his free hand, Desmond pretended to adjust his glasses while he pinched away new tears. "I'm so relieved to see you awake." He reined in his maudlin show with a quick sniffle. "Our flat's been too quiet without you."

"Well, I'm home now for a good while," Miles assured him. "You'll be tired of me before you know it."

Desmond gave Miles's hand a gentle squeeze. "Never."

Around the two men hummed a collection of medical machines, all linked by thick-coated wires to leads taped onto Miles's chest and torso. Nearest the bed stood the cardiac monitor. Its repeated animation of peaks and valleys was accompanied by a soft, regular *boop*. A chill in the air added to the sharpness of its mingled odors of ammonia and antiseptic.

Daylight slanted in between the window blinds behind Desmond, crowning him with a honey-colored halo. "The doctors won't tell me about your injuries," he said.

Miles offered his love a smile. "You'll see the scars soon enough."

"And will I get stories to go with those scars?"

A shrug. "Ply me with gin and I'll reward you with heroic fictions."

His pledge did not seem to satisfy Desmond. Concern creased the man's high, pale brow. "How many more of these close calls must we endure?"

"What would have me do, Dez? Resign?"

"Of course not. But a transfer?" He cocked one eyebrow. "After all, there must be a safer billet *somewhere* in Her Majesty's Ministry of Agriculture and Fisheries."

"Indubitably," Miles said, taking in stride Desmond's gentle ribbing about the transparent nature of his occupation's official diplomatic cover. Though Miles had never explicitly admitted to Desmond that he worked for MI6, it hadn't been a difficult mystery for Dez to sort out.

Before Miles could reply, they both tensed at the sound of the room's door being opened. Desmond pulled his hand from Miles's in a snap reflex and stood tall while fumbling to pull a clutch of papers from inside his jacket, all to preserve the pretense of this being a business visit. He affected his driest monotone. "And then there's the matter of restructuring your trust to allocate twenty-three percent of your accrued interest and thirty-two percent of new deposits annually for investment on the London Exchange. Given your projected date for retirement—"

"Pardon me," the visitor said, his voice rich, his accent Middle Eastern.

Miles pulled back the privacy curtain beside his bed to see the man. He appeared to be in his sixties or perhaps even his seventies. Skin the color of mahogany. Beard, brows, and short hair, all as white as new snow. His eyes, in spite of a rheumy cloudiness, had a piercing intensity. He walked slowly, with the aid of a cane. Beneath his beige wool overcoat he wore a simple suit of dark brown over a white shirt and a golden tie with a diagonal grid pattern.

His smile revealed yellowed teeth. "Miles Franklin?"

"Who's asking?"

The old man hobbled closer. "Forgive the intrusion, Mr. Franklin. My name is Khalîl el-Sahir. I've come on behalf of our mutual friend, Cade Martin."

"Cade!" Miles leaned forward as if to get up, only to be reminded by sharp pains from deep inside his body, and from all of his surgical scars, why he needed to stay in bed. Dez steadied him with one hand, and then he eased Miles back onto his pillows. Composure recovered, Miles asked in a more measured tone, "Where is he? Is he all right?"

"Mr. Martin is in good health, as are his compatriots."

Miles nodded. "Did he sort out that business with Dragan?"

"The crisis is resolved," Khalîl said, "and you will not hear from Dragan again." He pulled open his overcoat and dipped a few fingers into an inside pocket. Miles noted the care with which the old man made sure to let him see what he was doing, no doubt to allay any fear that he might be reaching for a weapon. Khalîl produced a folded letter, which he offered to Miles. When Desmond tried to take it from him, he pulled it back. "For Mr. Franklin only."

"It's all right," Desmond said, "I'm his solicitor."

"We both know you are far more than that." Once more Khalîl extended the letter to Miles. "But this missive is meant for you alone."

Miles accepted the letter. Opened it. Read it in silence.

It was brief. In a handful of sentences, Cade wished Miles a speedy recovery, assured him using prearranged code words that he was safe, and resigned from MI6 with immediate effect.

Numb with emotional shock, Miles folded the letter and set it on his lap. He cast an imploring look at Khalîl. "Did he tell you why?"

"The time has come for Cade to answer a greater calling." Khalîl regarded Miles and Desmond with a knowing look followed by a cryptic smile. "And perhaps for you, as well." He produced a small hand mirror from one of his coat pockets and handed it to Miles. "You have seen Cade use one of these, yes?"

"I have."

"And you know how to use it yourself?"

"I do."

"Good. Keep it with you, always. When Cade is ready, he will contact you." From his coat's front pocket he pulled a wool flatcap, which he set upon his head. "Until then, rest well, Mr. Franklin. And may the hand of God defend you in all the empty places you walk."

The old man turned and shuffled toward the door.

For a moment Miles stared at the mirror in his hand, and Desmond watched Khalîl, each of them in his own way bewildered and transfixed. Then Miles called out, "Wait!"

Khalîl was already out the door.

Desmond left Miles's bedside, hurried to the door, and opened it. From the doorway he looked to either side, and then he cast a perplexed look at Miles. "Miles? He *vanished*."

Miles sighed. "Of course he did." *Bloody magicians.*

Desmond returned to Miles and once more took his hand. "Any chance you'll ever tell me what that was about? Or why that old man spoke of this cheap mirror as if it were a radio?"

"As soon as I can think of a convincing lie, I'll let you know."

"Please do."

"In the meantime," Miles said, "see if you can get the nurse to bring me a phone. Time to ring my boss. I think it's high time I made a move to join the home office."

Delight widened Desmond's brown eyes. "Are you serious?"

"I am."

Overjoyed but ever-cautious, Dez stole a celebratory kiss from Miles. "Don't move, you beautiful man. I'll be back in the flashest of flashes." He hurried out, a man on a happy mission.

Let someone else save the world from now on, Miles decided with confidence and relief. *I've earned the right to enjoy the rest of my life . . . and after all these years, so has Dez.*

～～

Briet found it almost comical to watch Frank climb stairs. She had arrived several minutes early for their 2:00 A.M. meeting at the top of the steps to the Lincoln Memorial. He was tardy, as usual. Fourteen minutes past the hour and he was still huffing and wheezing his way up to her.

By the time Frank reached the top, his shirt had come untucked, his left shoe was untied, and his face had acquired a mask of sweat bullets. "Next time," he said between gasps for air, "let's meet . . . down by . . . the pool."

Put off by his unhealthy spectacle, Briet averted her eyes while Frank put himself back together. Instead she admired the distant majesty of the Washington Monument, whose needle-like profile was mirrored in the long reflecting pool that lay between it and the Lincoln Memorial. Beyond the obelisk-shaped monument glowed the dome of the Capitol. Both landmarks looked luminous against the clear and moonless night sky.

A biting wind gusted and set Frank's open jacket to flapping. He pulled it closed and buttoned it. "You owe me, Bree. I hope you know that."

"Feel free to dock my pay."

He palmed sweat from his forehead. "Har-dee-har. You're just lucky your stunt at the safe house didn't cause any fatalities, or you'd be in a shallow grave by now." Noting her sullen, sidelong look, he continued, "That's right: I cleaned up your mess in Arizona. Took almost all the favors I was owed on the Hill, and more than a few IOUs." As she looked away, he added, "You're welcome."

She faced east, toward the pool and the Washington Monument. "What about Shemya?"

"Be glad your fingerprints aren't on *that* mess. Over a hundred dead mercs on a former Air Force base? At the same time a bunch of eggheads at the PPG are screaming bloody murder, saying someone tampered with the Castle Bravo test? The House and the Senate each have a secret subcommittee trying to figure out what the fuck happened." Frank faced west and looked up at the great statue of Abraham Lincoln, grimly majestic between two rows of Doric columns. "If they ever figure out who brokered the illegal sale of the base to Dragan, heads'll roll."

"I doubt they'll find anything actionable," Briet said.

"What makes you so sure?"

Briet lit a cigarette to calm the chittering of demonic voices lurking behind her thoughts. "Someone far more powerful than a mere congressman has been manipulating events." She exhaled through her nose. "I thought the ODP got shut down by someone on Dragan's payroll. I was wrong." She took another drag. As she continued, smoke spilled from her mouth. "I talked to everyone who should've known something. Even when I forced the truth out of them by magick, they didn't know anything specific. All they could tell me was that someone high up was applying pressure through channels."

"High up?" Frank looked perplexed. "You mean, like, the president?"

"Higher," Briet said. "Whoever did this is beyond my reach."

"But the Silo's been reopened," Frank said. "We're back in business."

"For now. Which tells me that whoever pulled the plug last time no longer thinks we're a threat. Or thinks we don't know that we're being manipulated." A long drag. "I followed every lead I had to my former adepts. All the ones who vanished. I can't prove they're linked, but I heard variations on the same story, over and over again, from people who knew them. Someone approached them. Told them about a job opening. Mentioned the possibility of an interview. And then . . . nothing. More than a dozen of my best students, never seen again."

Frank sounded incredulous. "How can that be? They must've turned up somewhere."

"Not yet," Briet said. "No forwarding addresses. No financial records. No tax returns."

Now her Silo supervisor sounded alarmed. "Were they turned? Or murdered?"

"Either-or. Maybe both." She watched the end of her cigarette flare red as she pulled in another lungful of smoke. "Whoever poached them from the Silo left no paper trail, which in the context of the federal government is tantamount to a miracle."

She exhaled and dropped the stub of her Gauloises, which she snuffed under the toe of her boot. "All I know for certain is that *someone* is working against us. Someone powerful. Well-connected. Rich. And whoever they are, they know how to pull strings from the shadows." She turned her head to catch Frank's eye. "The Silo's back up and running, but we can't go back to business-as-usual. From this moment on, we have to assume that a deadly adversary tracks our every move. And until we know that enemy's name? We have no friends except each other."

∿

Anja stood next to Cade on the hillside, gazing at the fog that had turned the valley below into a milky sea. She was half in shock as she tried to make sense of all he had just confessed to her about his mysterious absences from MI6 over the past nine years. They were alone in the soft rain and far enough from the villa that she was sure their voices wouldn't carry back to Luis, but she spoke in a fearful whisper all the same. "How many?"

"Ten so far. I'm considering three more."

It was worse than she had thought. "Have you told Miles?"

Cade took a drag off his Lucky, which he held between his thumb and forefinger, cupped under his hand to shield it from the cold drizzle. "Too dangerous. The CIA grilled me about it in Arizona. Odds are they aren't the only ones who noticed my disappearing act."

"Who knows about this?"

"Only you and me. I kept the others in the dark."

She turned away as if to pace, but she had nowhere to go. Burdened now with his long-hidden truth, she felt trapped. She fixed him with an accusatory stare. "Why? Why do this?"

"You know why."

The pain behind his eyes was as raw and vivid as ever, and as soon as she recognized it, she understood his motives perfectly: "Dresden."

A hard frown. "Dresden." The city where they and Adair were betrayed by the Allies.

The implications of what Cade had done filled Anja with a fear she hadn't known since the war. "Cade, you are not the only one at risk here. If the governments of the world or any of their spy agencies find out you have been training secret apprentices—"

"I know. . . . They'll kill us all."

GLOSSARY

adept—*n.*, an initiate into the Art of ceremonial magick; often used synonymously with "apprentice." The lowest level of adept in magick is a *novice*; a journeyman adept is an *acolyte*; a master-level adept is a *karcist* (see below).

Art, the—*n.*, capitalized, a shorthand term referring to Renaissance-era ceremonial magick.

athamé—*n.*, a black-handled knife with many uses in ceremonial magick.

dabbler—*n.*, karcists' pejorative for an amateur or a poorly trained adept of ceremonial magick.

demon—*n.*, a fallen angel; demons provide the overwhelming majority of magick in the Art, with the remaining small percentage coming from angels.

Enochian—*n.*, the language of angels; *adj.*, related to or originating from angels or their language.

experiment—*n.*, in ceremonial magick, technical term for a ritual involving the conjuration and control of demons or angels.

familiar—*n.*, a demonic spirit in animal form, sent to aid a karcist and amplify his or her powers.

grimoire—*n.*, a book of magickal contracts between a karcist and the demons with whom he or she has struck pacts in exchange for access to them and the powers they grant.

incubus—*n.*, a low-level (i.e., nameless) demon, a creature of pure meanness and spite, whose function is to seduce mortals or, in some cases, act as their sexual servant; an incubus can take any of a variety of masculine forms. When so desired, it can assume a feminine form; in such an event, it is referred to as a *succubus* (see below).

Kabbalah—*n.*, a system of esoteric theosophy and theurgy developed by Hebrew rabbis; it is considered a system of "White Magick," though it has a "Black Magick" component known as *Sitra Achra*.

karcist—*n.*, a master-level adept in the Art of ceremonial magick.

lamia—*n.*, a low-level (i.e., nameless) demon summoned to act as a domestic servant; though lamiae can be compelled to behave in a manner that seems docile or even friendly, they must be carefully controlled, or else they will turn against those who conjured and commanded them.

Llull Engine—*n.*, a divination tool, often consisting of overlapping wheels made from stiff paper or cardboard, that can be called upon without invoking either demons or angels.

magick—*n.*, when spelled with a terminal "k," a shorthand term for Renaissance-era ceremonial magick, also known as the Art. Not to be confused with theatrical or stage magic, which consists of sleight of hand, misdirection, and mechanical illusions. All acts of true magick are predicated on the conjuration and control of demons or, in rare cases, angels.

nadach—*n.*, a human being whose soul has been spiritually bonded prior to birth with the essence of a demon; such a union persists for life and often confers one or more special abilities.

nikraim—*n.*, a human being whose soul has been spiritually bonded prior to birth with the essence of an angel; such a union persists for life and often confers one or more special abilities.

operator—*n.*, in the Art, the adept or karcist leading or controlling an experiment.

patient—*n.*, an antiseptic term of the Art for the intended subject (often a victim) of a demonic sending (see below) resulting from an experiment.

rabble—*n.*, karcists' nickname for the world's non-magickal majority of people.

rod—*n.*, in the Art, a wand; used to impose punishments on demons and direct magickal effects.

scrying—*n.*, a term for remote viewing, or clairvoyance (i.e., witnessing events in faraway places) by means of magick.

send—*v.*, in the context of magick, to dispatch a demon by means of an experiment, with orders to perform a specified task. Such actions can include, but are not limited to, murder, assault, recovery of valued objects, and the acquisition of information.

succubus—*n.*, a low-level (i.e., nameless) demon, a creature of pure meanness and spite, whose function is to seduce mortals or, in some cases, act as their sexual servant; a succubus can take any of a variety of feminine forms. When so desired, it can assume a masculine form; in such an event, it is referred to as an *incubus* (see above).

tanist—*n.*, a karcist, adept, or other person who acts as an assistant to the operator during an experiment. Most experiments are designed to be performed either by a lone operator or by an operator with two or four tanists.

ward—*n.*, a glyph, seal, or other sigil, whether temporary or permanent, that serves to protect a person, place, or thing from demonic or magickal assault, detection, or other effect.

yoke—*v.*, to force a demon or angel into the conscious control of a karcist. Yoking a demon often incurs deleterious side effects for the karcist; such effects can include, but are not limited to, headaches, nosebleeds, nightmares, indigestion, and a variety of self-destructive obsessive-compulsive behaviors.

THE INFERNAL DESCENDING HIERARCHY

SUPERIOR SPIRITS AND MINISTERS OF HELL

SATAN MEKRATRIG

PUT SATANACHIA (BAPHOMET)			BEELZEBUTH		
LUCIFUGE ROFOCALE	ASTAROTH	SATHANAS	PAIMON	ASMODEUS	BELIAL

Mortals cannot strike pacts with the Emperor of Hell (SATAN MEKRATRIG) or the other two superior spirits (BAPHOMET and BEELZEBUTH).

A karcist makes his/her first pact with one of the six ministers (governors) of Hell; subsequently, his or her future pacts are limited to the subordinate spirits of that minister, and no others. It is possible for a minister to act as patron to many human karcists at once. None of the six ministers (aka patron spirits) can be yoked by a mortal karcist.

The ministers, ranked in terms of power and influence, from most to least, are:

LUCIFUGE ROFOCALE (666 legions)
PAIMON (200 legions)
ASMODEUS (72 legions)
BELIAL (50 legions)
ASTAROTH (40 legions)
SATHANAS (38 legions)

The fortunes and influences of the spirits fluctuate as the demons vie for power in the Infernal Hierarchy. A karcist most often makes compacts with his/her patron spirit for such benefits as wealth, longevity with slowed aging, and immunity to disease.

ACKNOWLEDGMENTS

My deepest thanks are owed to my wife, Kara, for her unstinting support during the plotting and drafting of this novel. I also am grateful to my editor, Marco Palmieri, for his narrative guidance and patience; to my agent, Lucienne Diver, for her business advice; and to my story consultants, Aaron Rosenberg and Ilana C. Myer, and my historical consultant and beta reader, Scott Pearson.

THE DARK ARTS SERIES WILL CONTINUE IN

THE SHADOW COMMISSION